Also by Tom Wilson

Black Canyon
Desert Fury
Final Thunder
Black Wolf

BLACK SKY

Tom Wilson

A SIGNET BOOK

SIGNET
Published by New American Library, a division of
Penguin Putnam Inc., 375 Hudson Street,
New York, New York 10014, U.S.A.
Penguin Books Ltd, 80 Strand,
London WC2R 0RL, England
Penguin Books Australia Ltd, 250 Camberwell Road,
Camberwell, Victoria 3124, Australia
Penguin Books Canada Ltd, 10 Alcorn Avenue,
Toronto, Ontario, Canada M4V 3B2
Penguin Books (N.Z.) Ltd, 182–190 Wairau Road,
Auckland 10, New Zealand

Penguin Books Ltd, Registered Offices:
Harmondsworth, Middlesex, England

First published by Signet, an imprint of New American Library,
a division of Penguin Putnam Inc.

First Printing, January 2003
10 9 8 7 6 5 4 3 2 1

Again the time has come for our military personnel to place themselves in jeopardy. This book is dedicated to those who dare to fight to keep the American dream alive.

Thank you.

ACKNOWLEDGMENTS

The formative years of the Northwoods of Wisconsin and UP Michigan is obvious. Fly over it and your mind's eye imagines great glaciers scraping the terrain like a giant bulldozer, then melting and leaving countless pristine lakes and streams. Dense arboreal woods soon followed, as did a profusion of animals that either adapted to the deep snow and bitter cold of winter, or perished. That hardiness was exhibited by Siouan bands who came for the plenty, and then by the Fox, Ojibwe, Ottawa, Potawatami, Iroquois, and others, driven before the Europeans to the east and south. The tribes were often at one anothers' throats, fighting for the best hunting grounds and most plentiful lakes or for the rights to trade furs with the whites. The French and English arrived as entrepreneurs, Scandinavians to harvest the forest, Irish to build the railroads, and Welsh to work the mines. A number stayed behind after their endeavors played out, but the Northwoods wilderness areas (thankfully) remain sparsely populated.

In the nineteenth century a north-south Indian path that bisected the Northwoods from Wausau to Lake Superior was widened into a wagon trail for settlers. Today the path has become Highway 51, but during Prohibition it was dubbed "Capone's Highway" for the spate of trucks hauling Canadian and kerosene-quality locally distilled spirits. Few Northwoods residents liked the dry times, and they made up their own minds about who was and who was not the good guy. Capone's Highway was maintained in good repair and was seldom patrolled. Chicago "outfit" bosses built vacation lodges in the Northwoods and were respected for their community largesse, regardless of loathsome reputations elsewhere. Marge Engel, the community of Winchester's resident historian, reminisces about giving a city fellow a push out of the snow with her jalopy by repeatedly crashing into the back of his fancy sedan. Between thumps he angrily yelled, "Hey, ain't you ever done this before?" "Never," the saucy teenager replied. After he'd pulled a bill from his roll and departed, Marge learned that Al Capone was visiting his brother in Mercer.

Following a disastrous (for the lawmen) shootout near Manitowish Waters between the Dillinger gang and the FBI, Machine Gun Nelson was hidden and hosted by an Ojibwe chief at the Lac du Flambeau reservation until things cooled off. No one should be surprised. The odious practices of robbing, withholding, and redirecting American Indian assets at the whimsy and gain of politicans are older than our nation. The relatively recent advent of gambling casinos has provided new opportunities for abuse.

I make it a point to experience the places I write about—this time the Northwoods. For several years I enjoyed their four seasons and met so many helpful individuals that it would take far more than my allotted space to properly credit everyone who made this Westerner feel at home. Of especially notable help to this effort were the ladies of the libraries at Winchester (led by the irrepressible Barbara Bull), Manitowish Waters, and Mercer. Another gracious lady, at the Lac du Flambeau reservation museum, provided accurate sources for the Chippewa language, customs, and legends. Visits to their annual powwows are enlightening and just plain fun. Lac du Flambeau is a working model of how a modern reservation can and should be administered to the benefit of its people.

Prologue

It was during the murky hour that precedes dawn, when shadows and gray tones present the imagination with suspicions and half-truths. United States senator Eddie Little-Turtle Adcock had the engine backed off to a low, rumbling idle and looked with care as he steered his twenty-eight-foot craft past the jumbled chunks of concrete that formed seawalls at either side of the inlet.

His head moved with a start. Was somebody crouching in the rubble, waiting in ambush? Finally he discerned innocent shadows, but knew to remain wary. For weeks he had been followed, both by automobile and by foot. Near-miss bullets had hissed past his head from muted weapons. The first time he'd flung himself to the ground, the Secret Service agents had believed him. The next time there had been doubts. The third time Eddie had told no one.

The launch throbbed into the small harbor that he'd selected for the meeting. The park was on Lake Superior, not far from the border separating the Upper Peninsula of Michigan from northern Wisconsin. It was sparsely populated, heavily forested, and bisected by the river. High cliffs overlooked a deserted, wind-blown sandy beach, and Superior stretched into the distance as far as the eye could discern. The Black River—so called because of the dark color imparted by fallen tamarack needles—flowed into the inland sea. When the bay wasn't frozen, as it became during the harsh winters, a handful of canny visitors from the various Great Lakes were often found tied up at the protected pier. If a storm blew up, the boats felt hardly a ripple.

Eddie had picked the park because of the security it offered. A single access road offered a ten-minute drive from U.S. 2, and if trouble arose, few boats could keep up with his venerable Chris-Craft. Eddie had added the latest electronics, and replaced the stodgy Marine six with a Ramcharger ten-cylinder engine, making it a screamer. It was a dinghy compared to the Bertrams and such owned by the big boys, but he was pleased with his fifty-year-old beauty.

When confident that nothing was stirring, he eased in between two larger boats and tied up at the long riverside pier, keeping his engine idling, using slipknots in anticipation of a quick getaway.

Eddie was in his late fifties, not tall but powerfully built, with a caricature of bold features: large ears, a prominent proboscis, a boxer's lantern chin, and high Indian cheekbones. In his youth his athletic ability had bolstered the popularity imparted by an easygoing nature and high intelligence. A tenacious running back, a first baseman with a golden bat, rambunctious enough to make up for a few inches of height in basketball, a rough-and-tumble defenseman on the ice. Yet it was his oratory skills that had set him apart. Reporters still called him one of the most naturally charismatic men in the country.

The sturdy build and copper skin were gifts of Eddie's heritage. He felt the term "Native American" was inappropriate and could be claimed by anyone born in the hemisphere. He was an *American Indian,* and damned proud of it. Not only did he cherish his Chippewa blood; he was humbled at his fortune to be born a citizen of the greatest nation in the world.

Eddie fiddled with the idle setting, simultaneously scanning the park for his "guests." He remained in the cockpit, for he was too well known to go unnoticed. Still, it was his way to confront danger rather than send another. In 1966, fresh out of college and ROTC, he'd deployed to Vietnam as a U.S. Marine Corps lieutenant. His proudest achievement—far outweighing the medals he'd received—was that he never lost a man on his recon team, although they'd been in harm's way often. Part of the reason was that he'd personally participated in the most hazardous missions. Later, as a federal prosecutor, he'd taken on the toughest investigations.

A Green Bay Packers knit cap lay atop the radio console. Green for go, the prearranged signal that all was okay. The bright red Kansas City Chiefs cap beside it would alert them to turn back. Not imaginative, but easily remembered by the two employees of the mob who would soon bring him dark secrets.

He noted road activity—two cars pulling into the parking lot across the grassy area. It was too dark to make out details, only that a male emerged from one vehicle, a woman from the other. Each carried a plain brown briefcase, as Eddie had specified in his instructions. They peered curiously at one another. At water's edge they stopped, checked names on shadowed sterns until they found the Chris-Craft parked between two yachts.

Eddie switched on hidden video cameras, emerged in his Packers knit cap, and examined the sheet of paper each offered. They were the ones he'd sent.

"Inside," he told them. Spoken tersely. There was no time for niceties.

The woman was a looker from Vegas, possessed of high-riding silicone breasts that would never sag, and had served a stint as a showgirl. Her true talent was unknown to most, for she'd never been caught at it. She was said to be the best break-and-enter artist in America, so good at it that the mob called upon her for the most difficult tasks.

The man with her was a foot shorter, balding, with a bulldog's face and grimace. He was from Cleveland. His reputation as a safecracker was unsurpassed.

As Eddie searched them thoroughly the woman joked that if he kept it up she'd follow him anywhere. Neither was wired, and he found no weapons, so he went out and cast off fore and aft. Came back in, eased the boat away from the pier, then headed toward the seawalls.

Across the grassy expanse a new automobile arrived. A state police cruiser, yet its presence was not reassuring. Eddie trusted no one.

He glanced at his guests. "Either of you think you might have been followed?"

"No way," said the thief from Cleveland. *Too sure of himself,* thought Eddie, who knew their adversaries better than this man who was one of them.

The woman from Vegas didn't think she'd been followed, but wanted to get on with it.

Eddie wagged his head. "Not yet." He maneuvered the zigzag channel between the seawalls and, as they emerged, ran the throttle up to one-third. The Chris-Craft squatted briefly before rising onto the plane. They roared northward, directly away from the shore.

"Where we headed?" asked the Cleveland hood.

Eddie just smiled his answer.

"Okay," Cleveland blustered, "long as there's no funny business."

The woman was staring at Eddie. "I never guessed it was *you* I was dealing with."

Eddie continued at the fast clip, steering manually despite the fact that he had preset the coordinates of way points and destination, the integrated GPS and radar display showed every hazard known and unknown to man, and the autopilot worked flawlessly.

If a suspicious airplane or watercraft appeared, he would push up the throttle and head for the radar blip that had appeared at 350 degrees, six miles distant.

Fifteen minutes later they came upon the U.S. Coast Guard cutter cruising eastward. He throttled back; they wallowed as he turned to parallel the cutter's course. If there was funny business he wanted it done in sight of big-time help.

Eddie started with the woman from Vegas, asking to see what she'd brought.

"Not until I have the money," she said.

*   *   *

An hour later, everyone had come out a winner. Eddie handed each a cashier's check drawn on one of his banks. In return he transferred the contents of their briefcases into a waterproof canvas gym bag. Eddie advised them to lay low and, when the news broke, make amnesty deals with the FBI. Neither appeared interested. While he did not particularly blame them, he wanted his actions, being captured on video, to be appropriate.

He brought the Chris-Craft around, pressed NAV 2 on the GPS panel, and followed the steering needle back toward the park. Feeling down. Their information confirmed his fears. His nation's justice system was turning a blind eye as his people were enslaved.

7:15 A.M.

Eddie let the engine idle as he reentered the small bay, feeling tense.

When he pulled into the same vacant space at the pier, nothing seemed amiss. A sport fisherman was preparing his bass boat for a morning foray. There were more vehicles in the lot, but it was after all a park and had its share of summer visitors. Like a couple and their child crossing the walking bridge on their way to the beach.

"Go ahead," he advised his two guests, and they stepped off and started across the luxuriant lawn. Something nagged him about the situation, and he delayed his departure.

Eddie's heart sank as four men rose from picnic benches and started toward the informants. He was reaching for the air horn to alert them when the woman began to run toward her auto, and the man split off toward the distant road. Both were hotly pursued. Neither had the slightest chance of escape. As Eddie drew the shift lever into reverse, a uniformed policeman rushed across the grass, waving for him to stop. He deftly maneuvered about, and nudged the lever forward. The boat charged for the channel. More men running, all pulling side arms, which he hoped would be inaccurate from over fifty yards.

He bent lower, heart thumping as they aimed. There were no sounds of gunfire as the silenced weapons bucked in their hands. Two pursuers scrambled into the bass boat, shoving aside the owner. The small craft roared from the pier, but by then Eddie was approaching the zigzag seawall. Only at the last moment did he note the figure standing on one of the huge stones dredged from the lake. Eddie crouched until he could barely see over the instruments, maneuvering deftly as a spray of bullets sliced through cabin walls. He swung the wheel right, then left. Waiting to be shredded as more rounds zipped through bulkheads.

Eddie rose slightly to negotiate the final seawall. More bullets whispered past. Miraculously those too missed, although the gym bag beside him was repeatedly hit.

When free of the seawalls he looked aft at the pursuing bass boat approaching. A shooter was standing, aiming an automatic weapon. Eddie ran the throttle full forward. The stern dug in at the shock of raw power; the craft skittered, then shot forward. The speedometer showed the boat was passing through thirty knots. He turned for a look at the dwindling jetty and bass boat, and let out a victory whoop, as an Indian ancestor might have made as he escaped death. The boat engine was screaming, the speedometer now showing fifty knots!

Should he head for the Coast Guard cutter?

He tried the emergency frequency, but discovered that both radios were inoperative. The rounds that had missed Eddie had not been so kind to his boat. The radar and GPS panel were shattered, and the manual indicator revealed that fuel was draining from the main tank.

He was reaching for the AUX TANK switch when his right leg literally flew out from under him. For a moment of confusion he lay on the hard deck, thinking it was some impossible joke until he noted the bright crimson pool beneath him. A single lucky round lobbed by a shooter on the jetty or in the bass boat.

With effort Eddie drew himself up, balanced on the

good leg, and blinked about. The boat was moving north at unbelievable speed. He turned eastward to parallel the shoreline, back toward his point of departure and the automobile waiting there.

He felt a chill. Ignored it. The wound bled profusely, but his first priority was to place as much water as possible between himself and the shooters, and remain watchful for aircraft. Anything was possible. His adversaries had virtually limitless resources.

Got what I came for! The thought succored him, made the wound worthwhile.

He switched to AUX TANK, and observed the needle. It began to rise. *Got gasoline.*

Finally he paused to inspect his wound. The round had passed through his thigh, but something—an artery?—had been nicked, for blood spurted in profuse pulses.

The engine was screaming, the indicator up to sixty knots, his objective only a few miles ahead. His priority shifted: time to tend to the wound. As he opened the first aid kit, he was surprised at the amount of blood on the cabin deck. When he applied a tourniquet about his thigh and twisted the plastic handle, the crimson flow diminished.

7:45 A.M.—*Black River State Park, Upper Peninsula, Michigan*

The woman called Sydney sat in the Honda minivan, hardly believing the debacle she had witnessed. She was nondescript, approaching middle age and clad in a modest black dress.

As she waited for her phone to ring, Sydney looked about, thinking of public perception. The informants had been removed in another van, to be questioned away from public view by two specialists who could extract any secret. Twelve civilians had been in the park: five in the big boats tied up at the pier, the sport fisherman whose bass boat had been confiscated, two on the beach, and four on various hiking trails. State troopers were taking names and briefing them about the "realistic training exercise—no live bullets or anything dangerous, ma'am—to intercept drugs or contraband that might be brought in from Canada." Sydney foresaw no problems, even from the owner of the bass boat. Citizens liked to be a part of such things.

Her phone buzzed to life, the connection made possible by radio repeater network. Cell phones were useless throughout much of the sparsely populated Northwoods.

"I hear you're unhappy. What's going down you don't like?" asked Tonio Gracchi, who she swore sounded like Al Pacino in *The Godfather*.

"Of course I'm fucking *unhappy*. So far nothing's going right." Sydney explained how his people had mishandled things. How they'd taken the informants but let their information get away. How they'd riddled the senator's boat but had not slowed him down. "Now your man in charge is off questioning the informants, when he should be worrying about Eddie."

"Sly Paquette's awfully good at getting answers."

"We need to find the senator. *That's* priority one, not quiz games."

"Fucker actually got away?" Gracchi muttered, as if it were impossible.

"Look, there's nothing from him on the scanner, meaning his radio is out and he can't call for help. I still may be able to put the pieces together, so I'm taking control."

There was a moment of pause. Likely as Tonio Gracchi tried to recall if anyone had ever spoken to a big organization boss like Sydney just had and got away with it.

"Okay," he whispered, as if the word had been forced from him. "I'll call my guys and tell 'em you're in charge."

"Good. How about your helicopters?"

"The pilots are standing by. I say the word, they're on the way."

"Send 'em. Tell them to contact me on the radio and do as I say."

"Have you considered the fuckin' senator might just wave down another boat?"

"He's too spooked." Until he'd disappeared two days before, Eddie had intentionally been kept *very* spooked. Constantly followed, phones obviously monitored, observers positioned to stare. A unidirectional sound projector broadcasting sounds so only he could hear them. During a critical political debate his water had been spiked with LSD. Sydney had ordered those things to keep him in a state of paranoia. *Her* part of the operation had gone smoothly. Gracchi's people had made the fuckups, like losing track of him.

"What else you need?" Gracchi asked.

"Just make sure all your guys know to do what I say." Sydney terminated, not waiting for Gracchi's response or worrying about his sensitivities as a big bad crime boss.

Sydney examined the reaction as Gracchi's men received the news over their radios. *"The woman's in charge,"* she heard over the scanner. They looked at her uneasily. Dumb as horse turds. Two of them approached her minivan, trying to look dutiful as she drew the veil into place and rolled down the window. "We just got a call. Mr. Gracchi said . . ."

"I know what he said," she interrupted.

A radio call came from the second van, parked a few miles distant, where Sly Paquette worked on the informants. "I was told to put you in the loop," he said in a low voice.

"Fuck *in the loop*. He'd better've said I'm running the goddamned show."

Sly Paquette released a sigh. "Yeah."

"How many people can you get your hands on?"

"I got maybe thirty waiting in Ironwood." The small Upper Michigan town was not far.

She told him to deploy cars with searchers and shooters to drive the lakeshore. "Tell 'em to look for the senator's boat. Once they find it, bring me everything he's got with him."

Sydney heard the high-pitched sounds of approaching jet helicopters. The first was a commercial model, the kind used by television stations. The other was larger, sleeker, and faster, virtually bulletproof, the best the military had to offer. Both were painted dark green.

One of the pilots called for instructions.

"Split up and look for a blue-and-white twenty-eight-footer heading north or east."

Sly Paquette came back on. "Both of these dick-heads are talkin'. Can't shut 'em up now they've started." When he explained what they'd revealed to Eddie, her heart hastened its beat.

Sydney started the engine. "I'll be right there."

"I'll have the Junkman waiting."

Minutes later she pulled off on a dirt side road, continued for a hundred yards, and pulled in behind an identical van. The dense foliage muted sound, but she could hear piteous sobs from farther along.

The Junkman, a massive man with a face like a wad of lumpy dough, approached to tell her Paquette was with the rats up the road.

As Sydney walked, she steeled herself for what she was about to see.

A pilot reported that they had several boats in view, none resembling Eddie's.

"Fly the shoreline. Look at marinas, docks, places he might have put in."

The man and woman had been stripped and lay crying like babes, their upper limbs broken and awry, their flesh marred by ash-covered cigar burns. Sharp-faced Sly Paquette stood by, puffing a fat Churchill and using the female's panties to wipe blood from a two-foot length of metal pipe. He handed over two cashier's checks, and explained what the rats had provided in exchange. Documents, photos, videos and audiotapes, all transferred to Eddie's canvas bag.

"See if they know where he went," Sydney said.

"I asked. They said no."

Sydney lifted her eyes. "Do you have a problem with your hearing?"

Sly Paquette responded by drawing hard a couple of times to fire up the cigar, nodded so the dough-faced giant knew to hold the male down, then applied the business end to the man's penis. An animal's scream resonated in the forest. The cigar was pressed into the woman's genitalia. More squealing. The smell of burnt flesh was pungent. He asked questions. As the informants babbled answers he looked to Sydney.

"That's good," she said, assured that neither knew Eddie Adcock's whereabouts.

At 8:40, one of the pilots discovered the boat, which had been hastily tied up to a private pier, and landed. The cockpit was awash with blood. Bright footprints led to where a vehicle had been parked. There was no gym bag, no one in residence at the nearby home.

"Search the boat again, then take it to deep water and scuttle it," said Sydney.

The pilot dropped off a crew for the task and joined the other helicopter in the next search phase, made difficult since they didn't know what kind of vehicle they were looking for. It was the same with the ground army driving the highways and back roads with orders to find Eddie and the bag. Facilities were as sparse as humans in Upper Michigan, so they posted lookouts at medical clinics, airstrips, and police stations.

Sydney walked down the dirt road for separation—the informants were still noisy—and radiophoned a number in Washington. She gave the address where the boat was docked. "I need the homeowner's name, and a description of vehicles normally kept there."

"Give me half an hour."

She called Tonio Gracchi. Told him what they had so far.

"There's telephones. How come the senator's not calling for help?" he asked.

"He can't distinguish friends from enemies. The blood loss is heightening his paranoia."

"Meaning he's nuttier'n a jar of crunchy Skippy. You pulled that part off okay."

"I know." Sydney seldom passed up a chance to strut her stuff.

"Be nice if we can find him before someone recognizes him."

"But not essential. Before evening I'd have 'em thinking they saw Barney the dinosaur. No matter who gets
to him first, we take him from them and explain later."

"If you need anything, just ask Paquette."

"And if he isn't helpful, I'll get back to you." She
disconnected and stalked back.

The dough-faced giant was off to one side, observing
what remained of the aging showgirl, who had been reduced to making an unnatural high, keening sound.

"We done with them?" Sly Paquette lit a fresh cigar.

"Stuff something in her mouth to shut her up. I need
them alive."

10:29 A.M.—*Wayside near Watersmeet, Upper Michigan*

Eddie Adcock was parked under a sprawling canopy
of sugar maples. Fighting to remain sufficiently alert to
operate the tourniquet, which had to be relaxed every
few minutes. He wished he could think more clearly,
better analyze his situation and the information he possessed. Even in this era of blatant official lies, the contents of the bag would shake the public.

He picked up the tape recorder on the seat beside
him, pressed the REC button, and began: "I am United
States senator Edward Little-Turtle Adcock." His normally deep and resonant voice was reedy and hesitant.

Eddie's intent had been to explain it all, the discovery
and his new proof, but even the simplest task was difficult. His mind wandered and just speaking was a chore.
He continued, often wandering afield, and wondered if
he was making any sense at all.

A family drove into the wayside; a woman led a young
girl toward the toilets. Should he approach the man who
waited in the car? Offer identification? Beg him to somehow get the gym bag to his assistant in Washington?
Out of the question. The two mob informants had surely
talked, and the search for the gym bag would be under
way. Eddie might get the family killed.

He drew a long breath to replenish the oxygen carried

to his brain, so he could better think. Dark orbs formed
and danced. The reservation! He'd somehow reach the
reservation.

"Follow me," he muttered into the recorder. Senator
Eddie Adcock started the engine of the aging Jeep Wa-
goneer and left the wayside, driving south toward the
Spirit Lake Reservation.

Eddie spoke into the recorder, veering back as the car
wandered to a side of the road, and desperately repeated, "Follow me." Trying to think properly.

Halfway to the reservation he pulled to the side of the
road, ejected the audiotape, and sealed it in a stamped
envelope that already contained lists of names. He
placed it in a rural mailbox, and painfully pulled up the
flag. Eddie then drove on, still muttering, "Follow me."

11:20 A.M.—*Black River State Park, Michigan*

There'd been no sightings, although they now knew
Eddie was driving a 1983 Jeep station wagon. Sydney
was running out of ideas when she got the wild notion
that Eddie might try for the reservation where he had
spent his childhood. When she ran the possibility by Sly
Paquette, the torturer felt it was unlikely. "It would be
like running at a firing squad."

"Eddie's got heavy balls, and if he's dying
anyway . . . ?"

She had Paquette contact the reservation casino, tell
the casino bosses to drive the roads and ask questions
and look for Senator Adcock. He called the tribal police
and told the captain to have his patrolmen do the same.
Find Eddie and the gym bag. After a few minutes reports from Spirit Lake started coming in to Sydney, and
were added to those she was already receiving.

At one o'clock a casino boss reported that an hour
earlier Eddie had been recognized by residents. He was
driving the old Wagoneer, but had not been seen since.
Sydney's joy was tempered by the fact that now she
must come up with a cover story about what he'd been

doing at the damned reservation. She called for the pilot of the sleek and stealthy military helicopter to stop his search and take them—herself, Paquette, the Junkman, and the informants—closer to the action.

Since they mustn't be seen, they landed in a field at the east side of the reservation. As they waited, Sydney thought of how Senator Eddie had explored the reservation on bicycle and foot as a youth, and knew every path, lake, and marsh. They might have trouble finding him.

6:30 *P.M.—Spirit Lake Indian Reservation*

Five hours later, Sydney was beginning to believe that Eddie had eluded them, when the same casino boss called. They'd spotted the Wagoneer on a back road, headed away from the community *toward Sydney*. Two cars were in pursuit, a police vehicle and a sedan. He said that Eddie was weaving, slowing and speeding, driving erratically.

The blood loss, Sydney decided. "Stick on him like glue until he's out of town, then stop him and get that damned gym bag!"

She yelled for the pilot to start engines and fly closer.

A long minute passed before she heard, "Aw shit, he saw us and he's speeding up."

"Are people around?" Her heart was thumping; she was charged with adrenaline.

"Just trees and dirt road." The connection became static filled. Sydney cursed.

"*Catch* him!" she cried, hardly breathing as the jet engines whined to life.

"Jesus," she heard through static. "He's got that clunker up to ninety."

"Don't let him escape!" The helicopter surged and took off.

"He's fishtailing, goin' into a turn. Oh, *damn*! He rolled the fucker."

The crash had occurred just five miles from them. The pilot landed near a turn in the dirt road beside a sedan and a black-and-white Explorer with a police light bar.

Sydney was immediately out, hurrying toward the group crouched by the upturned Wagoneer.

They'd pulled Eddie free. He was pale and bloody . . . and still.

"The canvas bag?" Sydney immediately asked them.

"Nothing's in the car," said the woman from the casino.

Sydney told her to examine the path where the Wagoneer had rolled, in case it had been thrown free. "It's *got* to be around here!"

A battered pickup approached from around the bend, the driver braking hard to avoid running into the helicopter. Sydney saw only a single person inside. "Stop him," she cried.

Before they could react the driver managed to get turned around and flee in the direction from which he'd come.

"I know him," Sly Paquette hissed. "His name's Danny Eagle."

Sydney motioned. "Go after him. When you find him, call me for instructions."

She knelt. Eddie stared back through partially open eyes that held no surprise, as if he'd *expected* her to appear out of nowhere.

"You did great, Eddie. Now where's the gym bag so I can get it in the proper hands."

Eddie did not respond. Just lay there, mocking her with silence.

"You can trust me. I have the police here with us. Damn it, Eddie. Where is it?"

"I got the bleeding stopped," said one of the casino men, gripping the tourniquet handle.

"Looks more like he ran out of blood," observed a cop.

Sydney felt ill. "The gym bag?" she cried out. Eddie mustn't die without telling her.

But he did die. At 6:43, U.S. senator Edward Little-Turtle Adcock expired without word or whimper, only a brittle rattling sound.

Sydney delayed for five full minutes, thinking and chewing on a thumbnail. There could be no involvement

by anyone in government. The cover-up might be difficult because of who Eddie was, but of course that was
precisely what she was best at. Illusion and twists of
perception made truth whatever Sydney wished it to be.

She thought of the first ruse, which must be orches-
trated immediately. Then she contacted Tonio Gracchi
and told him to send his best burglar team from Chicago.
They must bring their tools, and arrive well before dawn.
They'd need to pay a visit to the museum.

Gracchi asked questions, but she had no time for
them.

Sydney had the informants brought to the overturned
Wagoneer. There was little life remaining in them—but
it did not matter. "Buckle 'em in back real snug," she
told the casino people. Eddie was next, his body
strapped into the driver's seat.

All the intricate pages and chapters must be seen to
support the lie she was preparing. Once she'd destroyed
Senator Eddie's reputation and credibility, it would be
easier to have the official inquiry—which was sure to
come—stopped in its tracks.

That must be done quickly, or investigators might
stumble upon the Warehouse.

As soon as the uproar subsided, she'd put her energies
back to locating the elusive gym bag, and use all necessary means to find it.

PART I

Senator Eddie

1

The Weyland Foundation was spawned during the tumultuous years of World War Two, begun by five persons of wealth—who were then, as now, called "the handful"—willing to sacrifice everything to make the world a better place. Through the years their investments grew a thousandfold, and in the process the world and its people benefited. Their Cultural Earth division promoted artistic endeavors, Mankind Earth initiated great charitable causes, and Habitat Earth's wildlife and flora councils purchased vast tracts of ecologically ruined lands around the world and returned them to nature.

Without the financial board, now consisting of the original members' heirs, none of those things would have been possible, and they were extolled for their humanitarian efforts. But other, quieter, projects altered the world even more. The handful's underlying tenet was that democracy and capitalism were the best possible institutions for mankind, and the United States, although it had its warts and problems, was an excellent model. One avenue was to establish viable industries in those nations that had proved to be deserving. At other times their actions took a more direct, more covert form, called special projects, and while there had been more failures than successes, a number of despots had been toppled and a number of struggling nations nourished. Currently, Special Projects, including all offices on the restricted twenty-fifth through twenty-seventh floors of the massive Weyland Building, was administered by Abraham Lincoln Anderson.

Anderson, called Link by his friends, was tall and lithe. Half Blackfoot Indian, he felt most at peace when wandering about various wildernesses. Raised by a military family, he'd spent four years at the Air Force Academy, and repaid his tuition in full by spending an eventful combat tour in the Persian Gulf War. He still loved flying and the freedom of the skies, yet when asked to assume the position at the Weyland Foundation, he had agreed. Frank was not only the foundation's chairman, he was his closest friend, with whom he'd served in the same squadron during Desert Storm. With those diverse considerations it was not unnatural that he was often ill at ease working in the fourth largest structure in New York City.

Link was intelligent but not complex, and sought no added esteem. He was pleased at the fact that his title, executive vice president for Special Projects, was unknown outside the three floors of the building that were under his control.

Erin Frechette, Link's technical assistant, observed him from the doorway that separated their offices, and decided that he was the grumpiest she'd seen him during their two years together. While seldom enamored with his job, he enjoyed traveling in support of the projects. When possible he did so at the controls of one of the foundation's corporate airplanes, which included everything from light craft to Gulfstreams, even a stubby wide-body mobile command post (MCP) aircraft originally produced for the U.S. Army.

For the past eleven weeks he had been involved with construction of a steel mill complex half the world away, constantly shuttling between a Zurich apartment and a dismal office in Dhaka. With hard work and Erin's inputs, he'd established lines of credit for new Bangladeshi moguls, set up supply routes and essential trading partners, lived on soggy and stale sandwiches, and crashed nightly in briefing rooms converted to sleeping quarters.

The effort had been Herculean, but now control was being transferred to the new corporate management, and—AND—he'd finally be able to get away. Erin had done much of her part from home, accessing the foundation's mainframe server from her laptop while he played troglodyte, and wanted him out of her hair so she could tidy up loose ends and get her life back and under proper control.

Maybe take lunches with some nice guy she could meet if she didn't have a project to worry about. At thirty she was getting no younger, and had no eligible prospects. Tending to a precocious nine-year-old son did not attract qualified bachelors. Nursing a top-priority project was even worse. She too was getting damned grumpy and needed a break.

She'd given a name to the foundation's massive computer server, so when people asked she could look back seriously and tell them she spent her time with Helga, a cousin to Hal. The Hal she referred to was, of course, the star of *2001: A Space Odyssey*.

Erin Frechette was no normal computer geek. For starters, she was knockout good looking. Not so Helga, whom she described as weighing in at fifty terabytes (that's millions of millions) of memory, yet operated at incredible speeds in excess of three gigahertz.

She looked over his shoulder and noted that he was reading a story in the *Times* that had caught her interest that morning. A circuit court judge, indicted for accepting millions of dollars in bribes from two different New York crime families over the past decade, had disappeared. They were searching various Caribbean islands, looking for both the judge *and* the money.

"He could be anywhere," she kibitzed.

"Maybe I'll run across him in Montana," he joked. The mountains where Link was headed were primitive and wild, the way he liked them.

"Ten minutes until show time," she reminded him, which was why she'd come in.

He reluctantly put aside the newspaper, looked dubiously at his computer, pressed the wrong mouse button, and grumbled, "How do I get the damned slide to advance?" causing Erin to sigh loud enough to be heard across the room.

Link was technically minded, even held an engineering degree. He was also brilliant at managing personnel and assets—as he'd proved with the project they were wrapping—but he refused to learn the first thing about the computer on his desk, could not accept that they were just helpful machines, and refused to go on-line to retrieve E-mail—as if something might stretch an invisible head across cyberspace and bite him.

"Put the arrow on FWD and press the left button to advance the page. The right one activates animation within the frames. It's dummy stuff, Link."

He punched the incorrect mouse button and glared. "That's what I feel like after being cooped up for so long, a dummy. Got to get back into the real world."

"Amen to that. Ready?" she asked. Even visiting presidents showed up on time when meeting with the handful, and then often were asked to wait.

"Yeah. I don't need to take the diskette, right?"

"The briefing's loaded on the Weyland Classified Intranet. Just type in the code word, enter it, and press the proper mouse buttons. There are only *two* of them, Link."

"The one on my desk has three."

She *almost* raised her voice. "We're only using two of them, remember?"

He pulled on his jacket. Western cut, since Link Anderson seldom strayed far from his roots. Once she'd figured it was to irritate the chairman, since his longtime buddy expected his executives to wear subdued business suits. But Link truly preferred snaps to buttons and bolos to cloth ties, and felt the affectation among New York businessmen to wear Lucchese boots was folks finally coming to their senses.

"Explain the mouse buttons again," he told her as they started for the door.

She started to explain. Then sighed her loudest sigh, *wishing* he'd hurry and leave on vacation, and said, "*I'll* run the damned computer for the presentation."

He grinned victoriously. "Hey, don't get grouchy on me."

She felt like bopping him.

They walked down the hall on sumptuous, noise-muting carpeting, yet she could hear his light wheeze. This from a man who took pride in keeping his physical condition at a peak. But Link had been forced to suspend his workouts, and athletes went downhill faster than mortals. He complained that his muscles were mush. She believed him. He *needed* to get away.

"Joseph Spotted Horse called. He wants to know when you leave."

"Immediately after this briefing." He looked pleased at the thought of heading for Boudie Springs, Montana, where old Joseph looked after his cabin and mare. There were no strings to restrain him. His most recent lady friend, a petite FBI agent, had taken a promotion and a posting as ASAC at the San Francisco field office. It was easy to forgive her. Link was one of those rare male animals who bonded with a mate for life, and to her misfortune it had happened before she appeared on his scene. It was now thirty months since Marie LeBecque, a bright anthropologist from Browning, Montana, died just before they were to marry.

Heck, if he was *really* available, Erin might hog-tie him for herself. But she'd come to know Link, and when she found him staring out at the skyline, gazing at a soaring gull and wearing his vulnerable expression, she left him in peace with his memories.

Link was planning his escape. "I'll head for the apartment, pack, grab a cab to Kennedy, and board the first airplane headed west."

"Why not take a company plane and fly yourself?"

"Mmm, maybe," he considered.

"I'll get a list of available airplanes. So what's the first thing you'll do there?"

"Saddle Ms. Stubborn, and head uphill."

Ms. Stubborn was his mare. From what Erin knew she was not particularly fast, but had dogged endurance, a barrel chest, and "good wind for the high country." Erin hailed from Flagstaff, Arizona, and knew horses and

open spaces, yet she felt little envy. She was becoming
Easternized, and particularly enjoyed taking in the latest shows.

The receptionist posted outside the Summit Room offered an efficient smile. Security was thorough on all the
classified floors, but access to the Summit Room was
particularly tight. Erin, in succession, placed her palm
on a desktop glass screen, looked into a bug-eyed lens,
and touched a wand to her tongue. After the young
woman had changed the wand tip, Link did the same,
providing fingerprints, a retinal scan, and a DNA sam-
ple. Analyses took seventeen seconds, establishing identities with zero margin of error.

First one, then a second LED illuminated.

"They'll see you now," said the receptionist. A moose-
sized male guard wearing a blue Weyland Foundation
blazer opened the double doors.

The Summit Room was massive and elegantly appointed. Richly carpeted, done in California oak, with
portraits of American presidents and the Weyland Foundation founders on the walls. Frank Dubois, crippled in
a private airplane accident two years before and con-
fined to a wheelchair, greeted them from the head of
the small conference table. The others of the handful, all
descendents of the original five, joined in the welcome.

"Lincoln, as always, you are refreshing to these eyes,"
said the sole woman on the board. She was fiftyish,
hailed from Wyoming, and never failed to cast him a
coquettish smile. "Welcome home. We hear you're
about to leave on vacation?"

"Yes, ma'am. As soon as we're done here."

"Good. Don't let them talk you out of it." She was
also the chatterbox of the group and had trouble keeping
secrets to herself. Meaning, Erin knew, that something
was afoot.

Erin went to the podium, typed in a classified password, and clicked a button on the cordless mouse
pointer. The big screen came alive: the words PROJECT
GREEN 311 were superimposed over a photograph of the
enormous industrial complex in Bangladesh. Satisfied,

she carried the mouse back to the side of the room and waited as Link took the floor and began. As was his norm, he was frugal with words, yet he had accumulated in-depth knowledge of Australian Hamersley Range iron ore, coking coal from Tumbler Ridge, British Columbia, and the burgeoning need for steel forms and beams in Pacific Rim countries.

The incoming project monitor, a VP from the fifth floor, lauded Link for shepherding the twenty-seven-billion-dollar project "to fruition," his congratulations taking as long as had all of Link's descriptions. Erin was betting that behind his wan smile, her boss's mind was wandering the high country of Montana.

Finally the members of the handful teleconferenced with the CEO of the huge new corporation, who also voiced praise for Link's work, although he did not know his name.

As the video link and the meeting concluded, the new project monitor excused himself. Link and Erin also rose to their feet, but Ambassador Baker, one of the handful, asked if they would stay for the next session. The ensuing silence was heavy.

Erin wondered if Link would decline, knowing he was anxious to depart. When he hesitated, she knew it was due to his esteem for the ambassador. The title was an honorarium for posts he had once held—Doyle D. Baker was a scion of the Philadelphia Bakers, who for the past two centuries had provided top diplomats to serve their country. While he was often the most garrulous of the handful, today he appeared especially subdued.

"Please stay," Ambassador Baker repeated. "I've invited Gordon Tower to give us information on a matter of concern, and I would like your advice on a proper next step."

Supervisory Special Agent Gordon Tower was an assistant director in charge and was also their FBI liaison at the New York bureau office. Under every president since FDR, even the government's most sensitive files had been open to the senior officers of the Weyland Foundation, who served their country well.

"What subject?" Erin asked.

"The circumstances surrounding Senator Adcock's death."

Link gave a small start, and Erin wondered if he had been aware of the matter. Adcock—called Senator Eddie by admirers and opponents alike—had been the first full-blood Chippewa senator. He had been popular—a gifted orator, a human rights zealot, a thorn in the side of organized crime, an advocate not only for the American Indian but for all Americans.

Ambassador Baker cleared his throat. "You may wonder at my interest. Eddie was married to my daughter until she died in an automobile accident a few years ago. They had three wonderful children—my grandchildren— all now adults. I cringe to think of the impact the scandal is visiting upon their lives. Then there's Gloria, his second wife. She doesn't deserve to hear the vilification. And finally, I believe he was innocent of any wrongdoing."

Link was frowning, obviously wondering, *what* scandal and vilification?

Frank Dubois, chairman of the board and Link's longtime friend, spoke. "We worked with the senator on programs of mutual interest, ranging from the preservation of Native American languages to inner city crime solutions, and on every occasion we were impressed with his integrity. That's why the scandal is difficult to comprehend."

"When did he die?" Link asked in a quiet voice.

The ambassador looked surprised. "Two months ago. You didn't know of it?"

"I've been focused," Link said truthfully. When running a project he purposefully shut out news from the outside. "How did he die?"

"Mmm. Surely you heard the senator was a presidential candidate?"

"I was aware, but I didn't follow any of them closely."

"He collected only a fraction of the funds available to major party candidates, but he was giving them a good run. His platform was built around honesty and morality

issues, and a promise to put an end to justice meted out
to the highest bidders."

"People listened," said Frank Dubois, "until a debate
in June when it seemed obvious that Eddie was unstable,
perhaps drunken. It was painful, watching him commit
political hara-kiri. He chastised the audience for their
so-what attitudes about the lapses at the nuclear labs,
saying, 'You'll *wish* you'd cared when missiles with
American-designed warheads rain on our cities.' He was
slurring, saying things politicians don't dare mention.
How the Kennedys should pay for their damned burials
at sea until our sailors no longer qualify for food stamps.
How our government's for sale, and what country do
you want the military to bomb or prop up next. How
the Justice Department goes after fourteen-year-old
junkies, but ignores the rich crooks. How there's a devil's contract between organized crime and high-ranking
members of government, and he'd prove it."

"What did he mean by that?" asked Link.

"No one's sure. About then his team was able to pull
him off camera."

"I heard something about that," Link said. "It just
didn't seem very important."

"It was after the media got hold of it," said the
woman. "A *Post* article called him mean-spirited, reduced to dredging up old issues. *Time* suggested he was
a closet racist, and the Chinese were everyone's whipping boy. A White House spokesman advised that he
seek professional help." She paused. "Senator Eddie
quietly retired from the race."

"That week in June," said the ambassador, "he went
from being a contender for the presidency, to a political
embarrassment. Still a lot of Americans believed in him.
At the time of his death Eddie remained one of the
most popular public figures in the country. He was considered an icon for honesty. His patriotism couldn't be
denied, nor his pride in his Indian heritage and his
nation."

"But that didn't last," said the woman. "Within days
of his death, new rumors flew. There were planted sto-

ries of his womanizing with young staff members. Someone nicknamed him Fast Eddie, which they'd never have
dared to do when he lived, and intimated that he'd taken
money for political favors. Another story was circulated
that he'd cheated on taxes."

"Not one of those was substantiated," said the ambassador, "but as fast as one rumor was disproved, another
appeared. The public grew tired of hearing about him.
They wanted to move on, and so the media did. They
branded him a crook and forgot him."

Link had met Senator Adcock only once, when he'd
visited the remote Blackfeet reservation in Montana for
Marie LeBecque's funeral and given her eulogy. He had
described her death as the extinguishing of one of America's brightest young stars.

Following the funeral, Marie's friends and colleagues
had proceeded to the home owned by her uncle, who
had reared and educated her. Link had been besieged
by well-wishers, and the senator had waited unobtru-
sively. After allowing Link a quiet moment, the senator
had come over to search his eyes and grip his hand. He
was a head shorter than Link, yet he had exuded cha-
risma, a phenomenon once described by Marie.

"She spoke of you with respect," Link had told the
senator.

Senator Eddie's voice held a sad and resonant rumble.
"Marie convinced me to support some very worthwhile
projects. On others we disagreed, but she always fought
the good fight. She'll be sorely missed by the native peoples of America."

The senator told him how Marie had offered unique
insights concerning the old Indian cultures that they
might otherwise have not explored. "She never let us
forget . . ." he'd begun. Then his words had caught and
he'd taken a breath, tried to go on but was unable. He'd
remained silent, too wrought with emotion to speak as
tears coursed freely down his face of granite.

Finally the senator had drawn a ragged breath. "I lost
my wife more than a year ago, Lincoln, but I am healing.
Grief diminishes with time. Treasure Marie's memory,

but move on as she'd have you do. If I can be of assistance, officially or as a friend, don't hesitate to call."

Link had not questioned his sincerity, yet he'd been sure that his own grief was too overpowering, his love too strong, to ever diminish. He cherished their time together more than any other in his life, but as the Senator had said, time had indeed been the great healer. He no longer thought of her every waking moment. She resided somewhere deeper within.

Now Senator Eddie Adcock too was gone, and a voice inside Link whispered that something was wrong with what he was hearing. The senator was not the kind to cheat or turn criminal. Marie's judgment and faith in the man, and the tears the senator had shed over her passing, combined to make Link care.

2

Frank Dubois interrupted. "Link, we understand how much you deserve your vacation. Get out of here and relax. The senator's dead, and that won't be changed when you get back."

"How did he die?" Link asked. "I'd really like to know."

Frank gave his friend a look like he was being foolish. "Let's get it from the horse's mouth. Gordon's waiting in reception to brief us on any latest developments."

He pressed a button built into the tabletop.

Supervisory Special Agent Gordon Tower was large and black, and stood neatly groomed in a fawn-colored suit. His primary duty as the deputy assistant director in charge (often shortened to deputy ADIC) at the New York district office was to act as liaison and information conduit to the foundation. As he took the podium, he nodded gravely to the board, and deliberately avoided looking at Link and Erin—odd for a man they considered a friend.

"I have little to add to what I told you on my previous visits, just more substantiation of the senator's guilt after his wife discovered a series of entries in his computer notes."

"Gordon," said Frank Dubois, "Link's been out of pocket. Could you fill in the events surrounding the senator's death?"

"Yes." Tower stiffly withdrew a folder from his brief-case, not at all his friendly self.

Erin leaned toward Link. "The senator's new wife is Gloria Vasson. Her father was the founder of the Pierre Vasson cosmetics house, and she's heiress to the whole enchilada. She's filthy rich, striking for her age, and shuns publicity."

Gordon found the notes he was after, and began: "On the evening of August fourth, an overturned, burning vehicle was discovered on the Spirit Lake Indian Reservation in northern Wisconsin. The fire had been fed by accelerant from the ruptured gas tank, and the occupants were burned beyond recognition. Their identity was unknown until the tribal police found certain items that had obviously been thrown from the vehicle, including two partially burned cashier's checks signed by Eddie L. T. Adcock, one made out to Patricia Gilroy, the other to Edwin Gamble, each for one hundred thousand dollars. DNA analysis later confirmed those three as the vehicle's occupants.

"The following morning they discovered an empty thirty-inch aluminum tube, designed to preserve fragile documents. Taped to its side was a legend describing the contents as the original peace treaty between the Manido-Chippewa band and the United States, signed by President Jefferson. A search of the reservation museum's safe showed seven other documents were missing. Included among them was a 1634 trade agreement signed by a fur-trading factor commissioned by the king of France. All are priceless, and were—and still are—missing.

"At ten a.m. an FBI advance team deployed from the Milwaukee field office. When they arrived the integrity of the accident scene had been corrupted, but they were able to come up with new data. For instance, the '83 Wagoneer had been borrowed from an Adcock supporter with a vacation home on Lake Superior, where the senator had spent the two nights preceding his death. The senator's boat, seen by neighbors tied up to the private pier, remains missing.

"Some pertinent facts. Records in the senator's office included addresses for Ms. Gilroy and Mr. Gamble, both of whom were known for their ability to illegally remove high-value items from difficult locations. The treaties qualified, since there were multiple sensors to defeat. No melted aluminum or parchment ash was discovered, leading them to assume the other treaties had not been consumed in the fire.

"Altogether those were enough that the team forwarded a most likely chain of events, and offered a few unofficial preliminary conclusions." Gordon looked up from the notes. "It didn't take Sherlock Holmes to surmise that the senator had hired Gilroy and Gamble to steal the treaties and then exchanged the checks for the documents, which Adcock secreted somewhere on the reservation he knew so well."

"Their conclusions were awfully convenient," said the ambassador. "Also too obvious, considering that Eddie was a highly intelligent man."

"Perhaps. It doesn't really matter since we're no longer involved. Two weeks into the bureau's investigation the tribal council requested that our assistance be terminated and the attorney general ordered us off the case."

Link frowned. "Doesn't the FBI have investigative authority on Indian reservations?"

"Normally you're correct, but the treaty with the Manido-Chippewa band is unique. Crimes *against* their people and perpetrated *by* their people are to be investigated by their tribal police. Since the thefts occurred on the reservation, and since Senator Adcock was a full-blooded Manido, they have legal jurisdiction. The bureau withdrew its participation, and transferred all working files to the governing council at the reservation."

"Ridiculous," muttered the ambassador.

"There's more. This morning I was advised that any and all further questions are to be referred to either the BIA or the tribal police. This is the final briefing on the matter."

Ambassador Baker was incredulous. "This is outrageous. We're talking about the violent death of a United States senator under mysterious circumstances."

"We've received our orders, and we will comply." Gordon put his papers away. "We'll assist the Manido only if they so request. That has not happened, and we don't expect it."

Link spoke up. "Can you provide a copy of your reports up to the time you dropped out?"

"The investigation should not have been opened. Nothing is releasable."

The FBI supervisor was using government babble talk, which was not like him.

"Gordon," Frank Dubois said, "we've always honored our side of the gentleman's agreement to share sensitive information. The least you can do is . . ."

He shook his head. "Not on this one, Frank." Gordon looked at his watch. "I have a meeting." He nodded to the group and, without another word, departed.

Hastily, Link believed. Certainly rudely.

Frank Dubois stared at the door.

"They've been noncooperative on this from the first," grumbled a member. "We should request another briefer."

"Gordon goes by the book," said Frank. "Be assured, that was the official word."

The ambassador sighed. "When the FBI was pulled off the case, I engaged a private investigative firm there in the Northwoods. After a week they returned my retainer, saying they refused to associate with persons of Eddie's character. I was astounded. Next I tried a legal firm in Madison. They *jumped* at it, and a week later came back with precisely the same response."

"Perhaps it's the mudslinging," said the woman. "The media went at Senator Eddie like wolves after a wounded sheep."

The ambassador gave her an ironic smile. "I've encountered few law firms that wouldn't take money to represent the devil. And to merely look into the matter?"

Frank Dubois was thoughtful. "Gordon said the tribal

police assumed control of the investigation. I doubt they're qualified, and if the Bureau of Indian Affairs has anything to do with it, forget it. They're political appointees who change with the wind."

The ambassador sighed. "*Someone* must look into Eddie's death."

Erin saw his look and quickly shook her head. "This is out of our realm, Mr. Ambassador. The security department has investigators who are *trained* for this sort of thing."

"We considered them at our last meeting," responded the woman on the handful. "Utter secrecy would be paramount on such a project, and that isn't their game. Your department's quite good at keeping things quiet."

Link thought about his mare and how badly he wanted to visit the high country.

Frank Dubois read his mind. "Go to Montana. We'll discuss it when you get back."

"I have a better idea. I've never been in the Northwoods. I'll take the first couple of weeks of my vacation in Wisconsin, then head west."

Erin glared. "You need rest, damn it."

Link looked at her. "Since there's no official project, you'll be out of this one."

"That's bull," snorted Erin. "Don't even think of doing it without me."

The ambassador smiled, openly pleased. "I'm glad you changed your mind."

"I owe the senator a favor," Link said quietly.

Ambassador Baker arched an eyebrow. "I received an envelope mailed from northern Wisconsin the day Eddie died. Inside is an audiotape—mutterings from someone claiming to be him. There are also lists of names."

"You didn't show them to the bureau?" Erin asked.

"By the time I realized what I had, the FBI was off the case. I'll send them to you as soon as we adjourn."

As they walked back down the hall, Erin shook her head. "Two hours ago nothing could have kept you from 'saddling Ms. Stubborn and heading uphill.' What changed your mind?"

"Marie considered Senator Adcock a friend."

Hoo boy, Erin thought. Marie was involved, so argument closed. "What do you want me to tell Joseph Spotted Horse? He thinks you're on your way to Montana."

"Tell him I'll be there in two weeks. Maybe sooner."

"Take a laptop. It might be helpful."

He snorted to exhibit disgust at the thought.

"Where do you want to start?"

"Get the list of available airplanes. I'll take off this afternoon, spend the night somewhere along the way, and be in the Northwoods by tomorrow morning."

Seventeen blocks distant, at the Jacob Javits Building at 26 Federal Plaza, an olive drab helicopter with an American flag emblazoned across its nose settled onto a rooftop helipad. On six of the floors below, nine hundred FBI agents, the largest assemblage outside Washington, were assigned to various offices, miniempires, and bureaucracies. Four hundred others worked in liaison and undercover assignments around the city.

Supervisory Special Agent Gordon Tower dismounted and hurried forth, then slowed as a man with a refined and tailored look emerged from a door on the east side. The man spotted Tower, and shooed his several aides out of earshot.

"How did it go?" he asked, his voice hardly audible over the sound of the helicopter. He was a cautious man, appointed in an acting capacity after the resignation of the previous director. "Do you think they'll try to dig into it?"

Gordon believed it was probable since Link Anderson had been sitting in.

"I doubt it," he said, and felt better about himself.

"Good. Our orders are specific, Gordon. It's one of those instances where we heed the rules and trust that our people at the top are acting for the general good."

"I've never been great at that." Gordon immediately wished he had not spoken.

"Yes. I've read your record." The acting director observed him with a withering stare. "When we were ordered to withdraw, it was implied that there's a major operation under way there by—ah—another department."

Gordon stared back. "Outside of Justice?" He was not at all sure he believed him.

"That information was not offered and I didn't ask. I know the sound of a direct order from a superior. Do you, Gordon?"

A knot of muscle worked at the side of Gordon Tower's jaw. Finally he nodded.

"Good, because it was made clear that careers could be jeopardized if we interfere, and I can promise that yours is more vulnerable than mine."

The acting director motioned to his cortege of aides. "I have to return to Washington, Tower. I don't want to hear any more on this unless you find that the Weyland Foundation is interfering in some manner. In that instance, you will let me know immediately."

3

Link had been away from flying for several months, and the Baron was a good choice for getting back with the program. Twin engines, but they ran sweet. Nimble, but not so quick that it could get an out-of-practice pilot in trouble. The integrated avionics package was so capable a check-out pilot said if you treated it right it would wash your socks and fry your eggs in the morning.

He touched down ten feet past the threshold mark, let the airplane run down the tarmac past lush, multicolored fall foliage, and turned around at the far end to taxi back—feeling the rush as he always did when he'd done a passable job of piloting.

"Baron ten-twenty, taxi back to the operations building. How long will you be with us?"

"I'll prepay for two weeks. Do you have covered parking?"

"With the kind of winter weather we get? You bet. Pull into the third hangarette in the second row. Will you need fuel?"

Twenty minutes and he'd secured the bird and was walking toward the operations shack. He wore weathered, button fly jeans, a lightweight flannel shirt with snaps, comfortably worn boots, and one of his seasoned Stetsons, feeling free of the city, and not wishing to be mistaken for an executive of any kind at all.

A sign said the small, no-frills airfield served the com-

munities of what was collectively called Lakeland. At
the top were Minocqua and Woodruff, at the bottom
Lac du Flambeau and Spirit Lake, the two large Indian
reservations in the area.

Ten more minutes and Link had signed the airport pa-
perwork and was outside, inspecting the Toyota midsize—
several years old, dark in color, and unspectacular—Erin
had somehow arranged for him. He drove back to the
Baron and retrieved his bag and a cardboard box containing items he considered essential for vacationing,
among them a bottle of scotch and several good wines.
After consideration he left the .357 Magnum revolver
locked in the storage compartment.

As he drove through dense forest toward the exit, he
raised Erin on the flip-top satellite phone. The foundation provided them for clandestine government users
who did not wish to be overheard—and for their own
covert operations. Unlike the bulkier units used by Irid-
ium and Globalstar, these were indistinguishable from
normal cellular phones—and could be used in the cell
mode as well. The phones were deemed so secure that
they could be used for sensitive conversation.

Erin came on the line, and explained she was examining the items that had been mailed by Senator Eddie
Adcock—the cassette tape and list of names. She asked
about his flight, and he responded that it had gone fine,
not mentioning how the sense of freedom had been ex-
hilarating after the long incarceration with the Bangladesh project.

For the past hour the terrain beneath had been mostly
flat—Erin said the highest point in Wisconsin was two
thousand feet—yet the scenery had been anything but
boring. As he'd turned north, the greens and blues had
turned to the variegated shades of autumn. There were
endless forests, countless marshes and bogs, and chains
of lakes that glittered into the distance for as far as the
eye could see. More than one writer had described the
Northwoods as the Everglades of the north.

"I'm at Highway 51," he told her.

"Turn right, go through Woodruff and over the bridge
into Minocqua." She gave the location and address of

a downtown office. "You'll speak with a man named Ron Doughty."

When Erin had suggested that they start with a visit to the PI who had declined the investigation, Link had felt it was time wasted. Erin argued that since he'd be there anyway, they may as well turn over all the rocks. As was normal, he could not dispute her logic.

"What does Helga say about them?"

She read from her computer screen. R. L. Doughty was a widower who had been medically retired from the Milwaukee PD after being wounded on the job. For the past nine years, Reliable Inquiries—the PI and his alarm installer daughter—primarily did investigative work for legal and insurance firms. He had a good reputation, but prosperity was always around the next corner. During his best year, he'd netted forty thousand. Last year he'd brought in twenty. If not for his pension he would have gone under.

"Only two jobs in the past month," said Erin. "A councilman's wife had her husband followed because he was coming home late. She refuses to pay the bill because she *knows* he's up to something. The other's a five-hundred-dollar alarm system, and they still owe the supplier. I just looked at the Doughty bank account. He's been steadily dipping into savings. Either he gets more business, or changes occupations."

"Yet he turned down a fifty-thousand-dollar retainer from the ambassador?"

"Yeah, which would have been his most lucrative single contract *ever*."

Link was eternally amazed at the information Erin could glean. "I don't know how you do it," he muttered.

"Of course you don't. You won't even work a *mouse,* for God's sake. He's expecting you. I was vague when I called, like we agreed. Remember what to say?"

"Sure. Use my own name?"

"No reason not to, as long as you don't mention who you work for."

The Weyland Foundation paid obscene amounts of money for Special Projects personnel to remain out of public scrutiny. Except for family and a few official con-

tacts like FBI ADIC Gordon Tower, Link's connection
with the foundation was unknown outside the building.

Minocqua was an island town. It was touristy—clean,
picturesque, and working hard to stay that way—but the
streets were sparsely populated after the departure of
the summer people.

He followed Erin's directions and located a rambling
wooden structure near the courthouse. Black lettering
on the window explained that RELIABLE INQUIRIES provided PRIVATE INVESTIGATIONS, TRACING, BAIL BONDS,
DEBT COLLECTION, ALARM SYSTEMS INSTALLED, and even
NOTARY PUBLIC. A gamut of services.

Inside, a pleasant young woman was rearranging a display of burglar and fire alarm paraphernalia, explaining
their operation to a middle-aged man. She looked up
inquiringly.

"Lincoln Anderson." Keeping his voice neutral, neither friendly nor cold.

She leafed through a ledger, then smiled as if she'd
found his name amid hundreds of others. "Oh, yes. Your
friend called."

The man, shorter but beefier than Link, stepped forward and offered a heavy paw. "Ron Doughty. World's
greatest investigator, barbecue chef, Packers fan, and
Brewers rooter. Used to be a superb leg-wrestler, until
my daughter broke one of my knees."

Joking about the wound that had retired him from the
Milwaukee police force.

The young woman shook her head in mock disgust
and motioned them toward an open door. "Don't run
off potential clients, Dad."

Doughty limped to the door, closed it behind them,
took a seat behind a scarred desk, and leaned back,
hands tepeed on a comfortable gut. "How can I help?"

Link was studying Doughty's "I Love Me" wall.
Among the collection of youthful photos and mundane
licenses was a framed Bronze Star, with a *V* device for
valor. Beside it a citation from the U.S. Army for heroism at a place called the Ashau Valley, Republic of

South Vietnam. Also a collection of awards for meritorious service from the Milwaukee PD.

"You caught us at a good time, Mr. Anderson," said Doughty. "I just wrapped up a surveillance, and I'm free." Small laugh. "You from here?"

"Not really."

That did not slow him. "And your problem?"

"Let's say I've got a friend with a problem."

"A friend," he mused. "What kind of problem does this *friend* of yours have?"

Link watched Doughty closely. "Let's say he has a prison record. Maybe served considerable jail time for dealing heroin, and a few years more for killing a man." Link paused, examined the reaction, decided it was minimal.

The investigator nodded. "Go on."

"Interested?"

"Does this friend of yours have folding money?"

"Let's say he can go as high as twenty-five thousand for your services." *They'd set the figure at half what the governor had offered.*

Ron Doughty formed a grin that belonged on a cat finishing off a mouse with cholesterol problems. "I charge sixty bucks per investigative hour plus limited expenses, like meals and mileage. For twenty-five thou, your friend can buy a whole lot of my time. Now, what's it for?"

"Let's say he wants to prove he was at another location when someone was murdered."

"Was he?"

"He says he was."

"Where'd all this happen?"

Link shrugged. "Up north?"

"Once you leave our city limits, there isn't a whole lot of north left." Ron Doughty squinted. "Something your friend should know. I'm a legitimate private investigator, and I won't risk my license by manufacturing evidence or doing anything illegal. *But . . .* what a client's done in the past doesn't keep me from inquiring into situations."

It was time to move to the next level. "Do you like kids, Mr. Doughty?"

The investigator immediately glared. "Let's leave my family out of this."

"It's an easy question. Do you *like* children?" Erin had told him that Doughty had two grown children, including the daughter in the front office. Also four grandchildren.

"What I don't like is the direction this discussion is headed. Let's get back to business."

"Everything I just told you was bull manure. Senator Eddie Adcock had three children, and they'd like to know if their father really was a criminal."

Ron Doughty slowly shook his head. "Why, you tricky son of a bitch."

"You just agreed to take on a convicted dealer and murderer, yet you turned down a contract involving a *possible* first-time offender."

Doughty stared. "Who are you?"

"A friend of the senator's. *Will* you reconsider?"

"No." The investigator's voice crackled with emotion.

"Why?" Link examined the man's bleak expression. "You're no coward. I saw the Bronze Star citation on the wall."

"I got that a long time ago." His face was dark. "Damn you, I *can't.*"

"Can't what? Do the right thing?"

Link waited for a few more seconds, then leaned forward and wrote his satellite phone number on a notepad on the desktop. "If you care to share anything, I'd appreciate a call. It's guaranteed to be secure."

Doughty looked at the number on the pad, nose wrinkled like he smelled something unsavory. He rose, went over, and held the door open. "Get out."

Link pulled a money clip from his pocket, unfolded three twenties and dropped them on the desk beside the pad. "For your time."

He nodded to the daughter on his way through. Outside he paused on the sidewalk, wondering what his next step should be. Fly down to Madison and talk with the lawyers who had turned down the Adcock case? Skip it and go on out to the reservation?

He walked to the Toyota, got in, and was trying to make up his mind when Ron Doughty emerged from his office and hobbled down the street as if he was on a holy mission. For a foolish moment, Link wondered if he shouldn't follow him. But Doughty was the detective, not he. In a forest it would have been different, but in an unfamiliar town?

He noted a sedan parked behind him, and a big man observing the PI just as Link was doing. *Really* big, eating Cheez-Its from a cellophane bag. He had the black hair and copper skin of an Indian, a face with lumps rather than features, and was so immense he utterly filled the driver's seat. He refocused his flat gaze on the office from which Doughty had emerged, and tossed back another fistful of Cheez-Its.

Link looked at the plates. Illinois. He started up, and drove back toward Highway 51, the north-south artery once called "Capone's Road." Erin had mentioned in her descriptions how during Prohibition, Al Capone's people had lobbied to keep the road in good repair. His truckers took it up to Lake Superior, rendezvoused with fishing boats filled to the gunwales, then hauled Canadian label whiskey back to Chicago. Lots of money changed hands. Lots of bodies were disposed of in countless marshes and bogs along the way.

The sat phone buzzed. "Anderson," he answered, expecting Erin.

He heard labored breathing, then, "You sure this is secure?"

"Guaranteed."

"I felt like shit, not being able to speak up," said the investigator's voice.

"Where are you?" Link asked, wondering where he had been rushing off to.

"Pay phone in back of a restaurant. I don't *think* my office line's bugged, but I can't take the chance. I know I'm being watched. The same car shows up. Usually a butt-ugly house-sized Indian, sometimes it's others. They park near my house or office for a while, then leave."

"I saw the big guy. Face like a lump of dough?"

"That's him. You're really legitimate? Not here to harm my family?"

"Yes to the first, no to the second."

"Where are you?"

"Driving north on Highway 51. I just entered the town of Woodruff."

"How about pulling over while I tell you a story."

Link turned into a motel entrance and parked. "Okay, I'm listening."

"Last month when I got that contract to look into the senator's death, I felt like I'd hit the jackpot. First there was the money, which I needed, and second, I liked Eddie Adcock. Liked him staying P.O.'d about the Washington politicians having their hands in our pocket. Must've been true 'cause they were always mad at him. And if he exaggerated about them during that debate, so what? It's like a call girl gettin' upset when someone calls her a whore. I also had trouble believing he stole anything at Spirit Lake. I met him a couple times. You could look him in the eye and see an honest man inside. So I felt damn good about getting that contract."

"But you turned it down."

"Wait for me, okay? First thing I did was drive up to the reservation so I could talk with the FBI agent in charge, but nope, they were already outa there. I spoke with the tribal cops, and found they only had two guys on it and they weren't interested. Right then I decided I had a lot of work in front of me to earn the ambassador's money. I came back to my office, set up the case file, made a call to a legal investigator buddy in Eau Claire to see if he'd give me a hand, and started writing down everything I knew. Went home late, and came in early the next morning, all eager to get started. That's when I found the note on my desk."

"Someone had broken in?"

"Yeah, and not a peep outa the alarm system. We may not be fancy, but we take our work seriously and keep our client information confidential, so my daughter put us in an alarm setup that would make the CIA proud. Everything's redundant, with acoustic, Doppler-shift, and infrared detectors, backup batteries, *and* autodialers that ring both my home and the police."

Doughty paused so long that Link had to urge him on. "What was in the note?"

"Directions to go someplace and visit a person—then: *'The same misfortune could happen to anyone. Man or woman. Adult or child. You and yours. You should not help a dirty politician. Turn down the contract.'* There were two final words. *'Burn this.'* "

"So who did they want you to visit?"

"Make a little detour and take a look for yourself," said Doughty. He gave him an address and instructions, spoke a man's name, and hung up.

A minute later, Link pulled into a visitor's parking slot near a pristine white sign that read PLEASANT MANOR, LONG & SHORT TERM MEDICAL CARE. The glass on the door displayed visiting hours. Twenty minutes remained before they'd close for lunch.

Inside he found a counter, and a woman in nurse's whites.

"I'd like to see a Mr. Daniel Eagle."

She pulled out a form. "Except for his wife, he doesn't get many visitors. You're from the Spirit Lake Reservation?"

Link just smiled. Lying had never been easy for him.

"Your people are paying for his keep, so I got no argument. Name?"

"A. L. Anderson."

She had him sign in, and pointed him down the hallway. "Room thirty-eight. He's the only one inside. You guys won't pay for a private room, but no one wants to be in with him."

Link's boots made scuffing sounds on the tiles. He found the door to room thirty-eight cracked, and stepped inside. A scarecrow with coppery skin was strapped into the nearest bed, all four limbs in casts. His age was indeterminable. Forty? Perhaps sixty? His slit eyes were milky and sightless, and burn scars warped the heavy lids. The clawlike fingers that extended from the casts trembled continuously, and periodically he'd release a birdlike chirping sound. He would lick his lips, then

chirp, lick, chirp, again and again. Saliva trickled from
the corner of his mouth to accumulate on his chin.

"The misfortune can happen to anyone," someone had
written in the note to Ron Doughty. *"Man or woman.
Adult or child. You and yours."*

There was no hint of lucidity about Daniel Eagle. Link
watched the ruined man for a moment, then went back
out to the desk, where the woman was laboring over a
form. She looked up. "Leaving so soon?"

"What happened to him?"

"You don't know?"

"I've been out of the area." Somewhat true, since he'd
never been *in* the area.

"Owner of the Big Buck Tavern—up next to the reservation—was closing, and found Daniel outside in the
bed of his pickup. Someone'd used a club on his arms
and legs, then beat him in the head until his brain was
jelly. Would you believe seventeen skull fractures?"

"Who did it?"

"No one knows. Hard to imagine anyone that mean,
regardless if he was a troublemaker. They poked a live
cigar into Daniel's cornea. He's permanently blinded and
has a near-flat-line brain. He's lucky to be breathing."

Lucky? Link wondered. "You say he was a
troublemaker?"

"An elder on the Spirit Lake council said that right
on channel twelve, and again in an interview with the
Lakeland Times."

She abruptly stopped and nodded to a woman entering through the double doors. "Good morning, Mrs.
Eagle."

The newcomer passed quietly by and continued down
the hall. She was sturdily built, with rounded chipmunk
cheeks and an air of gentle radiance.

"His wife?" Link asked, although she appeared much
younger than Daniel.

"Yes. Doris is here most of the time. He's lost weight
so she tries to feed him, and doesn't understand that
he's getting nourishment through an IV. She keeps it up,
she'll end up choking him. Between you and me, it
wouldn't be a bad thing."

Link thought about it all as he went back down to room thirty-eight, where Doris Eagle had taken the chair beside the husk that was once her husband. Lick. *Chirp!* Nothing had changed with him except that she'd wiped the accumulation from his chin.

"Mrs. Eagle?" Link asked after a quiet moment.

She examined him. "I do not know you. Are you of the People?"

Most Indian tribes spoke of their own as "the People." The Blackfeet and Manido-Ojibwe were linguistic cousins, members of the Algonkian-speaking family, with common ancestral roots buried somewhere in prehistory.

"Yes," he replied. "Do you mind if we talk?"

"No. Daniel and I were raised in the forest on the north side. People there were friendly and liked to talk. Only in the towns do people have no time to talk."

4

Link turned onto Highway 51, trying to erase the image of Daniel Eagle from his mind.

The sat phone buzzed. "Anderson," he answered more brusquely than normal.

"You're driving north." Erin tracked the sat phone's location. After a moment of silence she added, "A few more miles and you'll see a resort called Little Bohemia, where John Dillinger and his gang stayed when the heat was on back in the thirties. Another resort owner called in the FBI, and they shot up some innocent guys who'd dropped by for a drink. Dillinger and his crew gave 'em a whupping and got away, and the bureau *still* doesn't like to be reminded of it."

"Yeah?" Link was thinking about Daniel Eagle's scarred and sightless eyes.

Erin broke the silence again. "The Northwoods was a playground for the old Chicago mob. Some thought Capone's eldest brother made the arrangements for Dillinger, since he owned a fishing lodge only a few miles north of there."

A pipe, or some sort of metal club, had been used on Eagle's head and limbs. He would never regain basic bodily functions, let alone think. "I just saw something," he said.

"Would you please tell me. I'm tired of talking to myself."

He explained the visit with Doughty, then about seeing Daniel Eagle.

Erin was appropriately horrified. "Hey, pardner. I come from northern Arizona, where liquored up cowboys and Indians line up to duke it out over girls and football, but they don't do things like *that*."

"I spoke with Daniel's wife. He called home the evening Senator Adcock died, excited about seeing an accident, saying he was with a buddy at the bar."

"Gordon Tower didn't mention that in his briefing."

"The FBI may not have believed Daniel. He'd been drinking when he called her. She said he was celebrating, but when I asked why, she felt she'd said enough."

It was the eyes that bothered Link most. Someone had used a lit cigar to burn out Daniel Eagle's vision. His own ancestors had reserved that treatment for their worst enemies, so they wouldn't be able to see in the next life. Was this somehow related?

"Link, I'm wondering. Someone hurt Daniel Eagle . . . and someone used what happened to him to warn off the investigator . . . and Ron Doughty feels it's the same people, right?"

"I haven't talked with him since my visit with the Eagles."

"Sure he does, or he wouldn't take the threat so seriously. Back to the break-in, and the security alarm installed by his daughter. They probably have a good one, as advertising."

"Yeah. In fact Doughty claimed they use three different kinds of sensors."

"Then whoever got past them had to be an expert. I have trouble matching a dweeb with the know-how to get past all that technology with a badass who burns out people's eyes. *My* conclusion? There are a number of someones involved, working together."

"Including the biggest Indian I've ever seen," he said, and described the man outside the investigator's office. "Doughty says he's been parking there off and on since the break-in."

"Did you get a license plate number?"

"Only that it was issued in Illinois."

Erin typed data into her computer. "I'd say, considering all of this, it's mighty odd that the FBI bowed out so quickly."

"From what Gordon said they were *kicked* out." He mulled it over. "Erin, give me an estimate on how many agents you think the FBI had assigned to the case?"

"A high-vis, high-profile senator's death? I don't know. Fifty? A hundred?"

"How about six? Now that they're gone, there are two reservation policemen assigned, and Doughty says they aren't interested."

"I'll call Gordon and see what he thinks of all that. First, follow me on another thought. Before the break-in at Reliable Inquiries, someone stole the documents from the Spirit Lake museum, which was *also* crawling with alarms, right?"

"Yeah. Supposedly done by the two crooks who died with Senator Adcock."

"They couldn't have done both jobs, since the break-in at Reliable Inquiries happened after they were dead. So it sounds to me like the place was just crawling with top-notch break-in experts, which I would offer is not normal for the boondocks."

"Agreed."

"So why did the FBI feel it had to be the crooks with Senator Eddie who robbed the museum? It could have been the same ones who later broke into Reliable Inquiries."

"I've only been here a couple of hours, and you've got everything solved?"

"Maybe not everything. Where are you headed?"

"You can't tell with your magic computer?"

"Hmm. Since I doubt you'd stop at the John Dillinger exhibition—they display the guns and stuff he left behind—how about the Spirit Lake Reservation?"

"Bingo. Thought I'd nose around some, then find a motel room."

"Well I've been putzing around in people's computers up there, and there's two problems with that, pardner. One of those is the reservation police aren't taking kindly to outsiders *nosing* around their back roads. They have roadblocks set up so outsiders don't run around looking for stolen documents."

"Tourists are *supposed* to nose around."

"Only at the main lake. No one can go into the north side, including the Manido Indians. Also, it's Friday. Every room, cabin, and cubbyhole is filled for the weekend, *and* the casino-hotel's booked."

Link had not thought of that. "So what do I do?"

"Enjoy the scenery, and if you do that slowly enough, Helga and I'll be back with answers before you get there. I will also tell you about the brand-new Link Anderson."

When Erin next buzzed him, Link reported that he'd dawdled as instructed, even stopped for coffee and wild blueberry pie at a roadside pastry shop called Michael's Parlor.

"Part of your physical conditioning program?" she asked.

"Now *that's* mean."

"Ready to hear your new background, Dr. Jekyll?"

"Fire away."

"You're no longer a Blackfoot savage. You're a member of the Manido-Ojibwe band—which is related to but not a part of the Lake Superior Ojibwe nation. That's the same tribe most of us white-eyes call Chippewa. Umm, you'd better turn right."

He turned off U.S. 51 onto a nondescript county road. A small sign read SPIRIT LAKE, 47 MILES.

"Until age three you lived in a cabin in the north side wilderness. Then your family moved to Ohio, where your pop was a carpenter." She went on to describe parents who had moved often, leaving few roots behind.

"They died when you were small, and from there on we'll stick close to the truth. You were adopted by military stepparents. Good athlete. Air Force Academy. Flew combat in Desert Storm and got out. Bummed around as a ski instructor, woodchopper and hunting guide, then got the wonders and made numerous trips to visit the reservation there at Spirit Lake, which is how you got to know it so well. Recently you've lived in New York—but here's another switch—you've been flying charters out of Teterboro in a variety of airplanes."

"That works." He had logged four thousand hours flying various military and corporate aircraft. His stepfather owned a charter airline based at Ronald Reagan International, in Washington.

"You've leased the Baron and you're striking out on your own. You're considering a move to Spirit Lake, hoping to get charter work out of Chicago and Milwaukee."

"What about records? Birth, school, employment, bank account, that sort of thing?"

"I'm punching the right buttons as we speak, kemo sabe. *There.* Until I change it all back, if anyone looks, you're the real thing."

"Great for the past. Now I need a bed for tonight."

"You're staying at Hideaway Bay Resort, on Spirit Lake. I'm talking about the lake, not the town. Check in and register. They'll put you in cottage eight."

"An hour ago you said there weren't any vacancies."

"People really shouldn't leave their computers on. A Mr. and Mrs. Schneider canceled their two-week stay, and a Mr. Lincoln Anderson was at the top of the waiting list. The desk clerk called for verification and I told them you were already on your way."

"So what do I do when the Schneiders arrive?"

"I'm appalled at your lack of confidence in your vivacious young assistant. They won't arrive, so don't question. Your abode has two rooms, a great view of the lake, and maid service twice a week. Of course, if you'd rather look for a place yourself . . ."

"I humbly apologize."

"That apology will be processed with all the others. Next point, the reservation has three major areas. The south side, which you'll see first. Next there's the town on the lake where they built the casino. Finally, there's this vast wilderness area they call the north side, because it's north of Spirit Lake. That's where they suspect Senator Adcock hid the gym bag and the old treaties, and the police do not appreciate tourists *nosing around* there, as you put it."

"So what do you suggest?"

"Start by getting someone to back up your story about being from there."

"I'm game. How do I do that?"

"Just continue relying upon your brilliant but modest assistant. I'm having a local fellow drop by your cottage this afternoon."

"How did you find him?"

"Recall the package Senator Adcock mailed before he died? I've loaded the voice tape into Helga for analysis, but there's also a long list of names, all tagged with descriptive notes. Some are well known; most are not. Some he suspected of wrongdoing. Others are sources and informants—including the two who died with him in the crash. There's one group Eddie felt were especially trustworthy, including a fellow named Jason Toussaint, whom he listed as very helpful. I rang him up while you were battling the blueberry pie, and he's agreed to meet you. Your cottage, at four this afternoon?"

"Sounds good."

"You'll use passwords. He'll ask if you need a fishing guide—that's what he does—then you ask if he provides the boat."

"Isn't that a little overdramatic?"

"Maybe not. Here's an interesting fact. About a quarter of the names Senator Adcock listed as trustworthy *can't* talk. They've either disappeared, died, or were hurt in accidents."

"I'll use the passwords."

"I think it's wise. Turn right on a road called County H, just ahead."

For the next half hour, Link drove in silence as he passed through state and national forestlands. There was little traffic, no roadside homes, and the dense forest grew close to the roadway. While he gravitated to wildernesses, he had seen few that made him feel so isolated.

He passed Big Buck Tavern—unremarkable and set back into the trees—where the husk of Daniel Eagle had been found. A quarter mile farther he entered the Spirit Lake Reservation, and passed row after row of small, paint-faded homes, all precisely alike, some with battered pickups, old snowmobiles, and appliances littering the yards. He slowed for a man and woman staggering along the edge of the highway, desperately clutching paper sacks.

In the space of a few blocks he passed three parked black-and-white Ford Explorers. Uniformed men stared out at residents who lolled about small porches. The policemen seemed wrong somehow. While their vehicles were marked RESERVATION PATROL, none were Indian.

Erin called again. "What you're seeing is the back way in, out of the view of tourists and official visitors. Whattaya think, pardner?"

"Poverty and small cookie-cutter homes."

"Back in the sixties, most of the Indians lived in the wilderness on the north side, which they'd called home for the previous three hundred years. Then political activists arrived—not a local in the group—raising hell about the way they lived. Congress ordered an investigation by HUD, newly formed as part of the Great Society. Ignoring the fact that it was a Manido tradition to live with nature, the inquiry found they were living in primitive conditions and built the housing you're looking at. When no one moved, the elders tried to explain that they preferred to live as their ancestors had done. Since that wasn't the plan, HUD yelled at the Bureau of Indian Affairs, and the BIA coaxed the Manido with money and handouts. Finally the Department of the Interior declared the north side an unsafe habitat, and *forced* them to move. Almost four thousand people were relocated. Most just kept on going to cities or other reservations."

"All that room up north, and here they're crammed like sardines into a filthy can."

"They can't even visit their old homes. Remember what you're seeing, okay? Then turn right up ahead, and keep going until you get to the highway, which is what

Chicago tourists see when *they* come to visit." She gave
more directions.

As he turned onto Bear Lane, she said, "Gotta go.
I'm heading for the Meadowlands so Johnny can watch
his Giants get their butts beat by the Cowboys. *Ciao* for
now, pardner. "

"Say hi to Johnny," Link told her, and dropped the
sat phone into his shirt pocket.

Bear Lane meandered out of the inhabited area and
passed through forests for several miles. On an isolated
stretch, he watched a black-and-white Ford Explorer pull
over a sedan. A patrolman emerged from either side of
the SUV and swaggered forth.

As he passed, the woman in the sedan appeared so
shaken that Link considered stopping.

He decided that with two cops present the woman
should be safe enough, and drove on.

The big, florid-faced cop named Willie pulled in behind the woman's car, and looked around. A single,
dark-colored Toyota proceeded past toward the main
road. He was not surprised at the lack of traffic. There
was too little income among south siders for more than
essential travel, especially with gasoline being so out-
rageously expensive.

Willie winked at the scarecrow-skinny ex-hood from
Saint Paul who was his partner. "Ready to see how it's
done?" He hitched his pants and strode to the driver's
open window.

She was Indian, in her thirties. A little overweight,
and looking panicky.

"Where the fuck you headed, goin' so fast?"

"Home. I went for cigarettes at the Smoke Shop."

"We clocked you doin' fifty in a twenty-five," he
growled. "Outa the fuckin' vehicle."

She cringed. "I wasn't—"

"Don't fuckin' argue and make it worse. I said outa
the car."

"Please . . ."

"You don't hear?" He grasped the handle, yanked
the door open, stepped just slightly back, and placed a

menacing hand on his pistol. "Any more argument and we haul your ass in."

She climbed out, so frightened it appeared she might fall.

Willie grasped her arm, deftly spun her about, and shoved her hard against the door. While she remained off-balance, he nudged his boot between her legs and kicked her feet apart.

"Oh, God . . ." Her voice was wavering and high.

"You carrying a weapon?" he asked, grinning over the top of her vehicle at his partner as he popped off a button while shoving a heavy hand into her blouse.

She tried to twist away. "Stay *still,*" he roared. She cried as he felt her.

"What caliber's she carryin'?" joked the other cop.

"Big enough. Stay outside and keep the traffic moving while we check out the backseat."

"Don't wear it out. I'd like some of that myself."

As Link joined the traffic heading back westward toward town, the change from the south side was dramatic. The roadway was newly paved, the buildings freshly painted. There were signs of prosperity, and none of poverty. Most of the license plates were from Illinois. According to Erin, Chicago residents felt the Northwoods was their private fiefdom. In return, more than a few folks in northern Wisconsin and Upper Michigan called them FIBs, which in local patois meant "F'in' Illinois Bastids." But while they were short of industry and agriculture in the Northwoods, there were loads of deer hunting, fishing, and water and snow recreation. Most reservations, like the one at Lac du Flambeau, were doubly prosperous because of gaming and tourism incomes. While the Spirit Lake reserve was much larger, it drew only a modest tourist trade.

Link learned about the Hatchet Club from billboards. He found that the slots were set "loose" for the enjoyment of their guests, that they gave away a new SUV every month, that "real men play craps," that "Headline Stars" he'd never heard of played weekends at the lounge. The world's largest hatchet—the record had

been submitted to Ripley's "Believe It or Not!" for verification—was situated at the casino entrance. "Look
for it!"

By the time Link spotted the towering blaze-orange
hatchet he'd been conditioned to expect Las Vegas gran-
deur, but there was nothing grand about the gaudy casino and attached three-story hotel. In the sprawling
parking lot were scores of buses and vans, and hundreds
of automobiles. The Hatchet Club complemented the
beauty of the surrounding forest like a plastic gem in a
platinum setting.

Beyond was a dazzling blue lake, and on it a variety
of watercraft, from jet skis to pontoons to motorboats
pulling skiers to canoes and sailboats. Humans walked
littered beaches and, despite the crisp air, sunned themselves in chaise lounges on docks lining the shore. Still
there were not all that many tourists compared with similar resorts he'd seen.

The lake covered ten thousand acres—the combined
reservation and state and national forest land beyond
occupied three thousand square miles. On the north
side—including the top third of the reservation that extended into Upper Michigan—were a plethora of smaller
lakes, numerous creeks and bogs, and dense forest, yet
all of the thousand-odd residents lived either in the town
or on the slummy south side.

Link pulled into the casino parking lot to get a feel
for the reservation's major attraction, and drove through
slowly. Taking in the buses (one marked GAMBLER'S SPE-
CIAL) and RVs parked in neat rows near the back.

He counted three of the black-and-white Explorers,
all manned by male cops. None of them appeared to be
Indian, and all looked hard and unkempt. He wondered
about the relationship between the law officers and the
casino. He even detected something different about the
tourists. The males appeared too shifty-eyed, too slick,
and the women too gaudy.

Link had completed his circle of the building and was
turning toward the exit when one of the policemen
walked over from a side hotel entrance and held up a
hand, signaling for him to halt.

A green van had stopped before him. Moderately nosy, Link rolled down the window.

Another car pulled up beside him—an Indian family, parents in front and kids in back—and the driver eased forward as if to pass. "Get back!" the reservation policeman barked angrily. When the driver hesitated, he stared him down and yelled, "Move your red ass."

Not an ambassador of goodwill.

First out of the van were two men swathed in facial bandages. Next came several dweeb types of each gender, with PalmPilots in belt holsters and laser pointers in pocket protectors, wearing uniformly green jackets and trousers. Some sort of engineers? Last out was a slender male with unkempt blond hair, a scraggly beard, and eyes so intense they could be used to cut metal. The dweebs hovered about him as he hurried to the side entrance, as if they'd not wanted the blond to be seen. *Why?* he wondered.

The policeman walked up to his window. "The fuck you lookin' at?"

"Good day to you too." Link said softly as he put the Toyota in gear. He drove around the van, noting a subdued logo, reading ECOL-REC, LTD.

After a quarter mile on the highway he turned off on the road that circumnavigated the big lake. He counted a dozen resorts, all infinitely nicer than the squalor he'd noted on the south side.

The pavement turned to crushed granite. Half a mile farther he encountered a sign reading HIDEAWAY BAY, FAMILY RESORT. He purposefully drove on, toward the north side wilderness, until he arrived at the roadblock Erin had told him about, manned by two mean-looking apes in police uniform. He turned around without arguing, and returned to the resort.

Whitewashed cottages were aligned along the lakeshore to the left and right of the lodge. He went inside, registered, and was assigned to—big surprise—cottage eight. The manager, a prim-looking man, said it had come available only a short time before.

Link mentioned that he was about to move from New York.

The manager narrowed his eyes at the smell of money. "I dabble in real estate. What sort of home will you be looking for?"

"Something remote, on a nice lake away from town?"

"I know of some acreage on Rock Lake. Nicely wooded, ten minutes from the casino."

"How about the wilderness area north of here."

The manager shook his head. "The Department of the Interior declared it unfit for habitation. The primitive fools went on living there until they were forced to leave for their own good."

"Any way I can drive up there for a look?"

"The police have it blockaded. How about looking at Rock Lake?"

"No, thanks. My parents were a couple of those primitive fools. I thought I'd have a look at the cabin where I was born." He took his key, touched his hat, and departed.

Link drove to number eight, where he toted his bag and cardboard box inside. The kitchen-dinette-living room was tidy, the queen-sized bed in the back room freshly made. With an hour remaining before his meeting with Jason Toussaint, Link took a leisurely shower, dressed, pulled a bottle from the "vacation" box and a tumbler from the kitchen cabinet. He settled on the porch with three ounces of Johnny Walker Black, taking it neat like he preferred.

He thought about the way the north side had been cut off, and wondered how he might avoid the roadblocks.

The scenery was pleasant, the cottages set into a forest of birch, tamarack, and pine.

While there was not nearly the amount of water traffic he'd expected, a hundred yards distant on the lake two young women on water skis showed off their hard bodies, wearing what was either the skimpiest of bikinis or body paint. He could not decide which, and stared intently while enjoying a savory sip of scotch. The sat phone buzzed inside the cabin where he'd placed it in

its charging unit, and he wondered if he could get away
with ignoring the thing.

After the eighth buzz he decided the caller was serious, and went inside. "Anderson."

"Now you've seen Daniel Eagle," rasped Ron Doughty's voice, "maybe you can understand. I've got
grandkids, and no big-city police force to back me, like
I had in Milwaukee."

"I sympathize," Link responded. Understanding was
a different matter.

"You never said how you figure into it."

Link didn't answer, thinking silence was better than
a lie.

The private investigator sighed. "Shit. I'm getting
sucked in."

"Not true. Hang up, and this is the last you'll hear
of me."

Doughty paused again. "It'll go no further? Just to
you?"

"Anything you tell me will be kept between my assistant and myself."

"Who's this assistant?"

Again Link chose not to answer.

Another sigh. "What would you like to know?"

"For starters, who hurt Daniel Eagle?"

"There were people in the bar with Eagle, but no
one remembered an argument. Daniel stayed to himself,
except for talking to a buddy and a member of the council who dropped by. No one recalls Eagle leaving. The
place closed at ten from lack of customers, and half an
hour later the owner was taking out the trash when he
looked into Daniel's pickup."

"How about the buddy? Does he corroborate
anything?"

"No trace of him since that night. Some say he left
town."

"You got that from the bar?"

"Coldspring County Sheriff's Department. I maintain
a relationship with them."

"What do *they* think happened?"

"Keep in mind there's eleven deputies to handle an

area larger than Connecticut. They may be saying they're developing leads and such, but they're buffaloed. They *think* it was someone from the reservation with a grudge, but when they try to talk to people in Spirit Lake they get nowhere because of jurisdiction problems. The cops out there say they need permission to even pass *through* the reservation. Bottom line—after a month they stopped looking."

"How about the reservation police?"

"Worse than awful. The beating happened off the reservation, or there'd be no investigation at all. The cops there are rotten and the council doesn't want any bad press."

"I spoke with Daniel's wife. She said he called her at home, and mentioned seeing an accident." Doris Eagle had seemed reluctant to say more.

"She tell you about the people at the accident waving pistols, and how he almost ran into a helicopter?"

"A *what*?"

"She claimed Daniel had told her he'd seen a helicopter on the road, until a tribal elder hushed her up. He said Eagle's drinking and fighting had brought disgrace to the tribe, and anything he'd told her was a lie."

"She told me Daniel was celebrating. You know why?"

"Not really. The deputies just figured he was off on a binge. Some out there do that."

"I could use your help, Doughty. A phone call like this once in a while?"

"I don't think so. I'll give you one more thing, then I'm gone. The county cops are not only buffaloed, they don't *want* to look hard."

"What do you mean?"

"People here have long memories, like back to when if folks saw something they weren't supposed to, and wouldn't shut up, they'd get done like Daniel Eagle."

"Who is *they*?" Link tried.

"There're rumors about heavy-duty mob involvement at the reservation, but no one likes to say it too loud." He paused. "Jesus, why did I make that first phone call to you?"

"Because it was the right thing?"

"No more, okay?" With that, the private investigator hung up.

Link went outside and settled into the chair on the porch. As he sipped more good scotch and stared out at the hard bodies on water skis—now joined by a third who he figured was *definitely* wearing only body paint—his mind kept returning to the conversation. What was the *mob* talk about?

He considered the people he'd seen dismounting from the van at the casino-hotel. Most memorable was the blond man with the penetrating eyes. He thought about him for a moment, then returned to the more pleasant tasks of sipping good whiskey and observing the skiers.

5

Link was wondering if his visitor would show when a red Firebird, with roof panels removed, pulled up. The occupant stepped over the door and sauntered over, looking no older than twenty, black hair pulled into a ponytail, a silver bear symbol hanging insolently from his left ear, wearing Nikes, jeans, and a sleeveless shirt that showed off lean muscles.

"Hear you're lookin' for a fishing guide?" His voice held a cocky ring.

"Depends. Got your own boat?"

"You betcha." A grin beamed as he stuck out his hand. "Jase Toussaint."

"Link Anderson."

"Got a call from a sexy voice named Erin. Said she was your assistant and asked if I'd help you get the skinny about Senator Eddie's death. She look as good as she sounds?"

"Guys get whiplash when she walks down the street."

"Then I'm headin' for wherever she's callin' from." He grinned. "How'd you get my name?" He wore a look like he knew the answer and was checking.

"The senator kept a list of people he trusted. A member of his family gave it to us."

Jason digested the words. "Senator Eddie was the greatest thing that ever happened to this country. If you're on his side, far as I'm concerned you were born on the north side." Jase Toussaint gave Link a once-over. "Won't be a hard sell. You look Indian."

"Piegan Blackfoot. Language experts say they and the Ojibwe once lived close together, maybe were even one nation."

"We call ourselves Manido-Ojibwe," Jason said. "The Spirit People. We were the traditional keepers of the faith, the Holy Rollers of the Ojibwe tribe. Now they're in the twenty-first century, and we're stuck in the nineteenth. Used to be, all the Chippewa bands came to our powwows to hear our speakers talk about the days when we whipped the Iroquois and Sioux, and made the world safer for them. When our elders spoke, they showed respect."

They settled into chairs on the porch.

"And now?"

"Not many of us left. Four thousand before we were evicted from the north side. Now we're only a thousand and more leaving every month. When we hold powwows, the other bands are too busy spending their money from gambling to attend. Now we've got the fever. People were tired of being poor so we sold our souls for a casino, like Senator Eddie begged us not to."

Jason wagged his head dolefully, then looked up sharply.

"While you're here, watch out for the tribal police. They're outsiders brought in from places like Chicago and Milwaukee, and they're mean as hell."

Link let him talk on about how the move to the south side had changed everything, and with Senator Adcock gone, their lives were miserable. "The talk about Senator Eddie stealing treaties is bull. He hated dishonesty, and didn't mind steppin' on the toes of people who were. He was a real orator, talked like he had honey in his mouth. He honestly cared, not just for the Manido, but for America."

"I met him once. An impressive man."

"My folks died in a flu epidemic when I was little, so my aunt helped raise me. Back when I was fifteen, I was getting into trouble—not awful stuff, but smoking dope and popping all the pills I could get my hands on—and he visited. Big man, famous and all. Told everyone he was home to relax and get the Washington baloney out of his system. My aunt was tired of me fooling around and took me to him and asked if he'd talk to me.

"Senator Eddie told my aunt not to wait up, ordered me to get my butt in his pickup, and drove us up to the lakeshore cabin where he was raised. He was this incredible positive force, whistling and smiling all the way, explaining how important it is for us to carry on our traditions. He showed me an old dugout canoe he'd found as a kid, and said how back some two, three hundred years ago someone had weighted it with rocks and sunk it for the winter. That's how they kept their canoes safe from ice damage. When the person died, it had been left there all those years until he found it. Next he showed me a collection of fishing spears with metal heads that he explained were old French trade goods. After we'd tightened the spearheads, we used dried grass, tree pitch, and wood to make torches, just like the ancient Manido-Ojibwe.

"He'd ask if I was hungry, and I'd say yeah, and he'd say, 'Me too so we better catch something. We're gonna have to *work* for this meal.' "

The young Indian stared out at the lake, seeing another vision.

"Eddie told stories while we rowed out to a place he said was good fishing. By then it was dark, so we lit the torches in their holders at the ends of the canoe. We waited and stood real still, and whispered like little kids while we watched for fish. I think he fixed it somehow, but I was the one who speared a big walleye pike that swam up to the surface. It was something—just like the old, old days. When we got back to the cabin we sliced off fillets, and charbroiled 'em with some fresh corn he just happened to have in the truck.

"He showed me this," Jason said, and displayed a worn wooden flute, ten inches in length. "It's called a *bibig-wun*. He'd made several of them the old way. See how there's six finger holes and five holes around the end? Our museum people say it's a replica of the ones used in the old rituals. This one was lowest in tone, like the bass, even though it sounds high-pitched without something to compare it with. He showed me how to play it, and we even tried a duet. He was good, like he was with most things. After a while he said it was mine if I'd just practice the old tunes so we could play together when he visited."

"Could you show me?"

Jason played a few bars. The sound was haunting. Link was impressed.

"I never slept so well as I did when he dropped me off at home that night. Think of it. A great man like the senator taking time for a screwed-up kid. Afterward he never missed a birthday without calling. Even helped set me up in the guide business, and every year he'd keep after me until I'd signed up for college courses. I haven't looked at a joint or a pill since."

"Don't most of the Manido think he stole the treaties?"

"Most just say whatever Sly Fox Paquette—he's the council elder in charge of the casino committee—wants them to."

Link registered the name as Jason told him more.

"Sly went off to the army after high school, and came back sixteen years later—four years ago—tossing money around like it was free. A couple weeks after, Charlie Eagle, a council elder, fell out of his boat, hit his head, and drowned just a hundred yards from shore."

"Eagle?" Link repeated, remembering the ruined man in the hospital bed.

"Yeah. Paquette's hated the Eagle clan since high school when Daniel stole his girlfriend Doris. Anyway, Paquette ran for Charlie's seat using his Indian name. 'Vote for Sly Fox Paquette,' he told people, a *real* Injin. Whoop-whoop. Ugh. Heap big chief. All that fake stuff, like he was making fun of the band and didn't care what they thought."

"I'm surprised he won."

"My aunt was already on council and thought he didn't have a prayer. Then this army buddy of his, huge guy, big as a house, spread the word that Sly had been a hero in the Persian Gulf War. Spent time as a prisoner of war before he wiped out a bunch of Iraqis and escaped. Got a bunch of medals. Military service is big here, and there was talk that not voting for him would be unpatriotic. Just to make sure, his big buddy and some others cleaned out all the bars inside and outside the reservation and drove 'em all to the polls. They even made threats saying they'd know how people voted, and anyone that screwed up would pay the price. Sly only won by twelve votes, but it was enough and he smiled a lot when he took Charlie Eagle's seat on council."

"You knew the Eagles?"

"Just to see them. I was raised in town, and they were on the north side near Frenchman's Lake." He dropped his voice. "The night Senator Eddie died, someone beat Daniel almost to death. Sly Paquette said Daniel was drinking and fighting, and brought shame on the People. Daniel's wife said he was just celebrating. She's pregnant, and the doctor had told them it was a boy, so Daniel went out for a few drinks with a friend."

Pregnant? Link kicked himself for thinking she was built *sturdy,* not recognizing the radiant look for what it was. "Any chance I can talk to the friend?"

"He moved without leaving an address. Quite a few have done that. Some scared of the police, others just tired of putting up with things. Spirit Lake isn't a good place to live.

"As soon as Sly Paquette got his council seat he started talking about a casino, saying he had connections, and how anything was possible if we donated to the right politicians. He said it would be like printing money. We'd get free schools and services, and everyone with the blood could just sit back and collect. The council was skeptical, but Paquette had a team of lawyers come in with fancy presentations, and pretty soon *everyone* was talking about what we could do with the money. Like the council president wanted to upgrade the pow-wow grounds, and my aunt wanted the schools. Something for everyone."

"You don't sound too happy about it."

"I've never trusted anything that came out of Sly's mouth. I called Senator Eddie about the hundred thousand the council was about to hand over to the politicians. He flew back and went in front of the council and called it bribery, but Paquette's lawyers argued there's nothing illegal about contributions. That's the way American politics works.

"Senator Eddie called a meeting at the hall to debate it in front of the People, and even let Sly and his lawyers go first. Then he spoke in that deep rumble of his, saying that no casino, even if it paid back *double* what was promised, was worth the People's soul. He pleaded for us to bribe *no* one, because that's what it was, and *if* they got all the facts and decided on a casino, go through the proper channels. Nothing's free, he said. Then an aide came up on stage and whispered something, and he left. Later we learned his wife had been killed in an auto accident."

A couple pulled up to the next cottage. Middle-aged, wearing brightly colored shorts—she bulging out of a halter, he from a flowered shirt. Both called out greetings, and Link waved. As they began hauling luggage, Link noted Jason had grown quiet.

"Would you rather go inside?"

"Yeah," Jason said, looking at the Illinois plates. "Hard to tell the real tourists."

Link led the way into the kitchen table, picked up the scotch to try and clean up, and noted how Jason's eyes had become fixed on the bottle. "Care for a drink?"

"Maybe later." Still, his eyes remained hungry as Link put away the bottle.

"When the senator left, did the council make the contribution?"

"They voted to wait, like Senator Eddie wanted, so Paquette called in reinforcements. An undersecretary of the Interior just *happened* to drop in to talk about the ecol-rec zone, and . . ."

"The *what*?"

"Ecology recovery zone. Back a hundred years ago some mining developers talked the council into leasing a ten-mile square of property up at the northwest corner of the reservation. When they stripped out the surface iron ore and left a mess, council sued, but the mining company won. Couple years back, the Department of the Interior popped in, declared the old mine area a disaster zone, and ordered the People out of the entire north side for their own good."

"That was why they had to move?"

"Yeah, because of the ecol-rec zone, and how the poisons might have spread there. Then Interior hired a company to reclaim the zone by the use of bio-engineering."

"I saw a van with ECOL-REC, LIMITED printed on its side at the hotel. There was a blond guy with a beard that they didn't want anyone seeing."

"I haven't met him." Jason's gaze was noncommittal. It was not worth pursuing. "Go back to the meeting with the government official."

"Sure. The undersecretary told council that Senator Eddie was out of touch, and what Sly Paquette said was true. We were *eligible* for the casino, but there were so many other requests being processed it might take years. The only way to jump line was for the elders to get to know the decision makers, and *that* meant buying thirty seats to a dinner party in Madison. After he departed the elders added up the numbers—thirty seats at five hundred a plate. The ante had just gone up by fifteen thousand dollars. Paquette told them if they wanted all that free money, they had to prime the pump, and they better do it before the price went up again."

"And?"

"The measure passed, and the tribal fund was cleaned out."

"How did your aunt vote?"

"Against, but by then she was spending most of her time in Washington, working for a congressional committee. None of us knew the real price of the casino back then."

"So what is the real price?"

Jason Toussaint started to explain, then changed his mind. "My aunt's moved back from Washington. I'd better check with her before I go any further."

"Mob involvement?" Link tried, remembering the private investigator's concern.

Jason looked troubled. "Let's wait until I've talked to my aunt."

"During the investigation of the senator's death, did the FBI ask about the fight over the casino?"

"After a week most of the agents were sent back to Milwaukee. The ones left concentrated on the theft of the old documents. Now the tribal police are investigating, which is like leaving your Ferrari with a car thief. They won't find anything, and the reporters have dragged Senator Eddie's name through so much mud, no one cares."

"Why did your council order the FBI out?"

"They didn't. Sly Paquette sent complaints on council letterhead to both the attorney general and Indian Affairs, saying the FBI was meddling in Manido business, which went against our treaty. By the time the rest of the council got wind of it, the Washington politicians were already agreeing that the FBI was meddling in the noble red man's business."

"Doesn't sound like you have one big happy family here."

"Things are bad. *Really* bad. The new cops are crooked, and there's no one to turn to." An "oh yeah" look crept over Jason's face. "You ever hear of Gloria Vasson?"

"Senator Adcock's second wife?"

"She's a rich lady. The police have been searching the north side for the old treaties, but they don't have a clue. Tomorrow Gloria will talk to the council, and offer to bring in a team of professionals. It's all hush-hush. No one but council members are supposed to know."

"Tell me about her."

Jason shrugged. "I never met the lady. My aunt doesn't like her, but Senator Eddie told me she was one of the best things that ever happened to him."

"What does Sly Paquette say about her proposal?"

"He's arguing to let her go ahead with it, and he's the man. He runs the casino committee, and they're about to release their first year's earnings. Then the infighting will *really* begin. My aunt will be in there slugging for a new grade school, and two others want—"

Link interrupted. "How many people are going on the document search?"

"Three or four. Paquette's telling everyone on council to keep it quiet."

Link thought about it for a moment. "How about a local area guide?"

"I don't know, but it makes sense. I'll see what my aunt says."

"How much clout does she have?"

"Zero if it has anything to do with the casino. On minor things she and the council president get their way so the others can feel better about selling out to Paquette."

"I'd like to meet her."

"Good idea." Jason looked relieved, as if he'd been talking above his pay grade.

"How about now?"

Jason glanced at his watch. "Let's make it later."

They decided on eight o'clock, which was two and a half hours away.

Link stepped outside so Jason could call his aunt in privacy. The activity on the lake had changed. The cooler air had driven away skiers and jet skis. There were more parties on pontoons, more fishing boats, the occupants casting carefully as swifter craft darted by.

Jason emerged. "Erin told me you're a pilot. Sounds cool."

"We get a chance, I'll take you up."

"I'd like that. Once they reopen the north side, I'll take you out to a couple lakes where the bass are spoiling for a fight and the muskies are giants."

"I've never seen a live muskie."

"Muskellunge's the largest fish in the pike family. They grow to fifty, sixty pounds, and fight like a marlin— or that's what I hear, never having caught a marlin."

Link followed him to his car. "While I'm waiting, I'll take a turn around town."

"Watch out for the cops. I'm not kidding when I say they're bad. They hand out beatings, and demand bribes and such. Since Senator Eddie left they've been sellin' dope. *Heavy*-duty crystal meth. We've had pot around, and kids sniffin' gasoline and glue, but this crank is different. They almost give it away, then keep sinking the hook deeper. Bad!"

"No one says anything to the Bureau of Indian Affairs?"

"Tell you something true. Now that Senator Eddie's gone, no one in Washington gives a damn about a band of backwoods Indians in the middle of nowhere. People who get inquisitive have accidents or disappear, and no one wants to end up like the Eagle clan."

Jason described the town of Spirit Lake. There were a few outlets. Curio shops, Indian jewelry stores, the biggest moccasin outlet in the Northwoods, a bead and buckskin clothing store going in. All were owned out of town by friends of Sly Paquette. The powwow center, museum, tribal council building, supermarket, and meeting hall were used by locals. Jason told him about the home where he lived with his aunt. Erected by a French-Canadian trapper in 1820, the first Toussaint at Spirit Lake. Burned down twice. Now there were dozens of Toussaints.

The youthful Jason stepped over the door of the topless Firebird in a practiced display of cool, and settled into the seat.

"See you here at eight," said Link.

"You got it." Jason started the engine, which idled in a lusty rumble. "You'll like my aunt. She got the brains in the family." His eyes shone with pride. Then his look darkened. "If you hear anything bad about her, don't listen."

Link called the New York office's recorder and summarized his discussion with young Toussaint. He said he was going into town to buy supplies, take a touristy look around, and return in time for the meeting with Jason and his aunt. He finished by asking Erin to look up Ron Doughty's bank account—child's play for her—and deposit a thousand dollars along with the message "Error in your favor, Anderson Investments." Who knew what it might reap?

Aside from dodging an inattentive tourist, the drive

into Spirit Lake was uneventful. After stopping at a Quik Mart for coffee and sandwich makings, and making a circuit around the town for familiarization, he pulled into the half-filled casino parking lot.

He purposefully took a space at the farthest corner of the lot, walked briskly, and was winded by the time he got to the casino entrance. He was disgusted with his physical state. Tomorrow he would get back into his exercise regime to change all that.

Inside, the Hatchet Club was a cookie-cutter replica of the cheaper class of gambling emporiums found in Vegas and Atlantic City. He roved the floor, was made to feel at home by losing fifty dollars at a crap table, and strolled again, idling and watching the action and the crowd, who did not look at all like other gambling tourists he'd seen, thinking how Jason had called them crooks from the cities. Also thinking about Ron Doughty, the private investigator, and about the broken Daniel Eagle. He did not catch sight of the engineer types in green uniforms or the skinny blond man, yet the entire time he felt like he was being watched.

He left. It had been a busy day, and there was still the meeting with Jason's aunt to come.

6:30 P.M.—Pleasant Manor, Woodruff

Doris Eagle emerged from the nursing home, completely void of the slightest trace of happiness. Before her man had been ruined and her life's purpose lost, she'd been forever cheerful, with a kind word for everyone. Now there was nothing but bitterness.

As she walked toward the old car her sister had loaned her for her daily trips, a huge man with a featureless and lumpy face—Indian, but not one of the People—approached her from the side. Roughly he grabbed her arm and steered her toward a Lexus sedan. He opened the door and gave her a shove. "Get in."

Doris obediently climbed in back and stared at the sharp-faced man there. She'd known him since childhood, yet was so frightened that she fought the urge to urinate even though she'd felt fine only a moment before. The ugly giant crawled into the front seat, and handed back a long paper-wrapped object. The eyes of the evil man were emotionless as he accepted it.

He spoke quietly. "Tell me about your husband's visitor."

Doris was too frightened to respond.

The evil man methodically pulled back a portion of paper wrapping. A length of pipe, two feet long and an inch and a half in diameter, was revealed—the metal permeated with dark stain. She did not have to be told it was the same one he'd used to ruin Daniel.

"Once more," the man beside her said in an ugly monotone. "Who was the visitor, and what did he want? Or do I persuade you, like I did your precious husband."

Then a miracle occurred, for as quickly as Doris's fears had risen, they disappeared. Did he not realize that her life had already been stolen from her, and there was nothing he could do to make it worse? Her heart had been ripped out when she'd seen what he had done to Daniel. Now he offered pain, as if he'd forgotten that only agony could ease her sorrow. Women in her ancestry had cut away strips of living flesh to mourn the loss of family members.

The child within her was without heritage. Its good Eagle clan name destroyed before it could even draw its first breath. It would be just as well that it did not survive.

This terrible man she had once known saw only a woman with a broken life. He could not see the new spirit that filled the void where only a moment before she'd known terror.

She could do no more for her husband. She must honor his name.

Doris Eagle hawked, taking her time with the task and gathering residue from far back in her throat, and spat in his face. Then, as Sly Paquette's jaw still drooped, she launched herself, fingers like talons, raking and clawing. Going for his eyes, as he had done to her Daniel.

6

The woman called Sydney was bored, bored, BORED, so bored that she wanted to scream, although she'd only been back for a day. It was the place and the people— oh *God* how she missed Washington, with its intrigues and undercurrents of power. She missed the familiarity of the office—after all she'd spent fifteen years there— even the way the chief peeked into her lab each morning and said, "So who shall we be today?"

Seated at the window of the suite, looking out over the dark forest, it was difficult to realize that she could never go back. When her boss had been "made," she had been dragged down with him, as if she were some rank amateur and not the Assistant Master of Disguise. She'd been indicted in absentia and secretly, since it was in the interest of national security that her prosecution be kept from the public. There were high officials with whom she quietly remained in contact, of course—those avenues would remain open so long as she breathed and had piles of dirt on them—but the indictment meant she was banished.

On the brink of slipping into a darker mood, Sydney decided to amuse herself by going to dinner as a cutesy dumb blonde. She went into the dressing room and pulled out her artist's wooden case. Inside were a variety of wigs and latex-based human features.

As she applied gum spirits to position apple cheeks and perky nose, Sydney opened a notepad and examined scribbled entries, indecipherable to a casual reader, as if reviewing a Sit Rep back at the office.

Her effort to destroy Senator Eddie Adcock's reputation and credibility was complete. Even forced to operate in the shadows—after all, she was a fugitive—Sydney had found it easy, considering her leverage over so many powerful individuals. She'd done it gleefully. Adcock had been the one on the Senate subcommittee who had gone after her like a bulldog. The silly twit had not realized how deadly she could be.

The FBI had been ordered to cease all monitoring of the senator's death.

Now that she was back, everything on the reservation must be watched closely. She would expect periodic reports from Sly Paquette and his police. Without absolute control of Spirit Lake and the Indian reservation, the rest would be impossible.

The casino-hotel was lucrative, but she had little interest there. It was the activities at the Warehouse—not one, but *three* of them—that would generate spectacular revenues. Tonio Gracchi and his mafiosi would swim in money, and Sydney would progress from modest wealth—funds she still channeled from agency operating accounts—to obscene riches.

It was absolutely necessary that the Warehouse remain secure and unknown. Already it was protected from observation from the sky, and soon it would be impenetrable from the ground. The engineers who designed the systems were being rewarded with a night in the private big-roller's casino, down the hall from her penthouse suite.

Sydney had decided to see how they'd react to a buxom blonde in their midst.

As she labored on her appearance, she continued reading from her notes. Although Sly Paquette's police had searched while she'd been away, Senator Eddie Adcock's gym bag and its incriminating evidence remained unfound.

She paused as she interpreted the next, and final, entry. Senator Adcock's widow, Gloria Vasson, believing the gym bag contained something entirely different, had offered to hire a professional explorer and organize a search.

Sydney's interest was aroused, as it had been since she'd learned that Eddie's widow was coming to Spirit Lake. She was striking and extremely wealthy—and Sydney was *so* tempted.

So who shall we be today?

Middle School, South Side, Spirit Lake Reservation

Evening shadows were darkening as Jason pulled up to the side of the old schoolhouse, doused his lights, and looked carefully about, tingling with anticipation, since meeting with the secret "*Muk-wah* society" was perilous. Still, he knew they were the only remaining hope the Manido had to survive this, the worst crisis since the Iroquois had come in force to destroy the Ojibwe nation two centuries ago.

He was the sentinel, the first to arrive. As such he would keep his engine idling and be watchful. Since he hadn't seen a police patrol car in the area there should be no problem starting on time. That was good, for he intended to leave early. He'd been unable to reach his aunt by phone, and they had the eight o'clock meeting with Link Anderson.

Jason was forced by sacred oath to tell the Bear Society leader about Link. He wondered if Storyteller would want to meet the pilot and judge for himself.

His attention was drawn by motion in the rearview mirror, and he stared until he recognized the dark shape of the beater pickup that idled past and parked fifty yards distant. He blinked his parking lamps once, telling his friend that he'd identified him, then remembered how Storyteller had said that everyone was to keep their lights off. "Damn," he grumbled. Another screwup. Too many more and Storyteller might ask him to drop out of the group.

As a second vehicle rolled by in the gloom, Jason held his forehead as a numbness came over him. He knew what was happening and tried to push the dream-time away. His breathing intensified as sensations trembled through his shoulder, his arms and head.

He was unaware that more shadow vehicles rolled past in the darkness, knew only that somewhere a woman screamed as she was broken and ruined. Finally, although not nearly quickly enough, the sensations faded.

Jason sat very still, rigid as stone, arms wrapped protectively about himself.

He'd been frightened after the first dream-times as a teenager, and even wondered if they might be epileptic attacks.

Not many knew of his dream-times—only his aunt, his best friend, and a few others he trusted. Senator Eddie had been aware without being told, and Storyteller, leader of the *Muk-wah,* had somehow learned of them and wished to be told of every incidence. The Manido took dreams seriously. It was a part of their heritage.

A few times Jason too had *almost* believed, after realizing that following the dream-times he knew things that were impossible. Then another part of him argued how foolish that was. A dream was just that, regardless of when you dreamed it.

This time there'd been no mystery. A woman of the People had been horribly beaten.

During the vagueness of the dream-time the parking lot had become darker, and he wondered how many *Muk-wah* had assembled. The Firebird's engine was still idling. He prepared to shut it off and walk to the practice football field where the society would meet.

He noted a flash of illumination on the side of the school building, and swiveled his head. A new vehicle appeared, this one with lights on and the shadowy shape of a light bar on top.

The enemy—about to discover a meeting in progress!

Without thought Jason jammed the shifter into reverse. The Firebird spewed gravel as he cranked the wheel and swung back around, then rocked in place as he switched on his lights, illuminating the black-and-white Explorer now directly in his path.

The red and blues came on, and the Explorer nosed in to block his escape.

He clawed under the seat for his prop, unscrewed the cap and took a swig of wine, and got out, staring stupidly. It was not difficult to act inebriated, just coming out of the dream.

A bulky cop emerged and sauntered toward him. "What the fuck you doin', Injin?"

Jason motioned with the bottle. "Havin' a little Thunderbird. You want a . . ."

The cop batted with his hand and sent the bottle flying.

"Aw shit," Jason said in a maudlin tone.

The patrolman pulled him by his shirtfront and slammed a ham-sized fist into his gut. Jason had tensed, but the blow was fierce and doubled him over. He staggered and sucked for air.

"Dumb shit," the cop said as Jason wheezed. "Get your red ass out of here."

Jason groaned piteously, drawing it out to make sure the other *Muk-wah* had sufficient time to escape. Finally he painfully climbed into the Firebird, waited as the Explorer moved out of his path, and slowly drove forward.

As he turned onto the highway, the patrolman followed, remaining a car length behind.

Where now? Jason wondered gloomily. No way he could lead the goon to the meeting with his aunt and Link Anderson, or any of his Bear Society friends.

After a few blocks he turned into the Hatchet Club parking lot. The cop parked and watched, leaving Jason no option but to go into the casino bar. He had a deserved reputation as a boozer, despite the fact that he'd recently sworn to cut down.

Storyteller would realize that he was doing it for the *Muk-wah*. He hoped his aunt would be as charitable. Her meeting with Link Anderson would have to wait.

8:30 P.M.—Hideaway Bay, Spirit Lake

There'd been no miscommunication—Jason had set the meeting time—yet he and his aunt were increasingly late. After ten *more* minutes Link reminded himself he was on vacation, poured an inch of scotch, and relaxed. He would not have worried had not the image of Daniel Eagle niggled in his consciousness along with the concern that something might have befallen Jason. He liked the brash young man.

Link rummaged through various drawers until he found a phone book, counted twelve Toussaints in Spirit Lake, but no Jason. The number was obviously in the aunt's name, which Jason had not mentioned. He gave up and settled back again.

At nine fifteen he went onto the porch—looked out at the lights of pontoon boats and overheard conversations that drifted over the water. The brightly lit casino shimmered in the distance. The next-door tourist couple arrived home, the woman laughing gaily and bragging about beating the slots. The man grumbled that it had been a long day—meaning he'd lost.

Link made up his mind. Jason had told him where they lived.

He drove into and then on beyond the town of Spirit Lake, then slowed to examine the mailboxes lined up on the road. The sixth one was labeled Toussaint.

He pulled in before a home with an illuminated porch and parked beside a late-model Honda, noting the absence of Jason's Firebird. Link crossed a well-tended lawn, and heard canned television audience laughter. He pressed the door chime and stepped back into the light. There were muffled footsteps; a woman in a robe cracked the door.

She was slight, with raven's wing hair, a vaguely Asian cast to ebony eyes, and delicate features. With only that too-brief glimpse his heart thumped in his chest.

"May I help you?"

"My name's Lincoln Anderson," he said awkwardly, wanting to see her more clearly.

She displayed not a hint of name recognition.

"Jason called you about a meeting."

"A meeting with whom?"

He could not help staring. "You *are* Jason's aunt, aren't you?"

Suspicion passed like a shadow across her face. "Who are you looking for?"

"Jason didn't give your name, only that you were on the tribal council."

She made up her mind. "My nephew did not call me, I know *nothing* about a meeting, and I have no earthly idea who you are. Good-bye." She prepared to close the door.

"Lincoln Anderson," he repeated—wondering how he'd got off on the wrong foot so quickly. "Jason wanted to set up a meeting between us." His heart pounded like a love-struck teenager's. She was so like the person he had cherished more than any other in his life.

"No one's telephoned me."

"We discussed the casino, and Senator Adcock's wife's visit, but there were things Jason wouldn't get into without you present." The perfect features and intelligent eyes. She looked so *much* like his Marie!

She tried to shut the door, but Link applied enough pressure to keep it cracked.

"Please," he began. "I'm concerned . . ."

"You *should* be concerned," she said through the opening. "Have you noticed that my left hand is out of your view? I'm holding a pistol. If you continue to try to break in, I swear I will shoot you—not once, but repeatedly. Now, good *night*."

Being the rational sort he prudently stepped back, and the door was closed in his face.

"I'm staying at the Hideaway Bay Resort," he called. "Cottage number eight."

"Congratulations. Enjoy your stay." The lock clicked. A chain rattled. A dead bolt was thrown. He heard her mutter something uncharitable.

They were so similar. Marie had had a burn scar. Otherwise . . . Link wondered if there might still be a way to get through to her. Perhaps ring the doorbell and start over?

He noticed motion at a curtain. Heard an angry sigh.

"Mr. Anderson, if you do not leave I will call the police. I assure you they're not humored by visitors who stalk members of the council. Good *night*."

10:15 P.M.—Little Martha's Marsh

The bog was well off the road, in a remote part of the reservation yet not difficult to get to, thus good for their intent. It was not the first time Sly Paquette had been here for this purpose, yet he was much more sullen than usual as he watched the Junkman open the sedan's trunk.

The trunk light revealed Paquette's face and a swath of gauze covering his left eye. His right eye gazed upon the lifeless body of Doris Eagle, whom he'd clubbed mercilessly in the lot outside the rest home. Broken a leg so badly it was turned back at an angle like her left arm. Ribs, neck. Then he'd beaten her fucking head in with the pipe.

She'd deserved worse. If the Junkman had not restrained her when he had, she would have got to his other eye as well.

He'd called Tonio Gracchi about what he'd had to do, and the mob boss had screamed curses. The bitch was going to raise hell when she found out, he said. Meaning Sydney, who had just returned from *somewhere* to the casino-hotel's penthouse suite.

Damned but his eye hurt!

A blood bubble formed on Doris's nostril, revealing that she was not quite dead.

A jolt of pain fired through his eye. He gritted his teeth, trembling, praying it would stop. Slowly it receded, but left enough residual agony to remind him that it would return.

"You okay?" asked the Junkman, who was as intelligent as your standard garden radish. Sly almost swung the pipe at the idiot. Of *course* he wasn't fucking okay.

A new wave of pain erupted in the eye, and he could not help releasing a new moan, shuddering, even dropping to a shaky knee.

"Jesus, Sly," the Junkman whispered.

"Shut the fuck up," he managed. Then the agony worsened and he moaned louder.

Hurting other people was fine by Paquette. He'd been doing it for Gracchi since he'd gone to Chicago after high school, and those he'd killed, broken, or burned always had it coming. Working with the Junkman made it easier, the way he held down their victims, and often Sly didn't get a speck of blood on his clothing. But this time when Doris had dug in her claws, bloody fluid from his eyeball had drooled all over his shirt.

When the agony diminished a bit, he returned to the task at hand before the next wave could hit. Twenty yards distant, a pair of his thugs-turned-cops looked out while a floor boss from the Hatchet Club prepared the disposal of Doris's car—rigging the accelerator so it would proceed under its own power down the incline into the mud bog. He'd done it enough lately that he was becoming proficient.

"Hurry," he told the Junkman. "I gotta get some help."

The dough-faced Junkman pulled Doris from the trunk, carried her around to the opened rear hatch of the other car, and stuffed her inside.

"Jesus, she's alive," said the casino boss.

"Somebody ask you?"

The Junkman closed the Pinto's hatch.

"We're ready," one of his mobster cops called out.

"Sink the fuckin' thing," growled Sly Paquette.

The Pinto was filled with furniture and belongings from Doris's home. Its engine revved as the chunk of wood was wedged in place. The casino boss reached through an open window and slipped the lever to DRIVE. The Pinto lurched forward, almost taking him along. A minute or so later there was nothing, no car, no belongings, not even many bubbles.

"Let's go," Sly said.

The Junkman would drive him to a clinic in Wausau, two hours south. There were closer medical facilities, like seeing a doctor at the Warehouse, but that required Sydney's approval, and explaining to the bitch was the last thing he needed. The other clinics were too near the reservation, and he might be recognized. He would check into the Wausau emergency room under a fake name and give them a story about how it had happened. Tell the doctor about the milky sap that had oozed from the eyeball and pray it could be repaired. Problem was, he had to be back for a council meeting in the morning.

Sly cast a final glance at the edge of the bog, where his cops worked to mask tire tracks. His eye hurt. He yelled for the Junkman to get his big ass in gear—they had a long drive ahead of them.

He had a last fleeting thought of Doris Eagle, sort of wishing he'd put her out of her misery since she'd been his first girlfriend and all. He wondered if she was talking with her husband, or maybe with the baby in her gut. Was that what happened at the moment of death?

The agony returned, and Sly hurried into the Lexus.

7

Link was late rising—after all, he told himself, he was on vacation—and yawned mightily before pulling on cut-offs, a T-shirt, and runners. He trotted down to a se-cluded area on the lakeshore for his morning workout. Starting with side stretches to limber up. Intended to do fifty push-ups, but reduced the number to twenty when he felt pain stitches in his sides. Next, thirty leg lifts . . . pausing after every ten to huff. Beginning his sit-ups, doing them in sets of twenty, finishing two sets and want-ing to die. Finally he rose onto wobbly pins and set off up the lane, slowly picking up the pace on a graveled road leading north and away from the lake.

The forest was a medley of birch, pine, alder, maple, tamaracks, all fighting for dominance, most turning to bright fall pastels, shading thick undergrowths of brush, ferns, ground lilies, and ivy.

A red fox darted across the road, paused, and stared insolently. White-tailed deer peered from the roadside. Does, with fawns craning their necks behind them. A raccoon family scampered homeward after a night of plunder.

While all that was well and good, Link wondered how long it would take for someone to discover his carcass after he collapsed. The run was torture. His normal mini-mum was five miles—more if there was time—but he'd been stagnant for far too long. He'd gone only a mile when he pleaded with himself to turn back. He pressed on—and on—until his legs were leaden and he felt every jolting step. He turned finally, and on the trip back experienced muscle tremors that threatened to topple him. He was grateful when he saw the Hideaway Bay sign, by then reduced to a torturous sort of stumbling. Once in sight of cottage eight, he slowed to a walk. Wondering if, at thirty-six years of age, he was sinking into permanent decline.

A blue Honda was pulled up by his rental car, and Jason's aunt—he recognized her although he'd only had the glimpse—leaned back against the front fender, watching with obvious interest. Link was too weary to greet her, just stopped and bent over, hands on trembling knees, head down and blowing like a runaway steam engine.

"You do this often?" she queried dubiously.

Link searched for an apt reply, found an appropriately scathing one but gave up when he realized he could not speak. Instead he continued trying to regain his breath.

"Take your time," she said, displaying a trace of sympathy.

"I—let myself—get out of—condition."

"Jason said you're from New York," she said, as if that explained it.

He found a hint of strength. "He musta—got home?"

"Not yet. When I woke up, I rang my office. He'd left the message on my voice mail at work yesterday. All about the call from your assistant and meeting you. He asked me to keep it quiet, which wasn't real smart. Anyone with my access code could have listened in."

In the daylight she looked less like Marie—taller, more slender, hair that hardly reached her shoulders, while Marie's had cascaded—yet the similarities remained unsettling. Her eyes were sparkling obsidian, quick and intelligent, and the hint of a smile resided there.

"I'm Jenifer," she said, "spelled with one *n*." A playful imp curled the corners of her lips—another distinct similarity. "I suppose I should apologize for pulling the gun."

He did a set of leg stretches, both to regain composure and to settle the long muscles that threatened to seize up. Finally he found his wind. "Link Anderson . . . last night I didn't . . . handle the introduction well."

"True, but Miss Manners says one should not shoot guests." The smile played on her features as he showed her into the cottage. Cute, no matter what you wanted to call it.

"Got to clean up," he said, still panting more than breathing, and disappeared.

Link showered quickly, as he'd learned in his early days at the Academy. Five minutes for the complete toilet, this time motivated not by harrying upperclassmen but by an attractive woman. He pulled on jeans, boots, and a short-sleeved cotton shirt with mother-of-pearl snaps, and emerged to find her putting the finishing touches on a pot of coffee.

"Hope you don't mind. I've been so concerned about Jason I've gone without my normal caffeine fix."

"Be my guest," he said, thinking that Jenifer Toussaint exuded competence, yet there was sensuality in the way she allowed her eyes to linger, as if she could not take them away.

"What did you and Jason talk about?" she asked.

"I mostly listened." He explained how Jason had extolled Senator Eddie Adcock, disdained Council Elder Sly Paquette, and his concern about the casino and the reservation police. He did not use the word mob. "He felt there were outside influences," he said, then remembered something Jason had said about her. "You're a schoolteacher?"

"A counselor. I handle troubled kids for the school district. Until a few weeks ago I spent most of my time in Washington, working with congressional committees about problems with our Native American youth. Then I learned about a new drug problem here at home—a flood of methamphetamine—and I decided my help was needed." The coffee pot gurgled excitedly. "Jase said you were a pilot but he wasn't specific. Why are you here, Link?"

"I met Senator Adcock a couple of years ago, and

found him to be a decent man. I'd like to learn more about his death."

She spoke quietly, "Do you know what you're getting into?"

"Jason mentioned that the reservation police are out of control."

"They're a major part of the problem, drugs and otherwise."

"On my way here I heard something about the Mafia being involved. Didn't the news media claim they were extinct?"

"They're as big and bad as ever, just quieter. They control things. Contracts, unions, drugs, businesses that outwardly seem legitimate. Anywhere there's money to be made, you'll see them skulking around with their hand in some other guy's pocket. Here we've got a casino and there's too much cash exchanging hands. No one's big enough to keep them out. Even the gamblers they cater to are mostly criminals. The gaming commissions in Nevada and New Jersey won't let them in, so they come here and don't have to worry about being hassled."

"Why not have the casino managers run them off?"

"All the key employees are mob people. The Manido only hold the menial jobs. Anyone who complains to the council has a change of heart or moves away in the night."

"How about your connections in Washington?"

"They're mainly educators. When I call the high-powered staffers, none want to hear our problems. Some won't even accept my calls. You'd be surprised how politicians tune out when you mention Native Americans. It's even a Washington tradition to siphon off tribal funds. Even Senator Eddie couldn't stop it. When he heard about mob involvement, he jumped in, and Sly Paquette trod lightly. With Eddie gone, the People are being terrorized by our own police.

"Before, there was a guideline that tribal policemen had to come from the reservation, but Paquette claimed we needed more qualified peace officers. As soon as he got it changed, he brought in scum from the cities and we haven't been able to get rid of them."

She poured coffee and they sat across from one another at the table with steaming mugs. Sipping and reflective, quietly sharing a warmth they knew was mutual.

"You gave the senator information about what was going on?"

"I was in Washington and didn't see it. Jason made the phone calls. It had to be done quietly, so Sly Paquette wouldn't know. Now there's no one to tell. No one wants to know."

"How about help from Madison?"

"Once the casino license was approved, the federal honchos told the state to butt out. Complain to the state and they send you to the feds. Complain to a fed or a pol about anything—rampant drugs for instance—and they tell you to see the BIA. Go to the BIA and you're told to forward it in writing through channels, meaning our council. Do that and the cops pay a visit, because nothing gets past Sly Paquette. He not only runs the team; he owns the ball. We're a splinter band tucked way back in the boondocks, and there are a lot of deaf ears."

"Any ideas about Senator Eddie's death?"

"Hundreds of ideas, but nothing anyone can prove. If you act suspicious, the rotten cops start looking at you. They even use illegal wiretaps."

Link mulled all that over. "You don't think the senator was guilty?"

"Of course not. Eddie wore his honor like a badge. Someone set him up so it looked like he stole the treaties."

She pulled her eyes away from his, and regarded her cup. "Now I'm concerned about Jason. He's not always reliable, but to set up a meeting concerning his hero—he worshipped the senator—and not make it? I called the police and asked if anything unusual happened last night, like I was checking as a part of my council duties. They said no, but I can't trust anything they say."

"Do the cops know Jason works against them?"

"I hope not. Sly Paquette's scary. One week a person comes out against him; the next they're either in his pocket or they've moved away. People are deathly afraid of him, and wherever you see him you see Billy Junkins. That's the one they call the Junkman. He's *huge*."

"The army buddy?"

"Yes. Sly was medically retired from the army as some sort of sergeant. He won't talk about it because he says it was tough losing all his buddies in combat. They must pay him well because he drives a new Lexus and throws money around like it's water."

"It doesn't come from the military. They're parsimonious with retirees." He paused thoughtfully. "What can you tell me about the Eagles?"

"Only that Charlie's dead and what was done to Daniel was horrible. Thinking about it makes me more concerned about Jason. He's—" Jenifer was interrupted by a buzz. She drew a pager from her purse, went to the kitchen phone, and punched in the number.

She spoke a few words, listened, and released a long sigh. "When he wakes up tell him I've met his friend from out of town. He'll know who I mean."

Jenifer hung up, her relief obvious. "Jason showed up at his buddy Lonnie's, and crashed on his couch. He'd partied all night."

"Does he do that often?"

"More frequently since Senator Eddie's death. It affected him."

"He told me he hasn't done drugs for a long while."

"He doesn't consider alcohol a drug. It's a problem with some of our people. I enjoy a glass of wine or two, but I don't have the demon. If Jason has a single beer he can't stop." She refilled their cups, and examined her watch. "I've got council at ten, and I still have to change."

"Jason mentioned Gloria Vasson's proposal to organize a search for the treaties."

"He talks too much. You're not supposed to know."

"They'll need a guide," he said. "I'd like you to nominate me."

Her eyes were on him again. "That's crazy. No one here knows you."

"I'm at home in the forest, and I can handle emergencies. I have the right military and survival school training, and a couple of years ago I served on a search and rescue team."

She smiled at his audacity.

"I'm experienced. Three years as a big game outfitter in Montana."

"That's impressive for Montana. How about here?"

"Give me a couple of days, and I'll be an expert. I brought detailed maps, and I'm a quick study. I'm also a pilot. I intend to look the place over from both the air and ground."

"Jason mentioned the pilot part. He's infatuated with flying."

"I've been that way since childhood."

She gave him a long, cup-to-lips stare. "It would involve doing menial chores."

"I'm not allergic to work."

"Let's stretch the truth and say you're qualified. Now the big question. Why?"

"I don't think the senator stole anything. The bad guys know that, yet *someone's* putting a lot of effort into this search."

"You're acting on a feeling?"

"Yeah. *Something's* up there."

"I agree," said Jenifer. "Especially considering all their secrecy about the search. None of us on council are supposed to even mention it."

"How about my participation in the search? Think it over?"

She continued her examination of him. Finally gave a little nod. "If the council allows it, you're on. Jason also said you'd like us to back up your story about being born here."

He waited.

"I'll do it, even if I have a problem thinking you're just a concerned citizen who's worried about Senator Eddie's reputation."

He smiled. "Thanks."

"Don't presume your story will work just because I go along. Someone may demand a background check with the Indian registries at Madison and Washington."

"I have an assistant who's great at fixing that sort of thing."

She nodded out the window. "They'll have to hurry if they want to find the treaties before the snow flies. Gloria Vasson wants authorization quickly so they can start Monday. Assuming I convince the council that you're real, you'll have today and tomorrow to get to know the place."

"Then I'd better get busy. Do me a favor? There's a restriction to overflying the reservation below five thousand feet. I'll need permission from the council."

"We grant it all the time. Give me your aircraft identification and the time you'll need the clearance."

He jotted the information onto a notepad.

"Just avoid Spirit Lake. If the tourists complain, it might raise questions. Also stay clear of the ecol-rec zone."

"Jason told me about it."

"Ecol-Rec, Limited's also the contractor's name. Their briefings are so technical we get headaches. Phase one was to isolate that first zone, and try to stop any wider contamination. Now they're in phase two, applying enzymes, which is the sensitive period. The government prohibits *all* overflight so nothing can affect the balance."

"Gotcha." He tore out the page and handed it over.

Jenifer started for the door. He followed. On the porch she looked out at the lake, then swung her gaze back to him. A new volume of unspoken communication flowed between them.

Her voice was soft. "I'm pleased you're here, Link. We've needed someone like you."

"I like your Northwoods." And the present company, he did not have to add.

The pixie curls played at the corners of her mouth. "I really was holding a pistol."

"I didn't doubt it for a second." He took a resolute

breath. "I'd like to get together later. Discuss how things went in the council meeting?"

"I'd like that too." The smile tugged harder, as if it had taken Link too long to ask. "Six o'clock at my house. We'll try out a new pasta dish. You bring the wine."

"How about Jason?"

"He'll be there," she said as she walked to the Honda.

"Too bad," Link said so low she could not hear, admiring everything he saw.

South Side, Spirit Lake

Jason came awake, taking a long moment before realizing that Lonnie was shaking his shoulder. He sat up slowly, holding his head.

Lonnie grinned back. "That was a close call with the *naud-o-way* last night."

It took a moment before Jason connected the meaning of the word. *Naud-o-way* meant enemy of the People. Lonnie was talking about the bad cop. "Too close. I dreamed again."

"Your dream-times are coming every couple of days now. Cool."

"I wish you were the one having them." Jason looked at Lonnie through burning, bloodshot eyes. "A woman was killed in it." His head pounded unmercifully—he had a terrific hangover. "I led the cop to the bar. End of tale."

"That's all cool, but Storyteller doesn't like you getting plastered. Better clean up, Jase. He's calling for another *Me-da-we* initiation ritual and wants you there."

Jason got to his feet. "What's the word?"

At each ritual, Storyteller gave them a word of old Ojibwe and asked that they practice its usage. Two of the first ones they'd learned were *naud-o-way*, which meant enemy, and *Muk-wah*, meaning a member of their own Bear Society, or trusted friend. To say someone was *Muk-wah* meant you could entrust them with your life. The *naud-o-way* were the bad guys. No trust.

"Che-she," said Lonnie. "It means rattlesnake."

Jason shook his head to clear it, and created a new throbbing. "Who's being purified?"

"Marvin Yellowbird."

"He's a good choice." Marvin was one of few Indians still serving on the police force. He was honorable, tough as a nail, and would make a good member of the Bear Society.

Jason felt there were not enough *Muk-wah*. None of them except Storyteller knew the true numbers, but they were all aware that there were more than fifty *naud-o-way,* including reservation cops and casino bosses, and *they* were all armed. They'd need a lot of *Muk-wah* to stand up to them. Storyteller said the caliber of people they selected was more important. Another factor was discipline and rigorous training. But two or three to one?

According to Storyteller, since the earliest days, Eagle, Turtle, Bear, and Loon society warriors had readily sacrificed themselves during emergencies. When the current trouble had begun there had been others who had stepped forth to confront the mob. Sly Paquette had destroyed Charlie Eagle, leader of his namesake clan, then his cousins and nephews, and finally his brother, Daniel. The prestigious Loon Society had been next— their leaders had disappeared almost before they'd formed. Other able men and women had disappeared whenever they'd tried to assert leadership.

It was closely held that Storyteller was head of the Bear Society, just as it was that selected men and women were being purified with *Me-da-we* rites, then inducted into the *Muk-wah,* to one day defend the Manido-Ojibwe against the latest *naud-o-way*. Only Storyteller knew who they all were, for they met in smaller groups. They were told of the old ways, learned forest skills and stealth tactics from those who knew them. He organized weapons classes—not only firearms, for he demanded that each also learn to use a silent weapon. Lonnie and Jason joked about their lack of skills with knife and hatchet. Not archery though. Lonnie had a pair of great compound hunting bows he knew how to use, and Jason was catching on.

Jason was called on to play his flute at rites and training sessions, and the others learned to react to tunes or animal sounds that told them to attack, fall back, or remain unseen.

Storyteller told them tales, such as one the previous week: "Have you wondered about the origins of the name of our band? 'Manido' means spirit, of course, for we are the Spirit People, but what about 'Ojibwe'?" He'd looked at them gravely. "Once the Ojibwe were regarded as the fiercest of tribes, and their enemies fled in fear before them. Why did the enemy run? One reason was because they were often defeated. Another was because we roasted their captured warriors alive. That is the old meaning of 'Ojibwe'—to roast until puckered up. Now we have a new enemy, and soon we must teach them a lesson they will not forget."

Storyteller reminded them of another time, when the Ojibwe were made almost extinct by Iroquois pressing in from the East, crushing them against the Dakota to the West. He told them how the Manido band's heroism had helped save the entire Ojibwe nation. "Now we must save ourselves. I have learned that two more of our people have disappeared from the south side."

Soon Storyteller would appoint an assistant, to be called Young Storyteller. Jason knew he had no chance at that honor, but headache or not he would attend the *Me-da-we* rite for Marvin Yellowbird, and tell Storyteller about his dream of the woman who had been so savagely beaten. Then he'd tell him about Lincoln Anderson, and about Erin, his assistant, and the help they might be bringing to the People.

The *Me-da-we* hut, a framework of branches covered with thatch made of woven grass, was purposely located a mile from the nearest road. There it was more or less safe from discovery by the bad cops, who were far too lazy to walk that far. The interior of the hut was laid out with stations, each of which represented a phase of the band's history and of life itself. Initiates must stop at each station and recite the appropriate oath of purity and allegiance.

The *Me-da-we* ritual was the most sacred of those that could be attended by the Manido-Ojibwe, the Spirit People. The initiate would emerge cleansed and ready to serve.

Marvin Yellowbird stood at the opened door of the hut, awaiting the signal for his ceremony to begin. Storyteller delayed, as he often did to build anticipation in the young people, and came over to speak with Jason.

He asked about the dream, which Jason described.

"I believe it was Doris Eagle," said Storyteller, who put importance on the dream-times. He looked at him quizzically. "You say she was in pain. Was she telling us something?"

"I can tell you about the dream-times, but I'm not good at interpreting them." He did not add that he wasn't convinced they meant anything at all. He was his own chief doubter.

"Try," Storyteller encouraged, staring as if prepared to wait him out.

Jason attempted to recall the dream-time. "I don't think she was frightened. She was angry, I think, and wanted—I don't know—justice?"

"For herself? Her husband? The People?"

"All I know is what I've told you. Even that memory is fading."

"From this time on, when you have a dream-time, try to make sense of it. What good is a gift if it isn't used? What good is it if you cloud it with alcohol?"

"I led the cop to the club," Jason reasoned, "away from the rest of you."

Storyteller's voice was harsh. "Don't betray us with your good intentions, Jason." He stared sternly, "Now play your *bibig-wun* and we will have our ceremony. Afterward we'll talk about how the police are passing out drugs again, then about your visitor from New York."

Jason pulled out the flute, pleased that the subject was changed.

8

Link drove southwest from the reservation, feeling good. Wondering what was happening at Jenifer's council meeting. His thoughts were interrupted by the sat phone's buzz.

"Anderson," he answered.

"Johnny said to tell you the Giants whipped the Cowboys *bad*."

Erin and her nine-year-old were devoted Giants fans. "How did my Broncos do?"

"They haven't played yet. Big game with the 49ers on Sunday. Headed for the airport?"

"Yeah. I spoke with Jenifer Toussaint. There's a chance I'll be named to the search, so I'd better get to know the area."

"A FedEx package is waiting for you at flight ops. Got some things for you. Umm. I just brought up Jenifer's photo. She's cute."

"I thought 'cute' was a put-down to womanhood."

"Just to those who aren't. The lady's brilliant too. Youngest psych master's degree recipient in the class of ninety-two at U of W, Madison. She then furnished the key ideas for a national policy to interdict troubled youths early, before they turn violent, and Senator Adcock sponsored her to come to Washington to work on various congressional advisory panels."

Link was surprised. "All she said was that she was a counselor for the school district."

"That's her present title—also tribal council elder, of course—but she was on a Senate advisory panel and only two courses and a thesis away from a doctorate at Georgetown U when she quietly gave it all up and returned home."

"Why?"

"Who knows? Maybe for the same reason you keep wanting to go back to Montana and walk the mountains. By the way, did Jason show up?"

"He was at a friend's. I guess he has a drinking problem."

"Damn, and we confided in him. A boozer's a loser, pard."

"Some of my heroes were boozers, but they came through when it counted. General Grant, Winston Churchill, Colonel Pete Peterson."

"Drunks are unpredictable."

"I wouldn't call him a *drunk*. More like a kid with a problem."

"How about Jenifer? She's not shown on the senator's good guy list."

"Which list is she on?"

"None. She's conspicuously missing, since it's obvious she knew the senator."

"I trust her."

Erin paused, as if considering his quick response. "I've been looking through the items the senator mailed. Security examined the envelope, and found fingerprints and secretions in all the right places, so we know he was the one who closed it and licked the stamps. There were also blood smears. *His* blood. He placed the envelope in a mailbox on a county road not far from Presque Isle, Wisconsin, about six hours before he was found in the burning car sixty miles away."

"Anything more about the lists?"

"Nothing I haven't told you."

"The tape?"

"Lots there, but it's unclear so I worked it over with a couple of heavy-duty audio analysis programs. There's no doubt, Link—it's Senator Adcock's voice. Then the mystery deepens. He mailed the tape before he went to the reservation, but he was already physically hurting and showing considerable mental stress."

"You think he was injured *before* the accident?"

"Yes, and so does Helga."

"How about the message?"

"Twenty-six minutes of audio. He starts with, *'I am United States senator Edward Little-Turtle Adcock,'* spoken sadly, like he knew what was in store, and all through the tape he keeps repeating, *'Follow me.'* He talks about a warehouse and says, *'Our true worst enemies will never know justice until we drag them into the light.'* "

"What worst enemies?"

"He doesn't explain. I'll take a look at his previous speeches and look for a match."

"I'll check out the local warehouses." He paused. "Dig up the background on a 'Sly Fox' Paquette. He claims to be a medically retired army NCO—highly decorated, prisoner of war in Iraq. He controls the Spirit Lake tribal council, and may be involved in something larger."

"Larger as in politics?"

"How about larger as in mob."

"Chicago mob?"

"I thought it was all one big, happy *cosa nostra*."

"Lotsa differences. I'll dig up what I can on the mob and Mr. Paquette. Anything else?"

"Might as well add Paquette's sidekick to the list. Billy Junkins, aka the Junkman. I've seen him and he's really, *really* big. Looks at you like you're not there and if you are he doesn't care. American Indian, I think, but not from here. Supposedly served in the army with Paquette."

"Gotcha. How's the vacation going?"

"Hard work." Link turned off on the access road to the Lakeland Airport. "Last night I lost fifty bucks at the casino, and this morning I tortured myself trying to get back into shape."

"Forget the exercise and lose more money. That's what Americans do for fun and happiness. Speaking of which, I dropped the thousand into Mr. Doughty's account, along with the error-in-his-favor message. I assume we're priming the pump so he'll call you again?"

"That would be nice, but I think he's too worried about his family."

"Understandable, after what you told me about Daniel Eagle. I'll get to work. *Ciao.*"

He checked at the Lakeland Airport ops desk, and picked up Erin's package—containing a pocket-size hand-held GPS receiver, an approved application for charter airline service based in northern Wisconsin, an updated instrument rating card and pilot's log showing he was qualified in the Beech Baron, and business cards describing his charter service. Also a dues-current card showing his membership in the North American Guides and Outfitters Association.

The crusty old fixed base operator, Link recalled his nickname was T-bone, said he had received a message providing formal PPR—a pilot's acronym meaning "prior permission required"—indicating he was granted overflight authority for the Spirit Lake Reservation. Jenifer had come through as promised. He filed a visual flight plan for a "local area familiarization," handed it over to the FBO, and brought up the NOTAM, the "Notice to Airmen" he'd just read.

"Anything new about the two airplanes that disappeared north of here?" he asked.

"Nope, but there was bad static over the radio both times. You start getting static, watch your damned instruments," he said in a growl.

Link did a thorough preflight, and took off in the Baron. He maintained two thousand feet above the treetops for the en route period, then stayed there for a circuit around the reservation's perimeter. It was rectangular, forty-five miles north to south, with a girth of fifty. Spirit Lake—both the body of water and the town—were centered near the bottom. The north side, much of which was in Michigan, was all wild forest and lakes.

It was that north side wilderness—where the senator had spent his childhood and had most likely cached the documents—that interested Link most. If he was to pass himself off as an expert on the reservation, he must know it well.

During his first circumnavigation Link found Spirit and Portage Nord and Portage Sud to be the most imposing lakes, but others, large and small, were scattered everywhere.

The ecology recovery zone was easily distinguishable, an eight-by-eight-mile square that appeared contrived and unnatural. The treated water was milky and opaque, while outside it was emerald green or a blue topaz reflection of the sky. The foliage inside was yellowing, while that outside was verdant. He'd seen enzymes and microbes in action at other reclamation areas and oil spills, often exhibiting bizarre or improbable colors. This one simply looked dead.

On the map the ecol-rec zone was overlaid with red stripes, and bold lettering that announced PROHIBITED AREA, NO OVERFLIGHT. Later, if there was time, he might venture close enough for a gander at No Bottom Marsh, Woman's Hat Lake, and Dead Man's Creek, all within the ecol-rec zone, and memorize their features. Yet he doubted the zone would be a player in the search. Even a man desperate to hide stolen goods would find such a place forbidding.

Link switched functions on the Collins integrated navigation system until an electronic map appeared on the flat-screen display on the instrument panel. The reservation—town, lakes, and all—was displayed in detail. He set in boundaries of the entire area he wanted to examine, excluding the big lake and the ecol-rec zone, then selected SEARCH GRID. Routes and turn points appeared in bright blue, zigzagging across the presentation. He examined, decided it would work, and pressed an ENTER button. Finally he descended to five hundred feet above the earth and followed steering needles on the navigation system toward WP 1 (way point one).

He began to sort and categorize features. Big Fish and Little Fish Lakes were loaded with reeds. Portage Nord and Portage Sud had begun life as a single body of water, but over the years the two sections had become separated by a narrow isthmus. Rock and Turtle Creeks;

Shining Button, Moose, and Frenchman's Lakes; Big Marsh and Martha's Marsh, slowly became unique and distinguishable, and were stored in niches of memory.

As his eyes grew accustomed to details, he noted abandoned structures, overgrown with green. The inhabitants had moved, either into the south side or away from the reservation. Except for a deserted old cranberry bog at the northern east corner, and the pale ecol-rec zone at the northwest, the north side had been reclaimed by nature.

He was throttled back and was carefully scanning below when he noted that the IFF light was illuminated, meaning that someone was interrogating and receiving his aircraft data. Odd since there were no FAA radars around.

The light flickered off, and Link went back to his search.

After an hour of it the terrain features began to run together. With sore eyes, and with his mental faculties rebelling, Link pushed the throttles forward and climbed to a safer altitude to rest.

The sat phone buzzed. "Anderson," he responded.

"I've got a few answers. Is this a good time?"

"Great time. I'm taking a break to rest my eyes."

"First subject, we're talking about the Chicago-based mob like I thought. That's their turf. For your info, *Checagou* meant foul-smelling skunk cabbage in the local Indian lingo."

"Is that on the test?"

"Hey, that was my opening humor. Do you want this, or do I press the delete button and get rid of an hour's hard work?"

"Sorry."

"*Any*way, let's go way back to 1900, when Chicago's already known as the most corrupt city in the country. Crooks, rotten politicians, police on the take, most of it in the poor neighborhoods. Then in 1909, a twerp from New York named Johnny Torrio comes along and starts to organize the hoods, opening cheap brothels, gambling parlors, you name it. He's a little guy with a big idea:

how all the factions should cooperate and make a lot
more money."

"That was then, Erin. What's happening *today*?"

"Hey, it's *my* story, and I'll tell it, skunk cabbage and
all." She humphed indignantly, and continued. "In 1919,
a twenty-year-old bully named Alphonse Capone shows
up, running from a badass New York Irishman and carrying a recommendation for Torrio to take him on,
which he does. Al's a quick study, and with his help
Torrio's 'cooperate and graduate' idea begins to gel. So
when Prohibition comes they're ready to make the most
of it." Erin paused. "Follow me?"

"Yeah," he fibbed, wondering how many lakes were
in his view. A hundred?

"In 1925, Torrio's shot up by a gang that isn't eager
to listen, and judiciously decides to retire. Al sets him
up with a super 401(k) plan and takes over, and brings
the rest of the mobsters in line. A few he has killed, like
the ones in the garage on Valentine's Day, but most he
talks into joining in and sharing the profit. Why fight the
authorities, he says, when we can just buy the ones at
the top. And they do. The police brass are in on the
action, so are the big politicians, and so are the newspaper publishers, and *boy* does the money roll in."

"It sounds a lot like what's going on here, on a different scale. Now, what's the difference between the Chicago mob and other mobs?"

"Here in New York we have five Italian crime families
and a big Irish faction. We have Chinese, Vietnamese,
Russian, and Mexican Mafias, *plus* all the street gangs.
In Miami there are three major factions. In L.A., five.
But in toddling Chicago, the lessons taught by Capone
are still gospel. Get along and get ahead. There's one
mob, period, and while there's a sea full of different
gangs, they work at the mob's sufferance and everyone
gets a cut."

"Centralized command and control."

"Hey, you're catching on. Also less opposition and
risk. During Prohibition the outfit raked in huge sums—
billions in today's dollars—and well over half went in

payoffs to cops, judges, politicians. Capone felt it was the cost of doing business. Think about if you were an honest cop, out to stop him. Who could you turn to? He had you beat before you started."

"Did the Northwoods figure into it?"

"You bet. Capone used the highways to haul whiskey, and set up safe houses where his hoods could get away, relax, and keep an eye on the traffic. Outfit guys up there kept a roll in their pockets to pass out, which kept the locals' mouths shut regardless of what the cops and G-men asked. Northwoods people called the mob the 'men with the folding money.' "

"Did they visit the Spirit Lake Reservation?"

"They tried to get in there more than the others. It's a great hideout, and the tribe has a treaty that makes it even better. No one can come looking without their say-so. Also, customs officials can't examine what they carry when they visit Chippewa bands in Canada. The mob tried to get their foot in the door at the reservation for years."

"They've succeeded. Jenifer said even the gamblers at the casino are criminals."

"That's interesting. Here's another tidbit, Link. I've got FBI records about activities at Spirit Lake from years past, since it's one of their mandates to keep track of the reservations. Recently it's like the place doesn't exist. You've heard about all the bad things going on there, yet there've been no bureau reports about activities of *any* kind, good or bad."

"And you think it's deliberate?"

"You bet. When I discovered all that neglect I called Gordon Tower at the bureau to share my news, but guess what? As soon as he heard what I said, he was too busy to talk. When I asked when was a good time to call back, he said he'll be busy for the foreseeable future. I argued, so he said take it up with the professional responsibilities office in Washington, and hung up. Can you believe that? They've pulled our information plug."

"Does he know I'm here?"

"Not from me. If you're telling me to let him know, I will."

Link thought for a moment. "Let's wait until we have something firm."

"I agree. By the way, the FBI isn't the only agency that's turned their backs."

The ecol-rec zone was dead ahead.

"Who besides the FBI?" Link asked.

"How about the Marshals Service and the U.S. Attorney's Office. There's nothing current in any of their files. I peeked."

"You're saying they're all corrupt?"

"Of course not. Too many incorruptible people there. Same for the Department of Interior and the Bureau of Indian Affairs, but they're a blank too. I don't know how or why it's happening, just that it is. That means *someone's* involved in keeping everyone away from the Manido, and I don't mean someone junior."

"They'd have to be fooling a lot of people."

"Maybe that's what's happening. This is the age of the spin-meister and misinformation. The Manido are being wronged big-time, but they're a natural target for something like this. Indians and reservations are dull subjects to politicians. Not enough votes."

9

Link was about to start his right turn when something inside the zone caught his eye. A fuzzy rectangular area? Maybe just tired eyes?

Erin continued with her revelations. "A final note on the mob. They have territorial rules. For years Miami and Las Vegas were safe havens. No killings allowed—had to wait until the 'hittee' went somewhere else. The rules for the Northwoods were different too. If someone was to be eliminated, they'd quietly disappear into one of the lakes or bogs, never to be seen again."

"Were you able to learn anything about Sly Paquette?" he asked, staring as he approached ever closer to the rectangular patch of ecol-rec foliage near Woman's Hat Lake that was different from the surrounding forest.

"Did you ever doubt? John Sly Fox Paquette graduated from high school in 1980, and the next month left for the military induction center in Chicago. But how's this: he'd fought a lot with his parents, and two weeks after he left they were found with their heads beaten in."

"No one suspected him?"

"Sure they did, but there wasn't enough evidence to bring him back. When Paquette showed back up in 1996, the Eagle brothers brought up the old murders to the reservation police, and we know what happened to them. Also, everything Paquette's claimed on every form since he returned, from driver's license information to his bio for the council, is a lie. For starters, he said he was in the army and showed a discharge form, but the armed forces repository in St. Louis has no record of him ever serving. He claimed to be a POW in Iraq, but the Prisoners of War Association's never heard of him. Nothing tracks."

Link turned to avoid overflying the zone, and lost visual contact with the odd-looking fuzzy area. "Where was he?" he asked.

"Certainly not in the army. Same with his buddy, the Junkman."

Link rolled out, flying parallel to the ecol-rec zone. He scanned the skies for air traffic, then the ground to pick out landmarks.

Erin went on. "Paquette's got a balance of a hundred eighty thousand in a Farmers and Merchants bank account. Every few months he loads his account with another fifty thou. Meaning he has some kind of great day job, but a retired army sergeant he is not."

"Kickbacks from the casino?" He tried to reacquire the fuzzy anomaly.

"No telling."

"Is that all?" he asked.

"Give me a break. I give you the impossible, and you want more?"

"Yep. Anything else you can get. Paquette's a key to what's happening here." He continued examining the ecol-rec zone. Gravel roads led in from the north, the Michigan side, and from the west, the national forest. Both ended at the zone's perimeter. He wondered about their use—access so the Ecol-Rec, Limited people could administer their chemicals?

Link turned, and was again flying at just five hundred feet above the trees. "My eyes are rested, so I'll get back to work."

"And I'll go back to digging up dirt. Sorry about getting the grumpies."

"What grumpies?" Ahead he noted Moose and Little Fish Lakes.

"Jeez, I fuss at you and you don't even notice it? I'm

slipping. Been single too long and not getting my quota
of nagging time."

"Thanks for all the information, Erin."

"Don't mention it until time for my next raise. *Ciao,*
pardner." She disconnected.

A lone pine tree marked one end of Big Fish Lake.
Reeds covered a side of Portage Sud Lake. Crazy Man
Marsh was pocked with ugly sink holes. Link observed,
and memorized details.

It came to him what he'd seen back at the ecol-rec
zone. *Camouflage netting.* He hadn't seen it in quantity
since the Gulf War, where there'd been miles of the
stuff. In fact, desert camo fit right in with the pale, dead
colors below. With the riddle solved Link felt better, and
only idly wondered what Ecol-Rec, Limited might be
hiding. But then, all corporations had their secrets.

While scanning the ground the airplane's shadow
caught his eye. He peered harder. There were two shadows, a second one immediately behind him, as if locked
into position there. There were no wings on the shadow,
yet no average helicopter could tag along so easily. He
eased in more throttle, adding twenty miles per hour.
The helo held its position.

Interesting, he thought, for he was scooting along at
180 miles per hour, down in the weeds, yet the shadows
showed the helicopter was doggedly holding its place a
few feet behind him. Not your average whirlybird. Like
all fighter pilots Link despised being a target. The helicopter was in the tracking position. If it were a MiG,
and he an average pilot, he'd be dead.

But Link did not consider himself average. He paused
for another moment, giving the other pilot even more
of a sense of confidence, and prepared to maneuver.

Link turned just the slightest bit to his left, and the
helicopter pilot was still adjusting when he rolled to the
right, suddenly and violently—continuing up and over in
a high-speed barrel roll that bled off just enough energy—and rolled out wings-level behind the chopper.

The maneuver was accomplished so quickly, so precisely, than he could not keep a grin from forming. He
pulled in close to the tail rotor of a sleek military copter.

Then he violated yet another of the rules of flight and selected the emergency guard frequency on his radio—121.5 MHz was reserved for emergency use only—and broadcast, "tracking . . . tracking" in a monotone voice, as a military pilot does when he has bested another in a dogfight and is at his six o'clock in the killing position.

When the helicopter darted to the left, Link disengaged with a hard turn to his right. There was no way the Baron could turn with a chopper. After a moment he dipped his left wing for a look, and thought he saw a distant glimmer of the green helicopter flying northward.

He found himself chuckling, thinking he'd not lost all of his skill.

A blast of hissing noise erupted over the radio—and he recognized the once-familiar sound of electronic jamming. *Coincidence?* he wondered.

The noise in his radio was annoying, so he turned down the volume. He told himself to be more watchful, and went back to flying the grid and memorizing details on the earth below.

The blond man trembled with shame and fury. One moment he had been exulting at remaining unseen, having the Baron at his mercy, and the next the other pilot had maneuvered so quickly and adroitly that he still could hardly believe it had happened.

Howarski was still burning as he approached the zone, and used his secondary radio, on UHF band, to order the technician first to turn on the VHF jammer, then to open the shield.

Ahead the camouflage netting began to ponderously move, as he determined to land quickly and teach the Baron pilot the lesson of his life. He would die unseen and unnoticed.

Howarski blanked out the ignominy of what had happened, and mentally prepared for the kill. "Load four KW warhead missiles," he told the technician.

Link was too distant to see the helicopter land in the new opening in the camouflage, or the two rapid-fire cannons and four deadly missiles on a transporter-erector-launcher that whirred to life and tracked his course. Nor did he know that missile intercept data was being constantly updated in a tracking computer, or that the impact point of his airplane's debris was being studied by an engineer-operator who was preparing to shoot him down.

11:35 A.M.—*Manido-Ojibwe Tribal Council Meeting Room*

John Sly Fox Paquette listened with half an ear to the boring questions posed by the elders to Senator Eddie Adcock's widow. The painkillers that numbed his agony—without them it was as if someone held a thumb gouged into his raw eye socket—made his thoughts mushy and caused his attention to wander.

Adcock's widow was responding to questions when the cell phone on his belt buzzed.

Sly offered no apology as he stumped out into the deserted anteroom. There he pulled out a cigar, and switched on the phone. "Yeah?"

"There's an airplane up here looking around." Billy Junkins's anxious voice.

Tomorrow there was to be an important meeting at the Warehouse, and he'd sent the Junkman ahead to help with any necessary preparations.

"Just a minute." He peered into the adjacent office to make sure no one was listening, and closed that door. "Someone's flying overhead?"

"Not really *over,* but pretty close. Howarski went—"

"Damn it, I told you not to use that name!" Sly clipped the end off the Churchill.

"Sorry," the giant said. "Anyway, *he* went up in a helo for a look, then came back all upset, saying the airplane oughtn't to be there. Mr. Gracchi's not here and . . ."

"No fuckin' names!"

The Junkman took in a breath, trying to figure out how to talk without using names. "I think you'd better know, Sly."

"Then tell me!"

The Junkman spoke rapidly. "This guy's about to shoot the fuckin' airplane down so—so I called you."

Paquette almost dropped the cigar. "He's going to *what*?"

The Junkman's tone became defensive. "He says Mr. G put him in charge of protectin' the place so he's gonna shoot it down."

Howarski was as loony as a bag of donut holes.

"He says he'll do it so it lands in a lake, and nobody will ever—"

"Put him on the phone!"

A moment later he heard a nasal, "Yeah?"

"This is Paquette. The council gave a guy named Anderson permission to fly over the north side, 'cause he's gonna be the guide for the fuckin' expedition. We *need* him."

Howarski remained quiet. He had an ego like Sly Paquette had seldom seen.

"You hear me? We *need* this guy, so leave him the fuck alone."

"Gracchi didn't tell me about any guy named Anderson snooping around in an airplane."

"He didn't know. Hell, we just approved him two hours ago."

"Next time, tell me," said Crazy Howarski, and the line went dead.

"Nutty bastard." Sly turned off his cell phone, lit the cigar, and puffed angrily.

Howarski wasn't bluffing. On two other occasions light airplanes that had mistakenly flown over the Warehouse had *disappeared*. Their radios had been jammed so they couldn't tell anyone, and some kind of computer trajectory formula had been used to make sure the airplanes fell into deserted lakes. A genius hacker was required to do such a thing. Crazy Howarski qualified.

Tonio Gracchi thought it was great, being able to shoot down airplanes, kill everyone aboard, and have no one suspect where to start looking. Sly Paquette did not care one way or the other, but he wanted Anderson around for a while longer.

Anderson had superb qualifications, and having him on the expedition increased their chances of finding the gym bag, which they all wanted.

Sly puffed his Churchill until the Junkman called back. "Things're shut down and back to normal, but he's still mad as hell."

"Ask him to *please* not do anything like that unless he checks with me."

"He don't listen much," said Billy Junkins. "Last week somebody drove just kinda close to the Warehouse, so he's put up cameras and gates, and even mines on the roads out here."

Mines? Still Sly held his temper. Tonio Gracchi did not care that Howarski was crazy, so long as he kept intruders away from the Warehouse.

"Find out where he put the fuckin' mines," he told the Junkman, "so *we* don't get blown up." Sly pressed the END button, rubbed cautiously at the bandage covering his empty socket, and felt the deep ache begin. He wished he could check back into the hospital he'd walked out of at five this morning, after being cut on, bandaged, and told to rest.

He took a pull on the Churchill, considered another pain pill, and decided against it. They'd be talking about the search for the gym bag.

The woman called Sydney had shown her genius, orchestrating things so the FBI had been pulled out, which meant the investigation into Senator Eddie's death was over. The moment the agents had gone, she'd told Sly to send his cops to scour the north side for signs of the senator's gym bag, with all its damning tapes and sworn statements. They'd found nothing. Now the search was being turned over to a professional who knew how to find such things—even if he believed the gym bag contained old treaties.

Sydney was a bitch, but she was smart as hell.

When the bag was located, Sly's people would take it. The damning evidence would be destroyed, the old treaties substituted in their place.

He thought about the pilot flying near the ecol-rec zone. The council had discussed and checked out Lin-

coln Anderson. They were lucky to have him. Still Sly
Paquette had enough of an uneasy feeling to warrant
keeping an eye on him.

He stubbed the cigar out, and returned to the briefing.
There he took his seat quietly, and listened as the expedition leader spoke passionately about how he would
find and return the valuable lost treasures of the Manido people.

11:55 A.M.—*Airborne, near Frenchman's Lake, Man-ido Indian Reservation*

Link was all but sure that it had been an H-60 Hawk.
They were fast, rugged, and carried an assortment of
sensors and weapons. A less capable variant, the H-70,
had been sold to foreign countries. No H-60s he knew
of were piloted by persons outside the U.S. government.

The helicopter was long gone and the electronic jamming had been shut off by the time he called Erin and
passed on what he *thought* he'd seen and heard. She
said she'd check to see what government agencies were
around that were assigned such aircraft.

They chatted.

Link described the lush wilderness, and told her about
the brilliant blue lakes in his sight. He asked how things
were going in the city.

Erin said it was a rainy day, then read him a news
article from her computer screen. A Miami Beach police
captain had been accused of diverting large amounts of
cocaine from various drug busts over the years. The previous afternoon he'd told his wife that he'd be late,
lugged a heavy, expandable briefcase she'd never seen
before out to the family automobile, and not returned.
The vehicle was discovered several blocks distant with a
few smears of blood on the seat. They were running
DNA tests.

"Interesting, huh?" Erin loved mysteries. "My bet is
the blood's a red herring to put the cops off his trail. I
wonder what he had in the briefcase."

"Maybe a change of socks?"

"Hah! How about cash and negotiable bonds?"

"You think he got away with it?"

"That's been happening lately. I'd better get back to work. *Ciao,* pardner."

Link returned to memorizing details. Frenchman's Lake was clean and clear, and at one end a collection of fallen-in cabins—where the Eagle clan had lived—was being reclaimed by forest. He passed over Big Marsh, which was covered with sedge and horsetail, then Martha's Marsh. As he gazed down, an incomprehensible sense of sadness came over him. As quickly as the melancholy had come, it faded from his consciousness.

Link flew on, imprinting landmarks into his mind, and periodically smiling at the thought of the brief dogfight with the chopper.

10

Link followed the Firebird into the Toussaint driveway, then parked as Jason climbed out. The young Indian grinned at him like nothing was amiss, but bloodshot eyes and unsure steps told the real story. "Good seein' you again, man."

"Same here," said Link, emerging with a bottle of wine in hand.

"Told some buddies about you," said the younger man. "Mentioned how I'd heard about you when I was little, and now you're moving back and all."

He opened the door, and Link followed him in.

"Sorry I didn't show last night. Had a couple too many," Jason explained. "You know. BS'ing and forgettin' the time?"

"Is that you, Jason?" Jenifer's voice.

"Link's here too, Jen." Spoken like he might need the support.

She leaned out of the kitchen doorway, took in the wine Link carried, and motioned with a wooden spoon. "How about a glass while I finish the linguini."

"Not me," said Jason.

"You *bet*, not you. You're doing penance, Jase."

"Whatever you say." Jason did not argue, and lost none of his jocularity. "Gotta call Lonnie. I left my jacket at his place. Least I *hope* I did."

"Don't expect any sympathy if it's stolen."

While Link wrestled with the corkscrew, Jenifer sampled the pasta, adjusted the flame, and stirred some more. "Northwoods linguini," she explained. "I'm improvising." She nodded at the bottle. "Where in the world did you find good Valpolicella?"

"I brought a survival box from New York."

"Wonderful. How did your flight go?"

"Well enough. I learned a lot."

She gave him an amused look. "Before the council meeting, I mentioned you to the elders—how you'd been born on the north side and were coming back. I almost fainted when Sly Paquette had the staff go through the records to look you up. Guess what?"

"I passed?"

"One of the old families had the same surname. Their four-year-old was adopted by a couple named Anderson—and they renamed the boy Abraham Lincoln. You're even shown on the national registry as three-fourths Manido."

He smiled as he filled two wineglasses with the blood-red wine.

Jenifer took her wine. "Your assistant did all that from New York?"

"Erin's capable." Link raised his glass to eye level. "Cheers."

"To new friends." She sipped and stared, communicating unsaid things as they'd both done since they'd met. Instilling a sense of pleasant warmth in Link that was more than sexual, although there was definite magnetism.

Jason came in and took in their intimacy. "Am I interrupting something?"

He was definitely interrupting.

"Of course not," Jenifer murmured.

"Good. I'm hungry. What happened at the meeting, Jen? What was Gloria Vasson like?"

"Striking for her age, distant. I met her when I was in Washington working for the senator, and we had our differences. I haven't changed my mind, and from the way she looked at me today, she hasn't either."

"Did she defend Senator Eddie?" Jason asked.

"Just the opposite. She said Eddie all but admitted

his guilt in his computer notes, and listed locations on the north side, like he was evaluating various places to hide the old treaties. I think she's sponsoring the search as a sort of penance."

"She thinks he was *guilty*?" Jason looked at Link. "I was wrong. Gloria's a lying, rich bitch. Hey, I *saw* the senator the day he died, and there weren't any fucking thieves with him."

"Jason, this is *not* a bar," Jenifer scolded, turning off the burner under the bubbling pasta.

"You saw the senator that day?" Link asked.

"Twice. Lonnie and I were over at his uncle's helping him patch an aluminum boat when Senator Eddie drove by and turned off on the Lake Portage road. I didn't recognize the car—an old Jeep station wagon with Michigan plates—so I wasn't positive. Later one of the outsiders working at the casino came by asking, and I told him I *thought* I'd seen him. Then a few hours later Lonnie and I saw the Jeep turn onto the road where they found him. So I saw him twice, and both times he was *alone*."

"You told that to the FBI?"

"Sure, but then they asked things like, 'Could the others have been crouched out of sight?' There was no way to say no. They *could* have been. And I had to tell 'em he was driving real erratic, like he was sick or something was wrong with the steering."

"Could he have been drinking?"

Jenifer interrupted. "No one here's seen him take a drop of alcohol. He said it was a problem with *some* of our people"—she gave Jason a look—"so he set an example."

"What about the time during the televised debate?"

"They lied about him that time too," said Jason.

Jenifer shooed them both back and used mitts to empty the pasta into a colander.

Link looked on. "Will Gloria get her search?"

"She's calling it an expedition, and council's already given approval." She sipped wine, and returned her attentions to dinner, transferring pasta to an earthenware bowl, adding mussels, white sauce, and seasoning, and mixing it all thoroughly.

"Looks wonderful."

She sprinkled on a handful of herbs and stared critically. "After it sets for a few minutes, we'll give it a proper test."

Jason cocked his head inquisitively. "So who's going on the search?"

"The expedition leader and four others. Gloria's paying for everything, but she'll stay in town here and visit periodically."

"Expedition?" Jason snorted. "That sounds awfully grand."

"Joseph Richards's an explorer, scuba diver, you name it. I saw him on Discovery Channel, looking for an ancient emerald mine on the Amazon."

"Did he *find* anything?"

"Yes, as a matter of fact. Mr. Richards is quite capable. This time there'll be no publicity, just the business of finding the treaties. I assume Gloria's paying him well."

"She'll release the senator's notes?" Link asked.

"She has them stored in a laptop computer. They're private and she wants to keep them that way. We'll start at locations around the old Adcock home, so she'll hand over those notes only. If we don't find anything, she'll provide notes about other locations."

"You keep saying 'we,' " Jason said. "You're going?"

"I'll represent the tribal council."

"I'm surprised Sly went along with it."

"Who else?" Link asked.

"Richards's assistant, and Dr. David Brogg, who's an expert on the treaties and the handling of old documents." She smiled. "Oh yeah, the council heard your qualifications and accepted your offer. They want to talk to you on Monday morning, before Gloria meets with the expedition members."

"I'll be there. And thanks."

Jason was surprised. "They don't even *know* Link."

"They trusted my judgment." She toted salad fixings, condiments, and cranberry sauce into the small dining room.

"He doesn't know the north side," Jason groused.

Link spoke up. "I looked it over from the air. Tomorrow why don't you show it to me from the ground?"

"The cops have it blocked off. We can't even guide fishermen up there."

"The police were told to let Link go wherever he wishes," said Jenifer.

"And I'd like you to come with me," said Link. "How about a trade? First chance, I'll take you up so you can see it from the air."

Jason smiled. "You got a deal."

Jenifer gave Link a pleased look as she placed the pasta dish on the table. "If you two don't sit down, I'll try this out on the neighbors."

The linguini was superb, and Jenifer accepted their praise with a pleased smile. When they were stuffed, she offered a fitting finale: a sliver of pound cake topped with wild raspberries and covered with sweet cream.

When he'd finished, Link sat back, pleasantly miserable.

Jenifer asked if they'd heard about Doris Eagle.

He noted that Jason developed a somber expression.

"She visited Daniel in Woodruff yesterday, but she didn't return her sister's car, and no one's seen her since. Some of her belongings from her home are missing, but it's not like her to go off like that, pregnant and all. Council's alerted authorities both on and off the reservation."

"And Sly Paquette went along with it?" Jason asked. "When people disappear, he's the one always saying to forget it, they just moved off somewhere."

"Be charitable. He was in an accident over the weekend and lost sight in one eye."

"Sorry, Jen, I've *got* no charity for the guy." Jason turned to look at Link. "Your place at five o'clock, and don't eat breakfast. We'll *catch* it."

Link noted the headlights coming on behind him as he drove from the Toussaint driveway. After stopping at the Quik Mart for a six-pack—local stuff called Leinenkugel Red—he pulled onto the highway, and a moment later noted the same array of lights in his mirror.

He performed a textbook maneuver to confirm a follower's determination—starting with a left turn, then another. The tail followed, closing until it was only half a block behind.

Link turned right onto a well-lit street, doused his lights, and pulled to the curb. A few seconds later the follower made the turn. The streetlamp illuminated the occupants long enough for a glimpse. He noted the driver's hulking figure and doughy features, the passenger's facial bandages. Sly Paquette mouthed curse words as the car passed back into shadows.

Link accelerated until he was a car length behind, and stayed there.

The license plate read MANIDO-OJIBWE, SPIRIT LAKE, OFFICIAL. The Junkman, who filled the driver's side, looked back, saying something that Link was willing to bet was impolite. As they turned onto the town's deserted main thoroughfare, Sly Paquette swiveled his head for another look. He was holding a microphone to his bandaged face.

Still in trail, they turned into a residential area. Another vehicle accelerated up behind Link. The three of them continued in procession until the one in back switched on its blue-and-red flashing lights. Link continued another block before pulling over, watching as the vehicle before him continued down the street.

An officer emerged from the patrol car, and took his time approaching as Link rolled down the window. He was large and beefy, with a burr cut and a florid face with runaway acne.

"Lemme see your driver's license and registration."

Link reached for the glove compartment. "Mind if I ask why you stopped me?"

"You got a *problem* with me stopping you?"

"I'd just like to know why."

The officer drew his revolver. "Outa the fuckin' car. *Now!*"

Link emerged slowly, hands up and palms open.

"Turn around." He shoved Link against the side of the Toyota, kicked his feet apart, and jabbed twice into his kidneys with the revolver barrel. Link leaned over, nauseous with pain.

"Stand up, asshole." The cop went through his pockets using procedures so sloppy Link could have taken him at any moment of his choosing.

A second patrol car nosed in directly in front of them. In Link's peripheral vision a thin and wiry man emerged. This one looked Indian and wore three stripes on his shoulder.

"What do we have, Willie?" asked the new arrival.

"Resisted when I asked for his ID." When Link turned slightly, he pressed with the revolver's muzzle. "Hey, asshole, did I say you could move?"

"Why did you stop him, Willie?"

"Councilman Paquette called in that he was being followed."

The sergeant mused on that, then spoke to Link. "Your name, sir?"

"A. Lincoln Anderson."

"Just read about you in the day log. Mr. Anderson's a pilot, Willie. Also a big game guide. He's home from the big city, thinking about moving permanently. All that correct, sir?"

"Yes."

Willie continued to frisk him, found the satellite phone in his shirt pocket, and extracted it using two fingers, as if he just might have discovered a bomb.

The sergeant took phone and wallet. "Mr. Anderson, *why* did you resist my officer?"

"I didn't resist him. I just asked why he'd stopped me."

"That true, Willie?"

"He's a lying shit. Said he had a problem with me stopping him. Ask him."

The sergeant considered. "Willie, why don't you go back to the station and brew us a pot of coffee. If there's a fresh pot, drink a cup, then go back on patrol."

"Damn it, Sarge, he—"

"Not tomorrow, Willie. *Now.*"

As Officer Willie stumped off, the sergeant tapped Link's shoulder. "You can relax."

Link turned and watched as the police sergeant shone a flashlight and glanced through the wallet, paused when he came to the Guides and Outfitters card, then closed and returned it. He examined the satellite telephone and misidentified it, as most did.

"Cell phones don't do well here. No reception north of town where the expedition's going to be looking."

"I'll keep that in mind," Link said as he slipped the instrument into his shirt pocket.

"Surprised you didn't know it." He mused for a moment. "I'm George Rose, in charge of the local law during the wild and woolly night hours. You'll have to forgive Willie's exuberance. He's young."

While Link did not feel sufficient charity for forgiveness, he shook the sergeant's hand.

Rose spoke evenly. "The council's giving you the run of the place to help find the old treaties." He raised eyebrows. "You must be awful good for them to do that."

"I've done some guide work, and I know the reservation."

Rose smiled. "Care for a cup of that coffee Willie's brewing?"

"Some other time. I was on my way to get some sleep."

"Good to have you back with your people, Anderson, but if I were you I wouldn't rile Willie, or any of the other officers. And maybe you should think twice before you go following important people around at night?"

Before Link could respond, Sergeant George Rose turned and walked away.

The patrol car trailed him to the resort. There Rose stopped at the entrance for a couple of minutes, as if watching him, then turned about and sped away like he had somewhere to go.

In the cottage, Link popped the cap off one of the Leinie Reds and took a healthy swallow. Good beer, he decided. He was pleased that he'd met more of the players. Willie, the worst kind of cop, and his "go with the flow" sergeant, George Rose. What was it Jenifer had said? Paquette had the police department stacked?

He'd also got a first glimpse of Sly Paquette, and another of the Junkman, whom he'd seen in Minocqua outside the private investigator's office.

Link went out to look out at the lake as he drank more of the mellow beer and thought over the encounters. He phoned the office and left an outline of the evening's events on the recorder. He checked voice mail. There was a message—secure, level one.

With the decryption circuit switched on, Erin's voice was fuzzy. She'd looked up the nearest H-60 Hawk helicopters. Two were in Chicago, painted olive drab, bulbous-nosed, and assigned to a DEA surveillance role. The closest military versions were MH-60 Black Hawks at a Kansas ANG base, and those were painted black. None resembled the one he had seen.

Link wondered if he'd misidentified the helicopter. It was possible, yet whatever he'd seen had definitely been sleek and fast. He drained the last of the beer as he listened to the night sounds and thought about the mini-dogfight. Not bad for an old guy of thirty-six.

Sergeant George Rose had followed Anderson to the Hideaway Bay Resort when Council Elder Paquette radioed for him to drop by his home at Rock Lake.

When Rose arrived at the highway he headed east, away from town. Spirit Lake was for tourists. The south side was home to the poorest of the reservation's population. In contrast, Rock Lake was upscale, the properties expensive. Sly Paquette owned the largest house there, situated apart from all others. It was dark-hued cedar, two stories with four large gables, and at night it appeared downright spooky.

Rose slowed as he approached the home, noting that the cruiser assigned to the captain of reservation police was parked in front. He stepped out, wondering if there was a meeting. A light was on in the large work shed. Billy Junkins emerged and waved for him to come inside.

As Rose stepped through the door, he saw Council Elder Paquette in the corner. He started over, and slowed. A man hung from a hook set into the rafter beam, bright blood draining from nose and mouth to form a crimson pool on the floor. A massive purple-and-red bruise marred the side of his head. George went numb as he recognized his superior officer.

Paquette spoke. "Last week the captain was awarded a ten-thousand-dollar prize for a suggestion sent to the Department of Interior. You'd think he'd be grateful."

George mumbled something appropriate, eyes glued on the captain.

Paquette had unbelievable connections. He'd make a phone call, mention a name, and an award would arrive from Washington along with citations ascribing ideas no one at Spirit Lake had imagined. A five-thousand-dollar check went here, a ten-thousand-dollar one there. Rose had been awarded two such payments, one for outstanding achievement he had not performed, another for a money-saving suggestion he had not submitted. Paquette promised more—saying millions were available from various dumb-ass government incentive and bonus programs.

"But today," Paquette explained, "the captain called an undersecretary's office in Washington, saying he was police chief here and had information about something terrible going on." He bent down. "You remember doin' that?"

"Yegh." The captain's whimpering continued with each harsh breath.

An undersecretary? George Rose wondered how Paquette had learned of it.

Paquette motioned. The Junkman lifted the captain off the hook and untied his hands.

Sly Paquette owned the reservation police. There were no more holdouts. Those had mysteriously "left town" months ago, replaced by mobsters and bullies brought in from Chicago, Saint Paul, and Milwaukee. The directive that all patrolmen be Manido-Ojibwe was rescinded. Only George, the captain, and one patrolman were Indians.

"Dumb shit's about to be involved in an automobile accident," Paquette said. "He'll be out of commission for a while, so you'll fill in for him. Keep the People in line, and keep them and everyone else out of the fucking north side."

Rose mumbled, "I'll do my best, sir."

A buzz sounded from the workbench. The Junkman answered a cordless phone that had been laid there, and hurried over. "It's Sydney," he said in a reverent tone.

Paquette took the phone gingerly, listened, and respectfully explained that the captain would pose no more problems. He agreed with something that was said, thanked the caller for letting him know about it, and switched off.

Sydney? Rose wondered.

There had obviously been a change of plans, for Paquette turned and swung the pipe viciously. The metal thumped into the captain's head with a meaty crack.

Unless a blow is delivered to an area of vulnerability, the brain can endure great abuse. The captain shrieked and thrashed. Paquette swung again, and the captain's body shuddered and became still.

Paquette picked up a rag and cleaned blood from the length of pipe. He regarded Rose. "Before I go in, what's your impression of this Lincoln Anderson?"

Rose spoke through numbed lips. "I think he's what he says he is."

"Good, we need him on the expedition, but keep digging. Have the feds check him out. Bug his place and see where he goes. I don't need any fuckin' surprises."

"Yes, sir."

Paquette nudged the captain but got no response. "See to him," the council elder told Billy Junkins, and left.

Sergeant George Rose regarded his old boss. "Is he alive?" he asked the Junkman.

"Who gives a shit," replied the giant. He grasped a handful of hair and a broken arm, and dragged him toward the police cruiser.

11

It was still inky dark when Link went outside to begin
the warm-up exercises. He labored to complete the torturous leg lifts, reluctantly began the sit-ups, and mar-
veled that they were so incredibly difficult. Finally he
set out on the run, this time pacing himself, *knowing*
how easily he could overdo it. Loping to the road, adjusting his breathing so he exhaled a measured, rhythmic
huff with each step. Concentrating on the dark roadway ahead.

He forced himself to go the full distance before turning back, ignoring the inner voice that argued that there
was no rationale for such torture. He was wheezing and
blowing well before he arrived back at the cottage.

When he'd showered and dressed, he set the sat phone
to silent ring—there was no cell phone service where
they were headed so if it buzzed it might confuse
things—and snapped it inside his shirt pocket.

Jason Toussaint arrived in a battered, four-wheel drive
Ford pickup, appearing infinitely more alert than the
hungover specimen Link recalled from the previous evening. "My buddy Lonnie's," Jason explained about the
truck. "I use it for clients, and he takes my Firebird
when he's got a warm date. Where do you want to
start?"

Link unfolded an aeronautical chart on the dash, held

the door ajar so the overhead light stayed on, and pointed at the upper left corner. "How about we head for the northwest corner up near the ecol-rec zone, go east all the way across to the cranberry bog, then just take as many roads as we have time on the way back, and look at anything you feel is important."

Jason grinned. "Get ready for a rough ride. The roads on the north side were never much, and now they've gone unused, most are next to unpassable." Jason turned left on the gravel road. "Some of 'em, five miles an hour and you're speeding. Lots of fallen trees. Most you can drag outa the way, but others you gotta use the winch or cut a path with the chain saw. The oldest roads are completely overgrown. No way with those."

"You have plenty of gas?"

"Tank's full and there's ten gallons in cans in the back."

After a short distance, a white-and-black Explorer was illuminated in the headlamps, blocking the road. A slovenly uniformed driver got out, yawning.

"The fuckin' road's closed."

Link showed his driver's license. "My name's Anderson. Council gave me permission to look around the north side."

The cop gave him a cursory look, and a surly nod. "I heard."

They drove around the Ford. "Not overly friendly," commented Link.

"Bunch of thugs from Chicago and Milwaukee brought in by Sly Paquette," said Jason. "Quiz time. You remember the names of the major lakes?"

Link recited: "Spirit, Portage Nord and Portage Sud, Frenchman's, Shining Button, Woman's Hat . . ."

"Woman's Hat's in the ecol-rec zone, which Aunt Jen says is full of poisons and chemicals. All I know is parts of it smell like dirty socks. We'll just skirt around the edge." He glanced over. "Are those all the big lakes you recall?"

Link picked up where he'd left off. "Moose, Big Fish, Little Fish, and Turtle."

"Also White Dog and Rock Lake. They're not quite as large, but you oughta know them."

Link taxed his memory. "White Dog's peanut-shaped, up on the Michigan border in thick forest. Lots of reeds. Rock Lake is more or less round, only five miles from Spirit Lake. An access road and boat launch on one side, and vacation homes on the other."

"And for your info, Sly Paquette has a place there. How about the bogs?"

"Including marshes?"

"Same thing. You should know the biggest ones. There are a thousand small ones."

"Big Martha, Little Martha, No Bottom . . ." Link recited names and gave descriptions.

They proceeded slowly because of the atrocious condition of the spiderweb of roads, crossed the narrow isthmus between Portage Nord and Portage Sud Lakes, then drove the southern edge of Moose Lake. Link used a penlight to follow their twists and turns on the map as Jason expounded about the places they passed.

They drove on, until the first light of dawn began to relieve the gloom. Periodically then they'd stop and walk a trail to the water's edge, and Jason would explain landmarks and the families who had lived there. He personalized his tales, saying how this stretch had been the site of a battle with a huge sturgeon, how an inlet that looked promising was lousy fishing, how a small island had been the site of an encounter between a woman and a foraging bear. A crescent bay at one end of Shining Button Lake was lined with treetop eagle aeries, as it had always been. An inlet was the nesting place for two families of loons, odd because loon families were loners.

They turned onto a narrow path and continued for a mile.

"There are hundreds of trails like this that aren't on maps," said Jason as they stopped at a small cove on Shining Button Lake. "Time for breakfast," Jason announced.

From the back he pulled out a rod and spinning reel, and a wire contraption he called a "cheater," which could be closed about vegetables or fish fillets for roasting over an open fire. They hiked to the shoreline as the sun's orb glared through the trees onto the lake, causing the water to shimmer in alternating shades of gold, silver, and blue. Link watched as three different eagles flapped up to hunting altitude over the end of the lake. Forget the Washington scheming and the corruption of the Spirit Lake officials. The scenery was spectacular.

A fish jumped just twenty-five feet from where they stood.

"Smallmouth bass," said Jason. He handed over rod and reel, searched the rocky shore for a few seconds, plucked a crayfish from the cool water, and baited the hook. "Why don't you make that guy's day while I start a fire."

As Link walked up shore to an opening in the foliage, Jason arranged a few stones for a firebed and gathered wood, all within easy arm's reach. He'd brought fuel-impregnated paper for a no-brainer fire starter. Link took care with his back cast. The crayfish plunked into the water a couple of feet farther out than where they'd seen the bass. Link flipped over the bail, and hardly had time to reel in the slack when the bass hit.

The line grew taut—the fish ran.

"First cast!" Link exulted. The bass danced and feinted like a flyweight contender.

"Gotta think like a fish," Jason said with a grin. "That boy was hungry for crayfish. They like it so much, most places it's illegal to use 'em for bait. Here on the reservation we have our own rules."

When Link finally pulled it out, he estimated it at three pounds plus.

Jason had the fire going. "Toss him over here, so I can get the fillets in the cheater while you catch another. Same size, please."

"I usually clean what I catch."

"Might as well act like a client. I'm gonna hold you to that airplane ride."

Before he made his cast, Link took out the sat phone and pressed RC, then button 1 to save the coordinates on Erin's computer for future reference. He also fixed the location in his mind.

On the walk to the pickup, Jason pointed out a large, moist patch of dark earth. "That's a mixture of mud and decomposed matter the Northwoods locals call loon shit. If you get caught in it, it's like sinking in a mixture of quicksand and snot. It's hard to get out of, and it stains your clothes. Sometimes it's shallow; other times it goes down forever. Once you're in it, don't fool around. Get out. If you're stuck, don't fight it. Lean forward, distribute your weight, and swim your way out."

"Is that what the bogs and marshes consist of?"

"Only the worst ones, like No Bottom and Little Martha's. Most of the marshes are just shrunk-up lakes, where the sides filled in with reeds and sediment."

Half an hour later they were off the trail and back on the difficult road, savoring the aftertaste of the breakfast, Jason talking up his aunt Jen, saying she'd been engaged once but never found the right guy. Not even with all of her traveling back and forth to Washington.

"She likes you." He glanced over. "Want to hear a Toussaint family secret?"

"Whatever you think," Link said, wanting to know everything about Jenifer.

"Sly Paquette is behind a lie that's going around so he can get her voted off council and replaced by another yes-man. You'll hear it, so I'd like you to know the truth."

Link held his tongue.

"When Eddie got home from Vietnam, most of the local girls were chasing him, including Jen's mother. A couple of months and he went off to Madison to get his law degree. A few weeks more and Jen's mom was sent to stay with relatives in Minnesota."

Link guessed where they were going. "Maybe you *shouldn't* be telling me this."

"You'll hear the lie, and Aunt Jen won't defend herself. All I ask is you don't repeat it."

He thought about it. "You've got a deal."

Jason nodded. "Eddie wasn't aware Jen's mother was pregnant. By the time she returned from Minnesota with the baby, he'd married his first wife. A few years later we had the big Asian flu epidemic, and Jen's mother sent him a letter from her deathbed."

"Telling him he was the father?"

"Jen's the only one living who read the letter. She was only nine at the time, but she promised her mother never to tell, and she's kept her word. Still it was obvious, the way Eddie smiled at the mention of Jen's name. I think he wanted to tell the world she was his daughter, but she begged him to leave it alone, like her mother had wanted, so it wouldn't hurt his reputation. Every time he visited, Eddie dropped by to check. When she went to college, got the house in her name, paid for repairs, bought clothes, *anything,* the money was there. He left her a good inheritance, which she will also not discuss. Even today, with Sly Paquette floating rumors that she was Eddie's lover, Jen won't discuss it. She's that hardheaded."

Also loyal, Link thought, and liked her even more. He thought about something. "The senator had a list of people he trusted, but she's not on it. Any idea why?"

"Eddie was scared she'd get hurt by his politics. He insisted that she never contact him with the bad things happening here, in case someone retaliated."

Jason grew quiet as foliage crowded in from both sides, the road so narrow that branches scraped both sides of the pickup. They idled along, periodically descending into chasms that were well beyond pothole status. Several times they passed old homesteads set back in the trees, often with a barn, sheds, stable, and corral. There were wagons, carts, pickups, tractors, snowmobiles, and boats of all description, overgrown by forest and fern and in various states of disrepair. Some structures were so fallen-in they appeared almost leveled. A few looked more as if the owners were only away temporarily and needed to tend to their gardens.

"Four thousand people lived up here," Link murmured.

"Yeah, for nearly four hundred years. That's a lot of ghosts." He gave Link a sideward glance, like he was half serious, and they drove on in silence.

As they approached a T intersection, Jason cranked the wheel to make a right turn, then slowed and halted, and squinted to their left. The stare became fixed, his breathing shallow.

Link did not interfere. After a moment he climbed out, walked to the intersection, and stood scanning the sky, remembering the previous day's flight.

Another minute had passed before he heard the truck door open, and the sounds of the younger man's footsteps. "Sorry," said Jason. "Sometimes I . . ." His voice trailed off.

Link pointed at the south sky. "I was there yesterday when a feeling of great sadness came over me."

"You have dream-times?" Jason blurted.

"Just a sad feeling this time, but I used to have them. Mine were like memories, past and future, that I couldn't explain. Like a sense of déjà vu that you *knew* you'd never experienced. A psychologist I know studies precognition. She feels if it's real, it has to do with neural patterns in specific parts of the brain, and that it's prevalent in certain Indian tribes."

"*If* it's real? She wasn't sure?"

"Nothing is sure with science unless it can be measured. She thinks that with certain people, short- and long-term memory work together to figure things out. The results are the same, but that's easier for me to understand and accept."

Jason looked thoughtful. "Jen's heavy into psych, but she calls them gifts from our ancestors. Me? I have the dreams, but I don't believe in 'em."

"I didn't either. I'm at the stage now that the how doesn't matter. If I come up with a helpful answer, I generally use it."

Link waited for Jason to explain more about what he'd just experienced, but it was not forthcoming. As they climbed back into the truck, the young Indian found his grin.

"You've had 'em too? Maybe I'm not crazy after all."

Jason turned north, toward the ecology recovery zone. After a short distance he slowed to cross a log bridge over a small, marshy creek.

"Dead Man's Creek," Jason explained. "Many lifetimes ago the People found a man there with so many arrows in him he looked like a porcupine. He wasn't

Manido, and no one could identify the arrows that had killed him. Later—who knows how long since it was Indian time—a peckerless white mine worker was found in the same place. Story was he'd raped two little girls, and their pa caught up with him. No one said anything. The People just carried the body over to No Bottom Marsh and dropped it in. That was what they did with the enemies they dishonored—made them disappear and never spoke of them again, like they'd never existed."

"Sort of a bad luck creek," Link observed.

"That's according to your viewpoint," Jason replied.

"You're good with the local legends."

"Storytelling is important to our people."

As they continued, a sour odor became distinct. "Welcome to the ecol-rec zone," said Jason, his nose wrinkling.

"The miners left it smelling like this?"

"They dumped their chemicals into No Bottom Marsh and there were seepage problems, but the smell didn't come until Ecol-Rec, Limited started adding their enzymes." He motioned ahead. "We won't get much closer."

A few minutes later he ran out of road and halted. Before them was a two-feet-deep, seven-feet-wide gully created with heavy equipment. On the opposite side a sign read NO TRESPASSING, BY ORDER OF THE U.S. DEPARTMENT OF THE INTERIOR. VIOLATORS WILL BE PROSECUTED.

A second sign, nailed to a tree, read DO NOT PROCEED. DANGEROUS POLLUTANTS HAVE BEEN DETECTED THAT ARE HAZARDOUS TO HUMAN LIFE. ECOL-REC, LTD. There was a skull and crossbones sign, and another, reading TOXIC WASTES.

Jason snorted. "Now the ecol-reccers are telling us where we can go on our own reservation. We see 'em around town every now and then, wearing green uniforms. They don't mix in, and even Sly Paquette's cops stay out of their way."

Link recalled seeing them at the casino. "Might be better to stay out of the zone."

"We'd have to backtrack ten miles. This way it's only

four or five." Jason pointed across the gully to a fork in
the road. Straight ahead, leading toward the heart of the
zone, the way was blocked by a high fence. Link had
seen no roads inside the zone, and wondered if there
might be more camouflage netting than he'd noted.

A second branch led to their right. "That's where
we're headed," said Jason, pointing. "A sort of perimeter road."

"Inside the zone?"

"Just barely, and we won't do any harm." Jason chose
four-wheel, low-range and proceeded to wallow into the
soft earth of the gully and climb up the opposite bank.
"Piece o' cake," Jason crowed as he took the right fork.
"A few more miles and we'll be out."

Link pointed out a platform several feet up on a tree
trunk. "We're on television."

"That's new. Some of them almost caught me last time
I was here. I heard 'em coming and didn't wait around
to discuss the matter."

A distant Klaxon horn sounded.

"I'd guess they're on to you again," Link said.

Jason accelerated. Trees and underbrush at the sides
of the road appeared pale, unhealthy, and almost trans-
lucent, contrasting with the verdant world they had left.
The good news was that the rotten odor diminished as
they continued.

The sat phone vibrated in Link's shirt pocket. He dis-
regarded it.

Jason was holding a steady forty miles per hour—ignoring the continuing sounds of the Klaxon horn and
making better time on the improved road—when he
braked hard and almost rammed into a chain link gate
that extended across the roadway.

They climbed out and eyed the laminated steel pad-
lock securing the gate.

"This is all new." Jason peered into the forest. "We
may be able to drive around it. I'll take a look." He
pushed his way into the brush and disappeared from
view.

As he waited, Link slapped at voracious blackflies, increasingly bold as the morning sun warmed the air, and

studied the gate's hardware. The hinge pins were two-inch lag bolts screwed into ordinary nuts, and posed little challenge, as if the gate was only there to slow them down.

He walked to the side of the road and abruptly stopped, eyes drawn to a single, fine strand, chest-high and in an unlikely place for any spider's web.

"I don't think we can make it," Jason said as he returned, walking the fence line.

"Stop!" Link said, pointing at the strand.

Jason noted his alarmed expression and halted.

The wire was shiny black—chest-high so it would not likely be tripped by animals—invisible unless viewed at the proper angle.

A marine gunnery sergeant had once explained the use of such filament to Link, who continued to hold up a restraining hand as he cautiously approached Jason. "Take a step back."

Jason saw it. "A wire?" He reached out.

"Damn it, *don't*! Take a step back."

Link used care as he followed the thin strand into a bush. There he stopped and stared, and silently thanked the gunny. A canvas-covered shaped-charge antipersonnel mine was strapped to a tree trunk with wide, black tape. The word ENEMY was stenciled onto the canvas, and an arrow indicating direction of blast was turned toward the road. Another two steps and Jason would have triggered an explosion that would have cut them in two.

The device had three killing options. If the wire was tripped by either a man or a vehicle, the detonator would set off the shaped charge. There were also timer and remote modes.

Finding no secondary booby traps, Link disconnected the wire and called Jason over. The young Indian's eyes grew as he explained what could have been.

Link checked the other side of the road. An identical mine was rigged there, that one connected by wire to the gate. If the gate was opened . . .

"Jesus," Jason whispered a couple of times as Link disarmed that one as well.

Link carried both olive drab, canvas-clad mines—each weighing forty-four pounds—to the truck and loaded them into the bed. He then put Jason to work removing the hinges on one side of the gate as he explored to ensure there were no more surprises.

When the hinges were loosened, they swung the gate back from one side.

"Go ahead and drive through," Link told him grimly.

"Jesus," Jason said for at least the tenth time. "Listen."

They heard the growl of an approaching vehicle engine.

"How far until we're out of the zone?" Link asked.

"Three miles?"

"Drive through and wait," Link told him.

By the time Jason stopped on the opposite side, Link was dragging the gate into place.

"They're getting close!" Jason yelled.

Link dropped a lag bolt into a hinge, ran the nut to finger-tightness, and went to work with a wrench. He finished that one, dropped a bolt into the second, and hand-tightened the nut.

"Hurry!" Jason yelled from the truck. "I can see 'em!"

Link chanced a look. In the distance was an open-topped Humvee, the passengers decked out in green and brandishing long weapons. As he vaulted into the pickup bed, Jason jammed down the accelerator. The truck fishtailed, spewing dirt until the tires caught and they leaped forward.

When they were out of sight around the first turn, Link called into the driver's window, "You can stop."

Jason looked back over his shoulder with wide eyes as he came to a halt. "Better be quick," Jason said. "They'll have a key for the gate."

"I doubt they hurry. It's their turn to worry about mines."

"One look and they'll know we took them."

Link smiled as he slid into the front. "Then they'll proceed cautiously, won't they?"

As he accelerated, Jason looked back. "Those things okay, bouncing around like that?"

"Probably."

"Jesus."

A couple of minutes later they came to another fork. Jason turned sharply, bounced across another bulldozed gully, and blew out a long breath of relief despite the fact that the road had again become so pitted it looked unpassable.

"We just left the ecol-fucking-rec zone," Jason announced happily.

12

They'd traveled five miles on the awful roads and were abeam Moose Lake before Jason relaxed enough to talk about it. "The place is fortified like a military base."

"More so. Military bases use electrified fences and warn you if they use deadly force. None I know of plant Claymore mines unless it's a combat zone."

Jason peered back at the devices. "Are those ours?"

"America's best and latest twenty-kilo Claymore mines. They produce a focused blast. You saw what the terrorists did to the USS *Cole* in Yemen."

"Jesus. What are we going to do with them?"

"We could turn them over to the reservation police."

"No way."

They continued at the slow pace imposed by the awful roads until Jason stopped at White Dog Lake, within sight of a half-collapsed cabin.

"A guy they call the old hermit lived here. People still see him now and then. He'll be naked sometime, sometime wearing deerskin or furs, ranting and waving an old rifle. No one knows if he has bullets—the talk is that he doesn't—but I wouldn't press the issue. He speaks some kind of strange language, like he makes it up as he goes along. Senator Eddie knew him since they were kids, and he'd come up here to visit. He was the only one who could get close or understand him. A couple years ago he talked him—or sign-languaged him or what-

ever—into moving into the old Adcock place, the one
he took me to that time."

"And the hermit's still around."

"Probably. People forget him until he steals things,
like shiny objects." Jason put the pickup into gear.
"We're going to the Adcock cabin now, so don't be surprised if a naked guy comes running out waving a rifle.
Like I said, I don't *think* it's loaded."

"He's harmless?"

"Except for the stealing. Sometimes he'll come out if
I sit quietly and play the flute."

A long while later they came upon a neatly kept cabin
that looked as if you could move right in and build a
cheery fire. Jason led him on, to the shore of Big Fish
Lake. "This is where Senator Eddie took me torch
fishing."

"I don't see the dugout."

"It's down the lakeshore. Whenever he left he'd fill it
with rocks and sink it, like he found it when he was a
kid. That way the winter ice can't crush it?"

Jason walked toward the cabin. "I'll look around for
the hermit. If you hear a shot, run like hell." He grinned
to show he was *sort* of joking.

When Jason was out of earshot, Link pulled out the
sat phone.

Erin responded on the first ring. "How goes the vacation, pardner?"

"I'm fishing. Did you try to call me earlier?" he asked.

"Must be another of your fans. I've been checking out
the Manido. They're a splinter band of the Ojibwe, but
not part of the Lake Superior Ojibwe nation, and that
means they don't have even minimal clout."

"Jenifer told me they have no one to turn to."

"That's a real bummer. I've got more on Mr. John Sly
Fox Paquette."

"Tell me."

"When he went to Chicago to join the army in 1980,
he was rejected for antisocial behavior, and dropped out
of sight for a while. Jump to 1986, when a punk mobster
named Tonio Gracchi was ordered by his uncle Carmine,
who's still the big boss, to bring the Chicago construction

unions back in line after a major defection. In the process Tonio's guys earned *respect*—which in mob talk means they scared the doo-doo out of folks. Two of his *most* feared were Sly Paquette and the Junkman. According to rumor, the Junkman held their victims down while Paquette asked questions and broke bones with a length of steel pipe. Sound familiar?"

"Daniel Eagle."

"Right down to the cigar, which Paquette added to his repertoire after he quit smoking cigarettes. As Tonio Gracchi gained power his specialists dropped out of the spotlight, but there were more rumors of killings by Sly and the Junkman."

"If they were such assets, why send them here?"

"I'd guess because they decided to take over the reservation, and Sly was their natural choice as a born and bred member of the Manido."

"It worked. He runs the reservation and the mob owns the casino."

"Now I've shown you mine. What have you been up to?"

He told her about the drive with Jason, dwelling on the bass breakfast, then . . .

"You found *what*?" she yelled into the phone.

"Claymore shaped-charge mines like I saw in Desert Storm, only newer and fancier. I think they call them focused-effect explosives now."

"Things are getting serious, Link. It's time to bring in the cavalry."

"What cavalry?"

"Yeah. Who *do* we turn to? I keep hoping it's some kind of big hairy government operation. Like they're on to a major crime and collecting information before they pounce?"

"Here's something for Helga." Link read the ID numbers from the mines so Erin could trace their history. "For the present we'll hide the things."

Link heard a high-pitched whine accompanied by *whup-whup* sounds, coming ever closer. He got a glimpse of forest green color and the distinctive shape going overhead.

"Whose is that?" Link called out to Jason, who was still nosing about the cabin.

Jason shouted back, "Ecol-Rec, Limited uses helicopters to dump their enzymes and stuff."

A twenty-million-dollar war machine for crop-dusting? Link wondered.

"This time I'm positive, Erin. That was an H-60. I hear a second chopper, but it sounds different. Jason says the Ecol-Rec people use them, but a classified military chopper?"

"I'll run the audio through analysis." She recorded their conversations—joked that he was on candid computer—and had a databank of several million sound sources.

"Check out Ecol-Rec, Limited. Jason says their people come to town once in a while, like they're on R and R. I saw a few getting out of a van at the hotel. A couple of guys in facial bandages, then some dweeb types like you'd expect in the enzymes business."

"Ecol-Rec, Limited," she muttered, probably for Helga's benefit.

"See if they have a young, skinny blond guy with long hair and a scraggly beard in their management. He appeared to be in charge."

"That one may be tough."

"You thrive on difficulty."

"Yeah, sure."

"We just saw some of them in a Humvee carrying M16s."

"Let me get this straight. You're on an Indian reservation run by a bunch of bad cops, *and* there's dweebs with weapons, *and* you stole a couple of their land mines?"

"Antipersonnel focused-effect mines. Seriously dangerous stuff."

"Some vacation. Have you thought of finding a nice Caribbean beach?"

"Sounds boring. Gotta go."

"Stay in touch. As the saying goes, this just keeps getting curiouser and curiouser."

The Warehouse

Two helicopters forest green with subdued ECOL-REC, LIMITED logos on their sides—hovered as if to land, although there appeared to be only pale forest below. A low warbling noise penetrated the area, a warning to stand clear while a portion of the vast camouflage netting shuddered and began to retract on tremendous rails. The newly exposed area measured a hundred yards on each side. Two tractor-semi rigs were lined up at one end, as were a heavy-duty forklift and several land-sea transportable containers.

At the other end were an ultramodern radar and a transporter with four sleek surface-to-air missiles, flanked by a pair of cannons that looked like scorpions' stingers. In the center of the area were three hangar-shaped structures fashioned of aluminized canvas, kept inflated by a network of air pumps. Each was forty feet in height, eighty in width, and two hundred in length, interconnected by enclosed walkways. Together these were dubbed the Warehouse. Smaller structures housed the security control center, a dining hall, a hut where the laborers slept, and an administrative office. There was a constant hushed rumble from the generators and air pumps.

Sydney entered the compound from the parking lot—today she was a plain-looking middle-aged woman, as she had been several times recently—and noted that two of Howarski's engineers were standing beside the concrete helipad, carrying stubby machine pistols and squinting up at the helicopters that poised overhead like futuristic creatures.

The two craft descended. As they touched down and their shrill jet engines began to wind down, the overhead netting rumbled ponderously back into position.

The man who stepped from the MH-60 Black Hawk looked like Al Pacino, precisely because he'd emulated the actor for so long. Tonio Gracchi was a consigliere of the Chicago organization, in line for the top role if his uncle ever decided to step aside. He'd seen the original *Godfather* movie sixteen times by his own count, and admired its authenticity—and even if it wasn't *really* accurate, it was the way it should be. Once he'd ordered a horse's head placed in a rival's bed. The guy had awakened, so the Junkman had held him down until they got the bloody thing situated. Only then had Paquette beaten him to death with his pipe.

The mafioso walked over to Paquette and the Junkman, who offered ingratiating smiles. In contrast Sydney gave him a single, cool nod.

Before they started, Tonio observed the passengers deplaning from the second helicopter.

First was an obese man who looked as if he suffered from gas. "A New York circuit court judge," Tonio explained. "Took kickbacks from two different families and made a bundle."

Next came a young man in jeans, sandals, T-shirt, and ball cap, who looked about through uninterested eyes. "Made forty mil on an Internet scam before the feds figured it out," Tonio said admiringly. He was impressed with what he called "cyberstuff."

As the new arrivals were escorted into the "Resort," one of the large inflated buildings that had been divided into small apartments, Tonio gave them a grave look. "Uncle Carmine should be here in half an hour."

Tonio was proud of the fact that his uncle Carmine was the boss of bosses, the most feared man in several Midwestern states, plus Nevada, Arkansas, and southern Florida.

"How 'bout now we have a trial run of what we'll show him?"

"You should start in the security control center," said Sydney.

"I agree," said Tonio, who often took her advice, and led them toward the end building.

When it had become obvious that they'd need airtight security for their endeavors at the Warehouse, Sydney had recommended a young genius named Howarski, who had evaded the federal authorities for the previous two years because he had a nasty habit of blowing up things when he felt threatened and disappearing in the confusion. One such explosion had interrupted a World Trade

Organization meeting in San Francisco, with considerable loss of life. At the time she'd made her suggestion to Tonio, the FBI had been closing in.

She understood the young terrorist. They shared tremendous egos. When he visited the casino-hotel, she'd make herself up into different young women and play the seduction game. He loved the attention she lavished, and never failed to give her a wild ride.

Now, at the Warehouse in front of the others, she was all business.

The group filed into the control center. Inside were futuristic consoles, with engineers hovering over them as if they knew what they were doing. Behind them Howarski, blond-bearded, with piercing eyes, sauntered into the room, fresh from the controls of the MH-60 Black Hawk, which he allowed no other to fly.

Howarski had had a lifelong fascination with flight that he claimed was genetic. His ancestral name in an ancient Slavic root language meant hawk, and he'd made it a point to learn everything worth knowing about rockets, computers, and flying, using sources from da Vinci to Acree. Who else, Sydney wondered, would stay in the boondocks, spend his time with his head buried in technology, and love every minute of it?

To assist him, Sydney had recruited a group who had once been America's top computer engineers, then had been barred from working in the defense industry. They'd been in China to observe PLA rockets boost their systems into orbit. When there were technical problems with the launches, their CEO back in the States—a buddy of the president's—sent word that everything was fixed; it was just fine to provide classified algorithms to fix the problems. When someone snooped and Congress screamed, the billionaire CEO had tossed the engineers to the wolves, and the attorney general yanked their security clearances and bonds.

They were unemployable, righteously bitter, and gave not a damn who they hurt.

While Howarski was utterly undisciplined, he commanded his fifteen engineers with an iron fist, and in a period of only three months they'd perfected a formidable integrated air defense system, which he had modestly dubbed the Howarski System.

Sydney had encouraged him, provided the latest equipment and the brightest engineers, but he had been the one to integrate the system in such a manner that when an airplane was destroyed no one suspected foul play, and all traces of the craft simply disappeared.

"Your uncle might be interested in Howarski's work," Sydney said.

"You think so?" Tonio Gracchi rubbed nervously at his jaw. He had put all of his marbles and banked his future on the operation at the Warehouse.

One of the engineers came over and waited and, when Howarski did not give him notice, cleared his throat for attention. "While you were gone, we had an intruder."

They all heard and gave their rapt attention.

"Who?" hissed Tonio Gracchi.

"Two guys in a pickup went around the perimeter road."

"You got all those fancy systems, and a fucking *truck* drove in?"

Howarski spoke up. "We're still putting in the ground defenses. Paquette's police are supposed to keep everyone away until it's completed."

Sly Paquette bristled. "My cops can't patrol out here. They'd get their asses blown off."

"What's he talkin' about?" asked Tonio Gracchi.

Howarski explained the interim system: alarms and cameras, and gates rigged with what he called focused-effect explosives. "It's temporary. In a week everything will be computerized."

That was the right response, for Tonio was captivated by computers. "So what happened?" he asked. When the engineer muttered a sheepish response, the mafioso regarded him with disbelief. "Someone stole your fuckin' booby traps?"

"Either that or moved them. By the time we responded they were gone."

The engineer showed a black-and-white video shot of the pickup and the intruders.

Tonio nudged Sly Paquette. "Can you tell who they are?"

"The picture's not worth a shit."

"It's a video contrast sensor used for targeting," Howarski snapped, "not watching *Sesame Street.*"

Paquette ignored him and squinted at the screen. "The driver's a local guide, I think. The other's Lincoln Anderson. Council gave him permission to look around the north side."

Howarski's eyes flashed with emotion. "The one flying the Baron?"

"Yeah," said Sly Paquette. "My cops checked with the feds. He was air force, then a ski bum and hunting guide. Now he's a pilot looking for work. Sydney said to leave him alone."

"He has all the qualifications," Sydney said firmly. "Unless he does something rash, leave him alone so he can help find the senator's gym bag."

An engineer reported that a limousine had pulled into the parking lot.

Before they went out, Tonio held their attention. "No one mentions *any* of this."

The first two men in dark suits to emerge from the limo were bodyguards. The third was much older, dressed shabbily, and had a sunken appearance and wary expression. He was not trustful of flying machines, and had just spent six miserable hours in the automobile.

Carmine Gracchi, Chicago's boss of bosses, controlled the same empire that had been welded together by Alphonse Capone seventy years earlier. When his nephew, Tonio, stepped up to take his arm to help, Carmine shook him off. He gave a disapproving look to his nephew, sighed, then motioned for his bodyguards.

The mafiosi walked past Sly Paquette, the Junkman, and Sydney with hardly a look, not even paying mind to the sleek missiles and scorpion stinger guns.

"This way, uncle," said Tonio, leading him toward the security control center.

Carmine grunted and followed, a henchman on either side of him.

Inside the control center everyone waited as Uncle Carmine swept his gaze about at the sophisticated consoles and flat-screen digital maps, as if looking for something.

Tonio cleared his throat. "First I would like to explain this room and the security . . ."

Carmine broke in. "Where is the return on my money?"

"This place is a gold mine, uncle. Another month and you'll be laughing."

"You said that last time we talked. You look me in the eye and lie like Clinton."

His nephew looked embarrassed at being criticized in the presence of others.

Carmine frowned at something stuck to his finger that he was having trouble flicking away, then looked again at the high-tech displays. Tonio noticed this and spoke eagerly. "You know what big defense companies do after they test a new weapon? Doesn't matter how much they spent, they toss it in the junk pile. Sydney paid off somebody up high so all I had to do was send trucks and haul 'em away for salvage. Then Howarski—"

"Nephew! I don't care about that—where is my money? When you came to me and wanted to take a reservation from a bunch of stupid Indians to build a casino, I said do it, just get me a return. Then you wanted to move all the Indians so you could cook more drugs than anyone ever before, and I said okay, but give me my share. Now you have this Resort—"

"Uncle, this place is perfect for hiding things. *Nobody* knows we're here. It is all ours and we can do anything we want and not have to worry that someone will see."

Carmine sighed at the interruption.

"Sorry."

"When one business is starting to make money, you begin another."

"It's called multiplexing, uncle. It's the latest . . ."

"I think nineteen million will be enough interest for now."

Tonio paled even more.

"And what about that gym bag with all of our secrets that senator stole from us? How do I know it won't go to some newspaper?"

"We know it's here, uncle. We have a professional coming tomorrow to find it."

"More empty promises, Tonio?" The old man shook his head dolefully.

"I swear it. I'll get you your money too, uncle."

Carmine Gracchi looked about the room with a disgusted expression and started for the door. The bodyguards scrambled to follow.

He turned back. "My birthday is in ten days, nephew, on the fourth day of October. That is all I give you." He swept his gaze through Tonio and Sly Paquette, and then through Sydney, who felt a cold, involuntary chill. "Give me my money and the gym bag for my birthday."

Carmine Gracchi did not have to add an "or else."

Big Fish Lake

Link and Jason had lunch a half mile south of the Adcock cabin, hungry after the morning's adrenaline rush. They dined on panfish, as Jason called the stringer of two-pound crappies.

Jason pointed out a small bay where a family of loons—a mating pair and three fluffy chicks—swam serenely. "See the boulder on shore, next to the two tamaracks? There's a drop-off in the water where the senator kept the dugout."

Link retrieved the canvas-clad mines from the truck bed, strapped one on as Jason did with the other, and walked down the shoreline.

As he peered into the water, Jason perched his mine on the boulder for closer inspection.

"Don't pull the lanyard."

Jason yanked his hand away, as if he'd touched a snake.

Link could clearly see the outline of the dugout. It appeared heavy, measuring thirty inches abeam and twenty feet in length. He walked three paces past one end and carefully tossed in the first mine. It sank, blending with the muddy bottom.

Jason dropped the other mine three paces from the opposite end of the canoe.

Link looked about, getting a mental fix on the location. "Ready to get on with the tour."

"No more meals. Aunt Jen wants you hungry for dinner."

He thought of Jenifer Toussaint. Who was arguing?

A while later they heard the sounds of a single helicopter passing by. Again Link wondered about its purpose.

13

They drove slowly beside a slow-flowing, narrow but deep stream. "No Sun Creek," said Jason. "It runs from Moose Lake to Portage Sud Lake."

The wild and overgrown north side was slowly revealing itself in Link's mind. "There's good fishing at Moose Lake. How about here?"

"Best stream fishing on the reservation." Jason grinned, showing white teeth. "But then every really good guide keeps the *very* best spots to himself."

They'd become easy with one another's presence. The younger Indian was intrigued by their similarities, like they'd both lost their parents at an early age, and both had once been ashamed of their blood. Jason had found a new champion.

"I've got a question, Link. Why would anyone plant the mines?"

"I can't say. Only the military are permitted to possess them."

"Meaning they're stolen?"

"I'd say so, unless there's some kind of government involvement."

They'd discussed Link's acceptance into the Air Force Academy, how he'd played on a Falcon football team that had beat their big three opponents—Army, Navy, *and* Notre Dame—and how at graduation he'd realized his dream: assignment to pilot's school. In response to

Jason's questions he explained both the academics and the primary flying training, and how his stepfather—a retired lieutenant general—had pinned his own silver wings onto Link's chest. He described his checkouts in F-16s and A-10s, and flying combat in the latter.

"Which one's better?" Jason asked.

"They're totally different. Vipers are slick and fast. In the Warthog you get close and personal with the bad guys. It's got a thirty-millimeter Gatling gun that can make a tank look like a sieve." Link was often reticent, but became animate when the subject was flying.

Jason confided, "I had posters of an F-14 Tomcat and an F-15 Eagle in my room." He was wistful for a moment. "I'd really like to fly."

"With desire, the rest is a lot easier." They discussed physical requirements. Jason knew of no problems. Link had been watching; the youth's reactions were cat-quick. "When we go up, I'll let you handle the Baron."

"What would I need to get into military flight school?"

"Finish your degree, then apply for a commissioning program because only officers can be pilots. The good news is that both the air force and navy are short of fresh blood."

"You'd help?"

"If you're willing to do the work, I'll help all I can."

"Think I should cut my hair, and maybe take off the earring?"

"There's no rush. A few centuries ago, young men in Europe wore codpieces the size of footballs, and tights with the legs dyed different colors. When the oldsters complained, they'd shave half their heads and let the other half grow long."

Jason laughed. "Is there anything I *should* be doing?"

"Yeah. You can't handle booze. Quit drinking."

They rode in pregnant silence, crawling along since road conditions permitted them to go no faster. Finally Jason nodded. "You've got a deal."

As they continued, Jason looked over. "Do the Blackfeet have secret societies?"

"Most have gone by the wayside, but there are a few left."

Jason looked thoughtful.

They stopped at an expanse of water.

"Portage Nord Lake," he said. "The best fishing's in the bay to our right. Fish cribs are set up on the other end—lots of fingerlings so we can't overdo it."

A dust-laden black-and-white Ford Explorer approached. The driver braked, and two men in reservation police uniforms got out.

Willie, the bad cop, approached the driver's door, stopped, and glared.

The other leaned into the truck bed. "Nothin' back here."

"Where've you been?" Willie asked.

"Who wants to know?" Jason answered.

Willie grabbed his shirt, yanked him partially out of the window, and held him there.

"Let him go," Link said in a quiet voice.

"Fuck off, city boy. Where you been, Jason?"

"Up near the old cranberry bog," Jason muttered.

"Fuckin' liar!" Willie grasped a handful of hair, as if he was about to slam his head into the metal window frame.

Link prepared himself for unwanted action. "Let him go," he repeated.

"Sarge said to check 'em and leave 'em alone," said the second cop.

Willie shoved Jason back inside and gave Link a smirk. The two cops climbed back into their vehicle and went on.

Link watched them leave. "I thought Willie was on night shift."

The young Indian did not answer, just stared with hatred glittering in his eyes.

6:05 P.M.—Hideaway Bay Resort

Jason pulled up in front of the cottage and let the engine idle.

"When's your aunt expecting me?" Link asked as he climbed out.

"Soon as you're ready. She had some kinda outa-town meeting, but she should be back. I'll gas up the truck and pick up my car from Lonnie. Maybe talk to him about what we discussed. The flying and all?" He looked at Link. "You were serious?"

"If you're willing to work, I'll make sure you get the opportunity." He handed over two twenties. "Gas money."

"I'll take it. *Gotta* save for school now." Jason grinned and waved, and as he drove off Link decided the world would gain another pilot.

He went inside and showered. When he'd pulled on slacks, shirt, and a pair of lizard-skin dress boots, brushed back his wet hair, and finished with a splash of Santa Fe cologne, he went out to the kitchen-dining room.

Time to call Erin.

He flipped the sat phone open—and paused, watching the light-emitting diodes ripple in sequence down the side of the instrument.

The sat phone circuitry had detected an electronic bug and was issuing its warning.

Interesting, he thought as he pushed MEM and 1, then SEND.

Erin came on line. "Hi, pardner." She paused, and finally added, "Looks like we have a listener. Wait a sec so I can get an analysis from Helga."

A full minute later her voice returned, along with a steady tone. "Your bug's a voice-activated VHF FM transceiver. I turned on the harmonic so we can talk."

Link considered. "Let's get rid of it. "

"You're vulnerable. Perhaps it would be better if they don't know we're on to them."

"I'm tired of shadow dancing. If they're not feeling warm and fuzzy, I may be able to get more answers. How do I find the bug?"

"There'll likely be more than one, plus the device they're feeding into."

"Then let's get rid of all of them."

She sighed in obvious disagreement. "Your call. Let's go after the first one. Hold the sat phone faceup, then point the antenna and check how many LEDs illuminate."

She walked him through the find-the-bug procedure. The first was taped inside the mouth of a grinning, wall-mounted muskie in the living room. He disabled it, then described it so she could enter the information.

"Got it," she said. "Now the other rooms."

Another receiver-transmitter was taped to the bed frame. When satisfied there were no more, Erin reminded him there were two hardwired phones. "Better check 'em." She guided him through the receiver-dismantling process. He pulled a bug from each.

"Next we look for the unit those fed into—either a tape or digital recorder, a retransmitter, or a telephone relay. I'm picking up noise on another frequency, so I'm betting retransmitter. Give me a minute to reprogram your sat phone."

When she'd finished, he spoke into one of the R/T bugs to activate it and followed the flashing LEDs. The retransmitter was taped onto a telephone box at the rear of the cottage.

One by one Link hurled the devices into the lake. He rocketed one of the bugs fifty yards.

"They won't like it," Erin said as he skipped the retransmitter like a flat stone.

He tossed the final bug underhand, watched it plunk into the water, then went back in and pulled on a jacket—it was cool enough—picked both a white and a red wine from the cardboard box, and walked out to the Toyota.

"Question?" Erin asked. "Why are the cops giving you special attention?"

"Because I followed Sly Paquette?"

"Okay, but why did he tail you first? What made him suspicious?"

"He was on council when they discussed my qualifications." He dug the car key from his pocket, inserted it.

"You just switched on the ignition," she said.

"How did you know?" Erin was downright amazing.

"Look at the LEDs."

He pulled the sat phone from his face. The lights were flashing in a different sequence.

"Locator beacon," she said. "It transmits when the key's on so they can keep track of you."

Link located the bug taped under the front bumper. When he'd added it to the litter at the lake bottom, he started the engine.

"So what did you do with the antipersonnel mines?" Erin asked.

"Ditched them in five feet of water, next to the dug-out." He drove toward the road.

"Do you have coordinates?"

"Mmm. Make it a mile south of where I called you, in a small inlet."

"Just a second." She worked with her computer. "I've got it marked. Next time use the sat phone to mark it so I can get a precise location."

He turned toward town. "I transmitted three other positions as reference coordinates in case I need them later. RC 1, 2, and 3."

"I got those. They're stored in Helga's memory."

RCs, or "ref coords," were marked precisely, and used in various ways on their projects.

"Jason knows where you hid the mines?" she asked.

"Yeah. I trust him. His aunt too." It would be only the third time he'd seen Jenifer—forgetting the one when she'd considered shooting him—yet there was a lot of chemistry at work. Going both ways, he believed, but was not sure.

"I've been learning more about Ecol-Rec, Limited. They're not traded on the major stock exchanges. I contacted a few of our Habitat Earth people who should know about such things, since they're one of the largest ecological watchdog organizations in the world. None had heard of Ecol-Rec, Limited."

"You're saying they don't exist?"

"Just that they're not a household name in the industry. I finally tried going in the back door. Since they have the project there, I looked up all Department of Interior bioengineering contracts on reservations. There they were—single-source contract, with no competitive bids."

"Is that proper for a government contract?"

"Only if they have a capability no one else can provide, or there's an emergency requirement. The statement of need reads the northern parts of the Spirit Lake Reservation have massive amounts of residual life-threatening pollutants. Was it that bad?"

"From what I saw, no. When I get the chance I'll pay the ecol-rec zone another visit. Anything on the blond guy?"

"Not yet. How about a better description."

"Medium height, slender, blond with a scraggly beard, a stare so intense it's like he can drill holes with it."

"Same as you gave me before. Here's an interesting fact. Ten years ago there were four thousand Manido, and Spirit Lake had a seven-man police force. Now there are only one thousand residents, but they have thirty-three officers. You hear about the big change today?"

"We spent the day stealing mines, remember?"

"Last night the Spirit Lake police captain was in a head-on with a tree, and he's not expected to live. A Sergeant George Rose is his interim replacement."

"I met Rose," Link said. "Paquette controls him." A police shake-up might explain why Willie was changed to the day shift.

"I see you're almost to town. On your way to see Jenifer again?"

"Next time I have dinner with a lady, I'll leave the sat phone behind."

"Don't. Things are getting interesting. Take care, pardner."

For the remainder of the drive, Link thought about George Rose and Willie, and how the police deck at Spirit Lake was stacked.

Town of Spirit Lake

The Honda was alone in the Toussaint driveway, and there was no sign of Jason's Firebird. Link walked to the porch. Before he could knock, the door opened.

Jenifer wore a sky blue sweater—a great color for her—and tight jeans.

She smiled. "Hello there, Mr. Guide."

The sat phone shuddered in his pocket, and he realized that he'd not reset it from the silent ring mode. He ignored it.

"Jason called from Lonnie's and said he'd be a while. They're having pizza, playing CDs, and talking about females. He said you had an eventful time."

"I'll let him tell you."

After yet another try the sat phone ceased to vibrate.

Jenifer stood close. "Guess we're on our own." Finally she drew her gaze away and took in the two bottles of wine. "Care for a glass?" Her voice was throaty.

"Sure."

They looked at one another often, as if unable to keep their eyes away for long.

"I picked up steaks on my way home from work. You mind doing the honors with the wine, and taking over the barbecue grill?"

"Not at all. I thought Jason said you were at an out of town meeting."

"Attending meetings is work." Jenifer led the way into the kitchen, glanced back at him.

He observed her compact derriere in motion. "Corkscrew?" he asked innocently.

Jenifer rummaged in a drawer, and placed the implement on the counter beside the wine he deposited there. A dreamy look altered her expression as she put her arms around his neck, and lightly brushed his mouth with soft lips.

They kissed, letting it start lightly, then turning up the heat.

She sighed deeply and laid her cheek against his chest, and he had the feeling that they'd known one another forever. "Did I tell you I'm very infatuated, Lincoln?"

Jenifer pulled his face back down, and her tongue searched hungrily. Not rushing things at all, he decided, enjoying the firmness of her breasts and the heat against his thigh. He ran his hands over her back, then lower, eliciting sounds that rumbled down deep in her throat.

He held her lean buttocks through the restrictive clothing.

She shrugged him off. He searched for words of repentance. "I didn't mean . . ."

"You *better* have meant it," she said in her sexiest tone.

Jenifer drew him into a dark and eminently feminine room, and slipped the sweater over her head. It landed in a chair, quickly followed by her slacks. Link was charged with excitement, had shucked his shirt, and was stepping out of his trousers as she came to him. She discarded her final remnant, then held herself to him and traced a delicate tongue across his muscular chest, making more of the throaty noises as she grasped his penis. Her purr became urgent as she moved an arm about his neck, coiled a leg about him, and raised herself, shuddering as his hands moved to her most intimate zones.

He shivered as she moved her wet mouth on his chest, arousing every nerve ending in his body. He braced himself against the wall, still grasping her buttocks. She refused to release her hold on his member—writhing and drawing herself higher, knees splayed, holding herself open, moist and ready. Her head went back, the cords of her neck prominent as she took in a harsh breath and slowly descended.

Link did not remember precisely the when or how, only that when they finished they'd moved to the bed, where she exhorted him to remain still and exercised particularly adept muscles. As he finally became active, she alternated between whispers and outcries.

He slowed, and they shuddered together as he released.

They breathed as one, she caressing his face, whispering endearments. He began to withdraw, but she held on, and fiercely whispered, "I'm not done with you, Link Anderson."

They'd rested for only a short while when she began to move her hips in the sensual rhythm, which he soon joined in.

"I've searched," she whispered, "and now I've found you."

Half a mile distant, on the south side, Jason Toussaint drank from one of the ice-cold bottles from the six-pack he had brought, and belched grandly.

He had been talking about flying.

"Tomorrow I go on the wagon like I promised Link."

"Cool," said Lonnie. "He's right, Jase. Sometimes you let booze get the best of you."

"Maybe." He did not like talking about it. He did like the fact that Lonnie had promised to quit with him. A knock sounded at the door. As Lonnie was rising to respond, a thin, athletic-appearing man slipped inside. Storyteller drew back a curtain to ensure no one had seen him.

"We will talk," he said simply and looked with displeasure at the beer in Jason's hand.

No one drank alcohol when they discussed business. Jason went to the kitchen and poured out the Leinie.

During this time of emergency, the Bear Society—the *Muk-wah*—seldom gathered in large numbers. Instead they attended two- and three-on-one training sessions and passed information to Storyteller, who disseminated it as was appropriate. Each knew only of their own specific portions of the attack plan.

"How did it go?" Storyteller asked. He was curious about Lincoln Anderson.

Jason outlined his day. Told his favorable impressions of Link—and about the discovery of the mines. Storyteller listened intently and did not interrupt.

It became Jason's turn to be quiet.

"Let us speak truths," said Storyteller. "The new patrolmen are despicable and stop at nothing, including murder. There have been twenty-nine disappearances in the past two years—eighteen in the last two months. Some were young people they addicted with their drugs. Others disagreed with Sly Paquette. A question now. Are those people all dead? If so, where are the bodies, the vehicles, and belongings?"

Jason paused. "Maybe they dump them in bogs, like mob guys in the old days."

"And as our ancestors once did to dishonor enemies." He looked at them both. "Your guide business will continue to be slow until the north side reopens."

"Amen," said Lonnie, rolling his eyes. He noted Storyteller's stony expression, realized his error, and added, "Pardon me for interrupting."

Storyteller impressed upon the *Muk-wah* that self-discipline and respect were as important as their rituals and training.

"You both know the north side. Go without being seen and find if there's been traffic at any of the bogs. If you see sign, wait for night and observe them at it. Remember to use caution."

Storyteller then regarded Jason. "Have you had more dream-times?"

Jason was embarrassed. "Only one," he muttered. "It didn't make sense."

"Where were you?"

"Near the bridge over Dead Man's Creek. There were just scenes. A man ran after a large dog—or maybe several dogs—and he almost caught them."

"Go on."

"That's all. It went through my mind over and over, but nothing made sense."

Storyteller mused on that for a moment, then turned to Lonnie. "I'm appointing Jason as my assistant, Young Storyteller. He will need your help."

Jason's mouth drooped with surprise.

"He's *got* it," said Lonnie, grinning at his friend.

Storyteller asked Lonnie to leave them for a while. Then one by one he told Jason the identities of all of the members of the Bear Society, as well as their talents and contributions. For a full hour he spoke in the low tone, telling about the training sessions, who was competent to handle specific duties, and then how the attack plan must be conducted and coordinated.

Although swollen with pride, Jason worried. He voiced his fear. "There are so many *naud-o-way.*" It was the ancient Ojibwe word for enemy, or more literally, "snake people."

"You must provide confidence. Remember the old truths of how our people once overcame other *naud-o-way*. Recall Bi-a-jig?" He referred to an ancestral figure who had used brazen determination to lead the outnumbered Ojibwe to victories against the once powerful Fox nation. "He was real, Jason. Someday our people will speak of you. Will it be with pride?"

Jason asked, "Why did you pick me?"

"A good question. You are too young for the responsibility," Storyteller told him cruelly. "You are cautious when a situation calls for boldness, and then you act when it is time to think. Worst of all, you have a weakness for alcohol, and when you drink you become a loudmouth and bray like a donkey. Listen to my words now. Someday you will betray us."

Jason pulled back as if he'd been repeatedly struck. "I would never do that!" When Storyteller just stared back, he cried, "Why did you choose me?"

"With the Manido it was always those who knew truth through visions who led our ancestors through bad times. That is our heritage. I cannot change it, despite my concern."

He went to the door, cracked it, and looked out. "Things are happening that require my full attention. You must coordinate information and supervise training, and hold our Bear Society together. I've told the others about you and told them to cooperate.

"Be careful, Jason. We aren't the first or even the second society that set out to fight Sly Paquette. The others were capable, and they've all disappeared, but know this—being careful does not mean being indecisive. It means reaching proper decisions and acting on them. If I'm discovered, I cannot promise not to tell Paquette everything, so you know what you must do."

"Send out the code and attack," Jason whispered.

"The code is '*Che-she* walks.'"

When the door closed behind Storyteller, Jason called Lonnie back in, and they looked at one another. "He's going to be busy for a while. I'll need your help coordinating the training."

"Cool," said Lonnie. "Give us something to do now we've stopped drinking."

"We'll begin searching the marshes as soon as Aunt Jen leaves on the expedition."

Jason was now Young Storyteller, but his pride had been badly battered by Storyteller's criticism. *Can I do it?* he wondered. He needed a drink in the worst way.

At ten o'clock Jenifer returned from the kitchen with a plate of quartered sandwiches and the bottle of cabernet. "You get off easy," she said. "*Next* time you barbecue."

They sat cross-legged on the bed to eat, drink from the bottle, and share personal vignettes. She explained that for a decade she'd lived in or commuted to Washington on business, until she'd burned out on Washington pomposity and egotism. Jenifer did not elaborate on how long it had been since she'd been with a man, or that she had never felt so attracted. There was something about Lincoln Anderson that made her feel warm and content.

He told her about his youth and realizing his dream of flying, and she listened intently, wanting to know every small detail. When the food was gone, she pushed him back, dribbled wine onto his chest, and licked it away. They took turns with the game, laughing often and moving their attentions and their puddles of wine—and finished with a very private toast that was mutually enjoyed.

"I'm shameless," she whispered, and almost said she loved him. Much too early, her mind chided, but she'd never—not once!—felt so giddy with attraction.

Link tried to leave at one a.m. Instead she opened the second bottle of wine. They made love languidly and napped together, fuzzy-headed with intoxication. At some dark hour Link awakened and guided her onto her back. A moment later she was crying out, knees locked about his waist, heels digging into his buttocks. He went on and on, alternating between wild and gentle, and she was wondering if he could possibly succeed again—when he did.

They lay side by side, gloriously happy, and Link said he'd not felt as comfortable with a woman since . . . he stopped himself abruptly, as if he did not dare consider it.

Jenifer was confused, even startled, by the intensity of her own feeling.

Link drifted off, and sometime later Jenifer awakened him with breaths against his thigh, and unhurried efforts. She pushed his inquiring hand away and continued, wanting it to be perfect for him. He stiffened and trembled, and she was pleased.

Finally she drew herself up, sighed deeply, and rested her head on his chest. Within seconds he was snoring lightly, and she felt utter contentment as she too drifted off.

Link had left the sat phone's ringer off. If not, he might have noticed that the lights were rippling in the sequence that showed eavesdropping microphones had been planted in three different locations inside the Toussaint house. Nor did he know that two patrolmen in a vehicle parked a hundred yards from the house had overheard their every utterance and outcry.

PART II

The North Side

14

Link pulled up before cottage eight, killed the engine, and stared out at the dark world through gritty eyes. The interview with the tribal council and the meeting of the Gloria Vasson expedition were next on his agenda, and although more than a little smitten with Jenifer Toussaint, he craved sleep.

He stepped out of the Toyota, prepared to go in and collapse on the nearest soft surface when he realized the front door was a dark, open maw. Link rubbed at his weary eyes, and groaned at the obvious: *Someone's been inside.*

Or maybe the someone was *still* inside?

Link reached through the doorway and switched on the porch light. His canvas bag lay open at his feet—his clothing pulled out and strewn all the way to the water's edge. The GPS instrument and satellite telephone charger had been stomped into shards. The cardboard box had been dumped. Wine and beer bottles were all broken, the food scattered.

Just what he needed when he was dog-weary with his head spinning like a gyro.

Link opened the bag, picked up a shirt that had been ripped apart, and tossed it in. He retrieved clothing all the way to water's edge, much of it torn into strips. A light leather jacket that he'd liked had been pulled apart at the seams. A ruined pair of Levi's. A single boot from a comfortable old pair of Justins was lying half in the water, the mate nowhere to be found. All clothing went into the bag, broken bottles and food into the cardboard box.

The spoiler had not bothered with subtlety. There was only one person he'd seen who was large enough to leave the distinct boot prints. *The Indian they called the Junkman.*

There were footprints from others. *The rotten cops?* He doubted Sly Paquette would come on such a trivial task. As Link looked for his second boot, he discovered his sweat-stained Stetson work hat. Something—the Junkman's fist?—had been rammed through the crown. Like the loss of the comfortable boot, the fact of the ruined hat was upsetting. It had history.

He stepped into the cottage, where pictures, the television set, and the wall-mounted fish were in a jumble on the living room floor. The mattress had been dragged into the kitchen and ripped open. Windows were smashed, a kitchen chair still lodged in one. Coffeemaker and dishes were reduced to floor rubble.

Link awkwardly carried the mattress into the bedroom, thinking how he'd told Erin he didn't want them feeling warm and fuzzy. Paquette obviously felt the same about him.

He leaned the broken door so it blocked most of the opening, pulled off his boots, and burrowed into blankets that he'd tossed onto the ripped and tattered bed. It was uncannily comfortable. "Wish I could find the other boot," he grumbled as he fell asleep.

8:24 A.M.

Something shuddered insistently against his chest, paused, then shook again. Link came awake, opened an eye, and tried to determine the troublesome source, and divined that the satellite phone was still in the pocket of the shirt he wore, vibrating insistently.

"Anderson," he croaked, eyes smarting from the glare through the broken window.

"You were *asleep*?" Erin's tone was obnoxiously chipper.

He replied with a rude yawning sound.

"Get moving, sleepyhead. There's no time for your morning run."

He considered telling her he'd exercised through most of the night, but did not.

"You're supposed to meet with the council, and attend Gloria Vasson's meeting at ten."

"Last night I had visitors while I was out," he said. He explained the mess. "Those were great boots," he groused. "They fit like gloves."

"Any idea who did it?"

"I found size sixteen footprints. I'd say the Junkman and some of the bad cops."

"I told you to cool it with their electronic toys."

"Don't rub it in." He fondly recalled his hat, boots, and supple leather jacket. "Better send another sat phone charger, and maybe a bottle of Johnny Walker Black."

"Hey, this isn't a send-out deli."

"Also a couple bottles of good wine. Can't get it here and I'm on vacation, remember?"

"They ruined the charger?"

"They ruined everything. I don't even have underwear."

"Guess you'll have to go commando."

"I will not discuss my Jockey shorts with a woman."

Erin laughed. "What time did you get in?"

Link acted as if he'd not heard.

"Interesting that the manager wouldn't interfere if they were trashing his cottage."

"There's a lot of intimidation going on."

"I've learned more. It appears the mob's into scientific corporations almost as extensively as they are into construction. Ecol-Rec, Limited's a privately held corporation loosely associated with a number of other firms, some fronts, others real. This company owns parts of that one and that one owns parts of this one, and so on until you're going in circles. Ecol-Rec is in there lock, stock, and enzymes. There's also a genetic engineering laboratory in Houston, a medical supplies firm in Minneapolis, a midsize health maintenance organization, and a couple of private hospitals, all huge firms registered and incorporated in Fernley, Nevada."

"All owned by the mob?"

"Probably. All I've checked so far look questionable. For instance there's Sundown Medical Center in Las Vegas that's been mob-owned since the place was built in the fifties. No one's rushing in to investigate because of their high-powered patient list. Movie people, mobsters, Saudi princes, and such. Once in a while a filthy rich politician sneaks in.

"Compared to these others, Ecol-Rec, Limited is a piker. They only have that one project, cleaning up the problem at the Spirit Lake Reservation."

"Who issued the contract? The Bureau of Indian Affairs?"

"Those records are unavailable. Part of some *minor* problem the Department of Interior experienced with Y2K glitches. I don't like what I'm coming up with, pardner. You're out there in the cold with the mob, and I can't even find a government official who'll listen."

He glanced at the time—only an hour and a quarter remaining before the expedition meeting, and he still had the interview with council. "Let's talk after the meeting."

"Nope, I still have things you should know. If you argue, it'll just take longer."

Link's head hurt and his stomach was unsettled. "Go on."

"I've been comparing what Senator Eddie said on the tape with his speeches. Subjects like reorganizing Indian Affairs, his concern about the release of rocket secrets to China, and the leaking of nuclear information at the national laboratories. He gave some great orations, but the words I was looking for weren't mentioned until two months ago, when he warned the nation to open our eyes because our government was selling out to our *present and future worst enemy*. Bingo! The words used in the tape, and guess who he was talking about?"

Link's head hurt too much for another quiz. "The Chinese? Libya?"

"Nope, organized crime, and the ways they ensure that certain politicians are elected using money, lies, muscle, anything it takes. He explained how they're more pervasive than ever, and how they control large elements of corporate America. There was a lot of skepticism in the media and not much coverage.

"I think when he used the same words in the tape, 'our true worst enemy,' he meant the mob. He kept saying to follow him, and he was on his way to Spirit Lake. I interpret that as meaning the mob had taken over the reservation."

"Maybe. My problem with it is that he could have handled it a lot better from the floor of the Senate, but he chose to come here and do battle. Why?"

"How about the warehouse he mentioned."

"There are none here, only a self-storage facility, and it's unguarded and most of the units look empty." He rubbed his aching brow.

"I analyzed the helicopter engine sounds. One was a standard Bell Jet Ranger. The other was an MH-60 Black Hawk like you thought, which happens to be the most capable military helo we've got. As far as I can find out, none are operated by civilians outside the government.

"I also traced the serial numbers of the Claymore mines you liberated at the ecol-rec zone. They were manufactured for foreign military sales. Part of a shipment of four hundred and fifty of them, meant for Argentina. That means they may have a lot more."

"If I get the chance, I'll take a closer look at the ecol-rec zone."

"Just be darn careful. From what you said they weren't very friendly."

"Mr. Anderson?" a voice called from the front door.

"Gotta go," he told Erin.

"I've got information about the expedition members."

"Later." Link switched off the sat phone and looked about. The bathroom floor was a mess where the Junkman had dumped towels and toiletries. He ignored the voice at the door as he retrieved toothbrush, toothpaste, razor, shave gel, deodorant, and cologne, placed them all in the sink, and turned on cold water. When he finally went out, the manager from the resort office was peering through the gap where the door leaned against the shattered jamb.

"What time will you be checking out?" The manager sounded frightened.

"I paid for two weeks."

"We'll return the amount that's outstanding."

"Nope. Just get someone in to fix the door and windows. Maybe replace the mattress, since it's got a hole in it. I'll need fresh sheets, another coffeepot, all that."

"But . . ." The manager was sputtering. He called repeatedly as Link went back in to shower, shave, and finish his morning toilet.

After pulling on the same clothing he'd slept in, he moved the front door aside and stepped out to face the day. The manager was dolefully inspecting the broken windows as an elderly Indian man picked up debris and placed it in a wheelbarrow. When he spotted Link, he mustered his best officious tone. "Mister Anderson, I'm afraid you *must* leave."

Link was growing impatient. "My personal belongings were vandalized. When I return this afternoon I'll want a full explanation."

The manager was taken aback. "I had *nothing* to do with it. It was the police."

Link feigned surprise. "My attorney will need a statement to the effect that you witnessed the police destroying my property."

The manager's brow furrowed. "I—uh—didn't actually *see* them do it."

Link brandished the lone boot. "I pulled this out of the lake, so the mate's likely close by. I suggest you take a good look."

"What if they return?" The frightened tone had returned.

"Who? The police?"

The manager stared, unwilling to answer.

"Where can I buy a couple pairs of Levi's and some shorts?"

The manager's voice was strained. "There's a general store in town."

"I've got a meeting to attend," Link said grimly. "I suggest you repair the door and find that boot. Or would you rather my lawyer contact you?"

15

9:55 A.M.—Conference Room, Hatchet Club

An obscure easel in the hallway announced the VASSON
BRIEFING. At the door was a Clint Eastwood look-alike,
decked out in shotgunner's shirt and trousers bloused
over oiled Browning boots, yellow shooting glasses, and
an expensive Breitling wrist chronograph.

He squinted Dirty Harry–like at Link's rumpled shirt.
"And you are . . . ?"

"Link Anderson." On the way over he'd dropped by
the tribal council building as Jenifer had asked, and spoken to two aging elders who *sort of* recalled his family.
Link supposed he'd passed scrutiny, since no one had
thrown him out.

"Oh yes, you're the guide. I'm Joseph Richards."
When the expedition leader gripped his hand in a display
of strength, Link considered breaking every small bone.
It had not been a good morning. On the other hand, he
enjoyed old Dirty Harry movies.

Richards said there were two four-wheel drive vehicles
and a trailer filled with gear in the parking lot. "If you
find something's missing, I'll have it flown in overnight.
Once we've deployed I'll want to minimize trips back
to town."

"When do we leave?"

"First thing tomorrow. Today we'll get to know . . ."
He interrupted their conversation to smile at a new arrival. "Good morning, Gloria."

Gloria Vasson had sculpted features and long blond

hair, was dressed in a simple black pants suit that accentuated turquoise and coral jewelry that glittered from neck and wrist, and carried a pale blue briefcase. She spoke in a soft velvet voice, and it seemed improbable that she was in her late forties as Erin had said. After offering Link a vague smile, she ignored him.

Link went to a side table and poured himself a stay-awake cup of coffee.

A new man came into the room. David Brogg was a middle-aged Native American, with dark horn-rimmed glasses and a wild bush of dark hair reminiscent of the hippie sixties.

"Dr. Brogg's our expert on the Ojibwe tradition and the treaties," Richards explained to Gloria. "He's on leave of absence from the History Department at the University of Wisconsin."

"I wouldn't miss it for anything," said Brogg.

A mustached man in a porkpie hat paused at the door long enough for Richards to introduce him as Turf Siegel, his assistant.

Siegel gave a pleasant nod before joining Link at the coffee urn. He said something but spoke with such a heavy Bronx accent that it took a moment to decipher the words. He bit into a donut and observed Gloria with an appreciative eye.

"Jees, *anudder* perfect ten?" he muttered as he watched Richards greet Jenifer.

There was a chill between the women. After they'd managed weak smiles and mouthed halfhearted greetings, Jenifer entered and looked about. Her eyes glided past Link with no betrayal of the fact that a few hours earlier they'd mated like frenzied bunnies. Just as he was feeling ignored, she turned back, mouthed the name Jason, and gave him her sunshine smile, letting him know that her nephew had shown up.

"Guess you know her," said Turf, like that was too bad.

Joseph Richards closed the door. "Time to start." He strode to the front of the room. "Before I begin, I hope you were all able to keep details of the expedition from others."

"All I said was that I was off to the Northwoods," said Dr. Brogg, "but I really don't understand the need for secrecy."

"Council feels we should be discreet until we've found the treaties," said Richards. "We don't want to be plagued by news media and treasure seekers."

He swept the room with his gaze. "Before we proceed, I'll offer everyone a chance to reconsider. This won't be a namby-pamby operation with hot showers and three hot meals. Where we're going there's no cell phone service or other communications, only a periodic drive back here so you can call home. We have a guide, and he'll maintain the camp, but he's not along to pamper you or roll your sleeping bags, and we'll be eating mostly canned and freeze-dried foods. *Everyone* is expected to join the search. Not only do I intend to find what we came for; I would prefer to do so quickly and efficiently. Finally, it's autumn in the Northwoods, and we're sure to see freezing temperatures. Now, does anyone wish to drop out?"

He paused to look around. Richards was something of a grandstander, Link decided.

The expedition leader wrote names on the chalkboard, and asked questions and listed capabilities. All but Siegel were scuba and dive qualified. Richards was a rock climber. Siegel was a spelunker. All except Toussaint had been on archaeological digs.

> J. RICHARDS—SCUBA/CLIMBER/DIGS
> T. SIEGEL—CAVES/DIGS
> D. BROGG—SCUBA/DIGS
> J. TOUSSAINT—SCUBA

Richards explained that they might have to use all their combined skills.

Link's name was not shown, and he did not comment about the exclusion. It was as he'd wanted; he was viewed as hired help, more background noise than a full participant.

Richards posed beside the list of names and motioned to Turf Siegel, who hefted a video camera. "Go for it,"

Turf said, as the red recording indicator light began to flash, and Richards opened his briefing.

At lunchtime, Richards covered the map and white board, and opened the door for a foursome of waiters. As they presented salads, pheasant, and a light white wine, the expedition leader said to enjoy. They were having the last good meal they'd have for a while.

He smiled in anticipation. "We'll convoy to Alpha first thing in the morning. I like to make my first search—go for the gold—on the first day."

As they ate, Dr. Brogg said he viewed the retrieval of the Manido documents as being of national importance, yet he wondered if the public cared at all.

"It's the connection with Senator Adcock," said Turf Siegel. "Crooked politicians aren't viewed with much enthusiasm these days."

An awkward silence followed. Jenifer's face darkened—no real surprise when Link recalled what Jason had said about her parentage.

Gloria Vasson brusquely rose to her feet. "I'll see you off in the morning. Good luck, and thank you for helping."

Suite 300

As Gloria let herself into her rooms, which she'd been assured were the finest the casino-hotel had to offer, she thought about Jenifer Toussaint, and decided it was time to end their petty squabble. She would make the first move, not easy for a woman of her nature.

Gloria knew full well that others regarded her as possessing an imperious nature. In fact it had surprised everyone when she had fallen for Eddie Adcock, who had been outgoing and warm. Very few knew what a wonderful match they'd been. He had teased her about her stodginess and made her smile and laugh as no other human was able to do.

When she'd learned of his death she had spent the following weeks in seclusion, staring with blank looks at nothing at all, unable to release the grief that even now welled inside her. She had not betrayed her weakness. Not ice-cold Gloria. The ice woman needed no one.

God how she missed him.

She placed the briefcase on the desk near the window and stared out at the shimmering blue water, not seeing the tourists who walked the lakeshore or drove the rental speedboats. Finally she opened the case and removed the laptop computer that held Eddie's notes, a tunnel into the soul of the man she still loved dearly.

Gloria read them often, fondly, for it was as if she were listening to his voice.

She went into the bedroom and had removed the exquisite squash blossom and bracelet—gifts from Eddie—when someone knocked at the door. Likely maid service, she decided, although the suite appeared freshly cleaned. The management had guaranteed privacy. She could turn up the television or CD player as she wished and not a sound would be heard outside.

Gloria looked at herself in the mirror and tried to eliminate the sadness in her expression before going to the door, where she peered into the peephole.

The councilman with the bandaged eye stood at the threshold—she recalled that his name was Paquette and that he'd been supportive of mounting the expedition.

Gloria opened the door. "Yes?"

He gave the door a harsh shove, sending her reeling across the room. Before she collected her wits, a pair of uniformed policemen had stepped inside and Paquette closed the door.

"What do you want?" she cried as the men pressed forward. They wore shoulder patches reading SPIRIT LAKE RESERVATION PATROL, and the closest one—scarecrow thin, with close-set eyes and receding chin, and exuding the sour odor of old sweat—grasped her arm.

"What do you want?" Gloria shouted, trying to squirm away.

Paquette ignored her and spoke to the men. "First the hair."

Scarecrow held her in place as the other, a grinning,

thickset blond with a florid face with layers of crusted pimples, opened a lock-blade knife.

Her head was forced down. The blond grasped a handful of hair and pulled hard.

Gloria screamed.

"Let her yell," Paquette said from the desk. "The room's soundproof."

She felt the knife blade sawing at her locks and screamed again, eliciting laughter as the blond yanked and sawed, and stuffed handfuls of blond hair into a plastic bag.

Gloria blubbered at the pressure. "Stop!" she cried, then, "Help me!"

The one holding her said, "Help her, Willie!" and laughed some more.

"That part comes next. Now be still!" The scarecrow held her even tighter while the one called Willie wielded the knife blade like a razor, scraping at the remaining stubble.

"You're cuttin' her pretty bad," observed Scarecrow.

"Old bitch is movin'. I *told* her to be still." Again the knife blade dug into her scalp.

When Willie was satisfied, Scarecrow released her.

Gloria stood half dazed, rivulets of blood streaming down her forehead into her eyes as she looked at the plastic bag filled with her hair. "Why?" she whispered.

Willie wiped blood from the knife blade with a lace doily. "We're done with the hair."

Councilman Paquette was seated at the desk, looking through Gloria's briefcase. He looked over with his single, uncaring eye. "You get an hour with her."

"Yeah!" breathed Willie, and elbowed the scarecrow one out of his way.

Gloria struggled as he pushed her into the bedroom.

"*Now,* take off your clothes, old woman," Willie told her.

Gloria turned to escape—he pulled her back and slammed a fist into her side. She doubled over, sickened by the awful pain from her kidney as he shed shirt, trousers, and shorts.

As he began tearing off her clothing Gloria Vasson methodically turned herself into the numb ice woman she was so often accused of being. When he ripped away the lace bra, she hardly noticed. *Good tits for an old broad,* she vaguely heard him announce, but she was drifting in an otherworld. When he squeezed her breasts she told herself she could not feel his rough hands or sense the piercing ache. When he shoved her onto the bed, she closed her eyes and slipped yet farther away, thinking of a Jamaican beach she loved to visit.

Willie was rougher and meaner than she could have imagined in her most horrible dreams, and it was impossible to remain detached. Every base act he performed was announced so the others could hear. He inflicted pain so she'd do as he demanded, including opening her eyes and looking as he used her. When Willie could go on no more, he held her so her legs were bent in excruciating positions, leaned down to kiss her mouth, and howled in laughter.

Willie backed off the bed. "Got used pussy here! Come and get it or I'll fuck her again."

Gloria's hips and legs throbbed. She felt ancient and utterly used, yet somehow she managed to mutter hoarsely, "I promise . . . you will . . . suffer . . . for this."

"Hell, you oughta pay me, old woman." Willie examined the Indian necklace and bracelet he'd tossed onto the floor, and stuffed them into various pockets as the scarecrow came in, hastily pulling off his uniform.

After they were done with her, as Gloria heard the hall door closing and painfully sat up, aching in every bruised muscle and stretched tendon, she felt their filth drain from her.

The sheet and pillow were streaked with blood from her mutilated scalp.

Why had they taken her hair?

Why had any of it happened?

She heard the hall door reopen, and could not contain shivers of fear.

"She's in there," Paquette said, and she tensed. There were more!

A plain-looking middle-aged woman entered, set down an artist's wooden case, and observed her, cocking her head this way and that as she examined.

"They took my hair," Gloria tried. "Then they raped me."

"Perhaps you should get used to it."

"Why is this happening?" she cried.

"No, no. I ask the questions; you answer. Where did your husband hide the gym bag?"

"My God. How would I know?"

"Because you have the computer and his notes." She mused. "Come to think of it, I have them now, but you spent all that time studying them like the sweet little wife you weren't."

"If I knew where it was, I wouldn't be funding the expedition." Having lived with the possibility of kidnapping, she added, "Please let me go. I have money."

"Not for long." She offered a droll look. "I'm going to take your beauty and every cent you possess. In the meantime, entertain me with answers."

Gloria Vasson could not believe it was happening, and as the woman continued, she decided she must not cooperate or she might accelerate her own death.

The woman asked about a safe in Gloria's Georgetown home.

"I don't recall," she responded.

The plain woman sighed. "I do wish you'd cooperate."

"I doubt very much that I'll remember anything," Gloria said icily.

"Oh, don't say that. After spending a few days servicing a bunch of psychotic Neanderthals, you'll be surprised what you'll want to tell me."

16

Link pressed MEM, then 1. Erin responded almost immediately. "Hi, pardner. How did it go?"

"I am no longer going commando. I bought shorts."

"The meeting, silly."

"As expected. I'm headed for the cottage." *Where I will get some badly needed sleep.*

"I briefed Frank this afternoon. When I told him about the mines, and how no one in any official capacity will work with us, he started talking about pulling you out. It's hard to argue, Link. When he asked how the senator's death might have been related to mob corruption at the reservation—what could I tell him?"

"It's just as murky up close, but I'm staying."

"What's next?"

"First some sleep. I'll head for the casino in the morning and load the vehicles. When the group shows up, we'll caravan to Big Fish Lake."

"Did Gloria release the senator's notes?"

"Only that the senator never mentioned a theft. He wrote about a 'transaction,' and how he was going to put the 'evidence' in a waterproof canvas bag he was taking along for that purpose."

"The 'evidence'?" Erin mulled it over.

"Face it, 'evidence' sounds better than 'loot.' And since the senator used a waterproof bag, he could have stashed the 'evidence' anywhere, including a lake or bog or even an old grave. Tomorrow at the base camp, Richards's going to give us his plan of attack. He feels the senator hid the documents in a familiar location, so he'll concentrate on those."

"Makes sense, especially if he was hurt and not operating on all cylinders." She paused. "I'd love to get my hands on the senator's notes."

"They're in Gloria Vasson's laptop. Is this a problem you and Helga can't solve?"

"Not if you turn her computer on, hook it to a phone line, and have her look the other way for a couple of minutes." She sighed, then switched gears. "Okay, pardner, I've got names and bios, but tell me more about the people on the expedition."

He began with egotistical Richards, and had moved to Gloria—beautiful and aloof, not especially likable according to Jenifer—when he pulled into the Hideaway Bay Resort, slowed, and muttered, "Damn."

"What is it?" Erin asked.

"I have official visitors."

A Spirit Lake police cruiser was parked before cottage eight.

"Gotta go," he said, and switched off.

Sergeant George Rose came out of the cottage and waited as Link climbed out of the Toyota, carrying the bundle of new clothing under his left arm.

"Heard you had trouble yesterday. Vandals."

"Yeah, vandals." Link let his sarcasm show. "And you're investigating, right?"

"We're here to serve."

"And protect?"

"Sure."

"You're still wearing stripes. I heard you were promoted."

"I'm filling in while they decide on a replacement for the captain."

Willie the bad cop emerged from the cottage, looking to be in fine spirits. He sauntered over, looking like a cat that had just devoured a nest of mice.

"I'll let you know the good news up front," said Rose.

"Something didn't set right about you, so we had the feds give us a background? I just got word that you're what you say."

"An asshole city boy," interjected Willie, smirking at his wit.

Link wondered if it was an act, or if Willie was really that dumb.

"If you don't have anything, I'm going inside," he said, and took the first step.

Willie moved into his path. "What's wrong, city boy? Tired from banging on the council bitch all night?" He stepped closer and gave him a shove. "She as good as the guys all say?"

Link stood very still.

Willie gave him another shove. "The guys say she was yellin' real loud, city boy, just like she used to do with that senator. What was you usin'? Wasn't your dick 'cause you got no balls."

"Call him off, Rose," Link muttered.

The sergeant remained silent.

Willie laughed. "Way they said she squealed, I figure you gave her a load in the ass. Since she used to be the whore for a U.S. senator . . ."

Link pivoted, his full weight behind the extended knuckles that struck Willie's left temple. He stopped midsentence, eyes crossing and unconscious as he wilted to the ground.

Rose peered down curiously. "Gotta learn there's a time to keep his mouth shut."

Link relaxed just slightly, thinking he might not be immediately tossed into jail.

The sergeant spoke into his collar mike. Asked for a patrol car to come out to the Hideaway Resort. Told them there was no hurry and not to use a siren.

Link revised his estimate and wondered what the local jail looked like from close up.

"Gives us a minute to talk," said Sergeant Rose. "Any idea who tore your place up?"

No more shadow dancing, Link told himself. "A big guy called the Junkman, with some of your cops looking on."

Rose smiled humorlessly. "Think about what you just said. If that was true you wouldn't have anyone to turn to, would you?"

"Do you mind if I go inside?"

"Better if you stay out here and talk while I figure out what's next in your future." He nudged Willie with his boot, got no response, and shook his head. "Hurt your hand?"

"Not really." He'd been trained to tense his knuckles until they were hard as iron. If he did not, the force of an extreme blow could break his own bones.

"Returning to our conversation," said the sergeant, "a mutual friend decided that trashing your place was a mistake. In fact he wanted me to ask if you need some cash to replace your things and maybe help you get started with your flying business and all. After you get back from this expedition, of course."

There it is, out in the open. "Who's our friend? Sly Paquette?"

Rose was deadpan. "He's offering a considerable sum."

"And what would he like me to do to earn the considerable sum?"

"Just do a good job guiding the expedition and help them find the old treaties, and keep us advised. Oh yeah, he wants you to return something that belongs at the ecol-rec zone."

"You know the mob owns the company that runs the place?" Link goaded.

"Whoever. They complained about you taking something of theirs."

"A couple of antipersonnel mines that could take out a platoon?"

Rose looked honestly surprised. "You've got these—mines?"

"I didn't like hauling them around so I dumped 'em in a lake up there."

A patrol car pulled into the resort and nosed in beside Rose's cruiser. Two policemen emerged, and did a bug-eye act when they saw Willie.

"He fell," said Sergeant Rose. After nudging Willie

with his toe again, he told them to check his pulse. They determined that he was alive.

"Take him into town. If he hasn't come around by then, drop him off at the clinic."

The cops cast inquisitive looks at Link.

"I said he fell," said Rose.

Willie did not stir as they picked him up by hands and feet, and hefted him away.

Rose watched them go. "Can I tell our friend you'll help?"

"Tell him to stuff it." Link started for the cottage.

"Wouldn't you at least like to know how much he's offering?"

He tried the door and found it open. "How much did it take to buy you, Rose?"

The sergeant observed him for a moment. "Not as much as I would've believed."

Link went inside, still carrying the package of clothing under his left arm, and closed the door behind himself. The place was tidy considering its previous condition. The two front windows had been repaired, and the rear two temporarily boarded over. Appliances, paintings, even the stuffed fish, had been replaced. There was a new mattress and fresh bedding, and his missing boot had been returned, set neatly next to its mate.

From the package, Link pulled two new pairs of Levi's, socks and underwear, a flannel shirt, and a denim jacket. He then flipped the sat phone open, did a walk-through, and found no trace of electronic bugs. After pulling off his clothes, he laboriously washed everything in the bathroom sink, and draped it all over various ledges to dry.

After a yawn he climbed into bed, drew up the covers, and dropped off to sleep.

5:45 P.M.—Rock Lake

Sly Paquette had never developed a sense of humor. As a youth, whenever his peers had cracked jokes he'd felt they were belittling him. That had not changed. He was suspicious and sensitive, and did not try to understand witticisms others tried to relate.

He had brooded since the previous day about the deadline that Carmine Gracchi had set to get his money and the gym bag. The money was being amassed in a room at the casino, brought in from every possible source, counted, and bagged. Nineteen million was not a small amount. They were also scrambling to ensure that the expedition was given every possible chance to succeed. So when Sergeant George Rose joked about how Willie had insulted Link Anderson and been flattened, he just stared.

Rose attempted again to relate humor. "Willie was out for so long I docked his pay for taking the day off," he joked, but Paquette did not even try to understand.

"So what did Anderson say to my offer?"

"He didn't take it."

"Some people are naturally dumb. How 'bout the things he stole?"

"He said they were explosives, and he dumped 'em in a lake up there."

Paquette thought about it. "That works." He hadn't wanted to give them back anyway, since crazy Howarski might blow up the wrong people.

"Anderson thinks the Ecol-Rec, Limited people are from the mob."

Paquette's voice emerged low and dangerous. "Who cares who's at the fuckin' ecol-rec. Know what I give a shit about? You asking questions alla time, that's what."

"I just want to know enough so I can cover your back."

"I got people covering my back. You do what you're told, which was to get Anderson's attention, and offer him money. Remember what happened to the captain? He was always asking questions. Forget the fuckin' ecol-rec zone and the fuckin' mines and any fuckin' other thing that ain't your business and do what you're told."

Paquette's eye throbbed when he grew upset, and the blood flowed faster. Like now.

The Junkman pushed away from the wall where he'd been hulking in the shadows, and stood behind Rose, who looked uncomfortable.

Sly Paquette phoned Gloria Vasson's hotel room and told the person who answered about the development with Lincoln Anderson. Sydney repeated what she'd said earlier, to leave the pilot alone to lend his expertise to the expedition. When she disconnected, Paquette growled to George Rose, "Get the fuck outa here, and handle the expedition like I said."

He had other matters to deal with. A female employee at the moccasin store had told her friend that she was going to seek help from authorities in Madison. Also, he had to remove Gloria Vasson from the hotel so there wouldn't be two of her.

Suite 300, Hatchet Club Casino-Hotel

Gloria had been made to sit in the bedroom, watched over by a casino employee who tried to act uninterested in her nakedness. All that time the plain woman popped in and out of the suite, as if setting things up to move in.

After an hour she returned to Gloria, opened the artist's case, and laid out several plastic bags and vials. "I'm good at this, you know," she said.

Gloria had no inkling of what she meant.

The plain woman mixed a concoction of powder and liquid and, after getting it to the consistency of her choosing, daubed Gloria's head and face with a thick layer of mudlike plaster, and ordered her to remain utterly immobile. As they waited she answered the telephone and conducted a brief conversation during which she was very obviously the person in charge.

She removed the hardened cast in front and rear hemispheres, using care, and then announced with satisfaction, "Perfect!"

After letting Gloria dress herself in slacks and blouse, she made a final point. "For the present I've decided you may be useful alive."

With that she deftly pulled a pillowcase over Gloria's head.

Others entered and left, bringing in belongings at the direction of the woman. There were periods of silence, but Gloria heard her moving about, as if getting accustomed to the place.

After a long while she was led into the hall and down an elevator, then hastily pulled outside. There she was shoved into the rear of a van, and the sliding door hastily closed.

As the vehicle was driven away, she realized that she lay against the body of another human. After a while of bouncing about, she whispered, "Who are you?"

The woman was hardly coherent, but she made out fragments. "Oh God it hurts. He beat me with a pipe. I'm broken everywhere. *Help* me."

After a while, Gloria was able to freeze her emotions. She thought of the sandy white beach and bright sun. "Help me!" the other woman whimpered, and began to shudder and thrash, like an animal entering its death throes.

Gloria walked the pleasant Jamaican beaches, driven by a single purpose: bloody vengeance upon Councilman Paquette, Willie, the scarecrow, and the plain woman behind it all.

7:15 P.M.—*South Side, Manido Indian Reservation*

Jason climbed into his Firebird, about to leave Lonnie's after scheduling the training sessions for Bear Society members.

The words came in incoherent bursts. *Oh God . . . hurts . . . beat me with a pipe . . . broken everywhere. Help me!* There was no sound, only a silent reverberation of emotion.

The dream-time had come without forewarning. Jason leaned forward until his forehead rested on the steering wheel that he clutched, not wanting to hear the voice echoing in his mind.

Someone help me! Help me! Help me!

"Who are you?" he tried, although it would do no
good. This was no communication, only a soul crying out
in anguish.

Storyteller told them of ancient death songs recited by
ancestors. Was this one of those?

Jason gripped the steering wheel as if it were a lifeline
to sanity as the chant resumed—*Help me! Help me!*
Louder and louder the voice came, until it was shrieking
in his mind—then it slowly faded away into . . .
nothingness.

After a moment he released a drawn breath, and also
his fierce grip on the wheel. The dream-time had passed,
and only remnants of sadness remained. He considered
returning inside to share the dream-time with Lonnie,
getting his friend to help fight the craving that was growing within, offering solace to push away the raw emotions that still coursed through him.

Jason's fingers were trembling on the car keys. He
started the engine.

An hour later he was seated in the familiar corner of
the Hatchet Club's main bar, finishing his third drink
and talking too loudly of things that should have gone
unsaid. In that manner he was able to forget the voice,
and everything else about the unsettling dream-time.

17

Link arrived early to load the equipment, which included
camp gear, scuba tanks, and light watercraft. The Grand
Cherokee and Range Rover were fully equipped, down
to dash-mounted GPS receivers, short-range UHF radios, and frame-mounted winches on the front. Both carried jerricans filled with extra fuel.

The day was chilled and blustery. Richards wore gray
cotton-lined acrylic coveralls with his name embroidered
in blue on the right chest. Turf Siegel, in a mackinaw
jacket and hiking boots, might have passed for a Northwoods logger if not for the brown porkpie hat. Despite
the cold Link was mildly surprised that Gloria Vasson
did not see them off as she'd said she would do. Gloria
had seemed the determined type.

The way was overgrown, a narrow, twisting maze, and
the built-in GPS receivers were all but useless as path-
finders since the roads were so inaccurately mapped.
Still, Link unerringly made all the proper turns, pleased
that he'd paid close attention the previous day. He drove
the Land Rover, with Richards on his right, squinting
ahead at the road, and Turf Siegel in back, trying to nod
off to sleep. Jenifer was last, in the Jeep Cherokee with
Dr. Brogg, who chatted over the short-range UHF radio
about autumn colors and the various animals he saw.

They crawled along on the atrocious roads and were
slowed even more by Richards's frequent stops so Turf

Siegel could videotape their progress. Three hours passed
before they arrived at "Alpha," a wooded area on Big
Fish Lake a quarter mile beyond Senator Adcock's
childhood home.

When all had dismounted, Richards pointed back.
"Everyone stay away from the cabin. There may be clues
to tell us where Senator Adcock hid the treaties."

They pitched in to help unload the vehicles. The tools
were unloaded first: shovels, hoes, hand trowels, ma-
chetes, and metal detectors. Also a case of thermal
flares, to be used to burn away underbrush since the
forest was so damp that wildfire was unlikely.

Link erected a dome tent for each of them, slipping
flex rods into place to form the frames, and over them
stretching the lightweight nylon fabric. Into each he
placed a day pack, mummy bag, catalytic heater, and
electric lantern. He tied a protective tarp over the outdoor kitchen, laid out rocks for a fire pit, and set up two
tables, several camp chairs, a large propane stove, and
four large, bear-and-raccoon-proof sealed containers
stuffed with freeze-dried and canned food. On the opposite side he set up a chem-toilet, complete with modesty
curtain, which Dr. Brogg admired as a wonderful conces-
sion to civilization.

Finally Link unloaded the Kevlar-fiberglass canoe,
snapped the sections of the lightweight collapsible boat
together, then carried those and a five-horsepower John-
son outboard to the water's edge.

He quietly gazed across the still water at the wild forest on the distant shore. A pair of otters frolicked on
the bank. Closer in, a row of ducklings paddled furiously
after their mom.

Lincoln Anderson experienced a sense of belonging,
as he did whenever he was close to nature, and decided
that he was much more comfortable as a guide than in
his role as a senior vice president for the world's
largest foundation.

In the corner of his vision a flicker of something
brown disappeared behind a tamarack tree no more than
a dozen yards distant. He turned to observe—quietly and
patiently. He'd seen *something,* yet he was unsure of

what it had been. He went to the tree, knelt, and looked for spoor, but found no trace of whatever it had been.

As the group gathered for Jenifer's briefing on the treatment of the flora, fauna, and Indian artifacts they came across, Link set out sandwich makings on one of the tables.

He then returned to the lakeshore, still curious.

The sat phone vibrated in his pocket. "Anderson," he answered quietly.

"Remember me?"

"Sure," Link replied, surprised to hear Ron Doughty's voice.

"I haven't seen the big ox out front of our shop lately," said the investigator.

"His name's Billy Junkins, and you were right—he's dangerous. Chicago mob."

"I figured it was something like that. Safe to talk?"

Link observed the group. "Go ahead."

"I've been nosing around the different cop shops in the area, bullshitting about the reservation. Seems for the past couple months the reservation police have stopped cooperating. They refuse to share information, and won't let deputies, even state troopers, in for any reason. If anyone argues, they claim treaty rights and tell them to call Washington."

"Did they cooperate before?"

"Couple years back they shared everything. Then they became hard to work with. Now it's down to zero. Locals don't like going there. Get off the main road and you're roughed up for no reason. Couple times when women were alone, they claimed a cop stopped their car and searched them bodily and intimately, know what I mean? There've even been talk of rapes, but the women were too frightened to press it."

Link thought of Willie, and how he would put nothing like that past him, then about Sergeant Rose, who was not the kind to make waves. He answered to Sly Paquette, who answered to no one but the mob.

"The Coldspring County sheriff's office tried complaining to Madison, and the state attorney general raised hell with the tribal council. They denied everything, said their visitors and their clientele at the casino had lodged no complaints."

"What if their clientele are mostly crooks?"

"That rumor's bounced around quite a lot." He paused. "Another reason I called—a few people outside the reservation have been reporting truck traffic in the early morning hours. We're talking remote areas and primitive roads, and moving fast."

"Where?"

"In the national forest adjacent to the reservation."

"Have the deputies tried staking them out?"

Doughty chuckled humorlessly. "On the graveyard shift there are only three or four on-duty deputies in the entire county, which is larger than some New England states, and at least one is manning the desk. There've been periodic reports for a couple of months, but no one takes them seriously. There's no reason for big rigs to use back roads when there's Highway 51 over to the west. The deputies joke about bar patrons on their way home, seeing ghosts of Capone's outfit making their nightly booze runs."

"So there may be nothing to the reports?"

"Maybe, but lately there've been more. Two last week."

"Are the deputies going to check now?"

"Unless someone gets hurt, I doubt it. Maybe I'll take a look."

"It's time for you to back out, Ron. You were right, this is a rough crowd."

"I'll watch my ass." He paused. "I got the deposit in my bank account. Don't know how you did it, but thanks. Money's tight right now."

"You earned it." Link recalled something. "Remember what you said about the phone call Daniel Eagle made to his wife? Did he describe the helicopter?"

"Let me get my notes." He paused. "Yeah, a green, military-style helicopter."

Bingo, Link thought. Daniel Eagle had not been hallucinating. "One last thing. Have you been trying to call me?"

"Yeah. No answer. This is the third time I tried."

"Thanks for the information," Link said. "Now drop it before you get hurt."

"You sound like my daughter. First I'll spend a couple nights parked on those back roads, lookin' at what goes by. Cheers." Doughty terminated the call.

Link observed the sat phone charge level before putting it away. The battery was down to thirty percent. Until he received a replacement he'd conserve power.

He looked back out at the lake, wondering again about what he'd seen earlier.

Jenifer walked up. "We found the makings," she said, and showed off a sandwich to prove it. "Keep it up and you'll make someone a good wife."

Link smiled.

"Dr. Brogg's pleased with the potty. I learned about his prostate problem on the drive out. Think how lucky I am, being the only female around to listen to all that male talk. How's yours, by the way?"

"It's getting embarrassed."

Jenifer grinned naughtily. "Let's go someplace and be alone?"

"Bad timing," he said, thinking it was cold enough to freeze their buns off should they do anything serious. He watched her as she left, looking back and giving him a twitch of her hips.

Near Big Fish Lake

Willie pulled the black-and-white Ford Explorer into the clearing and parked beside a similar vehicle. He crawled out, lugging a sealed cardboard box, and toted it over to where another policeman leaned against a tree. Both were in uniform, wearing Smokey hats and black leather jackets with big silver badges on their chests. Despite their frequent deviations from duty, Sergeant Rose demanded that his people at least look the part of proper policemen.

"Nice of you to make it," Patrolman First Class Marvin Yellowbird said sarcastically.

Willie, who was a patrolman *second* class, muttered something about bad directions.

They were there to make sure the expedition didn't go too near the ecol-rec zone—and also for another purpose.

Yellowbird pointed. "If they find what they're after, they'll take that road back to town."

Willie stifled a groan at a new jolt of pain in his forehead, which had ached for the past day, ever since Anderson had decked him. *"Hit me from my blind side,"* he'd told everyone. He'd wanted to find him and even things. Shoot the son of a bitch. No, first make him beg, give him a good stomping, and *then* shoot him. But Sergeant Rose had said to leave Anderson alone until they were done with the expedition. Not that Willie was afraid of Rose, but the order had come down from Sly Paquette, who was a different matter altogether.

He put down the cardboard box, used a knife to open the top, and lifted out an aluminum tube, twenty inches in length, two and a half inches in diameter.

"Didn't you listen?" said Yellowbird. "We aren't supposed to open it. We wait until they head for town, stop them, and see if they have the gym bag. If they do, I keep them occupied while you take it out of their sight, open the box, and make the switch."

"Well, now I don't have to open it, do I?" Willie examined the metal tube, noting how it had a metal nipple on one end. He wondered what it was for, but didn't want to ask. After all, Sly Paquette had picked him to be the caretaker of the box and its contents.

Marvin stared at the tube with distaste. "Put it away."

A light bulb illuminated in Willie's head, and his jaw drooped. "Know what this is?"

"I guessed. Put the box back in the vehicle and lock it up like we were told."

The two had shared a mutual dislike since Willie's arrival from Milwaukee, where he'd spent two years in the slam-bang for robbery. He hated the pleasant-natured Boy Scout.

Neither of them noticed the strange-looking old man who watched from beyond the swampy pond, admiring the silver tube that Willie casually dropped back into the box.

Willie replaced the box in the Explorer, then pulled the ornate necklace and bracelet from the center console, and wondered how much they were worth.

Marvin walked over and observed. "Where'd you get those?"

Willie smirked. "A rich broad gave 'em to me after I fucked her brains out." He got hard thinking about the woman writhing and hurting—then he remembered the stupid threat she'd whispered before he left her, and felt uneasy. Willie was superstitious, and hoped she was dead.

He had an odd feeling that he was being watched and turned to look, but by then the old man had already moved specterlike back into the forest.

1:20 P.M.—Base Camp Alpha

The sun had finally emerged from the overcast—announcing another nippy but pleasant day in the Indian summer—and the members sat about on camp chairs and munched carrots as they spoke of homes and families. Dr. Brogg spoke of a wife of twenty-odd years, Turf was happily single, and Richards was long divorced.

Jenifer said if they'd come in the springtime they'd be battling blackflies and mosquitoes the size of B-1 bombers. Most of the flying insects had laid their eggs and died off by late July.

Dr. Brogg complained about the lack of a telephone or even E-mail. Richards said every few nights Link would drive them into town so they could call home.

The expedition leader rose to his feet and gave Turf Siegel a nod to switch on his camera.

"I make it a practice to go for the gold the first day out. This time I feel we have an admirable chance of success, considering the vast size of the wilderness area."

"The north side," Jenifer corrected. "It was the principal homeland for my people, continuously inhabited from the mid-seventeenth century until recently."

Richards cast her an irritated look for the interruption and observed his watch. "In half an hour we'll gather back here and I'll explain where we'll begin the search. In the meanwhile, Mr. Anderson will pass out wet suits. We'll be going for a swim, folks."

"Scuba tanks?" asked Dr. Brogg, frowning and ready to complain.

"We won't need them." He asked everyone to return to their tents, finish putting their things away, and prepare for the swim.

Link passed out neoprene wet suits to Richards, Brogg, and Jenifer. A few minutes later he was cleaning up after lunch when he sensed someone behind him.

A hand groped his butt, and Jenifer whispered, "You've got great buns. How about we sneak off somewhere and sin?"

"Only fifteen minutes until Richards's next take. How about a rain check?"

"Depend on it." She walked away in her wet suit, twitching her hips and looking like a svelte sea otter.

Crazy Man Marsh

It was Jason and Lonnie's first attempt to find the mob's burial place for troublesome citizens, as Storyteller had bidden them to do. Lonnie had opted to begin with Crazy Man Marsh.

"Too hard to get to," Jason had argued. "They're too lazy for that."

"You think they'd pick something easy? They're not stupid."

"I think they're lazy *and* stupid." He was betting on Big Marsh or Martha's Marsh, both of which were on the opposite, western side of the reservation.

They'd wagered ten dollars and planned their route of travel.

Thirty years before, the Manido had moved their cranberry operation from the northeastern corner of the reservation to a large, drained lake bed north of Rock

Lake. Forgotten was the back road once used to transport the plants from one bog to the other. That route led past Crazy Man Marsh, and while overgrown, it was passable by foot.

They'd begun at midmorning, well after his aunt Jen had departed, hid Lonnie's old pickup in a thicket near the new cranberry bog, then set out. Each carried a pack and fold-down fishing gear. Lonnie had his Browning compound bow and a dozen arrows. There was only one firearm, Jason's Ruger twenty-two rifle with a ten-round rotary clip. A guide's special.

Lonnie was pudgier and softer. Jason could have easily outdistanced him, but as he'd done on such outings all their lives, he adjusted to his friend's slower pace.

The way was more overgrown than they'd imagined, and only after three hours of walking and climbing over obstacles did they finally approach the marsh. They then split up and made a slow circuit, one in each direction, looking for any slightest sign of vehicular activity.

When they rejoined at the opposite side, Lonnie unwrapped a Snickers, took a bite, and glared at the marsh.

"It's not this one," said Jason.

"Maybe Sly Paquette's telling the truth, and all of those people really moved."

"In the middle of the night, just taking light stuff and leaving most of their furniture?"

Lonnie looked out over the marsh. "If they're killing people and we get caught looking, I've got a feeling they won't just ask us to leave."

"Hey, man, you think that bunch of Keystone Kops could catch us?"

"Not unless they get lucky." He took another bite, and brought up the subject Jason had avoided. "Or unless you screw up again and tell them what we're doing."

Jason winced, thinking how dumb he'd been the previous night, and that it was a good thing Lonnie had found him and dragged him home. *Never again,* he vowed.

After the dream-time he'd gone straight to the Hatchet Club. When Lonnie had pulled him out, he'd been talking with a friend, asking about the various marshes and telling how he was going to flight school. Lonnie said he'd mentioned the Bear Society and bragged about being Young Storyteller.

"I was mostly talking about flying someday," he tried. "Anyway, Marvin's a reservation cop, but he's *Muk-wah* and won't tell anyone."

"Marvin's the one who called me, for cripe's sake. When he tried to get you to stop, you argued and started blabbing about your friend Link and how he'd take care of Paquette."

Jason tried to recall where the female bartender had been standing. Close, he decided.

"I don't want a visit from Sly Paquette and the Junkman. You can get all the *Muk-wah* killed with your big mouth. You gotta act more like Young Storyteller and less like a drunk."

The words stung, but Jason knew Lonnie was being honest. Storyteller had warned him that his drinking was a problem, and foretold that he'd betray them. Had he done that? He vaguely recalled that the bartender had seemed more attentive than normal.

Jason looked out at the marsh for a long while. "I'll stop drinking," he said.

He had no choice. His friends' lives depended on it.

"Your word?"

Jason nodded resolutely. "My word."

"Next time you get the urge, let me know and I'll help."

"I will." He started to tell him about the dream-time but held his tongue. It wouldn't help the poor soul who had been brutalized.

He turned southward, in the direction from which they'd come.

Lonnie followed. "I'm hungry. Let's fish Turtle Creek on our way back."

18

Richards pulled out the large-scale map, opened and displayed it. There was the same red mark as the previous day, but he had added an "A-1" with an arrow pointing to a lakeshore location.

Damn, Link thought.

Richards indicated the map. "As a boy the senator found an old dugout canoe that he mentioned in his notes as one of his fondest memories. He wrote how it was stable and reliable, how the ancient people knew a lot about boatbuilding that they could teach us today. Whenever he left, he weighted it with stones and submerged it." He pointed at A-1.

"Remember, both the gym bag and the tubes are waterproof. I feel that when we find the sunken canoe, there's a chance we'll find the bag. According to the digital map, it's two miles distant, so if you're ready for our first adventure, we'll be on our way." He raised an eyebrow. "Dr. Brogg, if you'd rather sit this one out and rest . . ."

"I wouldn't miss it for anything."

Richards said that he, Brogg, and Jenifer would all dive. Since the work would be done in shallow water, there should be little physical challenge.

All Link could think of were the explosives that he'd left at the dugout. The fact that they were submerged would not diminish their effectiveness. If one of the divers grasped the wrong handle . . .

He observed Jenifer, wondering if he shouldn't remind her about the mines. After a moment's thought he realized it did not matter. He should have plenty of time to move the mines.

Link caught up with Richards as he entered his tent. "Will you need me?"

"I'd prefer if you stayed here and looked after the camp."

Link was pleased with the response. His intent was simple—to run down the lakeshore, arrive before the others, and relocate the mines.

Richards had other ideas. "Better load a couple scuba tanks in the Rover, in case we have to go deep. I doubt we'll need 'em, but who knows?" He called out to Turf and said he wanted documentation. "I've got a feeling about this one," he said.

Link loaded the tanks, and was starting for the forest when Richards emerged from his tent in his wet suit and asked for the average water temperature at this time of year.

"Forty-one degrees," said Link, anxious to depart.

"Brrr. And the visibility?"

"Four to fourteen feet. There's sediment and discoloration caused by the tamarack."

"You know your stuff." Richards looked pleased.

Link slipped into the forest, hoping Turf would take his time with his "documentation" of their departure so he'd have more time. Richards and the others had vehicles. He had only his legs.

Link trotted steadily down the lakeshore, ducking limbs and pushing through thickets, hurrying across clearings, using game trails when they were obvious and available. Wishing again that he'd not allowed his physical condition to deteriorate so atrociously. Still, his wind improved daily, and the muscles of his legs were devoid of flab.

He continued the steady pace, periodically slowing to negotiate his way through a dense stand or go around a tangle of brush. He found a small trail and made good time for a distance, then found the way blocked again.

Pushing through that thicket was difficult—once he lost his balance and fell knee-deep into the water—but he pressed on.

And almost ran into an apparition clad in deerskins, with a rifle raised to eye level, the barrel pointed directly at Link's head.

"Hah," the old man shouted, his finger curled inside the trigger guard.

Link stopped cold, as any sane person would do, and tried to remember Jason's warnings about the hermit.

"Hah, Nek-kahhh." The utterances seemed to be more sharp exhalations of breaths than coherent words. "Nek-kahhh." He patted his chest, indicating it was his name.

He was hairless—with not a follicle visible on chest, arms, legs, or head—and ragged deerskin clothing hung from his frame. His copper skin was much darker than Link's, and a thousand wrinkles belied his age. His left arm was shriveled, his legs bowed and misshapen, yet he moved as gracefully as any forest creature. He motioned the barrel angrily. "Sid-nyah."

Link considered escape, but the old man's eyes glittered with alertness as he motioned southward. "Sid-nyah, sid-nyah." He came a step closer, peering hard.

Link slowly raised his hands. "My name is Anderson," he tried, speaking clearly.

The hairless old man sighed and disgustedly jabbed the barrel forth, as if he'd rather shoot him than talk. He circled, the barrel trained on Link's chest, a growling sound issuing from his throat. He stopped, pointed the rifle southwest, and his expression grew sad. "Do-rah." He shook his head and sighed. "Do-rah."

Link tried to remember what Jason had revealed about the hermit. He was crazy and sometimes went naked, and had moved into the Adcock cabin with the senator's blessing. He threatened those who came close, but Jason hadn't believed the rifle was loaded.

"Do-rah." He was perturbed at something. "Do-rah!"

Not just any rifle, but an old-time lever action. A Henry repeater, one of the earliest Winchesters, with a brass forestock. The bluing had been worn away, but it was otherwise pristine. Clean and without a trace of oxidation, it looked to be in firing condition.

The hermit appeared agitated. He pointed the rifle at Link, then directly southward, then back at Link. "Ed-yah!" He repeated the motions, and became very sad. "Ed-yah," he whispered.

They heard the vehicles on the road. Link took a step, knowing he must hurry or they'd arrive at the canoe site well before him.

The old man grimaced. "Sid-nyah." Aiming the weapon at Link again.

Jason could be very wrong. The old lever action might be loaded.

Link cautiously touched his own chest. "Anderson."

The man sighed, obviously frustrated at not being understood. He pointed westward. "Do-rah," he said sadly. He looked southward, shook his head forlornly, and repeated, "Ed-yah."

Jason had said he spoke in his own language, not Ojibwe or English, and what Link was hearing seemed like nothing he had heard before. Another Indian tongue?

"I've got to go," Link pleaded.

The hermit shook his head and pointed down the shore, in the direction Link had been going. "Nyah," he said, and shook his head again. "Nyah."

The old man then slowly circled until they stood facing one another. He sighed, and twitched his bald head back and forth as if frustrated.

The standoff continued as they heard sounds of the vehicles turning off the main road. No chance of getting there first now.

The hermit pointed the barrel directly at Link, who tensed, prepared to attempt to throw himself to one side if he saw the slightest pressure being placed on the trigger.

"Lin-kyah," said the old man of the forest, and for the first time, he formed a smile.

Before Link could question, the hermit took a backward step and shifted just slightly. He seemed not to walk but to flow like liquid into the trees, and was gone.

Link remained still, wondering. While he was certainly the hermit Jason had spoken about, the person he had just seen was not crazy at all.

He hurried to the forest's edge, and prudently hesitated. Still nothing. No sounds or sight of the man, or any other living thing. The hermit did not live in the wilderness. He was a part of it. Link would not find him. He was as good as the best of his Blackfoot tutors.

Then Link felt an alarm sounding inside as he remembered his own destination, and rushed forward. He had to stop them before they detonated one of the mines. Link came onto a game trail and followed it, running, praying he'd be in time.

The forest did not cooperate, but grew in ever worse tangles. More minutes passed before he emerged into the clearing. In the distance were the two trees, and the boulder at their base. Beside them the SUVs were parked in a neat row. Turf Siegel was standing at the lake's edge, the video camera aimed out at the water.

The three divers were in snorkels and masks, standing chest-deep in the frigid water. The two in front held their masks to their faces, bent forward, and submerged. The one behind—Dr. Brogg—shuffled out and waited, mask pushed up onto his forehead.

"Get them out!" Link yelled, envisioning one of them reaching for the canvas pack.

Brogg saw him, waved jauntily, then turned back to watch whatever the first two divers were up to.

Link approached, panting harshly, wondering if he shouldn't dive in.

Relief flooded over him. Richards and Jenifer were snorkeling down the shoreline, well beyond the location of the sunken dugout.

"Is there a problem?" asked Dr. Brogg.

"The dugout," Link tried, thinking something was odd about it all.

"It's not here," Brogg said. "The senator obviously sank it elsewhere."

Link observed. There was no canoe, only a vague indentation where it had been. He walked the shoreline looking for canvas-clad mines, saw only the silt-and-rock-covered bottom, and the swimmers as they traversed the shoreline in their search.

Turf Siegel looked disgusted as he switched off the camera.

Since he could think of no good excuse for his presence, Link turned back up toward the base camp, wondering what the hell was going on, and who had taken the dugout and the mines.

Town of Spirit Lake

The woman who had become Gloria Vasson was enjoying her new role. The wig she'd fashioned and the latex-based features were as good as any she'd fashioned in her previous life. When she'd appeared for her meals in the casino dining room, she'd felt not a bit of apprehension.

There were still cautions as she made the transition. For instance, she worked harder at her exercises and weights, since Gloria Vasson was blessed with a youthful figure. She wore ramps, although she doubted anyone would realize that she was two inches shorter than the old Gloria. The voice transition was good but needed a little work, so she complained of a cold. No one had suspected when she spoke on the phone to personal bankers and longtime employees. Funds were being shifted, although not so wildly that anyone might become too curious, and the two household employees at Georgetown had learned that she was thinking of making changes.

Sydney felt it might take a month before everything would be as she wished. By then she would control Gloria's fortune as well as own a new base of operations in Washington.

She'd spent hours going over the senator's computer notes, poring over locations where he could have hidden the gym bag, and made interesting discoveries. One was the warmth with which he'd written about Jenifer Toussaint. He'd avoided specifics, so Sydney filled in the blanks. No wonder there was rancor between the older wife and the much younger girlfriend.

She'd almost scrolled past an entry Senator Eddie Adcock had written about a funeral in Montana and a man named Abraham Lincoln Anderson. Could it be the same person? Another entry mentioned Anderson and the Weyland Foundation.

Sydney had once been in the employ of America's foremost clandestine agency and had heard rumors of a secretive side to the foundation. While Anderson may not have been connected with that small tentacle of the massive organization, she decided that she must learn more.

19

A word was whispered, so low it would have been almost inaudible even had Link been awake. It came again, "Lin-kyah," and he drifted to the surface and became aware.

Link eased the flap aside and looked out at the dark camp. He'd positioned his tent so he could view the others, as well as the vehicles, and after a careful scan he saw nothing amiss and went back inside.

Three days had passed. Under Joseph Richards's guidance they'd dug up each suspicious mound, diligently waded the shoreline, and explored every niche and cranny at the search sites near the Adcock cabin. While the daily weather remained pleasant, early morning temperatures dropped to twenty-five degrees. The search was a race with the calendar. They would be able to continue in the face of snow flurries, but there'd been other Septembers when the locals had seen the real things—and real things in the Northwoods included subzero temperatures, ice storms, immobilizing drifts, and winds that cut to the bone.

Yet life was certainly not drudgery. Just a few hours earlier Jenifer had given him a subtle smile, and they'd canoed to the island for a lovemaking session that would qualify in any gym as a full-body workout. Afterward Jenifer had snuggled happily and told him he made her feel alive. Even now he found himself smiling foolishly.

* * *

The man Link called the hermit watched from the darkness. He was no longer in tattered deerskins. Those offered concealment, but colder nights demanded heavier clothing. At the first bone-chilling freeze he would change to even warmer furs. For the few days each winter when it was so frigid that tree branches cracked without encouragement, he would crawl into a cabin and remain until the cold-noise time went away.

He was Nek-kah, which meant "Goose." Not named after the noble migratory bird, but for its sounds, for like the goose he could speak only utterances with forceful endings.

While Nek-kah was not at all quick-witted, ofttimes he knew the proper pronunciation of a word in his mind, although it would not emerge from his mouth in that manner. He had known at a very young age that he was both slow and different. Even his mother had been impatient for him to speak properly, and blamed him for not trying. But try he did, although it seemed that his impediment only worsened with the effort.

Only one childhood acquaintance had shown patience and understanding. Eddie, his true friend, had comprehended that Nek-kah simply could not speak like others, or even pronounce a name. He could get part of it out, but had to hiss out the rest such as Ed-*yah*!

Now Eddie was gone. Death was a state that Nek-kah understood. He'd watched from the forest as the one called Sydney had stood over Eddie as he'd died, then as she'd told others to put a man and woman in the car with Eddie, and burn them.

Nek-kah had searched out Storyteller, leader of the Bear Society, but while Storyteller was indulgent, he'd been unable to understand. He had not dared visit Storyteller again, since he was so often surrounded by evil ones. Now Nek-kah had come to this place to meet again with Lin-kyah, to whom he'd tried to explain things three days earlier. After watching the camp for a while longer, he decided it was not a good time.

Soon Nek-kah must return to the old Eagle settlement, where the old gardens still grew, and, despite fervent competition by badgers and squirrels, gather enough vegetables to sustain him through the coming winter. But just now he must sleep. All old creatures required a lot of rest, and tomorrow would be busy. He would return to try to see Lin-kyah, and bring gifts so he would know he was a friend and to listen.

This time he must not point the old rifle, like he often did when he became agitated.

The gifts? Old Nek-kah knew of something that Lin-kyah was sure to admire.

2:45 A.M.—*Loop Road, near Big Marsh*

Thirty-five miles distant, Jason and Lonnie had checked out their third bog and were on the way to a fourth. There was a new urgency about their search. For the past three days they'd looked for Marie, the popular assistant manager of the moccasin store, whose employees said she was tired of weekly payoffs to the rotten cops and threatened to go to the state cops. The *Muk-wah* had been searching, hoping she'd escaped and was hiding.

They'd parked and hiked past the westernmost roadblock, then taken game trails that paralleled the west loop road—a semicircular route that went by Frenchman's Lake, and both Big Marsh and Little Martha's Marsh.

At Big Marsh they'd found no trace of recent human activity.

"It's getting late," Jason complained. They'd walked for three hours.

"Little Martha's not that far." Lonnie poked Jason's arm. "You forget our bet?"

"Nope. I'm just tired of stumbling around in the dark on cruddy game trails."

Loop Road was only a hundred yards distant, but Lonnie argued against using it. Twice they'd heard sounds of vehicle engines.

"We've come this far without being seen. Why push our luck?"

Jason sighed dramatically and set out faster, hastily leading the way up the dark trail. "We could be . . ."

He cursed aloud as his footing gave way. As he sank in to his knees, Jason fell forward on his arms, and flailed to extricate himself.

"What's happening?" Lonnie whispered.

"Jesus, you smell it, don't you? I walked into loon shit."

"Loon shit" being the local patois for a mixture of mud and matter that had decomposed into viscous quicksand. The stuff was maddening enough in full daylight.

"You okay?" Lonnie asked from a distance.

"Hell no," Jason griped as he crawled free, and unsteadily regained his footing. "I've got on my good jacket and this stuff doesn't come out." Jason slapped at his clothing to remove at least some of it—and then stopped cold and stood very still.

Wavering on his feet as he wafted between dream-time and reality.

Lonnie was talking, but Jason could not hear. *He was another person, being sucked into another marsh, terribly frightened as he walked with difficulty, drawn ever deeper as a voice ordered him on. He turned, saw a man with a pistol.*

A mighty blow struck him in the back . . .

Numbing emotion continued to trill through Jason. He cried out in a guttural voice and slowly, slowly began to emerge and become aware of his real-world surroundings.

Lonnie was beside him, hovering, saying, "You okay, Jase?"

He spoke gruffly. "I dropped my flashlight. Shine yours around, would you?" He wiped a cheek with his sleeve and decided he was *covered* with the stuff! "Damn!"

"Keep your voice down," Lonnie hissed. "The road's just over there."

Jason snorted with bravado as the emotions of the frightening dream-time diminished. He was Young Storyteller, and mustn't waver or show fear.

"Even if they heard us, they're too lazy to come after us. Shine the light, okay?"

As Lonnie shone the beam, Jason retrieved a lump from the black muck, then proceeded to scrape away gobs of loon shit. After a moment, he tried it. There was a dull glow—the lens was coated with yellow slime.

"I don't want to be out here all night." Jason illuminated with the feeble beam, and walked toward Loop Road.

Lonnie followed. "This isn't smart, Jase."

"Neither is swimming in more loon shit."

As soon as he emerged onto Loop Road, Jason strode down its side, not slowing for Lonnie until he'd walked a hundred yards and calmed down some in the wake of the dream-time.

He hadn't had a drink since the foul-up in the Hatchet Club bar, when he'd talked too much. Knowing he must not imbibe made it seem harder. Lonnie helped, hung around and kept him thinking about the *Muk-wah* attack plan and the training.

Lonnie hurried up, and they walked on together, side by side.

Jason thought about the plaguing dream-times and decided to talk to Link more openly about them next time. It was hard to discuss them with those who hadn't experienced them.

"The turnoff to Little Martha's around the next corner," he said.

"Quiet," Lonnie snapped in a hissing tone. "Someone's on the road."

Jason peered forward in the darkness. The glow from the crescent moon was waning as it dropped lower in the sky. He was ninety percent sure that there was nothing there, yet . . .

A loud, nasal male voice exclaimed, "I heard somethin'!" A flashlight was switched on no more than thirty yards straight ahead—the light swept up the side of the road, and they heard the ratcheting sound of a shotgun as a round was chambered.

Jason froze into place, heart pounding wildly.

"Let's go!" Lonnie whispered as the flashlight beam

explored, but Jason was so petrified with fear that he hardly heard.

The beam shone into Jason's face.

Jason started to cry out, "Don't shoot!"

The beam moved away.

He felt sick. Through numbed senses, he heard Lonnie running.

Bam! The report of the shotgun was tremendous.

Jason staggered off the road and huddled beside a bush. *Bam! Bam!*

He crouched lower, praying that they did not see him, hoping beyond hope that they'd continue to shoot at Lonnie. *Him, not me!* his mind cried to them.

The two men were talking, but he couldn't make out their words. They walked closer, and he trembled with abject fear, knowing he was about to die.

They stopped not far from where he knelt, both of them now shining their beams down the road. He waited for one of them to turn their light on him.

As they continued talking, he realized that they were unsure of what they'd seen. One thought it had been a bear.

"I seen fuckin' bears. They don't wear jeans."

They decided to take the patrol car and drive the road. As they turned back, a flashlight beam swept across Jason again.

They'd not seen him. The layer of dark loon shit had masked him.

When they'd gone Jason was sick to his stomach. He stumbled back to the game trail that paralleled Loop Road, and began the long walk back. *Coward!* he screamed at himself. Lonnie was his best friend, yet he'd been ready to sacrifice him.

Was Lonnie alive? He began to run, periodically wanting to cry, fighting it and going on, needing a drink in the worst way.

He was almost to Big Marsh when a voice startled him. "You *made* it!" Lonnie emerged from the dark forest, grabbed him, and would not let go.

Jason laughed aloud, filled with relief, then remembered the shotgun blasts. "You okay?"

"I was running so fast shotgun pellets couldn't keep up."

They gibbered, full of happiness and self-reproach. Jason told him about the dream-time, which was why he'd been such an asshole. They tried to cipher what the dream might have meant, but came up empty.

"We're this close," said Lonnie. "We have to look at Little Martha's Marsh."

"Yeah. They're guarding something."

There were no arguments that they'd take the game path. They went quietly, and used the flashlights as little as possible. Half an hour later they emerged at the marsh.

While the patrol car with the two goons they'd encountered was parked at the turnoff, the road to the marsh was clear. They gave the vehicle wide berth, then followed the myriad of tire tracks that led to the edge of the swampy bog—and that disappeared in the dark mud.

Lonnie crouched to observe the ruts. "Looks like they've ditched a lot of cars."

"Let's look at the marsh." Jason shone the flashlight out at the murk, wishing he could see through the stuff. He moved the beam slowly, looking for irregularities, anything to indicate what lay beneath.

"Back to your left," Lonnie whispered. "Maybe ten feet out."

A mud-coated protuberance thrust up from the mire.

"A branch?" Jason asked, unsure.

"I don't think so." Lonnie stripped off boots and trousers, waded out a few feet, reached out with a willow fork, and snagged it. He dragged it in with difficulty—and drew back.

With some of the mud removed, the branch had become a slender human hand.

"Aw, *shit*!" Jason vomited, gagged, and vomited again.

"Not so loud," Lonnie groused.

After he'd got past the retching and the initial horror, Jason helped to drag the weighted body down the shoreline and into tall grass.

Knowledge came to him that this was the woman he

had heard in his last dream, and for once he did not
argue. Instead Jason forced himself to switch on the
flashlight and stare. The woman's face was so terribly
swollen and battered that identification was difficult, but
he knew that she had shared her final moment of life
with him.

They were also certain they'd found Marie from the
moccasin store.

"What do we do with her?" Jason wondered aloud.

"Hey, you're Young Storyteller. Tell me."

They returned the weighted body to the marsh, and
looked on somberly as she sank from sight. "We found
the right marsh," Lonnie said. "I wonder how many others are out there?"

"A few," said Jason, "but they're taking most of them
somewhere else."

Lonnie gave him a quizzical look.

"The dream-times," he explained, and Lonnie did
not question.

They said a prayer for Marie, and left.

The Warehouse

Thirty miles north of Little Martha's Marsh, Gloria
Vasson tried to sleep, knowing that tomorrow she would
need every ounce of energy. She was cold, clad only in
a holey T-shirt and too-large jeans held up by twine, and
a torn towel fashioned to cover her blood-crusted scalp.
Massive and vivid bruises covered most of her visible
skin.

Her life had become one horror after the next. Not
long after she'd been taken from the casino-hotel—
hooded with a pillowcase, ankles and wrists duct-taped,
lying against the broken young woman—the van had
stopped. The dying woman had been dragged out, and
she'd heard a male and female talking. A few minutes
later there was a splash.

As they'd driven on, she had wondered if the woman
had still been alive.

When they'd arrived at the Warehouse, the pillowcase-hood had been pulled away and she'd been pulled out onto the ground, still bound. The couple—she'd since learned they were the ones who controlled the laborers and assigned them their various tasks—had stood over her, prodding and examining.

"Where am I?" Gloria had asked.

Questioning had been the wrong thing to do. The woman—who constantly frowned and looked to be all gristle—kicked her in the side and, when she rolled away, in the back.

"Don't ask questions and don't make trouble," was the woman's order.

They'd freed her ankles, dragged and shoved her into a structure she'd later found was called Warehouse Building Two, or the "Resort," and down a hall to a door marked ARNIE.

An obese male, with green gauze bandages covering the top portion of his face and rolls of fat beneath his chin, had opened the door.

"Got one for you, Arnie," the angular woman had said. "Five hundred for a week?"

He'd looked Gloria over. "Her head's bloody."

"Yeah, and I doubt she's a virgin," said the hard-looking woman.

As they'd haggled over price Gloria's mind had screamed to her that it could not be happening. She was being sold! "No!" she'd screamed in outrage.

Gloria had been taken out and beaten and kicked. She'd scuttled about and cringed, crying out as the man struck again and again.

When they'd pulled her back down the hall Arnie had no longer been interested, so the woman had offered her to a short man whose entire face was bandaged. After settling on three hundred, the woman had given Gloria a violent shove, sending her reeling into the room.

The door had closed and the short man had approached with a look of curiosity.

"My name is Gloria Vasson," she'd said primly. "Would you remove the tape from my wrists?"

"Sure." The faceless man had a nasal and brisk inner-city voice.

When freed Gloria had rubbed at her wrists until the circulation was returned.

He'd asked a few harmless questions, which she'd refused to answer, then told her to take off her clothes so he could have a look at the merchandise.

"No."

He'd pushed her against the wall, and used a firm tone of voice as he undid her clothing.

Gloria had flailed and pushed and screamed, "No!"

The couple had returned. Outside they'd taken turns beating and kicking her, and Gloria had rolled into a ball and cried out for them to please stop.

The man had drawn a pistol, and aimed at her face. "You gonna do what he says?"

"No," she'd managed through bloody lips, wondering if she'd hear the kill shot.

The rawboned woman had stopped the man. "They want her alive for a while."

The woman had proven to be as sadistic as the man, and had beaten her just as badly, but she was more practical. They were short on labor. Gloria's new specialty was cleaning urinals and toilets, but she'd not been offered to another man.

Gloria purposefully made herself as unappealing as possible, not difficult with her scabbed head, broken nose, snagged teeth, and ragged clothing. Each day they gave her a Baggie of lumpy powder, which they insisted she eat or snort. The first time she'd felt a powerful rush, and her heart had pounded like a trip-hammer. "Meth," "crank," "rock," and "speed," she heard them call it, and she'd found it was even mixed into the chowderlike pasty soup they ate.

She dumped the stuff when possible, and improvised when they watched. Anything to keep it out of her system. When there was no recourse but to swallow her allotment, at the first possible chance she vomited to void her stomach. No one noticed. While she was giddy from the meth that was assimilated into her system be-

fore she could get to a commode or drain, her mind
continued to rebel against the horrors of enslavement.
The fact that she disgorged the food made her appear
like the others, rail-thin, with raccoon eyes and muscular
deterioration. At some point she would be too under-
nourished to function at all, but Gloria was determined
to never give in.

She spent her nights in a common room with a dozen
Manido men and women who slept little, just grumbled
and ranted and made little sense. They were all from
Spirit Lake, and spoke anxiously. They'd ask one another questions in rapid fire, lose interest before anyone
responded, and conduct meaningless conversations with
themselves. From their utterances she learned they
worked in the big meth lab or as whores for the guests.

Gloria Vasson continued to live within her mind and
wondered how long it would be before she went mad,
or if the methamphetamine would take over her mind
before she had a chance to escape.

And underlying it all, the thing that maintained her
sanity was her seething hatred and promise of vengeance
upon those she hated most: Councilman Sly Paquette,
cruel Willie, the scarecrow rapist, and the woman who
had stolen her life.

20

The morning was cold and threatened rain. Link ran steadily down the primitive and overgrown roadway, getting the lay of the place. Within four miles of the base camp he knew of every deer, duckling and raccoon, and many of the rodentia. He'd also observed a lone tribal policeman sleeping fitfully in the back of his Explorer just two miles south of the camp.

During the run he'd considered the merits of quitting the search party. If he did so he'd be free to pick up a battery for the sat phone and to investigate the increasingly intriguing ecol-rec zone. On the other hand, a big plus about staying was named Jenifer. The intensity of their afternoon mutual delights provided a compelling argument. When he was around her he felt downright cavemannish.

The engine sound from an approaching vehicle pulled him from his thoughts. He dived into the brush. As the black-and-white SUV passed he identified the driver: Willie the bad cop.

Link decided to follow.

The two patrolmen had been ordered to watch the road like hawks, but since the expedition was idle at night, Marvin hadn't minded when Willie went into town, promising to be back by daybreak. Now Willie was nowhere to be seen, which shouldn't have been a surprise; the lazy bastard wasn't much for punctuality.

Willie drove up at eight.

"You're late," Marvin grumbled. "We should already be in place."

"Why the fuck we gotta move?" Willie snarled, hungover and surly.

Yellowbird spoke slowly, as if to a child. "Because they'll be looking around the old racks at the south end of the lake, and they'd see us here when they drove by."

Willie yawned. "They ain't gonna find anything anyway."

Marvin Yellowbird studied the chart that Sergeant Rose had provided. He'd been selected as map reader because Willie could not make heads or tails of it. They would also have the box of aluminum tubes in their possession, which Sly Paquette had insisted that Willie carry.

Marvin wondered about that. It was not smart to be known as a thinker on the reservation police force these days. Yet as a spy for the *Muk-wah,* he intended to learn as much as possible, as Storyteller had asked.

He found the sheds on the map and traced a finger down to the location suggested by Sergeant Rose: a clearing with a pond on one side and a partial view of the road on the other.

Marvin folded the map. "Let's move out."

Neither were aware that their movements and utterances were noted not only by one, but by two individuals who stood only a few feet away.

Link looked on as Willie and Patrolman Yellowbird—identified by his metal name tag—turned their vehicles around and drove southward. Still Link did not move. When he'd arrived, Nek-kah had already been watching from the shadows.

Once the hermit had even approached Willie's marked vehicle to peer through a back window. The patrolmen had been unaware, for the hermit moved like a specter.

Nek-kah stepped out into the open and stared precisely at where Link hid. "Lin-kyah," came the man's strained voice, showing that he'd not been fooled. He turned and set out down the dusty road in his shuffling lope, following the two black and whites.

Link waited for a moment before establishing his own easy pace—heading back to the base camp. After half a mile, he heard engine sounds, stepped into the forest, and watched the Range Rover and Jeep rumble by with the expedition members.

He considered what he'd overheard. Somehow, despite Richards's secrecy, the patrolmen had known of the expedition's new search site at the south end of the lake. He decided to pay them another visit tonight. There were questions. How were they getting their information, which was secreted in Gloria's computer? What were they up to, and what had been in the vehicle to attract the hermit's interest?

8:45 A.M.—*Base Camp Alpha*

Link returned to an empty camp. He had just begun to dismantle the tents, preparing for the move that Richards had ordered for that afternoon, when a Suburban, adorned with a Hatchet Club Casino logo, pulled in.

Gloria Vasson was in the passenger's seat, wearing a heavy blue cashmere coat, matching deerskin gloves, and a jaunty, black Western-style gambler's hat.

"Leave us for ten minutes," she said to a driver whose jacket had the same logo as the vehicle. She motioned curtly to Link and smiled coolly as he approached. He started to speak, but she raised a restraining hand until the driver was out of earshot.

"Richards and the others are at the other end of the lake," he said.

"I was hoping that would be the case. I'd like a word with you alone." Gloria coughed and held a handkerchief to her nose, obviously suffering from a cold.

She pulled up the hood and huddled in her coat. "I get the idea that it could snow at any moment."

"It's possible. The local record for September is ten inches."

"How well do you recall my husband, Mr. Anderson?"

He paused, caught off guard. "I met the senator only once."

Gloria gave a vague nod. "At your fiancée's funeral in Montana?"

That time Link managed to keep surprise from his expression. "Yes."

"Eddie told me about it afterward. When Ms. Toussaint brought up your name at the council meeting, I wondered just how many Abraham Lincoln Andersons there might be?"

He held his tongue.

"Eddie was saddened by the death of—wasn't her name Marie?"

"Yes."

"Eddie felt she had an understanding beyond her years. At the funeral, he was worried that you wouldn't be able to move on and put her experience behind you."

The senator had voiced the same concern to Link.

"You and Eddie shared a tragic bond. You'd lost your fiancée, and he his first wife." Her face saddened as she spoke passionately. "Now I know how you felt. God knows I miss him."

Link pushed a hand into his jacket pocket, as if for warmth, and repositioned the mode switch of the satellite phone. In transmit-only, the phone would send but not receive.

Gloria continued. "Ms. Toussaint told the council you were born here on the reservation, but I recall that Eddie described you as a Montana Blackfoot. Was he wrong?"

"I'm part Piegan-Blackfoot," he said, and noted a flicker of expression as if she'd just given herself a mental high five.

"But you're without a drop of Manido blood?" she asked too innocently.

"Is it important?"

"Not really. I've lost my regard for the Manido. They

should be thankful to have had a champion like Eddie, yet they've already labeled him a scoundrel."

Gloria looked at him with tear-moistened eyes. The word actress ran through his mind, but he decided that was unfair.

"Eddie mentioned that you'd accepted a position with the Weyland Foundation."

Link did not show his dismay.

She observed him. "Is that an inappropriate subject?"

He wondered. Would Adcock, who had worked on the Senate Committee on Intelligence, have discussed sensitive subjects with his wife?

"I worked for them on a development project in Bosnia."

"But no longer?"

"I went back to flying."

"I was hoping you might have connections in Washington. No one there answers my calls anymore. I don't know if it's malfeasance or ineptness, but it's frightening."

"You're worried?"

She lowered her voice. "I believe it's possible that someone here killed my husband and manipulated evidence. If the Manido can do that to a United States senator and get away with it, would they hesitate to harm the rest of us?"

"The Manido? You think the tribe did that?"

She sighed again. "Jenifer is important to you, isn't she? Open your eyes, Mr. Anderson. Jenifer Toussaint prostituted herself for my husband, and she's doing the same with you."

He was careful not to display anger. "You're wrong."

She gave him a narrow look. "Jenifer really is important to you, isn't she?"

It seemed more observation than question, and he didn't respond.

"I wasn't at all sure about you, Mr. Anderson, until I remembered how highly Eddie regarded you. Despite your relationship with—*her*—I honor his judgment."

He decided that she was fishing for information, and wondered what he might gain from *her*. Link thought about the policemen, and how they'd known about to-day's search site even before Richards had announced it.

"Have you shared the senator's computer notes with anyone except Joseph Richards?"

She answered smoothly. "Possibly, but not intentionally. The other night I set up my laptop and went to dinner, and when I came back I had an odd feeling that something was out of place. I've not let the briefcase out of my sight since."

It was a handy answer that explained how the police had obtained their information.

"What do you know about Sly Paquette?" he asked.

"The council member with the eye injury? I've found him cooperative."

He tossed her a bombshell. "Paquette controls the casino and the tribal police, and he's connected with the mob."

Gloria looked skeptical.

"He's a very dangerous man," Link added.

"I'll look out for him." She did not sound convinced.

"I'd keep a close eye on the computer files." He paused. "Could I see them."

Gloria opened her briefcase to show him a thin, gray computer.

"Eddie kept two sets of floppy disks, one for official business, the other private." She brandished a pair of matchbook-sized wafers. "They're compressed onto these. He listed different locations on one, and on the other described everything on the north side. I've put the two together, locations and descriptions."

She pulled out a sheet of paper. "This is the printout of the new search sites. For Joseph."

Link examined a page with several sets of coordinates, each with a descriptive paragraph. The new base camp was north of Turtle Lake, near the abandoned cranberry farm. A note explained that the plants had been moved to a lake bed to the south. Another described a crude wagon path connecting to a highway in Upper Michigan.

Jason had said there were no back doors. He was obviously wrong.

Gloria locked both wafers and the printout into the

briefcase. She then offered her hand and a surprisingly firm grip. "It's good to know someone here is on my side, Mr. Anderson."

"Tonight I'll drive the others into town so they can make their phone calls," he offered.

"I'm in suite 300. Call me and we'll talk again." She waved to the waiting driver.

Link said he was surprised that she'd driven out in the cold.

"Perhaps you underestimate me," she murmured, and ran up the window.

The driver climbed inside. A moment later they were gone.

21

Erin watched on her computer screen as Link switched from T-O, meaning transmit-only, to T/R, which was the sat phone's normal transmit and receive operation.

"Did you hear?" Link asked on the other end.

"Yeah, but not well. Where did you have the phone?"

"In my jacket pocket."

"That explains the rustling noises," she said. "I was listening to your dumb pocket."

"The lady you heard was Gloria Vasson."

"I got that part." Erin observed the widow's photo and bio on her screen. Gloria was unblemished despite her middle age. "From what she said, she really wants you on her side."

"Maybe. Something seems odd about it all."

"Where've you been, pardner? Frank and I were about to send in the cavalry?"

"I thought we didn't have cavalry on this one."

"How about an angry single mom and a mean-looking guy in a wheelchair?"

"The sat phone's charge is down to twenty-seven percent," he observed.

"So I noticed. There's fresh batteries and a charger at the Lakeland Airport."

"I won't be able to pick them up right away. Tonight I'll try to transfer the senator's computer notes from Gloria's room in town."

"All you'll have to do is turn on the laptop, plug in the Clik wafer, and hook it to a phone line. I'll do the rest."

Erin used Helga, a computer server so powerful it could suck data out of a radish. She'd monitored Gloria's computer once in her hotel room, using the laptop's own operating system to inventory the machine and settings. It was a Toshiba Tecra, with a Clik II drive. Unfortunately the forty-megabyte Clik disk, the matchbook-sized wafer Link had just seen, had not been loaded.

"For your info," Erin said, "I'm doing a V-A on Gloria." Helga was a whiz at voice analyses.

"How much of what she said was truth?"

"The analysis is mixed."

"Gloria said she has a cold. Would that make a difference?"

"Maybe. I'll send the tape to Gordon Tower since the FBI lab has the largest audio comparison library in the world, and hope he cooperates more than he has been. For now there's a sixty-three percent probability that she was telling the truth. You can *probably* trust her."

Link paused. "I'm not sure I want to do that just yet."

"Here's an uglier number, pardner. Your battery's down to twenty-six percent, so this is your final transmission until you install a fresh one. The good news is you can periodically go to receive-only and continue listening all the way down to five percent."

"What's the procedure?"

"Helga will transmit at four, eight, and twelve around the clock—my time, not yours, so subtract an hour. Just switch to R-O and listen. I won't be able to receive your coordinates, so we'll use the ref coords to identify locations."

Meaning the three locations he'd stored in her computer and his memory.

She asked, "Do you have anything critical while we're connected?"

"Someone moved the senator's canoe, also the 'accessories.' "

"Any idea who?"

"Nothing firm."

When he started to tell her about the call from the investigator about the big rigs, she stopped him. "Helga recorded the conversation. Any guesses about what they're hauling?"

"I doubt it has anything to do with the reservation."

Erin reminded herself to drop another thousand into Ron Doughty's bank account. "How goes the search for the gym bag?"

"Joseph Richards is methodical. If it's up here, sooner or later he'll find it."

"You're down to a minute," she told Link. "A final consideration. How about we send the Mike Charlie Papa to keep an eye on things?"

MCP was an acronym for the mobile command post they used on large-scale projects. A stubby wide-body jet designed for the U.S. Army, the MCP employed advanced state-of-the-art systems for data collection. Erin could connect the MCP's sensor outputs with Helga and monitor distant situations as closely as if she were orbiting in the airplane.

"Hold off for now," said Link.

"Frank wants to do something. He's concerned. Uh-oh. You're at twenty-five percent. Get that fresh battery so we can talk. In the meantime, listen on R-O when you can and like you fighter jocks say, watch your six o'clock, pardner."

"Will do."

When Erin confirmed that the connection was terminated, a sense of foreboding swept through her. Silly, she decided. Link had not indicated he was in jeopardy. Still, Erin was uneasy. There was no way to support Link properly if he could not speak to her.

The Weyland Foundation was the richest private organization in the world. The Special Projects division had incredibly deep pockets, state-of-the-art equipment, modern aircraft, and a staff of trained personnel—yet they were legally restricted to operations outside the U.S. Now, because of the failure of a single battery, Link was as isolated as a castaway on a hostile island.

Frank Dubois had a standing request that she inform him of all developments where his good friend was concerned. When Erin contacted the chairman's office, he was meeting with the secretary of commerce. She left a simple message that Link had made contact, unable to relay the lingering feeling in the pit of her stomach that something was about to go very wrong.

Near Big Fish Lake

Patrolman First Class Marvin Yellowbird had been working on Willie's nerves, like finding fault because he'd curled up and slept in back of the Explorer.

"We've gotta be ready when they find the gym bag," Marvin carped.

Fucking Boy Scout, Willie thought as he sullenly tossed a stone into the swampy pond.

Pluck. He thought about the woman in the hotel room and the threat she'd made. He'd wanted to ask Sly Paquette what had become of her, but was afraid.

Thirty feet behind them, a vague figure stepped to the edge of the forest.

Willie tossed another pebble. *Pluck.*

"Don't do that," said Yellowbird.

Behind them, the vague figure moved to the Ford Explorer Willie had just vacated.

"Why?" *Pluck.*

Yellowbird shook his head in disgust. "You're like a kid. Tell you not to do something and you have to do it."

"Then stop telling me."

Pluck. At the instant of impact the figure pulled open the vehicle's rear door.

Willie tossed another stone.

Pluck. The figure moved away, his arms now full.

Yellowbird frowned as if he'd heard something, and turned toward the SUVs. "You left your car door open. Close it or the battery'll run down."

"You're just full of orders." Willie glared as he stalked to his vehicle. He started to slam the door, then peered inside. "Fuck!" he shouted, pulled out his 9 mm issue Beretta, and aimed at Marvin Yellowbird.

"Don't do that," Marvin said, flinching.

"Where'd you put the fuckin' box?"

"I don't know what you're talking about."

"The aluminum tubes. Where'd you put 'em?" Willie leaned over the backseat and vainly pawed around. He looked in the console box, found the necklace and bracelet he'd taken from the rich broad were also missing, and wanted to scream.

He turned and jabbed the barrel toward his partner. "I ain't shittin' you. You don't give me the fuckin' box an' the jewelry, I'll blow your goddamn head off."

"You had the box, not me. And would you aim that somewhere else?" Marvin Yellowbird stopped speaking and stared into the forest, mouth drooping.

Willie whirled. Saw a flash of brown, then—nothing. He had a helpless feeling in his stomach as he blindly squeezed off three shots. *Bam—bam—bam.*

There was only an echo.

"Who was that?" he cried, realizing someone had no-shit just stolen the box.

Marvin looked as shaken as Willie felt. "The hermit."

"Who the fuck is the hermit?"

"A spooky old guy who lives up here."

"Fuck spooky. I'll get it back." Willie started resolutely for the woods.

"Watch your ass. He carries a rifle."

Willie stopped, and looked about cautiously.

They both stared into the dense forest.

"The hermit?" Willie questioned.

"When I was a kid, we were told about a wild man up here who moved through the forest like a ghost. Ma used to scare us, saying if we were bad the old hermit would get us."

Willie walked to the edge of the forest. He tried yelling, ordering whoever it had been to bring back the fucking box!

After a couple of minutes he returned and stared dolefully into the Explorer. To hell with the jewelry, it was the box that could get him killed.

Marvin switched his mobile radio to base frequency.

"Who you callin'?"

"Sergeant Rose. He'll know what to do."

Willie's mind worked double time, trying to come up with alternatives. Rose had said to keep the box with him at all times, to act like it contained gold. But Willie knew where the real orders had come from. He had visions of being dragged before Sly Paquette by the Junkman, who was bigger than a side of beef, to explain why he'd left the box in an unlocked vehicle.

He pointed the 9 mm at Marvin's face. "Turn off your fuckin' radio," he snarled. A fuzzy plan was forming in Willie's brain, not a thorough or good one, but anything was better than being beaten to death with a fucking pipe.

"Turn around," he told his partner.

When Willie jerked his pistol from his holster, Marvin Yellowbird did not argue. But when he was then marched to the edge of the pond, which was filled with marsh plants and mire, and told to keep walking, he began to plead.

"Keep walking." Willie holstered his own gun and lifted the one he'd just taken.

"I'll sink in this shit, man."

Willie wasn't sure how to end it. Maybe with a good scaring so Marvin would keep his mouth shut? Maybe with a licking, so he'd say he was the one who had fucked up? Let him sink up to his eyeballs and tell him either change his story or go under?

When Marvin was knee-deep, thrashing in the muck to keep going, Willie wondered if he shouldn't order him to stand still so he'd start sinking. That ought to scare the piss out of anyone.

Somehow he had to get him to say it was him and not Willie who had screwed up.

Yellowbird twisted his head, showing frightened eyes.

"Turn back around!" Willie yelled, putting pressure on the trigger.

"Don't!" Marvin cried, just as the weapon discharged. The bullet struck his right shoulder. Yellowbird screamed in pain, unable to flee since he was stuck in the mire.

Willie's mouth drooped. The trigger pull on Marvin's weapon was lighter than his own.

Too late to stop! He hardly thought as he hastily fired three more times, aiming for Marvin's back. The first round missed, the second struck his left shoulder and pushed him partway around—and the third hit him squarely in the nape of the neck. Yellowbird wavered, clutching at his bloody throat where the bullet had emerged, mouth opening and closing as he attempted to speak. Except for a series of wet gurgles, he was silent.

Willie lowered the pistol and immediately puked. When he had no more breakfast to vomit, he looked again. Yellowbird was down, writhing in the muddy water, weakening as he bled out. No longer trying to get away. Just—dying.

"Oh *shit*!" Willie wailed, wishing desperately that he had not shot Marvin Yellowbird. Knowing he could not undo it. Finally he picked up the handheld radio that Marvin had switched to Sergeant Rose's frequency and keyed the mike. He stopped then, trying to remember the story he'd come up with as he looked out at Yellowbird's final shudders and twitches. Marvin was face down, floating more than sinking.

He became still as Sergeant Rose's voice came over the air. *"Did someone try to call?"*

"The box is gone," Willie whispered hoarsely, staring out at what he'd done.

22

The driver of the Suburban squeezed past an SUV on the narrow road. Jenifer Toussaint nodded from the other vehicle, but Sydney played her role and glared in return.

Sydney stopped at the search site just long enough to hand over the list of new locations to Joseph Richards, then begged off, blaming her cold, and departed.

She had ventured to the north side to learn about Anderson's relationship with Senator Eddie and any connection with the Weyland Foundation—and also to see if they were closer to finding the gym bag, since half of the time Carmine Gracchi had allotted them had passed.

Then too, she'd decided to have another lark in her role as Gloria Vasson.

Instead, the entire time with Anderson she'd felt uneasy, almost in jeopardy.

Sydney was not only a master in the art of deception, she was also uncannily good with interrogation. From the moment he'd approached the Suburban, her warning antenna had cried *Danger!* and after only a moment's discussion she'd known that Anderson was no guide, no charter pilot down on his luck. He was one of the toughest operatives she'd faced. He had beaten Howarski in the air, disarmed the all-but-invisible Claymore mines, and observed her with penetrating eyes. She'd considered having him taken alive, to learn about the covert arm of the Weyland Foundation, a group so efficient it was sealed even from her sources, but she did not dare take the chance.

Her mind asked, *Why did I allow him to go on this long?* but she knew the answer. Like Howarski, she regarded Native Americans as inferior.

Ten miles farther she would rendezvous with a helicopter. Sly Paquette would be aboard, and she would issue an order. She wanted Lincoln Anderson *dead*, and she wanted it done soon.

Sydney heard gunshots and immediately reached for the police radio.

Link returned to packing the camp for the move. As he thought of the odd visit and his discussion with Erin, he felt increasingly wary of Gloria. Another of his gut feelings.

He was hefting the outboard motor when Jenifer drove into camp.

"I passed *someone* on the road. What was she doing here?"

"She was on her way to the search site," he said.

Jen sauntered over, hips swaying sensuously in tight jeans. "Did I tell you how Manido gals handle guys who cheat?" She made a snipping motion. "Both of 'em. Think about it. You can run, but you've gotta sleep."

He laughed.

"Would you get the boat and motor ready while I slip into my wet suit. Something long and dark's in the water about forty feet from shore. Joseph thinks it's the dugout."

"Don't take chances." She knew about the mines.

"Why don't you come along and operate the motor while I . . ."

They heard distant gunshots, three of them in rapid fire.

"Hunters?" she wondered.

"Not unless they're using pistols."

Jenifer hurried to the Jeep and called over short-range radio.

Joseph Richards responded. The shots had not come

from the search site. "I'll check it out," he added in his stalwart tone.

Link shook his head at Jenifer.

"Mr. Anderson is responsible for our safety. Keep everyone there while we look into it."

"I think I should . . ."

"Please don't argue," Jenifer snapped.

Link started the Jeep's engine. "Wait here."

"I'm going," she said resolutely.

"I'd rather you stay. Two reservation cops are parked in that direction."

Her face darkened. "They're not supposed to be here."

Link realized she was not going to remain, and drove southward. "I got up close this morning. They even knew where we'd be searching."

"No one but Gloria and Richards were supposed to know that."

He drove as fast as he dared on the terrible road.

Another gunshot sounded. Then three more, in stagger fire.

"Nine millimeter," Link confirmed, "like the reservation patrolmen carry."

Jenifer's heart pounded as she hung on. They'd continued for a mile past the turnoff to the expedition search site when Link slid to a stop, turned the wheel, and backed into the forest.

He handed over the car keys.

"I'm going with you," she said.

"I want to approach them unseen, Jen."

"I was raised here. I don't exactly stumble around in the forest," she said caustically.

Link placed his Western hat on the seat, quietly closed the door, and eyed her clothing.

She wore a rust-colored jacket, black sweater, dark blue fanny pack, and faded jeans, which she knew was good camouflage.

"Try to be quiet," he said as he scooped up leaves and piled them onto the vehicle.

Jenifer pitched in, depositing debris. "Mind telling me why we're doing this?"

"Later. Same with any other questions."

She patted her fanny pack. "I have my revolver."

"Keep it there." With that he set out walking. Jenifer followed him across the road and into the forest, directly toward the source of the gunshots.

Link spoke in a hardly audible voice. "Damp leaves muffle sound. Watch out for twigs and branches."

"I know that." She felt irritation that he was treating her like a stumblebum. She'd been taught to be quiet when approaching game. Her eyes shifted to the ground before her, then back to Link, and she continued the drill as they went on.

She caught him observing her and wondered why he was being so critical. If he'd believed her when she said she knew how to be quiet in the forest.

As the thought echoed, Jenifer stepped on an unseen twig that cracked so loudly it sounded like a rifle shot. She froze and stared downward, shifted her weight, and then looked back at Link—or at least where he'd been. There was nothing there!

Jenifer looked about, not liking the idea of being left.

She forced herself to stop and calm down. *Think!* Link had been with her a moment before, and could not have just—disappeared.

Jenifer was breathing fiercely when she heard his quiet voice. "There's a clearing with a pond thirty yards ahead. Two men. One's dead; the other's waving a pistol."

Jenifer looked around frantically, yet she couldn't see Link!

"Be *still*," he whispered. She saw a deliberate hand motion and then Link, crouched beside a tree. Even when she knew where he was, he blended with the forest.

"Don't leave me like that," Jenifer whispered, angrier at herself for her panic than at him.

Only then did his words sink in. One of the men in the clearing was *dead*.

There were sounds of clumsy movement. "Who—" she whispered, but Link gave a shake of his head.

"Hermit?" came a plaintive male voice. "*Please* come back."

Link touched her hand and motioned for her to crouch beside him.

"I won't hurt you, man," the man's sad voice called. "You can keep the jewelry. Just bring back the box."

Jenifer knelt by Link, increasingly frightened.

A large man with a florid face and terrible acne appeared precisely where they looked. He was uniformed, and his face was twisted with fear even though he brandished a pistol and stabbed the muzzle this way and that. He stumbled forward for a few more feet, and she recognized the patrolman named Willie, known among the Manido as one of the worst.

"Aw, shit," he blurted, then fled back in the direction from which he'd come.

Link cocked his head as if he heard something new, then touched her arm. "Let's go closer." He crept forward, following the frightened policeman.

Jenifer followed, this time making sure she avoided twigs, wishing she'd not insisted on coming. Also wishing he'd taken the pistol as she mimicked his fluid motions.

He stopped. So did she. He started; she followed and decided they were moving in a circle around the clearing. It did not matter. No way he was getting out of her sight again.

They paused at the fringe of the clearing, and beyond a veil of leaves she saw Willie pacing and shaking his head dismally. Then she discerned distant sounds, and a moment later the *thup-thup-thup* of helicopter blades.

Link pointed at bushes clumped about the base of a pine tree. When Jenifer frowned in nonunderstanding, he pulled her down so she was curled against the base of the tree, then held her so fiercely she was unable to move.

"They're about to land," Link said into her ear. "At least one set of eyes will be looking down at us, so be as still as possible."

As Jenifer felt the violent downdraft caused by the blades, she realized that Link had covered the Jeep because of this possibility. The helicopter made several approaches before the blades changed pitch as the craft descended, and finally came to earth.

"Stay here," Link said into her ear. "Do not move."

23

After Willie's frantic radio call, Sergeant Rose had contacted Sly Paquette—his was the only radio with Paquette's frequency set in—but Sly was not interested that one of his men had been killed. When Rose added that the treaties had been taken, Sly squealed so loud the sergeant's ear ached.

"I'm driving out to investigate."

"That'd take forever. Get over here. I've got a helicopter on the way."

Ten minutes later George Rose and two M16-wielding cops arrived at Rock Lake to find a green chopper, the ECOL-REC, LTD. logo on its side, idling. The pilot accelerated beneath the overcast and took only fifteen minutes to get to the marsh pond.

On the descent Rose examined the partially denuded autumn forest, hoping to get an eyeball on the hermit—or whoever had killed Marvin Yellowbird. Willie was below, gawking. After a third pass he thought to move the vehicles so there'd be room to land.

As they touched down, George Rose clambered out. One of his best was down. Marvin Yellowbird had been one of few Indians remaining on the force. Rose knew his family well. He remembered that when he'd recruited him, he'd been pleased that he came from good stock.

Marvin was twenty feet out in the swampy pond, half submerged in muck that was as thick as chowder and painted with bloody streaks.

A sigh bled from Rose's lips as he stood at water's edge, feeling leaden hearted.

Behind him Sly Paquette asked Willie about the cardboard box.

"Me 'n Marvin was waitin' in case the expedition people started for town. I had to take a shit, so I went in the woods while he guarded the box an' watched."

Rose turned to observe. Paquette was giving Willie the X-ray stare that made people think he could see right through them. The Junkman stood by in case his boss decided on firmer questioning, making Willie so nervous he was visibly trembling.

Sergeant Rose recalled how Marvin Yellowbird had come to him when he'd learned his fellow patrolmen were taking bribes.

Willie continued. "I heard Marvin yelling something about a hermit, then some shots, so I ran back and saw this old bald guy in leather clothes runnin' like hell with the box."

"You chased him?"

"He had a rifle." Willie gushed words, his eyes wide with fright. "I got a couple rounds off, but then he took a shot, and I know better than to fight a rifle with a pistol, so I ducked in back of a tree. Next time I looked he was gone, so I checked on my—uh—partner."

When Marvin had told him about the bribes, Rose had said to go along. They'd take proper action when the time was right and he'd gathered enough evidence. He remembered how Marvin had looked at him, as if to say, *I believe you, Sergeant Rose.* Trusting him.

"So tell me again who took the box," Sly Paquette said to Willie.

"Marvin told me about this creepy guy lives here on the north side called the hermit."

"I heard of him, but never about him hurtin' anybody."

"This time he sure as fuck did." Willie's voice was high, his eyes shifting wildly.

Paquette stared at the forest, his expression unsure. He shook his head glumly. "First the gym bag, now the fuckin' box."

Rose wondered if right then Sly wasn't as afraid as Willie.

The Junkman came over and handed Paquette a hand-held radio. "Sydney wants to talk," he said. "She heard about what happened over the radio."

Long-range communications on the north side were provided by radio repeaters mounted in the Explorers. The system was insecure, for anyone with a fifty-dollar police scanner could listen in. Fortunately few people in the Northwoods were that inquisitive.

Sydney had a radio on Paquette's frequency? Sergeant Rose wondered, as Sly walked to the tree line, where others could not overhear.

Rose looked sadly out at Marvin Yellowbird's back, then at Willie. "You pathetic shit, why did you kill him?"

Willie's eyes widened. "I didn't kill nobody."

"The hermit steals things, but he's never harmed anyone in his life. Why'd you kill Marvin? To switch blame?"

"Hey, man. I . . ."

"You say the hermit shot at you with a rifle?"

"He did."

"You ever try to fire a rifle while you were carrying a cardboard box?"

Willie glowered. "*He* did."

"The hermit's carried that old rifle all his life. President Grant presented it to his great-grandfather after the Civil War for helping to keep the Chippewa on the Union side. Kids called him names, even hit him with sticks because he moved funny and made strange sounds, but he never once fired that rifle. I doubt he'd even know how to load it if he somehow got bullets."

Willie was sullen. "I don't give a fuck about his life story." He brightened then, and gave Rose a cunning look. "Maybe he stole Marvin's pistol."

Sly Paquette returned, looking more sure of himself. He returned the radio to Billy Junkins and motioned at the pond. "This got out—a scary old man on the loose, killin' police officers—we'd have reporters running all over. Next thing, they'd be interviewing people like the expedition members. We can't have that, so it didn't happen. *Nobody* got killed, okay?"

Rose kept an even face. "What do I say to Marvin's parents?"

"Tell 'em he took off down to Wausau on personal business, maybe to see some girl. Haul the body into town and stick it in his car trunk, and I'll have one of my casino workers drive it down. There'll be a trailer fire in the morning."

"He was shot. The Wausau coroner won't be fooled."

"There's others'll worry about that. We do our part. They'll do theirs."

Sergeant Rose knew not to argue further. He called out to the policemen standing at the edge of the pond, "Recover the body."

Neither man appeared pleased with the prospect, but while they might not be suited in their roles as cops, they were exceedingly well paid. Both began pulling off shoes and socks.

Sly Paquette looked at Rose. "Use Willie to help get back the treaties. Wasn't for him runnin' back like he did, we'd have never even known the hermit did it."

Rose did not remind him that Willie had been the one entrusted with the box.

The cops complained about the cold as they slogged into the pond. When they approached Marvin's body they had difficulty staying upright.

"Willie'll never get anywhere near the hermit," Rose speculated.

"Sure he will, 'cause you and Billy'll be with him." Paquette regarded the Junkman. "Think you can track him down?"

"Sure." The Junkman looked pleased at the prospect.

Paquette looked at Rose. "Sydney just said Anderson's dangerous. You see him, cap the fucker, but make sure Richards and the others keep lookin' for the gym bag. Soon as they find it, get rid of 'em all. No witnesses."

Rose's heart sank as he followed Paquette to the helicopter.

"I've got to pick up someone with the chopper," said

Paquette. He stopped thoughtfully. "If you hear from somebody named Sydney, do what she says."

"What does she look like?"

"Don't ask. She wants you to know, she'll tell you." He climbed aboard and the blades clattered to a roar. A moment later the craft lifted off.

The helicopter's sounds were still receding when a still benumbed Sergeant George Rose sensed motion in the periphery of his vision, turned, and watched as a slate gray Range Rover pulled up in front of one of the Explorers. Two men emerged, looked inquisitively in the direction of the helo noise, then walked toward him. The skinny one—Joseph Richards, who he remembered was the expedition leader—had a pistol strapped to his waist. He squinted at the pond while the second one panned with a video camera.

Sergeant Rose shouted for his men to "Stop!" Meaning to stop dragging Marvin Yellowbird's corpse from the pond.

"What the *hell* are you doing here!" he exploded as he strode toward the newcomers, hoping to block their view. When Richards craned to peer around him, Rose grasped his arm, spun him about, and propelled him toward the road.

"Let go!" Richards yelled, but Rose kept pushing him along for his own good.

"Was—is that man dead?"

"Of course not."

As his arm was released, Richards angrily pushed away. "We heard gunfire."

"We're running a training exercise. A couple of my officers got in some target practice, and a few minutes ago one fell into the pond. He'll be fine. Now *leave*."

"Council promised to keep everyone out of the north side during our search."

Rose glanced. The cops were shielding Marvin Yellowbird's body. When he turned back the second man was shooting more footage.

Rose yanked the video camera from his grasp. "Closed training session," he said, winging it. "No photography allowed."

"Fuck that. Give it back," the cameraman demanded.

Anger swept over Rose. The turning of his police force into a cruel joke was exacerbated by Marvin Yellowbird's murder. Now he was having to protect these fools from themselves.

"We weren't briefed about restrictions," Richards said imperiously. "I have authorization from the council to search the north side of the reservation without interference."

"That camera's private property," added the other man.

Rose spoke through clenched teeth. "Get—into—your—vehicle."

"We were authorized . . ." Richards began.

Billy Junkins had stalked forward to help. As soon as they saw the giant, the two men scrambled into the Range Rover.

Rose went to the driver's window. "Get on with your search. I'll return the camera later."

As they accelerated away, his anger diminished into foreboding.

The policemen dragged Marvin Yellowbird's body ashore, and wiped away mud and blood. Under Rose's supervision they wrapped the corpse in a tarp and hefted it into the back of one of the Explorers.

He told one of the patrolmen to return to town with the body.

"No way I'm going alone with some crazy guy out there with a rifle."

Sergeant Rose did not argue. After Willie had requisitioned one of their M16s for his "manhunt," the two men departed, the patrolmen peering cautiously at the road ahead.

He called the police desk and told the surly female dispatcher to expedite deployment of two patrolmen replacements. They should bring M16s and shotguns.

The Junkman stood gazing down the road where the intruders had disappeared. "You better tell Sly about those guys with the camera," he rumbled, "in case they run into town."

"Yeah," Rose said wearily. After ordering the dispatcher to alert the roadblocks to detain any expedition members who tried to return, he switched to Paquette's private channel. There was no feedback, an indication that the radio had been turned off.

"You shoulda killed 'em while they were here." Willie's answer to everything.

"There's a chance they didn't know what they were looking at."

Billy Junkins turned toward the forest and grew a suspicious look.

"Is something out there?" Rose asked.

"Maybe," Junkins said in his rumbling growl. He began to stalk the periphery of the clearing, moving with surprising efficiency for a man of his size.

Jenifer remained curled about the base of the bush as Link had told her. While she'd seen little, she'd overheard enough to be frightened beyond belief.

She did not see Link return, just felt his hand on her shoulder and heard his whisper. "The Junkman's getting suspicious. It's time to leave."

He helped her to her feet and started for the road. Jenifer followed, placing her steps carefully, remembering the snapping twig.

When they were far enough away not to be heard, he said, "You did well."

"Sly Paquette came so close he almost stepped on me," she said. "He was talking on his radio with someone named Sydney. I think she's in charge, Link."

There was no response.

"Aren't you curious?"

"Very."

"Just after the helicopter left, I heard Joseph Richards's voice."

"He and Turf showed up," Link told her. "Rose wasn't sure how much they saw or how to handle it. He's waiting on instructions from Paquette."

"We're in trouble, aren't we, Link?"

"Probably. We'd better get to the others before Rose and Willie."

"The Junkman scares the pee out of me."

He slowed as if listening for something, then picked up his step. "They just drove past, headed for the search site."

"What do we do now?"

"Hope Richards was smart enough to skedaddle back to the base camp."

24

The Range Rover had been hastily parked, and Joseph Richards, Turf Siegel, and Dr. Brogg were huddled in serious conversation.

As Jenifer dismounted, Richards turned on her. "You didn't tell us anything about a police exercise."

"There *was* no exercise. One of the policemen was killed and the others were covering it up, like they've done with everything else on the reservation."

Turf Siegel said, "I thought that guy was dead. Too much blood."

"Joseph feels we should go into town and lodge a complaint," Dr. Brogg said.

Jenifer shook her head vigorously. "They have got orders to shoot Link on sight, and as soon as we find the gym bag, they'll kill the rest of us."

"But you're on the council," Brogg reasoned. There was fear in his tone.

"That won't help. The reservation's been taken over by criminals and there's no way they'll allow us to leave the north side alive. We've got to get away *now*."

There was a hush of disbelief. Richards squinted nervously as he lit a cigarette.

"Know what I think?" said Turf. "We oughta get the hell off this entire *reservation*."

"The roads to town are blocked." Jen was exasperated with their reluctance. "Look, we'll tell you everything we know once we're out of danger, but for now, please just trust us."

Richards shook his head. "I spoke with their sergeant. It's only a misunderstanding."

"Misunderstanding? Remember the big man at the pond? The Junkman kills people for a living. Then there's a psychopath in uniform named Willie who enjoys hurting people."

Turf nodded solemnly. "Those cops were up to no good, Joseph."

"I don't like any of this," Brogg said in a high voice.

Richards tried to regain control. "I'm responsible for the expedition. The rest of you remain here while I drive into town and demand an explanation."

"Sorry," Link said in his quiet voice. "We'll need both vehicles."

Richards's face reddened with anger. "Damn you, Anderson, stay out of this." His fingers curled around the butt of the SIG Sauer.

"Don't be foolish," said Link.

As the pistol cleared its holster, Link grasped the muzzle with his right hand and pressed upward on Richards's wrist with his left. Done with sufficient force, the maneuver was designed to snap the radiocarpal joint. He used only enough to disarm.

Link ejected the magazine into his hand, checked to see there was no round in the chamber, and dropped the empty automatic back into its holster.

The only casualty was the cigarette that Richards had dropped to the ground.

"I suggest we travel light," said Link, walking past a disbelieving Joseph Richards. "Food, sleeping bags, catalytic heaters, and warm clothing. It's going to get colder."

Alpha-Six Search Site

When Rose arrived at lakeside, the expedition members were neither working nor in sight.

Back at the marsh pond, Billy Junkins had discovered

sign that someone had indeed hidden and watched them. *The hermit?* Rose had wondered.

The Junkman had surprised him. "There were two," he'd announced. "One was a woman."

Rose had remembered Paquette's order to shoot Anderson on sight and to force the expedition members to find the gym bag—and then kill them.

Not that they wouldn't get away with it. *Someone* had proven to be a magician at deluding the world about Senator Eddie's death. Was that the work of Sydney? He did not know how to categorize her, and still had no idea what she looked like.

When the Junkman had announced that one of the watchers was a woman, Willie had shown immediate interest. Rose trusted him not an inch around females. Complaints had been forwarded from various police departments around the Northwoods about his molestation of visitors, yet Sly Paquette allowed no punitive action. Bullying and rape privileges were a part of his men's benefit package. When they confronted the expedition members, Rose would be hard-pressed to protect fiery Jenifer Toussaint.

"I say we take them now," Willie had said, grinning and brandishing the M16.

Rose had compromised. "We'll move closer while we wait on our backup."

Now they stared out at the abandoned drying racks and storage sheds.

"What now, ace?" Willie asked, using his derisive tone.

"You wait while I think," said Rose. Had Richards moved his searchers to another site, or returned to their camp across the lake? It mattered little so long as they didn't run.

Willie began to fool with the M16, until it seemed likely that sooner or later he'd shoot something. *Hopefully himself,* thought Rose.

Billy Junkins filled the rear seat, staring out at the drying racks with his blank expression, popping sunflower seeds into his cavernous mouth from a sack.

Willie slapped the M16's clip into place, ejected it, slapped it in again.

Rose turned the Explorer around and headed back to the intersection. There he turned right and accelerated as much as he dared on the terrible road. The Explorer was one of their oldest, with worn springs and shocks.

"You gotta be in such a hurry?" Willie complained, after an impact that jarred teeth.

They smashed into a chasm that was worse yet, and Willie cursed louder.

While they'd packed essential items Link had topped off gas tanks from the jerry cans. He made a final walk-through to see if they were leaving anything critical.

Joseph Richards approached. "There's an abandoned cranberry farm a couple of hours from here, and a path that connects with a highway on the Michigan side."

"Maybe."

"How about taking the canoe?"

"No time."

"You had time to load a case of flares."

Link did not respond. He heard distant vehicle engine sounds headed their way.

Sergeant Rose slowed as they passed the old Adcock cabin. Not much farther and he killed the engine. It felt good, stopping.

He climbed out and listened, heard the sounds of distant voices. After a while there was a ditty of music. A radio? Polka music played, confirming it.

Unless it was purposeful deception, the expedition members were likely in camp, and he did not wish to confront them until he had overwhelming numbers and firepower. Joseph Richards was armed, and there were likely other weapons.

He kept his voice down as he radioed the patrolmen, still an hour away, and told them to proceed to the Adcock cabin. After a question and answer session regarding directions, he asked if they'd passed anyone. Only the other black and white, they said.

As he waited and listened, suspicions niggled in Rose's head. Policeman's intuition. Like his wife often told him, law officers are a distrusting lot. Still he waited.

Heavy mist began to fall. Rose opened the rear hatch, found his rain slicker and pulled it on, and remained outside, listening. Finally he rapped on the window to gain the Junkman's attention. "Their camp's less than a half mile. We need to know how many are there, how many weapons, that sort of thing. Try to stay out of sight so they don't see you."

Junkins popped a sunflower seed into his mouth, cracked it, and spat the shell onto the Explorer's floor, all the while staring at the foliage where Rose pointed. He climbed out with difficulty—being too large for the doorway—and set out in a smooth and easy gait.

"Guy knows his shit," said Willie, toying with the M16. "You see how he knew a woman had hid back there, and how he moves like he don't weigh nothing."

"Used to be, the Manido People were good in the woods."

Willie snickered. "All I see are a bunch of lazy drunks."

Sergeant Rose wished Marvin Yellowbird had been more alert and shot first.

Fifteen minutes later Billy Junkins returned. He'd seen no vehicles and no people, just empty tents, scattered gear, and a battery radio that was turned up.

Rose climbed back into the vehicle and resolutely started up. They were running.

The rain added to Rose's dismal mood as he walked from one tent to the next. Willie was close behind, examining every loose item he came across to see if it was worth looting.

"Would you leave their shit alone?"

"You're turnin' into an old lady, Rose. Next thing you know, your dick'll fall off."

There was little he could do about disciplining Willie this side of whipping his butt, and thereafter he'd have to watch his back, as Marvin Yellowbird had failed to do. Then there was the problem of how Sly Paquette and Billy Junkins might react. As usual Rose did nothing.

That the search group had fled was no longer a question. Not with their sleeping bags and heavy clothing missing. The problem was to determine where they'd gone.

The north side was vast. A hundred lakes, large and small. Dense forestland crisscrossed by hundreds of miles of roads and trails. The fortunate part was that it was deserted, with no inhabitants for them to turn to.

When the radio buzzer sounded, Willie rushed to answer. As Rose turned on his radio, Willie was saying how everything was fucked-up, and Sly Paquette was asking, "What the hell you talkin' about?"

Rose snatched the handheld from Willie, and spoke into his own radio. "Disregard that."

"What's going on?"

He explained how Richards and his assistant had shown up, then about the Junkman finding sign of two persons, one a woman, who'd been close enough to overhear everything. Finally he said the expedition members had fled from the base camp.

"They're running," he concluded. "I'm trying to guess where."

"What's the Junkman say? He's good with that sorta shit."

"He's out lookin' around the woods."

"Dumber'n a rubber mallet, but he knows trackin'. He's half Aleut."

Rose was surprised. An Alaskan Indian?

"So they're running," Paquette mused, taking it with surprising calm. Rose never knew what to expect. Given the same news, one time he'd come unglued, the next he'd shrug it off.

"If they heard everything," Paquette considered, "they know the treaties are bullshit."

"Probably."

Willie edged closer so he could listen in.

"You gotta bring 'em back, and convince 'em to go back to work and that we ain't *really* gonna kill 'em when it's over." Paquette paused. "Wait a minute while I call Sydney."

Rose waited.

"No changes," Paquette said when he came back on.

"She says to catch them and take out Anderson. Hurt him bad first and get their attention so they'll go back to work."

The sour taste returned to Sergeant Rose's mouth. While he'd done despicable deeds for Paquette, he had never slain anyone.

At his side Willie was grinning, liking what he heard.

"Sydney said you might want to look at the old cranberry farm."

"How about the hermit?"

"You see him, shoot him. Now give Willie your radio. I need to tell him something."

Willie took the instrument, turned away from Rose, and muttered a few "yes sirs" and "no sirs." He then shut off the radio and handed it back, wearing a sardonic smirk, and went back to stuffing everything of value into a plastic garbage sack.

The Junkman emerged from the forest, looking like he thought something was amiss but was not convinced what it was. He raised his head and smelled the air.

"Was someone out there again?" Rose asked.

"Maybe" was all the giant rumbled.

"Mr. Paquette thinks they're at the old cranberry farm. When we goin' after them?" Willie asked.

"As soon as our backup arrives," Rose answered, wondering why Sydney believed the expedition members might go to that particular location.

If they did so, Rose thought, *Lincoln Anderson had made a terrible choice.*

25

One mile north of the camp Nek-kah hurried his awk-ward but distance-consuming gait, feeling concern. The giant was a tracker with highly developed senses, and was quick on his feet. If Lin-kya underestimated him, he would be in peril.

At the camp, Nek-kah had made noises to attract the giant into the forest, then crept back to observe and listen to Rose and Willie. While he was not good with nuances, he had worked to interpret what he'd heard into the world he knew. "Cranberry marsh," he under-stood, and also that they awaited the arrival of more bad men, coming to harm Lin-kya.

Nek-kah arrived at the T intersection where Lin-kya had paused to decide on his route of travel. Ahead was the abandoned cranberry marsh, to his left the road into the heart of the north side. He went into the forest between the forks for a dozen yards and laboriously removed stones that covered a ground cache he'd burrowed into the side of an earthen mound. He then emptied the box's contents and replaced them with a single canvas-clad mine.

Weeks before he had observed the people at the "place that smells bad" testing one of the devices. When it had exploded he'd cringed, and his ears had rung for hours afterward. He'd been afraid of the ones they'd planted until he'd seen Lin-kya disarm and carry two away.

Lin-kya had left them by the dugout, before Nek-kah moved them to this better place.

When he had once again masked the cache from view—not taking much time with it since he would soon return—he hefted the box and set out.

Wilderness Road

The road was brutal and, with the constant drizzle, slippery. Jenifer drove slowly, carefully remaining in the center of the road. Link was beside her in the passenger's seat. The others followed in the Rover. At the T intersection Richards had called over the built-in short-range UHF radio, suggesting they'd made a wrong turn. When he called again, Link told him to stay off the air unless there was an emergency.

She reached over and squeezed his hand. "Wow, am I happy you're here."

"You're not afraid?"

"After this morning nothing frightens me."

"Not even being followed by a bunch of bad-tempered thugs?"

"You're pretty tough yourself, Link. You're also good at sneaking around in the woods."

He looked as if he was considering her choice of words, then had her stop at a fallen pine that partially blocked the road. After anchoring the Jeep and securing a pulley to a sturdy tree, he winched the pine across the road.

"Aren't you afraid they'll catch up?" Dr. Brogg called out nervously from the Rover.

"Sergeant Rose is cautious," Link said.

Another mile and they stopped to haul a second fallen tree onto the road, that one a large maple. Jenifer and Turf Siegel pitched in, getting soggy in the process.

"Joseph says they'll just drag them back out of the way," called Dr. Brogg.

"He's not being observant," said Link.

Jenifer explained, "The Explorers don't have winches. They'll have to go around or chop their way through."

"He thinks we should have looked for a road at a cranberry farm."

"I know." Link finished with the pulley and started the electric winch.

Back in their vehicle, Jenifer moved out slowly. "What about the cranberry farm?"

"It was on the list of search sites Gloria brought out."

"It's not a good idea to go there?"

"Jason said there were no back doors. He would have known about a wagon road."

"You're a regular chatterbox, Lincoln, but I love you anyway." She was pleased that he did not panic at the word. "*One* of us had to say it," she added.

Men had to be trained first to accept, then to say such things.

Jen grew reflective. "I'm gonna miss the Alpha camp. Remember the island? I went screaming right past the infatuation stage on our second visit to the island."

Not one to take the hint or become maudlin, and despite the fact that he must remember telling her they could not possibly have had sex that many times, Link said, "I have a question."

"Ask away. It might calm my nerves."

"I thought you were fearless?"

"Men forget flowers. Women change our minds. I'm a bit nervous. What's the question?"

"What's the trouble between Gloria and you."

"It's not something I talk about."

"It's important."

"Only because I love you, understand?" She took her time. "The last time I visited Washington, Eddie invited me to stay with them. They hadn't been married long and that night over dinner he told her something I'd wanted kept quiet."

She hesitated. "Go on," he prodded.

"Eddie told her that he and I were—related. Gloria had drunk a wine too many, and hinted that he should be prudent and ask for a DNA test. When Eddie said it was unnecessary, she argued. When things kept heating up, I packed and left to find a hotel."

They drove on.

"Gloria sent an apology, which I didn't answer, so she sent another. After a third try she stopped. The next time I saw her was at the council meeting."

When he didn't respond, Jenifer asked, "Why did you want to know?"

"Something Gloria said." He did not elaborate. "Tell me about her."

"I'd rather talk about us." When he didn't respond she sighed. "Gloria is the kind of female other women hate. For instance she hasn't had a dollar's worth of cosmetic surgery, but her skin is flawless and she uses little makeup. When I'm her age I'll have to use a trowel."

She waited for Link to tell her she had wonderful skin, but he just sat there.

"Also, so you don't feel you have to observe too closely, she has a figure any twenty-year-old would kill for." When again he didn't respond, Jenifer frowned. "Talk to me, would you?"

"She claims the senator told her about meeting me. She knows I'm not Manido-Ojibwe, and suspects that I work for the Weyland Foundation."

"Damn!" She thought about it. "So what did she want?"

"She said she needed someone on her side."

"You believed her?"

"Not especially." Link explained how he'd transmitted their conversation over a satellite phone. "Erin analyzed her voice and feels she was probably telling the truth."

"That's sneaky!" Then she realized what he'd said. "Your phone *works* out here?"

"Not any more." He explained the battery problem.

She drove in silence for a while. "I'm upset, Lincoln. I tell you things I don't tell anyone else, and you're holding back."

"Not much." His mind was obviously working hard. "What did Gloria give as the reason we don't get along?"

"Because you'd had an affair with the senator."

"That's *obscene!* Eddie Adcock was my father! He was also a gentleman." She glared at the road. "Sly Paquette's spreading that rumor, but he's a real low-life scumbag. Gloria *certainly* knows better." She muttered a few choice words.

2:20 P.M.—*White Dog Lake*

The narrow end of White Dog Lake appeared on their right. Another half mile and Link showed Jenifer where to turn off, then asked her to proceed down a twisting path to the fallen-down cabin that Jason had explained had been the childhood home of the hermit.

"Let's get out of the rain while we talk," he said.

As they filed inside, Richards found a place away from the others, and lit a cigarette.

"Joseph feels we should have gone to the cranberry farm," said Dr. Brogg.

"There's a way out," said Richards. "An old wagon path."

Link nosed around. The structure was small, with a living area and two sleeping chambers with hand-hewn bed frames.

"Are you listening?" Richards demanded. When there was no response he added, "If you're upset because of the pistol, I'm sorry. I *certainly* wouldn't have used it."

"That's reassuring." Link settled by a window.

Richards tried again. "Why don't we at least check to see if the path exists?"

"The cranberry farm may be a trap," said Link. "I'll learn more tonight."

Richards sighed. "Would you explain why we're running like a pack of thieves."

Intersection, Wilderness Road

The two policemen arrived late, yet Sergeant Rose was glad he'd waited. Impatience too often preceded error in life-threatening situations.

With the reinforcements following, he led the way

north for a mile to a T intersection, where he stopped
and pondered. A faded sign showed the cranberry farm
was a dozen miles ahead. To his left lay the bulk of
the reservation, with roads that twisted serpentine-like
through the forest. There were no distinctive tire tracks
in either direction—it had rained steadily for the past
two hours—yet he was drawn toward the heart of the
north side.

According to Sydney's suggestion, the group had
likely gone to the cranberry marsh, yet something inside
him argued differently.

"Jesus," griped Willie. "You heard Sly say to check
out the cranberry farm."

"We'll look at both," Rose decided. "I'll send the others on, and we'll take the turnoff."

Willie snorted. "I'm going with them," he said, and
threw open the door.

Rose did not argue. Getting rid of Willie for even a
short while sounded good.

Willie pulled out his plastic garbage bag of loot. He
then stalked to the second Explorer, barked out a terse
order, and replaced the driver.

Rose was about to turn off when Willie gunned past,
spewing mud.

The Junkman placed another seed into his mouth and
spat out residue. "Real asshole." The observation was
obvious even to his limited intellect.

Rose contacted the other vehicle on the repeater
radio. "Let me know if you see anything," he advised,
and Willie gave a predictably insolent reply.

He eased along the badly pocked westbound road,
looking for sign that the expedition vehicles might have
come this way. After two grueling miles, they came upon
a pine tree in the road. The Junkman got out, stalked
around for a bit, and pointed at cable marks on a standing tree. "New," he announced. Either the expedition
had come this way or Anderson had planted a ruse.
Rose was trying to decide which when the repeater
radio buzzed.

Willie's wise guy voice was loud and clear. "Guess

what, ace? We just stopped 'cause there's a fuckin' box in the road, like the one the hermit took. *Now* whattaya think?"

Rose waved for Billy Junkins to get in. "Don't touch anything. We'll be there shortly."

Willie laughed on the air. "Go screw a large duck. I got the guys out getting the fuckin' box, then we'll go after the fuckin' people like Mr. Paquette said. That's why he wanted to talk, so I wouldn't let you slow me down. Get used to suckin' hind tit, ace."

As Rose turned the vehicle around, he again tried to convince Willie to leave everything where it was so he could get a reading on the scene—and that they'd be with them shortly.

Then it was too late for reason.

26

The others listened in horror as Link described Daniel Eagle's vegetative state after his head was beaten in. When he said Sly Paquette was an enforcer for the mob, Richards was dubious.

"The reservation police may be corrupt, but the Chicago mob?" He shook his head. "You're asking us to believe too much."

"No, he's not." Jenifer told them how any Manido who argued "moved away" in the night and left no forwarding addresses. Authorities turned deaf ears and there was no one to turn to. She ended by repeating what they'd overheard at the marsh pond.

"I don't understand," said Brogg, obviously the most frightened. "If they had the treaties all along, what were we looking for?"

"Something we don't know about. I think it has to do with Senator Eddie."

Turf Siegel snorted. "You're sayin' we're here because of a crooked politician?"

"He was *not* crooked."

"Yeah, and Clinton did not have sexual relations with *that* woman."

Jenifer gave him a look that would freeze Popsicles.

Link's eyes were drawn to movement outside the window. He stared out incredulously.

Jenifer saw his look. "What's out there?"

"The hermit just stole Joseph's pack."

Richards, who was nearest the door, was first out.
"Gone," he muttered, sweeping his Dirty Harry squint
about.

Turf went to the Rover and opened the hatch. "Is this
the guy you said stole the canoe and then the treaties
from the cops?"

"Yes."

"Aren't you going after him?" Richards asked.

"There's no way anyone could catch him. This is his
home."

They hastily inventoried and found that both vehicles
had been pilfered. The hermit had dumped out Richards's backpack and added a sweater from Jenifer's, hiking boots from Dr. Brogg's, and Turf's heavy down coat.

"Why did he take *my* pack?" the once expedition
leader complained, but no one listened.

Jenifer lifted a turquoise and coral bracelet from her
pack. "It's Gloria's. Senator Eddie showed it to me when
he bought it for her."

"Same one she was wearin' at the briefing," said Turf.

"Look at *this*!" Dr. Brogg exclaimed from the opposite side of the Jeep. There, leaned against a maple tree
were a collection of aluminum tubes—the containers for
the Manido treaties.

Brogg bubbled with excitement. "The seals are still
intact."

And precisely then they heard a distant *Crack!* from
the direction of the cranberry marsh.

4:05 P.M.—*Wilderness Road*

Rose was racing back, the Ford bouncing and bot-
toming out, when Willie responded on the radio, whimpering and no longer using the wise guy tone, begging
for Sarge to hurry 'cause . . .

"Oh *shit,* Sarge!"

"Calm down, Willie. We're coming."

"There ain't nothin' left of 'em. One guy reached
down to grab something in the box, then *bang,* and they

weren't there. A foot! Jesus, I see a fuckin' bloody foot!"

There were sounds of vomiting.

"I can't hear good, Sarge. You coming?"

"We're on the way."

"The woman said I'd be sorry. Oh shit. I'm *sorry!*"

Rose had no idea what he meant, but despite the fact that he despised the thugs who charaded as policemen, "Officer down!" was the worst call he could imagine.

What had exploded? While various options were presented in his mind, only one made sense—one of the antipersonnel mines stolen from the ecol-rec zone. Anderson had admitted taking them and said he'd thrown them into a lake. Rose shouldn't have believed him.

He attempted to call Paquette on the repeater. No one answered, so he contacted the station—did not tell them what had transpired, just called for ten more reinforcements and told them to bring weapons and provisions.

The next time Rose tried, Sly Paquette responded. When he told him about the explosion and deaths, Paquette screamed curses into the radio. After a moment of breathing angrily into the mike, he said, "Anderson's behind it."

"Anderson or the hermit," said Rose.

"You find 'em, break their fuckin' arms and legs, and cut off their balls. Then have the Junkman twist their fuckin' heads off." His voice grew calmer, as if envisioning the mutilations was Prozac. "Then kick the others' asses and put 'em back to work. We need the fuckin' bag."

White Dog Lake

An overgrown path led from the hermit's cabin into a large copse of pines that abutted the lake. Link chose a location in the heart of the thicket, just twenty yards from the water's edge. When they'd stretched the green plastic tarps to shelter themselves from the elements and

scrutiny from the air, Link, Turf, and Richards walked
back to the main road to remove traces of their passage.

Rainwater coursed down their faces as they labored.
If the temperature dropped much more, it would turn
to snow. As Turf and Joseph eliminated ruts with their
boots, Link smoothed them over with fans of evergreen
branches and covered them with loose debris.

"The police *can't* be as corrupt as they're saying,"
Richards complained to Turf.

"Watch what you're doin'," Turf Siegel exploded.
"You're leaving more tracks than you're coverin'."

Richards tried his squint. "Remember who you work
for."

"Fuck off. I quit when you tried to pull the pistol."

Richards glared at Link. "You've got your hiding
place. *Now* can I take a vehicle?"

"No." When Link was satisfied that the rain would
eradicate any remaining sign, he led them back into
the thicket.

Jenifer and Dr. Brogg tended a concoction of freeze-
dried stew that bubbled atop the portable propane camp
stove. Jen said they could sleep either in the backs of
the vehicles or outside on beds of needles under the tarp
canopy. She'd dug a trench for their waste.

As they awaited dinner, Richards opened the large map
and found their location. "Unless we return to Spirit Lake,
we're sixty miles from the nearest civilization."

"Can we walk that far?" asked Dr. Brogg. His voice
sounded concerned.

"It's all wetlands. Bogs, swamps, and lakes. We'd need
a canoe, but if you'll recall, Mr. *Anderson* chose not to
bring one."

"We gotta walk, that's da way it is," Turf said. "Just
show me which way."

"Joseph's right," said Link. "It won't be easy. Three
miles north and we'd be off of the reservation and in
Upper Michigan, with no roads and nothing but lakes
and bogs for miles." Link pointed. "Fifteen miles west,
there's the ecology recovery zone."

"Which we promised to avoid," said Richards, "but

of course if you prefer to ignore toxic chemicals and enzymes . . ."

Jenifer broke in. "According to our council briefings, they're lethal."

"Ruling that way out," Richards said. "We're still ignoring the obvious. There's the cranberry farm and a wagon path, and if that's *truly* closed, it's only forty miles to Spirit Lake."

"You're forgetting the roadblocks."

"We can park and hike past them into town."

"Is that possible?" Brogg asked nervously. "I really would like to get out of here."

Turf directed a question at Link. "You're sure that was a mine we heard?"

"I plan to go back and find out."

"So *you* can use a vehicle but I can't?" asked Richards.

"I'll go on foot."

Jenifer announced that the stew was ready.

Link ate sparingly. He would have more when he returned. "It may get cold tonight, but don't build a fire," he told them. "Also no flashlights or lanterns, and don't run the vehicle engines."

"Ridiculous!" Joseph Richards muttered.

Jen said that Richards was suffering from a damaged ego following his demotion. Link did not care about Richards's sensitivities. The man acted like a brat and might get them caught.

Link placed several items into his day pack, adjusted the shoulder straps, and drew Jenifer aside. "I should be back by three or four in the morning," he told her.

She hugged him. "Be safe, Lincoln. I just found you."

5:20 P.M.—*Township of Spirit Lake*

Four days had passed since Jason had taken a drink. He had not believed it would be this hard. He'd never considered himself addicted to alcohol, but now he knew differently. There was no option but to stay away from booze. With Storyteller away, the Bear Society relied upon him to pass judgments and keep them together. There was a truth he knew deep inside—if he slipped once more they'd be compromised, and it could mean death for every *Muk-wah*. Now that he received the secrets normally passed to Storyteller, he had learned how dangerous his drunken utterances at the Hatchet Club bar had been.

Three Bear Society members worked at the casino—a janitor, a change person, and a clerk—and told how the bartenders reported on the activities of locals. They offered cheap drinks, poured them strong, listened to the prattle, and wrote a nightly report to be passed up the chain. Those the manager felt were of importance were forwarded to Sly Paquette.

He had been praying that his drunken words had gone unnoticed, but the clerk had said she'd seen a folder that was marked JASON TOUSSAINT on its way to the manager's office.

His heart had sunk to his knees.

"Is there anything dangerous in there?" she'd asked.

Jason had hesitated, not wanting to say it. Finally, "Yes."

"I'll try to get into the manager's office and remove it," she'd said.

"I've stopped drinking," he'd told her before she'd left, knowing it sounded lame. She hadn't commented. If she was caught in the manager's office, they both knew it would be fatal.

That afternoon six *Muk-wah* had met at the new cranberry farm, where Lonnie had given an archery lesson using a fifty-pound-pull, three-to-one-ratio compound bow. Another six had listened to an old-timer explain how to move unseen in the forest, and practiced throwing hatchets. The Bear Society included female members, and the women were just as accurate with the short axes. Jason had ordered larger-than-usual numbers in the classes, for he felt an urgency that they would soon need all of the skills and training they could possibly get.

More Manido than ever were being enticed with rock methamphetamines and, when they were seriously hooked, disappeared. Nightly he awakened after dream-times, drenched with sweat, hearing echoes of sad voices praying that someone would hear them.

Were those Manido being buried at Little Martha's Marsh, like the assistant manager of the moccasin store? Why did he believe they were serving some other purpose? There were so many questions without answers, but one thing was certain: the Manido were facing extinction.

As evening approached, Jason had had enough of seriousness and was on his way out to his Firebird—to head for Lonnie's to relax and listen to some CDs—when a clerk from the Wigwam Smoke Shop pulled up in her old pickup.

He went over, and casually looked to ensure she was alone. She was a *Muk-wah*—her specialty an unerring eye with both pistol and throwing-knives, her task to observe the police station, located across the street from the Wigwam. Storyteller had made a good choice. Before the crooked cops had replaced her with one of their own, she'd been the night dispatcher.

She spoke with grave concern. "Something's happened to Marvin."

Marvin Yellowbird was a new member of the Society. She was his older sister.

Jason smiled so a patrolman viewing from a distance would think she'd said something humorous. He was getting good with such theatrics.

"He's been gone the past three days. I've been watching his car in the station lot." She told how one of the worst cops had pulled an Explorer in next to Marvin's car the other evening, and he and his partner had transferred something bulky into the trunk. Then one had got in and driven off, while the other followed in the black and white.

"Marvin would never let those guys use his car." Her voice cracked. "I'm worried."

"Cool it," he whispered. A patrolman drove by on the main road, going slow and observing them. Jason felt a chill. He looked at the girl and laughed uproariously, as if she'd told a good joke. She tried to join in but was too concerned about her brother, so she kept her face averted as the Explorer continued past.

The telephone rang inside the house.

"What can we do?" asked Marvin's sister.

He did not have to tell her it might be too late to help her brother. "Keep gathering information. I got your early report. Two patrolmen went north at noon, carrying rifles."

"Ten more left at five o'clock, carrying mike-sixteens."

He digested the new data with due interest and foreboding.

"I'd better get back to the shop," she said.

He grinned like she'd told another joke. Waved and started for the house to answer the phone. There would be no music session. Something was going on at the north side, where a dozen rotten cops had deployed with M16s. Jason's concern mounted. His aunt Jen was there, along with his new friend, Link Anderson.

He went in and picked up the telephone, and noted a high frequency hum. "Jason."

A woman's voice said, "This is Erin. Your telephone's monitored. Go to the pay phone at the Quik Mart and I'll call you there."

The line went dead.

27

The rain had stopped and the full moon peeked through a cloud, casting a hazy glow. Link continued his easy but dogged rhythm, knowing better than to waste the moonlight.

He slowed to a fast walk, eyed his watch, and moved off the road and into the trees. It was almost seven—eight o'clock in New York—time to check the receive-only mode of the satellite phone. Link checked his Rolex GMT Master, a gift from his stepfather when he'd earned his wings. Lucky Anderson had bought it at a base exchange after being shot down over North Vietnam and escaping. It had been purchased at a time of good fortune, and his stepfather hoped it would bring the same for Link.

He switched to R-O mode and held the phone to his ear.

When the second hand swept to the top, the phone came alive. A digitally neutered voice spoke. *"The nephew reports the north side is shut off. A good guy cop is missing, maybe dead. Two bad cops were dispatched at noon. Ten more at five o'clock, along with firepower, but the nephew does not know why. Break. Last item, expect a cold front to arrive by morning."*

The message was repeated. Link closed the flip-top phone and, as he walked back to the road, thought of what had been said. Erin had used terms familiar to them both. Jason had relayed that the cops had tight-

ened control at the roadblocks. Two backups had been
sent out at noon, then ten more, all carrying automatic
weapons.

Link found a trail he'd been looking for and set out
running again.

At five miles—passing abeam one of the trees he'd
winched onto the road—he slowed to a fast walk to rest.
Ten minutes and he was running once more, back on
the main road, finding the way difficult on the slick grass
at the side of the roadway, where he'd leave the least
sign. He stopped at the pine tree that was still across
the road, and found tire marks where a vehicle had been
turned around. He searched in the moonlight until he
found a set of large footprints by the tree where he'd set
up his pulley. The Junkman's tracks led back to the road.

They'd come this far and turned back, driving fast,
according to the indented tire prints.

9:13 *P.M.*—the T Intersection

From his arrival at the T intersection, the reconnoiter
took two hours from first to finish.

His first act was to step into the bush to avoid headlights, and crouch by an earthen mound as the beams
illuminated the denuded autumn forest. The moon cast
so much light that he could easily discern that two persons were inside.

He also noted three large stones placed in a triangle:
the sign of a cache left by a woodsman. They'd not been
there when he'd passed by during his morning runs.

Link decided to investigate later. He removed his shirt
and watch and most of the contents of his jeans pockets,
and placed them into the day pack. After rubbing himself liberally with earth to mask the odors of civilization,
he resumed his steady trot, bare chested and chilled,
drawn toward a sky glow cast from the hastily abandoned base camp.

The several propane lanterns they'd left behind were
all lit. He counted nine bad guy cops lounging around a
fire, relaxing with beer and weed, listening as Willie told

about the badass hermit who had killed Marvin and
blown up two others. The bodies of the dead men were
wrapped in canvas off to one side of the camp. The thugs
avoided looking at them.

While Link believed that a few of Willie's gears had
slipped off their cogs, he seemed subdued as he described how the two had leaned over the box and been
blown out of their shoes. A bloody foot had landed close
by. He described it again, like it was hard to forget.

Link wondered if the hermit hadn't left the pack and
box on the road by mistake. Then he remembered that
the old man had methodically removed both mines from
the water, hidden them, then dropped one off in their
path.

The hermit had known what he was doing.

Link watched quietly for another ten minutes, measuring and taking it all in, willing himself to forget the cold
of the night.

Two thug cops went to the edge of the forest and
peered into the darkness, complaining about being assigned the watch. "I was up too late last night for this
shit," one bitched.

"How's Rose gonna know what we do?" said the
other. "He's in the cabin while we're out here freezin'
our butts off, looking at dead men." He called out to
Willie, "Where do you think the expedition people
went?"

"Prob'ly running scared, but it won't do 'em any good.
The Junkman's like a jumbo hunting dog. You oughta
see him when he's onto something."

"What's Rose been like?"

"Candy ass. We find 'em, I'm gonna fuck the councilwoman in front of him."

"I thought Paquette wanted us to put them back to
work."

"Mr. Paquette won't mind me havin' some fun. He
knows Rose is a wimp."

"Any ideas about the other one . . . Sydney?"

"She don't tell me fast enough, I'll fuck her too."

"Do that, and the Junkman'll twist your head off."

Willie was smart enough to remain quiet.

Link departed, thinking of their vulnerability and the way the vehicles were scattered helter-skelter about the camp.

10:04 P.M.—Adcock Cabin

The old homestead was cozy, with amenities like glass windows, a working hand pump in the kitchen, and a crackling fire in the hearth. Billy was pleased that Rose had brought only two others and himself. Willie was a pain in the ass.

Everyone was down to shirtsleeves as Sergeant Rose bent over a map, assigning search routes for the three teams he'd designated.

Ground rule: When the expedition party was discovered, contain them and call for backup. They were armed, and Anderson was especially dangerous. He described him, and said if he threatened in any slightest way, to shoot him.

Ground rule: Do not harm any of the others unless absolutely necessary.

Ground rule: Whether over radio or in person, if a woman introduced herself as Sydney . . .

Bored with such things, the Junkman wandered outside to the porch, let his eyes adjust, and looked out at the silver-on-black nightscape. He mulled over the day and how much he enjoyed being back in the forest.

He raised his head and inhaled through his nose. Smelled the odors of the men inside, and their noxious smoke. Smelled the pines around the cabin, and the mustiness of people who had lived here long before. Then . . . there was something new and unexpected.

He was not quite sure. A wild animal's spoor?

Link stood only eight feet from the Junkman, beside a large tamarack so the tree's shadow mingled with that of his torso. Become a part of your natural surroundings, his Blackfoot tutors had told him. A bush. The grass. A stone. Presently he used the tree.

Junkins turned and stared about, as if puzzled by something. Again he reared his head and drew a long breath through flared nostrils. He held his head back like that for a long moment, as if sorting various scents. Finally he lowered his head, looked about carefully, then turned and walked to the other end of the long porch.

Willie believed that Billy Junkins was a tracker? Link doubted that was true.

He'd hoped to learn the identity of Sydney, but from what he'd overheard, none of them knew. If necessary, she was to identify herself. If harm came to her, it would be their asses.

Rose's next words captured Link's attention. "Don't be concerned if you hear a helicopter tonight. Councilman Paquette's sending a chopper to try to locate the expedition for us."

"Tonight? The weather's supposed to turn shitty again."

"From my understanding, with this helo it won't matter."

The MH-60! Link thought grimly. It was all-weather, and had state-of-the-art IR sensors.

When Rose began to repeat tomorrow's plan, Link backed away in preparation for leaving.

He heard a rush of heavy footsteps and froze into place.

The Junkman ran on past to the corner of the cabin, stopped, and looked carefully about. Then he too became perfectly still, scanning with only his eyes.

Considering his bulk, the Junkman was faster than Link had believed possible.

Junkins drew his head back, again took in the breath through his nostrils, and savored it.

"Who are you?" he asked in his deep, rumbling voice.

Link remained immobile, thinking it would not be easy to escape, considering the man's speed and the bright moon.

"I'll find you," reasoned the giant. "Make it easy on yourself."

The door opened, and Sergeant Rose's wiry figure was outlined. "Was that you, Billy?"

Junkins squinted at Rose and the intrusion of light. "Something's out here."

"I'll bring a flashlight." Rose disappeared inside.

Link had moved with the first spoken words, smoothly and directly away from the light. The Junkman's moment had passed, his concentration interrupted. Link had melted into the forest by the time Junkins muttered his thanks as he received the flashlight.

It was fortunate that Rose had interrupted. Another few seconds and he would have been discovered. The Junkman was good, although not perfect. He'd said *something* was out there, so he hadn't been sure it was a human. He had also made more noise than necessary when he had run, although that was understandable for one carrying such tremendous bulk.

Link must be warier. He was exhausted from the trek and decided that was part of the problem. He should have rested before venturing close. If he was not more alert in future confrontations, he would surely be caught, and if the giant got his hands on him . . .

Link stopped by the base camp for only a short period. Willie and another of the thugs were still awake, talking, and neither noticed when he crept into their midst and took a Zippo cigarette lighter and a jerry can half filled with gasoline. A moment later he silently toppled the can and waited as acrid-smelling liquid gurgled and seeped under a vehicle and into the camp.

Willie frowned at the sound. "I hear something."

Link opened and lighted the Zippo, tossed it into the gasoline, and watched as the fuel flared. Willie stared with bulging eyes at the half-naked man beyond the flames. At the moment of recognition he frantically attempted to fire his M16, but forgot to switch off the safety.

By the time Link heard the initial burst, he was fifty yards distant, trotting down the dark road. Another and yet another weapon sounded as he continued.

He stopped at the T intersection, ignoring the dwindling cacophony of gunfire and the blaze of the burning Explorer that illuminated the drifting low clouds.

After retrieving his belongings and pulling on the flannel shirt, Link investigated the cache. A simple lattice of branches masked a tunnel at one side of the earthen mound. Inside he found furs, a sturdy, sharp hand ax, and at the back, the second antipersonnel mine.

There was no question who had left the trove for him. "Thank you, Nek-kah," he whispered, and wondered if the hermit was close enough to hear.

After a thoughtful moment he pulled out the ax, then carefully replaced the tunnel's cover and scattered the marker stones. He hefted the day pack and hand ax, and set out on a new course. He considered the challenge.

The helicopter, called a Black Hawk because of its nocturnal and weather capabilities, was in military jargon a force multiplier. The Junkman too was a dangerous opponent.

Link had an ally in Nek-kah the hermit, who was resourceful and not crazy at all.

After half an hour, Link stopped at a small, nameless lake and rested, listening warily for the dreaded helicopter sounds as he thought out a plan of attack.

28

Gloria came alert at the sound of loud voices in the compound. It did not take much to wake her for she was constantly nervous. While she avoided or disgorged the daily allotment of methamphetamine and meth-laced chowder, enough was assimilated that she experienced the rush and glow. Increasingly she had to force herself to vomit—and put aside the bliss, the illusion that she was impervious to harm. She understood why the desperate women performed depraved acts, and why the men could betray friends, do anything to get more drugs so the false euphoria would not end.

In her fog, she wondered about the voices. She shook her head briskly, ignoring a cranked-up Manido who had begun to chatter in a meaningless conversation. Then she crawled from under the blanket she shared with two others and went to the door of the shed, arms huddled about herself to ward off the chill. She pressed her face to the door to listen.

She heard the shrill whine of helicopter jet engines being started.

At night? she wondered. Could helicopters fly in such conditions?

She had visually examined the helicopters, and also the missiles mounted on launchers, and the futuristic cannon with barrels that looked like scorpions' stingers, and wondered if they truly would use them. A new thought intrigued her. If they were flying helicopters, wouldn't they be seen, and might not someone come to investigate?

The security people in their green uniforms, with their electronic organizers and close-mouthed ways, were an enigma. They appeared intelligent, had to be to understand the sophisticated systems, yet whenever they saw Gloria or other scarecrow slaves, they fastidiously looked away. Once the couple had beaten a young Manido so badly that he'd bled from his ears and eyes, but two security people had hurried past as if they'd seen nothing.

On her second day, when Gloria had ventured into the security center, a blond-haired, scraggly-bearded young man ordered her out. "I'm here to clean," she'd muttered like a vacant half-wit, and held her breath as she walked by with her broom, mop, cloths, and solvents.

From listening she'd learned that his name was Howarski, and despite his youth, he was the one in charge of the security control center, the helicopters and exotic systems. He was nasty-tempered and called the Indians aborigines. When the couple had noticed her emerging from security, she'd told them Howarski had said to clean there, and they'd hastily dropped the issue rather than question the intense young man. Gloria had become a daily visitor, cleaning floors and rest rooms in the security control post, just as she did throughout the Warehouse. Guests at the "Resort" and security people ignored her. She cleaned toilets and smelled of antiseptics.

Gloria made it a point to listen and be watchful, and learn everything possible about the compound and surroundings. The security people spoke freely, and electronic map displays showed the area within two hundred miles, the reservation, and details of the place labeled "Ecol-Rec," including the Warehouse, the meth lab a mile down the sheltered lane, and the impressive array of defenses. Daily they added to the networks of video cameras and heat sensors, shown as small squares. Red lines were charged fences, and red *X*s were explosive charges. Everything was computer controlled, except for those times when the security men patrolled the routes shown by blue lines in their Humvees.

The security people said the place was impenetrable by any human and would be even more secure when they were finished. Gloria tried to memorize it all. Seldom did she dream of Jamaican beaches. Now she had darker fantasies. If she was to get her day of vengeance, she must first escape. She could not afford to delay long, lest the drugs, starvation, and abuse combine to make it impossible.

As she crouched by the door, she defined sounds. The jet engines squealed louder as the helicopter took off. It was the special one, piloted only by Howarski. He boasted that it handled like a jet fighter, and that he could destroy any enemy in the dead of night.

Gloria Vasson wondered who the *enemy* might be.

White Dog Lake

The temperature in the Range Rover was cool, scarcely maintained by a single catalytic heater. The side windows were cracked to eliminate the possibility of carbon monoxide poisoning.

Turf Siegel was in the front seat when he heard the clip-clopping of blades accompanied by shrill jet sounds.

In back Dr. Brogg muttered a few words and returned to sleep.

Turf saw Jenifer Toussaint outside in the gloom, and went out to join her, taking his coat along to ward off the chill. There was no illumination when he opened the door. She'd thought to remove the bulbs from the dome lighting of both vehicles.

"A chopper?" he asked, his breath a fog of vapor. He pulled up his coat collar, held his arms about himself, and shuddered.

"Yes, in this bad weather at one thirty in the morning. I don't like it."

"You think it's da bad cops?"

"Probably. You saw the helicopter at the marsh pond."

"Yeah." He paused. "Somethin' you oughta know. Soon as you went off to sleep, Joseph started talkin' about leavin'. Doc Brogg's starting to listen."

"No one goes anywhere until Link gets back. I've got the keys."

"Yeah, so maybe you oughta watch your ass."

Wilderness Road

Link Anderson continued placing one heavy foot before the other. Time had blurred and his tortured body and wooden legs cried out for respite, yet he doggedly continued running.

He'd missed the eleven o'clock satellite phone transmission—he'd been on the reconnoiter—and the next one would not come until three. Then he would learn—

Distant helicopter sounds interrupted, whispering, *The Black Hawk is coming.*

The plan that had been taking form in Link's mind was incomplete. *Think!*

While the helicopter pilot would likely be drawn first to the burning vehicle, which was one reason he'd torched it, he'd have to do more to keep him away from the hidden camp.

The fact that he was unarmed mattered little. The military helo was all but impervious to ground fire. He was left with innovation and the contents of the day pack.

The helicopter sounds proceeded toward the Alpha camp and the burning Explorer, as expected. After a couple of overhead passes, the pilot began a zigzag search pattern, examining the forest about the camp, likely looking for heat sources, either by use of night vision goggles or an infrared scanner.

Thus far the helicopter had not flown toward the hidden camp.

Link refused to think of what might happen to Jenifer if she was discovered. He'd had difficulty accepting the fact that he was falling for her so hard, so quickly. He must not lose someone he cherished for a second time.

He stopped to examine different trees, soon found an old pine that was weeping sticky pitch, and drew the hand ax and a thermal flare from the day pack.

He vigorously chopped into the pitchy seam, ignited the flare, and applied the spewing flame to the tree wound and the exposed pitch. The wood caught quickly, but he held the flare in place until the flames flickered hot and the fire crackled with intensity. While standard railroad or highway flares burned brightly, the thermals burned much hotter.

When that fire was going, casting new brilliance into the night, he trotted fifty yards down the path, found another pine, and ignited that one as well. Soon four trees were burning, arranged in a symmetrical square so it would be obvious that they'd been started by human hand.

Link waited, close enough to one of the conflagrations that an IR detector would be blinded to his relatively meager body heat.

As the helo noises grew louder, he tried to inject himself into the mind of the pilot, wondering if the same person that he'd met in the sky the previous week was flying the MH-60. If so, Link already knew some about him. For instance he had proven that he was the better pilot, with better situational awareness and knowledge of tactics. His adversary—if it was indeed the same person—was competitive to the point of overconfidence, and in a fight tended to react before thinking a situation through.

There was a clearing a hundred yards distant, illuminated by the fires. What would the Black Hawk pilot's reaction be if Link got out in plain view and just waved like a fool?

Airborne over the North Side, East of the Warehouse

Howarski felt one rush of adrenaline after another as he circled the burning trees. He was after a home run. *Life*

is good and is about to get better, he thought as he prepared
to destroy a man whom he particularly despised.

He had overflown the burned-out vehicle at the tribal
police camp, and spoken to a sergeant named Rose who
had confirmed that Lincoln Anderson had been the one
to torch the Explorer. Howarski had immediately established an expanding search pattern, forgetting the expedition, concentrating on finding the aboriginal pilot who
had humiliated him.

The engineer beside him scanned the burning trees
on the infrared flat-screen presentation, zoomed in, and
manually adjusted the attenuation.

"See anything yet?" Howarski asked. He was tingling
with anticipation.

"The fires are so hot I can't see much of anything
that's close to them."

"That's what he's banking on. He's here." Howarski
tapped the side of his head. "I'm in his skull. I know him
as well as I know myself. Set the miniguns to bore-site."

"Bore-site," the engineer responded, meaning that instead of swiveling at his command, the two forward-
firing 7.62 mini-Gatling guns would fire their streams of
death directly ahead.

They circled the four burning trees, searching for Anderson's body heat signature.

"There!" The engineer pointed at a pair of fleeing
shapes on the screen.

Howarski switched the green image onto his head-up
display so it was superimposed on the windscreen, and
centered one of the shapes in the sight reticle.

The engineer relaxed. "Just a couple of deer."

Howarski depressed the trigger. Both guns responded.
Brrr-rrrrrr-att! Twin arcs of tracers spewed out before
them. The green shapes of the fleeing animals tumbled,
and did not move thereafter. He continued to fire the
miniguns, stirring them about wildly. *Brrr-rrrrrr-att!*

Finally he stopped shooting and flew in a tight circle
about the trees. "Keep looking," Howarski said coldly.
"Anderson's here somewhere."

They alternately examined the scopes and the forest

below that was illuminated by the flames. Twice more Howarski fired the guns at shadows. *Brrr-rrrrrr-att!*

"Why would he set fires?" the engineer asked.

"Anderson's an aborigine. He feels he can push my nose in it and escape again." He did not add that it was precisely the kind of defiant act that he would do.

The engineer pointed. "There!"

A man stood at the far side of a clearing, a hand raised as if hailing them.

"He's giving up. He wants us to pick him up," said the engineer.

"Then we shall." They flew closer, and Anderson did not run.

Howarski altered the nimble MH-60's position just slightly, so the man was squarely in the sight reticle. Something about it all niggled just slightly at his mind, but he refused to delay.

Brrr-rrrrr-attt! Twin arcs skewered Anderson, who jerked about and fell.

"Jesus, you shredded the poor bastard," said the engineer.

Howarski laughed jubilantly as he switched on the landing light, illuminating the clearing even more brightly.

"He fell into the bushes there." The engineer pointed.

Howarski turned the MH-60 in a 360-degree pirouette, feeling his elation mounting as he ensured they were clear of obstacles, then settled the Black Hawk to earth.

"Get out and drag his body into the light."

"What if there are more of them."

"He doesn't operate like that. Go on. I want to see him."

The engineer unbuckled, then went back and cautiously slid open the cargo door.

Howarski set the engine to idle so he could hear. "Hurry," he called. "We still have to find their camp." That would make it a grand slam!

The engineer walked cautiously into the glare of the landing light, then proceeded into the bushes. He bent down, grasped something, and frowned. "We got a problem, Howarski!"

He lifted a flannel shirt and jeans, filled with limber branches that had been bent and fashioned to resemble a human.

"Son of a bitch!" Howarski screamed, reaching for the throttle.

The engineer ran pell-mell toward the helicopter, followed closely by a naked male human wearing blue Jockey shorts and Western boots, brandishing a sputtering flare.

Howarski did not wait or hesitate. He lifted off, then tipped the nose forward and depressed the trigger. Both miniguns roared as they spewed rounds. *Brrr-rrr-atttt!* The engineer dropped like a bloody sack, sawed in two.

Howarski manipulated both the collective and throttle, cursing as he maneuvered and looked in vain for Anderson, miniguns still firing wildly. *Brrrr-rrrrr-rrrrr-att . . . Brrr-rr . . .*

Simultaneously both guns ran out of ammunition, but as the helicopter rose ever higher from the clearing, Howarski exulted. He was free. He had won!

In his vision's periphery a sputtering light arced up and through the open rear hatch.

As Howarski frantically leveled the craft and added maximum power, he could already smell the acrid smoke issuing from the aft compartment as the helicopter began to burn.

Link did not feel for a pulse. The man sent to retrieve his body was very dead. Neither was Link concerned that the pilot—whom he'd heard called Howarski— might soon return. He had other problems. He'd killed his own copilot and now had a live flare as a passenger.

He hastily went through the dead man's pockets, found nothing of use, and observed the time. Another hour remained before the next sat phone R-O transmission.

The temperature was rapidly dropping, yet as he drew on the tattered clothing, Link was pleased. He'd pegged Howarski accurately. Not only was he impulsive; he was such an egotist that he'd had to have a final look at his vanquished foe.

"Gotcha," Link said happily, wondering at the extent of the damage to the chopper.

He replaced the hand ax and unused flares into the day pack, pulled it on, and started for the camp at White Dog Lake, now several hours distant.

Link heard the helicopter in the distance, clop-clopping to earth. Howarski was landing early, likely to scramble into the rear compartment to extinguish the fire.

The helicopter was still idling, so the engine was not disabled. If he could take it . . .

He did not allow the thought to gel, just ran faster.

Howarski was exhausted, but the fire was out and the worst of the smoke had dissipated out the open side door, if not the acrid smells of warped plastic and melted metal. He dropped the second extinguisher, now emptied of the sticky foam.

So close! Another minute and it would have been too late to save the helo.

With that dismal thought came a new one. He was little more than a mile from the clearing. Would Lincoln Anderson give pursuit?

Howarski reached for the handle to the sliding hatch—and in the moonlight he could clearly see a dark specter running directly toward the helicopter!

"Oh God," he shrieked, in abject fear as he reached for the MAC-10 Ingram machine pistol in its bracket beside the pilot's seat. He yanked it free and turned to the doorway.

There was nothing where the shadow had been. Where was Anderson?

Howarski depressed the trigger and drew the muzzle about in a circle, spraying the empty roadway. The noise inside the compartment was tremendous.

He slid the door closed, latched it, and as he was still dropping into the pilot's seat, the dark figure reappeared outside. Anderson tried the door handle, then turned back and swung something in his grasp.

Thump!

The aborigine was swinging a tomahawk into the glass!

Thump!

Howarski's heart pounded as he pushed up the throttle, screaming, "Leave me alone!"

Thump! A bull's-eye fracture had appeared in the glass.

"Go away!" he shrieked as the helicopter lifted from the earth, leaving Anderson below.

Thank God! Howarski glanced back out just in time to see the dark figure hurling the ax.

Whang! The primitive weapon skittered off the bullet-proof glass only a foot from his head. He cringed and whimpered childlike as he ascended, higher and higher, until no tomahawk could possibly reach him, still half expecting Anderson to somehow follow.

He turned the craft and fled toward the haven of the Warehouse.

As he landed at the helipad, Howarski calmed enough to take stock of the Black Hawk. All except the primary instruments were unusable, and the sensor panels were dark. Much of the sensitive equipment had been disabled by the fire. It seemed unthinkable that anyone could wreak such havoc upon his beloved machine.

Anderson was a wild Stone Age aborigine, yet somehow he had managed to outmaneuver him again. Only slowly did Howarski's fear subside, replaced by slow-burning hatred.

2:58 A.M.—*Wilderness Road*

Another half hour had passed, Link jogging on the same road where he'd discovered Howarski tending his crippled MH-60. Finally he slowed to a walk, held the sat phone to his ear, and waited for the call with anticipation.

Helga's faint digital voice announced, *"The nephew reports no change; no one has returned from the north*

*side. Break. If there's a way to get your status to us,
please do so. Big boss remains concerned."*

As the transmission was repeated, Link shut the
phone off.

As he continued toward White Dog Lake, he once
again considered the situation. The damage to the Black
Hawk was a big plus. Still, the bad cops would eventually
find them.

He had told Gloria Vasson about Sly Paquette's
treachery. Would she grow suspicious and contact the
authorities?

Link considered another avenue: Ron Doughty, the
small-town private investigator, was looking into night
truck movement near the reservation. Was there was a
way to get word to him?

29

For the past several nights Ron Doughty had watched various back roads, running the engine with the heater going to ward off the increasing cold, playing country and western CDs, drinking tepid thermos coffee, and reading mystery novels. So far he'd earned a zero. No big rigs going hell for leather—in fact hardly any traffic at all.

Willie Nelson finished singing "Georgia on My Mind," which Ron felt was his best. The private detective was parked well out of sight, some twenty feet off the pavement. On three occasions he had seen black-and-white Ford Explorers—patrol vehicles of the Spirit Lake police—and while he wondered what they were doing off the reservation and out of their jurisdiction, they were incentive for him to remain out of sight.

Should they discover him on the road, he'd decided upon a cover story. He was on his way to Upper Michigan to visit a cousin's family in Ironwood.

Yeah, right. In the middle of the night?

Tonight's back road ran parallel to the western side of the reservation, up near the Michigan state line and across from a spooky place that everyone avoided, the site of a century-old ecological disaster, rumored to be the cause of increased incidences of cancer and tuberculosis for anyone who ventured there. He could smell its odors, and wondered if it might be affecting him even where he parked. Next time he'd pick a road farther away.

Ron was reaching for the button to replay the same CD when he heard a low rumble. As the road noise increased, his heart picked up a beat. Had to be a big rig.

A moment later a massive shadow passed on the road. A tractor hauling a double trailer roared past going like a bat from hell—but it was in total blackout, as they'd called it in the army. No running lights, no headlamp illumination, *nothing*.

So how the hell could the driver see? he wondered. Not only was it illegal; it was dangerous. He wondered how many deer the rigs were smacking off the roads.

His first urge was to call someone and share his discovery, but there was no cellular service, and certainly no all-night businesses in boondocks like this. As he put the lever into drive a chill ran through him, and he wondered if following the phantom truck was wise.

Ron decided to proceed, but not too closely; just get within sight and hang back.

He pushed it up to seventy and wondered at his sanity, since even with his headlights on there was no earthly way he could spot an animal in time to stop.

A small sign announced that he'd entered Michigan.

Five long minutes later, when he'd still not got a glimpse of the truck, he decided he'd used up his share of luck for the morning and slowed to fifty. A mile farther he climbed a rise and came to a halt before a sign reading NORTH-SOUTH CONTINENTAL DIVIDE.

The rig was obviously still running in blackout, for when he looked slowly about, there was nothing. The road ahead was precisely like that he'd just left—a narrow alley through dark, uninhabited forestland. He pulled off the road and got out.

The putrid odor was no longer in the wind, meaning he'd driven beyond the disaster area.

He reached back in and shut off the engine—and far behind heard the sound of gears shifting, and a diesel engine rumbling. As the sounds became fainter he wondered, for he remembered no side roads. *Where the hell could the tractor-trailer have turned off?*

Ron Doughty then heard the sound of another vehicle, this one close. Headlamps came on not a hundred yards distant. *Someone had followed him as he'd tailed the truck.* He cursed his inattention as he yanked open the sedan's door, and was just turning the key when a black-and-white Explorer pulled directly in front of him, blocking his way.

Reservation patrolmen emerged from either side, leveling side arms, and he had a nasty premonition that they were not going to believe his story.

Rock Lake

Sly Paquette had received his first call of the long, long night when the police dispatcher called to connect him with Willie, who had sounded excited and said Anderson had burned up a vehicle but he thought he'd shot him.

"Don't call me about that kind of shit. Take it up with Rose," Sly had said, and his missing eye had begun to throb when he'd tried to go back to sleep.

He had been awakened again a couple of hours later, that time by Crazy Howarski at the Warehouse with an even more unbelievable tale that made Sly wonder if they were all somewhere smoking dope and making funny calls.

Howarski had been screaming mad, saying he'd shot him to pieces and then Anderson had tricked him and set his helicopter on fire. "When are you going to get rid of Anderson?"

"Soon," Sly had answered, thinking that Howarski was nuttier than ever, but Mr. Lincoln-fucking-Anderson was becoming a real elbow in the eye. "We're going to need a helicopter," he had told Howarski. "How about getting the other one tomorrow?"

"Fuck off!" Howarski had angrily hung up.

Sly Paquette had been wide awake so he'd radioed Sergeant Rose, who was at the scene of the burned patrol car but knew nothing about Howarski's damaged helicopter.

"Find Anderson, Rose. The rest of them too, but Anderson's like a fuckin' plague."

"Finding anyone's going to be difficult without a helicopter."

Sly Paquette had actually slept for the next hour.

The next call surprised him just as much as the others.

Whenever a shipment of hijacked goods or ingredients for Tonio Gracchi's meth factory was scheduled to arrive at the ecol-rec zone, Paquette's cops patrolled to make sure they weren't followed, and no one saw them turn off into the camouflaged entrance. The detail was tedious. Not once had the patrolmen found anyone on the remote back roads.

Until now, that is. The police dispatcher said a private investigator named Doughty had been caught following one of the blacked-out tractor-trailers.

Even after a "meaningful, know what I mean" interrogation, the dispatcher said the PI stubbornly claimed he'd been on his way to visit family in Upper Michigan.

Paquette remembered the PI's name, and how he had sent warnings for him to stay out of the Senator Adcock affair. The Junkman even sat outside his office in an auto now and then to remind him. Some people never learned.

While he was trying to figure all of that out, Paquette received his final call of the crazy night that was now early morning.

Howarski's voice was begrudging. "I changed my mind. I'll send the other helo out in the morning, with a couple of shooters at the door."

Paquette was betting that Howarski had not changed his mind at all, but had been told to provide the helicopter by Sydney, or maybe Tonio Gracchi.

"Only kill Anderson," Paquette reminded him. "We need the others back to work looking for the gym bag. Also have your chopper drop by here first thing. I'll have a couple passengers."

Outside he heard the patrolmen bring the nosy PI named Doughty into the work shed. It was still dark, another hour until sunrise, but his night was ruined. He brewed a pot of hot tea—using strong loose-leaf like many did who were raised on the reservation—and poured a cup.

Paquette took along his radio and cell phone—Rock Lake was just at the outer edge of the area of coverage—went down to the shed, and told the cops to beat it.

He'd decided not to overdo it, to get his information and have Howarski's helicopter take the PI to the Warehouse. They needed more laborers.

Doughty was tied at knees and elbows, suspended from the rafter hook.

Sly sipped hot tea and eyed the way he'd been amateurishly beaten, with all the blows directed at his face. He looked bad with his eyes swollen closed, but he still had the strength to turn his head to follow the sounds of movements and mumble words.

"You say you wanna see a lawyer?" Paquette repeated.

"Yeah."

"I always considered most of 'em assholes."

"My right." His voice was surprisingly strong emerging from such a battered face.

Sly lifted his cup and decided he was too tired and sleepy to do anything physical.

"Before we get started, tell me something, Mr. Detective. I sent a note saying what would happen to your family if you interfered. Which one o' your grandkids you want me to do first?"

"Oh Jesus," the private investigator whispered.

"He ain't here, just you and me. I recall you got four grandkids. One of 'em's a three-year-old girl, right? Walkin', talkin' just like a big girl. Pretty brown eyes." Paquette paused.

Doughty shook his head disconsolately. "Please don't."

"Remember how I told you to take a look at Danny Eagle's eyes." Paquette rocked back. "Think your granddaughter's gonna look good like that?"

"What do you want?" He was pleading to talk.

"Everything." Sometimes, thought Sly Paquette, it was

almost too easy. He sipped and savored the tea. "Who you workin' for and how much do they think they know?"

The answers surprised Paquette, although he later realized they shouldn't have. Abraham Lincoln Anderson seemed to be everywhere he turned.

6:40 A.M.—*Town of Spirit Lake*

Jason Toussaint killed the Firebird's engine and just waited for a moment. Knowing the house was bugged—Erin had said by three different listening devices—had a sobering effect, regardless of the fact that she said they would only periodically be monitored.

He'd been up early, receiving a report from the night janitor at the police station that a beefy-looking man had been brought in and beaten. He'd been taken away after a phone call to Sly Paquette, and his auto driven off in the opposite direction, toward Martha's Marsh.

Each day Jason had been collecting reports and coordinating training sessions. He devoutly wished that Storyteller would return so he could turn it all back over. Something was happening on the north side—they just did not know what it was.

Marvin Yellowbird's sister had been right to worry—her brother's charred body had been discovered in a burned trailer house near Wausau. The unanswered questions were *Why had Marvin been killed?* and *Did it have anything to do with the Bear Society?*

Now another *Muk-wah* was in trouble. Jason had talked too much and too loudly that night at the bar. The clerk at the Hatchet Club had attempted to remove the folder marked JASON TOUSSAINT from the manager's office, but it had already been forwarded to Sly Paquette.

While he feared for his own life, Jason wondered how many others he'd jeopardized with his drunken prattle. Just as Storyteller had foretold, Jason had betrayed the *Muk-wah*. Now he must send them to battle before they were ready.

As he sat staring at the house, he felt that he'd passed into another realm. Like Manido chiefs of old, he was about to send his People out to fight a despicable and deadly foe. Unlike them he was unqualified and unworthy.

He prayed for guidance, to find a way to avoid the confrontation for which he knew the *Muk-wah* were not prepared.

30

It had still been inky dark when Link stumbled into camp, climbed into the back of the Jeep beside Jenifer, and collapsed. She awakened him at first light as he'd asked, with a kiss and a whisper that she was pleased that he was safe.

Jenifer eyed him. "I missed you. Want to see if we can both fit into my sleeping bag?"

She became touchy-feely and he was thinking agreeable thoughts when she drew back and stared at his shirt.

"There are *holes* in your clothing."

He looked down in mock surprise. "I *thought* I felt a draft." With that he pulled his backup shirt and Levis from the back of the Jeep where he'd left them, and went to the lake.

She, followed and asked questions as he waded into the frigid water, washed off, then hurried back onto dry land. "That's *cold!*" he announced as he changed.

"Damn it, Lincoln, how did you get holes in your clothes?"

"Actually I wasn't wearing them at the time."

"Thank God for that." As he returned to the camp she continued prying.

"Let's get everyone together," Link announced.

After urging them all into the Range Rover for warmth, Link began explaining. It had indeed been an antipersonnel mine explosion, he told them. Two patrolmen had died.

"That's terrible," exclaimed Dr. Brogg.

"Maybe, but they weren't nice people. Now they're sending three armed teams after us."

"We should consider turning ourselves in."

"I wouldn't suggest it. Their orders are that none of you are to leave here alive."

Richards, whom he'd believed would argue, was uncharacteristically quiet.

"We heard gunfire," said Jenifer. "It's time to explain the bullet holes, Link."

"Just once, then everyone get some rest. Tonight we'll move deeper into the north side."

When Link finished telling about the helicopter there were questions, and he had to explain it all for a second, then a third time.

"My God," Brogg kept repeating.

"Unbelievable," Richards said with a skeptical frown.

"You burned a cop car and damaged their chopper?" Turf asked admiringly.

"*Truly* unbelievable," Richards said.

Link held up his hand. "I hear another helicopter," he said.

They bustled out and peered from under the tarps suspended overhead. The Jet Ranger traversed in the distance, prudently flying several hundred feet above the trees. At their altitude the tarps effectively shielded the camp from sight.

This pilot, Link knew, was not Howarski. While the Jet Ranger posed a threat, it was not as capable as the Night Hawk and carried no sensors or miniguns.

He climbed into the Jeep to rest.

Jenifer joined him. "How about some company? I'll stroke your brow—or whatever."

8:00 A.M.—Town of Spirit Lake

Jason answered the door. "Are they coming for us?" he blurted.

"Not yet," said Lonnie. He was taciturn as they walked into the yard to distance themselves from the listening devices. "It's time to give the order, Jase. Sly Paquette has your folder. Once his cops start bringing in all the people you named, the entire plan is screwed."

"The *Muk-wah* aren't ready."

"We sure as hell won't know if we do nothing and let them knock us off one at a time."

"They outnumber us four to one. They have automatic weapons."

His friend said nothing, just stared and waited.

Jason peered at the horizon. Clouds were scudding low and fast. A high-pressure system from Canada was settling in. The forecast was clear and cold.

He sighed. "Go ahead."

"Say the words, Jase. Do it right."

"Okay." He took in a breath. "Tell them to prepare for *Che-she*."

Lonnie turned and walked briskly to his pickup, on his way to contact three *Muk-wah*, each of whom would inform three others, and so on. There would be no phone calls. It was a pyramid notification, as military officers and the Manido had used for centuries in time of peril.

Bear Society warriors would top off their fuel tanks and prepare their weapons. They would mentally gird themselves for a fight to the death, and then wait and listen. When they heard the phrase *"Che-she* walks," all would proceed to their gathering places and attack.

And then they would all be killed. No one faced that sort of odds and survived.

Jason decided he must go to the pay telephone and call Erin for a final time.

10:57 A.M.—*White Dog Lake*

Link had slipped into the forest for the R-O transmission. As he waited he occupied himself with stroking the blade of the hand ax on a fine-grained flat stone. He felt kinship with the old implement, as if it held a residual memory that had been passed on by ancestors. The head was fashioned of tempered, blue-brown steel, and the words HUDSON BAY CO. were stamped into the metal. The sturdy eighteen-inch handle was firmly seated, wrapped from top to bottom with resin-coated animal gut.

He'd battered at the Black Hawk's bulletproof canopy with such force that the edge had been dulled, but with each stroke it was becoming as keen as ever. *Thank you, Nek-kah,* said Link in his mind, and wondered if the elusive hermit was watching them.

Jenifer joined him. "Mind if I listen in?"

"No. You have the keys?" he asked.

"Yep." She handed over both sets to each vehicle. Neither of them trusted Richards.

"It's time." He put away the ax, and switched the sat phone to R-O.

She leaned close so they both could hear.

"Nephew said two more patrolmen deployed to the north side. Nephew also stated that this is his final phone call, and refused to explain. Break. Big boss has ordered you to terminate activities and get out of there. I repeat . . ."

Link observed the readout. The battery was down to fifteen percent.

"Let me see the battery."

He opened the back of the sat phone, slipped out a flat, rectangular object, and held it up for her inspection. She eyed it closely, then took one of the sets of keys. "Turf keeps an assortment for his cameras in the Jeep. If one looks like that, I'll bring it."

As she walked toward the camp, Link wondered why he had not thought of that.

After a casual look around and a pleasant nod to Dr. Brogg, Jenifer activated the Jeep's electronic door locks, slid into the passenger's seat, and inserted the key into the console.

Brogg silently climbed into the backseat.

Damn! she said to herself, wishing he wasn't so nosy. She was about to make an excuse about what she was doing when the driver's door opened and Joseph Richards hastily took a seat.

Jenifer stared numbly at the automatic pistol in his hand. "Please don't point that."

"Just keep your mouth shut." He pulled the keys from her hand.

"This isn't necessary, Joseph."

"Oh? I wanted to leave last night, if you'll recall, but your friend wouldn't listen. He got sloppy. I found the clip to my pistol in his pack while the two of you slept this morning."

"Where's Turf?" she asked, concerned.

When Richards did not answer, Brogg found his voice. "He's fine. We tied him up."

Joseph started the engine and shifted into drive.

"Let me out," she said. "I really don't want to go."

He ignored her and eased the Jeep forward.

"Damn it, Joseph, I'm not your adversary," Jen told him.

"I agree. You're our insurance so your friend Link won't try anything."

"We won't harm you, Jenifer," Dr. Brogg said in his wavering voice.

"Didn't you listen to anything we said? The reservation patrolmen are killers!"

"You wonder why we don't listen to your lies?" Richards accelerated up the narrow path. "I followed you back there and saw you both listening to a cell phone. If we're such buddies, why didn't you share it with the rest of us?"

She leaned against the door, wondering if she could escape while they were underway.

"Don't even think about it," said Richards, motioning with the pistol. "Buckle in."

She hesitated.

"I wouldn't kill you, but I swear I'll wound you. Would you prefer I shoot you in the arm?"

Jenifer latched the shoulder harness.

"We were rushed," he complained. "I should have deflated the Rover's tires."

"Where are you taking us?"

"The cranberry farm so we can look for the wagon path. If it's not passable, we'll turn ourselves over to the authorities like we should have done yesterday."

She turned to Dr. Brogg. "Reason with him. They'll kill us."

"I'm not young as you, Jenifer. I'm cold and miserable. I've always been law-abiding, so I'll take my chances with the police."

Richards nodded in agreement. "If they're as corrupt as you claim, we'll go over their heads and lodge complaints."

Jenifer held on as he maneuvered the Cherokee, scraping past some bushes and driving over others. They arrived at the main road, and he turned left.

"The patrolmen are animals," she tried. "What do you think they'll do to *me*?"

"They're the *police*." As he accelerated he transferred the pistol to his left hand and drove with it clasped against the wheel. The muzzle was pointed toward her.

What if we hit a bump and the thing goes off?

As Joseph made two more turns, Jenifer noted that they were no longer going toward the cranberry marsh. She did not correct him. It was the last place she wanted to go. Periodically she glanced into the rearview mirror and caught glimpses of the Range Rover with two occupants. The driver was hanging back, playing cat and mouse.

Turf had obviously told Link about Richards's mental instability.

Again she saw the Range Rover peek around the corner behind them and halt. *Stay back,* she said to herself, not at all sure of what Joseph would do if he knew Link was in pursuit.

They passed through a long, open stretch with grassy

meadow on each side. In the middle of the straightaway were a series of potholes so cruel that Joseph was forced to slow to a crawl.

"Put the gun away, Joseph," she tried.

He regarded the weapon somberly. "I don't think so."

"Then please let me out. I'm really frightened."

Dr. Brogg spoke up. "It can't hurt now, Joseph. Let her out."

Richards appeared to be considering it, then looked ahead. "Too late," he said, and nodded at two black-and-white SUVs coming around the bend ahead.

He stopped just fifty feet distant, as two patrolmen carrying long weapons clambered from the lead vehicle. One was scarecrow thin. The other, a fleshy man in uniform, stalked forward, shrieking, "Get your fuckin' hands in view!"

Jenifer recalled Willie's reputation with appropriate trepidation. The last time she'd seen him was at the marsh pond, after he'd killed another patrolman.

"*Everyone* out!"

Richards tossed out his pistol. He opened the door and climbed out, smiling, his hands raised. "We've been looking for you to—"

Willie swung the rifle butt hard into Joseph Richards's chest. Without an utterance the expedition leader crumpled onto the road.

Brogg dismounted, crying, "We're *friendly,*" his voice high and filled with fright.

Willie crossed to Jenifer's side, grinning now. "You heard me, councilwoman. Out!" As she dismounted, he grabbed her by the fabric of her jacket, kicked her feet apart, and shoved her against the Jeep. Before she could collect herself he'd jammed the rifle barrel into her belly so hard the air exploded from her lungs. As Jenifer bent over, desperately trying to breathe, Willie casually reached into the coat and grasped a breast.

"Man," laughed the scarecrow patrolman, "you've got that down to a science."

"I've been wantin' in the councilwoman's pants since I heard about Anderson fuckin' her brains out."

"Please leave her alone," Dr. Brogg pleaded helplessly.

Willie nodded at his partner. "Kick his ass while I take the bitch over in the grass."

The scarecrow shoved the shotgun's breech into Brogg's face. The doctor wilted to the ground, drooling blood and broken teeth.

"Back—off," Jenifer managed, although Willie pressed the rifle's barrel so harshly into her abdomen it was difficult to breathe.

He grinned and squeezed her breast. Jenifer yelped at the sharp pain, then grasped both the shotgun and his hand and forcefully shoved them away. *"Stop!"*

Willie made an exaggerated *Oooooh* look and poised a hand to slap her.

"Didn't Paquette tell you about me?"

His grin faded just slightly.

"I'm Sydney, you fool."

A pallor swept over Willie's face. He sprang back, as if confronted by a cobra.

PART III

The Warehouse

31

Not even noon and Gloria was already weary. She'd finished with the guest quarters and was outside lugging her cleaning tools, preparing to scrub another floor of the Warehouse buildings. She was rail-thin with weary undereye smudges and appeared so obviously to be a hopeless crankhead that they no longer bothered to ensure she snorted her ration of meth. She'd plead for more, and they'd not suspect that she dropped the powder into the mop water.

Stomach pains bothered her, which she determined was a symptom of starvation. The only food she'd kept down was the morsels of a Danish one of the guests in the Resort had discarded into a waste can. If he'd possessed polite eating habits, there would have been nothing.

Gloria still had every intention of escaping, yet she believed it would border on impossible to do alone. She needed an accomplice, but found no candidates among the raccoon-eyed addicts who would turn her in in a minute in exchange for a larger allotment of dope.

She'd left the security office cleaning for last, for something was afoot. Howarski appeared tired and his moods swung from jolly to morose. The military helicopter had been moved from its parking spot. Engineers had removed charred panels and black boxes, making her believe there had been an accident, which would account for Howarski's foul mood.

The second helo, the *normal* one, had been flown out at daybreak, the female pilot augmented by armed security people, and twice had returned for refueling.

Gloria paused at the entrance of Building Two as the sky net rumbled open, and the normal helicopter descended onto the pad. This was no routine refueling stop. Two persons deplaned, the first a woman whose countenance was obscured beneath the peaked hood of a blue coat, the second a large man so badly beaten his mother would not have recognized him. The hooded woman strode past him to the security control center, not wasting a glance as he was pushed into the crude laborers' sleeping quarters that Gloria shared with the Manidos.

Another slave-addict? she wondered. He seemed too pasty-fleshed to have Indian blood.

She changed course, dragging her cleaning gear—a difficult feat for a person in her weakened state—toward the security control center, where the engineers were gathering. At the door, she moved one heavy item at a time into the crowded room. Several engineers stood close by, but none assisted her.

All listened intently as Howarski used a video and electronic map displays to explain the just-completed security upgrades. "With our missiles and antiaircraft cannon we can destroy anyone who approaches from the air. Now we can say the same for an intruder on the ground. Our system is foolproof. The MBI concept, first employed by Siemens Industries . . ."

The hooded woman who stood near the front flicked her fingers dismissively. "Quickly. I have a busy schedule." Her voice was soft but forceful, and somehow familiar to Gloria.

Howarski pointed out the numerous colored boxes on the map. "Our system uses three types of sensors mounted on platforms scattered throughout the zone. To remember those, think of the acronym MBI, which stands for motion, body heat, and imaging.

"We begin by fixing the background, wind swaying the bushes and trees, rabbits, squirrels, and birds. That alone took a great deal of programming skill."

"Can we get past the chest thumping?"

"The system looks for large mammalian motion. Then, does it radiate body heat? If thermal imaging tells us it's of human proportion and intensity, we continue. If not, the contact is classified as background clutter, and ignored. We still have our forest pristine."

"Please," said the woman, observing a gold watch.

Howarski spoke sullenly. "Unless we're truly threatened I reject brutality to animals. Their protection is important to me."

"I understand. Now please continue. I really must hurry."

"Let's say we've determined the contact is human. Now the next big question: Is it friend or foe?" He explained the electro-optical sensors, then the interworking of multiple sensors, to obtain foolproof identities. "If any inputs matched with our records, the system creates a safe zone, just as it did with animals, and the person can pass."

The woman asked, "And if my—umm—appearance changes?"

"In the event of ambiguity the computer will ask for a password."

She laughed aloud. "So all of this boils down to remembering a word? I believe signs and countersigns were used by King David's army."

Howarski was not pleased with her demeaning tone.

"You've run tests, I assume," said the woman.

"Of course." Howarski switched on the VCR. The monitor showed a figure stumbling through the woods. One of the Manido Indian laborers that Gloria recognized, for she had considered using him as an accomplice until his physical condition rapidly deteriorated. The previous day he had not returned from work at the meth factory.

A loud and brittle mechanical voice sounded over a speaker. "MOTION DETECTED."

The man stopped. He was thin as a stickman, with dark eyes.

"BODY HEAT DETECTED."

The man frowned, and looked about with a dazed expression.

The monotone continued. "ONE HUMAN DE-TECTED. STOP AND REMAIN STILL FOR EX-AMINATION."

The man froze, the only movement his eyes that darted feverishly about.

"It's best if the intruder remains motionless during targeting," said Howarski. "The explosive's on a gimbal and takes a few seconds to come to bear."

"NEGATIVE MATCH. STATE YOUR PASS-WORD."

"Unless he tries to run he has a minute to react," said Howarski, lips pursed thoughtfully.

The group watched the large digital clock with its red numerals.

The laborer remained still, hardly breathing.

Crack! The man who had been center focus disap-peared in a spray of red.

The hooded woman gave a brisk nod of approval.

Howarski ran another video sequence, showing one of the engineers very cautiously entering the same area of forest. After the initial detection the system recog-nized him. The final sequence showed another engineer who was not recognized, but who uttered the proper word.

In both instances the system boomed, "POSITIVE MATCH. IDENTITY CONFIRMED. PROCEED."

Howarski began to explain how contacts that were recognized as friendly, such as innocent mammalia, were given a tracking number and ignored throughout their time in the—

The woman in the hood sighed. "Please hurry."

"I would also like to explain what an incredible task all of this entailed."

"I understand how brilliant you all are. Now please *continue*."

Gloria remained in back of the room, obscure, slack-jawed and uncaring. The truth of the matter was that she despaired. It would have been difficult enough to escape before, but now the blond-haired genius had raised the bar. Was it now impossible?

"We completed the field tests. Today, as soon as the

staff are processed by the computer and given a password, the system will be activated."

Gloria remembered that four meth slaves who had been too worn out for further donkeywork had disappeared. There'd been periodic *Crack!* sounds from the forest since her arrival.

"How long does this *processing* take," the woman asked, "so I won't become an accidental victim?"

"Less than a minute. Remove your coat, please."

When the woman handed her hooded coat to Howarski, Gloria heard only the roaring in her ears—for she observed an image of herself, or rather, the person she had been. She felt a cruel mix of helplessness and outrage, and wanted to scream in protest. Only after a few vulnerable seconds did Gloria force herself to return to the vacant stare. In the periphery of her vision she saw the woman glance her way, but the rail-thin cleaning woman in rags, with swollen nose and broken teeth, did not worry that she might be recognized.

Howarski led the woman to an *X* shadow-painted on the floor, where four digital cameras were focused, and regarded an engineer at the console. "Name, Sydney. Access unlimited."

The woman who had stolen her face was called Sydney.

The engineer at the console depressed a series of keys.

"Give your password. Something you won't forget."

Sydney spoke in a low voice. Gloria thought she heard the word "vengeance."

"How much longer?" snapped Sydney.

Howarski smirked. "You're done," he told her.

The woman took her coat back, looking thoughtful. "Even if they come you mustn't harm the expedition people. We need to return them to the search. As you know, time is running out."

What did Sydney mean, time is running out? thought Gloria. *For whom?*

"Do *not* harm them," Sydney repeated in the familiar voice, which like everything else about her was very much like Gloria's.

Howarski sighed dramatically. "You want to exclude *everyone* on the expedition?"

"Not Anderson, of course." She considered. "Richards and Siegel are the experts."

"Include their names as passwords," Howarski snapped at the engineer at the console.

Behind the gathering Gloria Vasson pushed her bucket toward the toilet. In her mind she repeated the words "motion," "body heat," "imaging," and tried to store everything she had heard.

Her double, Sydney, drew on her coat.

"There's a final subject," said Howarski. "The Code Red options, in case we're about to be compromised. There are three levels of alarm . . ."

Gloria listened and despaired. If they declared Code Red, escape would be impossible.

The moment Howarski finished, Sydney said, "Fine, now I'd like a helicopter tour of the north side, and an explanation from *some*one why no one's found the damned expedition."

Gloria entered the bathroom to clean, trying desperately to memorize it all by placing everything into neat categories—wishing she could forget the visions of the laborers being killed, and that of her own once-lovely face.

An engineer entered to use the urinal, and ignored the faceless woman who was perched on hands and knees, scrubbing diligently.

Wilderness Road

"I'm Sydney, you fool!" said Jenifer, her abdomen shrieking from the pain administered by the jab with the rifle's muzzle.

Willie sprang back as if confronted by a cobra. "Sorry!"

"You don't *know* how sorry," she warned as two more reservation police thugs approached from the second vehicle. She offered them the hard look she'd given Willie.

"She's Sydney," Willie said in an unnatural voice.

"Leave him alone," Jenifer said to Willie's partner,

who stood over Dr. Brogg. "He has information we need."

Willie groveled. "You say leave him alone, it's done."

Joseph Richards struggled to one knee. He had his arms wrapped about his damaged ribs and rocked to and fro, grimacing in pain.

"How about him?" Willie looked hopeful.

"Don't hurt him so bad he can't work. He still has to find the gym bag."

"Yeah."

"I'd better get in touch with Rose," said a new arrival. He had a large nose and wore a blustering look, as if he was the man in charge.

Willie gave Jenifer another ingratiating smile. She stared back sternly, using every ounce of her considerable psych training as well as her newfound acting ability.

"She's lying," Joseph managed. "She and Anderson are liars."

"What's he talking about?" asked Big Nose.

"They have a cell phone, and they're conspiring against the rest of us," said Joseph. "There's no one named Sydney. She made it all up."

"Guy's nuts," Willie said. "We were told about Sydney."

"He's delusional," said Jenifer, ignoring the nausea still rising from her bruised abdomen and the fire in her throbbing breast.

She endured the pain as she walked around and climbed into the driver's seat.

The thug with the big nose sent for his radio. "Don't leave until I talk to Rose."

"I don't have time for your games," Jenifer snapped. "If you don't trust me, follow me and call anyone you like." Her heart pounded wildly as she played out her game.

She adjusted the mirrors, half expecting one of them to open the door and drag her out. When that did not happen she pressed her luck again and pointed out at Brogg. "Load him in back. I'll take him to Paquette and get some answers."

"No sweat." Willie grabbed Brogg by the coat and dragged him toward the rear.

"Don't let her take him," Joseph cried. "He's escaping with me."

"Guy's nutty as a pecan bar," said Willie's scarecrow partner.

Willie hoisted Dr. Brogg into the rear compartment and slammed the hatch. "He's in," he called out dutifully.

Jenifer considered having them load Joseph into the rear as well, but decided she'd pressed her luck entirely enough. "Get out of the way so I can turn around."

"Wait while I call the sergeant," argued Big Nose as his gofer arrived with his radio.

Jenifer put the Jeep in reverse, cranked the wheel sharply, and narrowly missed running over Willie as she backed off the road into what appeared to be grass.

Instead the rear wheels settled into soggy marsh.

No! Jenifer cried inwardly, and her heart pounded even more fiercely. She jammed the lever into drive and hit the gas, causing the rear tires to make a whirring sound.

"Stay right there while I call in," Big Nose yelled ominously.

Willie argued, "Sydney don't have time for candy-ass Rose. They told us she'd tell us who she was, and to do what she said."

"Stay out of it."

"Fuck both you and Rose, ace. The lady even gives orders to Paquette, which is where she's taking that poor bastard." He snickered. "You *don't* wanta trade places with him."

Jenifer tried putting the Jeep into drive, tapping the gas—into reverse, tapping the gas—drive and reverse, rocking the Jeep to and fro. The rear tires settled deeper.

"Lemme talk to Sarge," Big Nose said into the radio. "Got a woman says she's Sydney."

Jenifer made herself slow down. Like all women of the Northwoods she'd been stuck a thousand times. *Stop and think!*

The large-nosed patrolman was still waiting for Sergeant Rose as she selected 4WD, LOW RANGE. A mechanical clank sounded as the transmission changed modes, and she fought the urge to vomit as she twisted the wheel and backed up just inches. Before the Jeep could settle into the same rut, she twisted the wheel to the right, put the lever into D-1, and crept forward. She progressed so slowly it was maddening, listening to the patrolman a dozen feet away who had finally raised Sergeant Rose.

"Naw, we didn't hurt 'em too much," Big Nose said into the radio.

The SUV crawled onto the roadway—Jenifer praying that they'd not become mired again. Big Nose walked in front of the Jeep and raised his hand. "Sarge and the Junkman oughta be here in fifteen minutes."

Jenifer carefully put the shifter in reverse, looked into the backup mirror at the three men and the vehicle directly behind, and pushed the accelerator to the floor.

The patrolmen yelled out as the Jeep roared into their midst. She heard a thump as the vehicle impacted flesh—then felt a terrific jolt as the rear bumper smashed into the front of the Ford and violently shoved it back and around.

There was no *way* they could follow.

Jenifer dropped the shifter into drive and pressed on the gas—the Jeep spewed dirt and stones as it fishtailed forward. The big-nosed thug leaped onto the Jeep's hood and reached about wildly for some sort of purchase so he wouldn't slide off.

A look into the rearview mirror showed that the ones who had made it out of her path were gawking at the thug who writhed on the ground, shrieking and holding a bloody leg. A moment later she watched as Willie drew down with his M16.

"Damn you, *don't!*" she screamed through the open window, and he actually lowered the rifle. Jenifer crouched, making herself into the smallest target possible, craning her neck to see past the big-nosed thug, who had a death's grip on both windshield wipers.

She glanced back to see Willie's partner aiming.

Boom! The rear window shattered, and buckshot showered the interior.

Jenifer swerved wildly, yet Big Nose hung on precariously. Why wasn't she going faster? She remembered then and slowed to shift into HIGH RANGE, hoping Big Nose would take the opportunity to jump free. He did not, so she accelerated again, praying the Explorer back there was badly enough damaged that it would block the way while she escaped.

They were a third of the way to the distant curve when Big Nose reached down for his pistol. She swerved hard. He forgot about the pistol and held on for dear life.

Jenifer decided to continue until they rounded the curve, then stop abruptly. If Big Nose did not go flying she'd let Link—who she knew was waiting there—deal with him.

A pair of bullets punched through the windshield from behind. Big Nose slumped and his blood streaked the fractured glass, yet he somehow clung to his perch.

She screamed into the back for Dr. Brogg to stay down, just as she smashed into a granddaddy pothole and bounced so hard she momentarily lost her grasp of the wheel.

Then there were no more sounds of gunfire.

She wondered why. They were only halfway to the distant curve. Were they out of range?

A look into the mirror showed that the two thugs who were diminishing in size were lowering their weapons. While the fact surprised her, she exulted. They'd made it!

Link had stopped at the curve in the road, backed the Rover into the thicket, and observed. He had tried to remain out of their view from the beginning.

Turf regarded the drama with drawn breath. "She's got 'em confused," he exclaimed, and Link almost said, "Me too."

Her game was working despite the fact that one of the thugs clung precariously to her windshield, and Willie and his partner fired wildly.

She was halfway!

Link was determined to wait, to pull out and follow her as she passed, yet inside he still felt a tingle of impending peril, the sure knowledge that she was not yet safe.

There! As the sounds of gunfire diminished he heard the staccato beat of a helicopter.

The forest green Jet Ranger flew directly into Jenifer's path, only feet above the roadway.

She swerved to avoid collision, unnecessarily, for the pilot maneuvered sharply up and away. It was too late for her to recover—the Jeep veered off the road, slammed into a lone pine, and careened back toward the road.

The Cherokee wobbled, bounced, and the man on the hood was flung off, his shriek truncated as he tumbled onto the road. The Jeep rolled onto its side, then its top, squarely onto the gunman, and continued sliding, leaving a bloody trail.

The overturned vehicle came to rest, a front wheel spinning aimlessly.

The helicopter set down just twenty feet from the wreckage. Two figures emerged and stood on either side of the chopper, wielding M16s and looking warily about.

A third person deplaned and approached the Jeep, a woman who pushed back the hood of her heavy blue coat, knelt, and stared underneath. She motioned for assistance.

Willie and his partner maneuvered the second black and white past the wrecked one and drove toward the helicopter.

"We'd better get out of here," said Turf.

Link ignored him as he continued to observe, unarmed and helpless to intervene.

When Willie drove up he gawked at Gloria Vasson as if he were viewing a ghost. She said something and pointed. After a moment's hesitation Willie and his partner crawled underneath and labored until they pulled two bodies free of the wreckage.

Both were bloodied, and above the noise of the helicopter's idling engines could be heard Dr. David Brogg's anguished outcries for help.

Gloria gave directions, then followed as they carried Jenifer Toussaint to the helicopter and deposited her inside.

"I saw her move," Turf said in a croaking voice.

"Yes," said Link, his voice cold as steel.

Willie asked a question of Gloria as she boarded the helicopter.

She looked back with an irritated frown and nodded.

The shooters were climbing back into the Jet Ranger when Willie stalked over, drew his pistol, and fired a round into Brogg's head. The screams were silenced.

"Jesus!" Turf Siegel whispered.

Two new black-and-white vehicles arrived at the distant turn, pulled around the damaged one, and proceeded toward the crash scene. Sergeant Rose drove the lead Explorer. The hulk beside him could only be the Junkman.

The helicopter did not wait. The craft lifted off, turned, and flew away.

Link drove from the trees where they'd been hiding, back in the direction from which they'd come.

Turf was shaken. "Why did they kill Brogg?"

"He was injured. A hindrance to them," said Link. He wondered about Jenifer Toussaint's condition, and where Gloria Vasson might be taking her. It did not matter. He vowed to follow her to the corners of hell and bring her back.

32

Weyland Building, Manhattan, New York

Erin's phone buzzed.

"Twenty-seven seventy-five," she responded, giving the office suite number.

"This is Tower," said a quiet voice.

She glanced at the V-A and confirmed that it was indeed FBI Supervisory Special Agent Gordon Tower. "It's been a while," she said.

"We should talk," he said.

"Official?" she asked, hoping it was not. When they'd last spoken *officially* there had been a brick wall.

"Nothing even close. I'm hanging my neck out just dialing this number. When are you planning on heading home?"

She considered her tasks with Helga the computer. "Two hours."

"I'll save you taxi fare. I'm driving a black Suburban. See you at the Garden Entrance."

The Warehouse, Manido Indian Reservation

Gloria examined the burly man who had been brought in on the helicopter. He appeared so badly beaten that she doubted he could have his senses about him.

"Where am I?" he muttered through swollen lips.

"The Warehouse."

"What the hell's that?"

"We'll talk about it later," she said, thinking it would be unwise to relate too much. "Are you a crankhead like the others?"

He snorted. "I hate that shit. I was a damned good cop most of my life."

Her recent experiences with policemen were unpleasant. "Where?"

"Milwaukee. Name's Ron Doughty." He took in a painful breath. "World's greatest investigator, barbecue chef, Packers fan, and Brewers rooter." Another raspy breath. "Used to be a superb leg-wrestler, until my daughter broke my knee. How about you? Want to leg-wrestle?"

For the first time in a long while Gloria smiled. "You're awfully beat-up to be so feisty, Mr. D. Who did it?"

"Tribal police took me to their headquarters and had their fun. Then a guy named Sly Paquette played with my mind."

"You're lucky he didn't kill you."

"No reason to." His voice changed to bitterness. "He threatened my grandkids and I told him everything he asked. I'm not very proud of myself."

Gloria decided to trust him just a bit. She desperately needed a partner for her escape, and he at least sounded sober. "How bad off are you?"

He grunted. "I'm hurting some."

She showed no sympathy. "So are all the laborers. There's a couple here who beat the spirit out of new arrivals, but they'll probably give you a pass since you aren't in such great shape to begin with. Put on a good act and they may let you heal for a day before they destroy your brain and load you down like a donkey."

"I don't understand."

"They'll give you a daily ration of methamphetamine, even put it in the food to keep you cranked up so you'll work like a zombie."

"Jesus."

"Try to get as little in your system as possible, but don't let them know."

"Who are you?" It was murky dark in the sleeping quarters.

"The cleaning woman. If you can stay off the dope, I'll be a friend."

She heard the sounds of the warning horn, and the net withdrawing on its tracks.

"I heard that earlier. What is it?"

"The sky opening. I've got to go." She pushed open the door.

"They don't lock us in?" he asked.

"No reason to. If we stray, they'll shoot us. If we get any farther, the sensors will detect us and they'll blow us up."

"Sounds impossible."

"That's what they believe." She formed her fool's expression, closed the door behind herself, and methodically began to push her bucket toward the next building.

The civilian helo was landing. She acted uninterested in everything but moving the cleaning equipment, yet missed absolutely nothing.

The woman called Sydney supervised the removal of an obviously injured female whom two engineers carried to Building One. It took a moment before Gloria realized who it had been.

A while later she cleaned there and found the room on the far end locked. There were no sounds from inside, and she wondered if Jenifer Toussaint was alive.

Gloria was not a technical genius like Howarski or his engineers, but she had more than her share of common sense and was methodical-minded to a fault, which—come to think of it—had been the reason she'd alienated Jenifer during their confrontation in Georgetown.

Jenifer was Eddie's daughter, and he'd been proud of her. At first sight Gloria had enjoyed Jenifer's lively spontaneity, so like her father's that there should have been no question of parenthood, but after a drink too many she had questioned too archly, and driven her away.

She wondered if there was a way to save her—if she was alive.

Wilderness Road, North Side

Link futilely tried to follow the helicopter that de-parted with Jenifer and Gloria Vasson. When it disap-peared from view and hearing, he focused on where Jen might have been taken.

The Hatchet Club, where Gloria was staying? An air-port outside the reservation? The Warehouse, whatever and wherever that might be? Turf periodically attempted conversation, but Link remained focused.

He dredged up the brief time in the camp shared with Gloria when she had observed, "Jenifer is important to you, isn't she?"

The words echoed. Gloria had succeeded twofold that day. She had determined that he was a threat, and found a weakness in his thick armor.

She'd accused Jenifer of prostituting herself, baiting him to get a rise. Gloria Vasson—*or whoever she was*—was a master at trickery. There, he had thought it. Was she someone other than Gloria?

Jen said Gloria Vasson knew that Senator Eddie was her father. The woman he'd spoken with had not known. She'd kept a hood in place so he couldn't examine her closely, and claimed to have a cold so he would not get close. She had departed hastily, and a short time later at the marsh pond, he'd overheard Sly Paquette saying that *Sydney* had just declared him dangerous. He was to be killed on sight.

Conclusion: the Gloria who had visited him at the camp, and who had taken Jenifer, was Sydney. She held the trump card. She could threaten Jenifer with harm or use her as bait and know that Link Anderson would react. Sydney was the puppet master.

Wilderness Road, North Side

Sergeant George Rose observed the overturned Jeep and the dead man named Brogg who still lay beside it. Two of his men were out of action, one dead and one being taken to town with a crushed leg, but the murdered civilian made his heart heavier than either of those.

Willie was off to one side, smoking dope and sullenly refusing to help haul the Jeep upright so they could get to the supervisor's body underneath. He and his skinny partner claimed to have done absolutely nothing wrong, blaming everything on others. No one was left to argue except Joseph Richards, who had broken ribs and was so frightened of Willie that Rose took everything he said with a large grain of salt.

Rose radioed Sly Paquette's private frequency, as he'd promised to do when he gave him the first heads-up call, and laid out the story he'd pieced together.

Sly was not surprised that the helicopter had appeared when it had, or even that a woman resembling Gloria Vasson had hauled off Jenny Toussaint. He seemed more interested in Billy Junkins's observation about a vehicle that had been parked around the bend.

"Anderson?" he asked.

"Whoever it was probably watched the whole thing."

"We got our orders, Rose. Get rid of Anderson."

Rose wondered, *Orders from whom? The woman named Sydney? Gloria Vasson?*

Instead he said, "I sent a crew up to the camp Richards told us about. They found a stove, a box of food, and some tarps, but Anderson and Siegel were gone. The north side's awfully large. Any chance we'll get the helicopter back?"

"Probably." Paquette paused thoughtfully. "Let me talk to Willie boy."

Sly was not trusting. He used Willie and the Junkman to look over Rose's shoulder.

Willie sauntered over as if expecting to be called. He complained that his radio should have Paquette's frequency set in so they could talk privately.

"I knew all along the councilwoman wasn't Sydney," he immediately told Paquette, "but the dumb shit in charge let her go and got hisself killed. An' Sarge didn't mention everything. This Richards guy says Anderson talked to someone on a freakin' phone."

Willie looked puzzled at a question. "Cell phone I guess."

He wore a smirk as he handed the repeater radio back to Rose.

"You didn't tell me about any phone," Paquette said.

"Because I don't believe it. Cell phones don't work up here."

Paquette gave a begrudging grunt. "I'll see if I can get the chopper back. Meantime, put Richards back to looking for the fuckin' gym bag. We got a deadline."

What deadline? "I'll call a few more patrolmen from town to help him."

"Whatever. Let me talk with Billy so I can get his take on things."

"He's gone," said George Rose. "He took a shotgun and one of the vehicles."

Paquette laughed humorlessly. "Better say a prayer for Anderson."

Wilderness Road, near Moose Lake

They were parked at the southern shoreline of Moose Lake, and for the first time in three hours heard the clop-clop sound of helicopter blades.

"We better hide da Rover," said Turf.

"Take your gear and stay here. I'll be back for you."

"Maybe I oughta stay wit' you. Where you goin'?"

"Helicopter hunting." Link put the Rover into drive.

"Aw shit!" Turf scrambled out, took his sleeping bag and day pack from the back, and started for the trees.

"Stay away from the road and out of sight," Link called after him. "They'll be looking."

"Yeah." Turf gave Link a glance and head shake like he was truly nuts.

Link drove west, then north, homing in on the sounds of the helicopter while he devised a plan of attack. He started with objectives. What was he after? *One, get the chopper to land. Two, capture one of the crew and learn where they took Jenifer.*

It did not enter his mind that either of those was impossible. All he needed was a good plan. At a fork in the road he again turned toward the sound, still trying to organize something that made more sense than building another scarecrow.

Link heard the surges of power and varying tempo of the rotor blades of a maneuvering helicopter. It was close by, and he decided the pilot had spotted the Rover.

How would they react?

Bap-bap-bap—brrraaaaatt. The back window shattered!

The helicopter passed over, going fast, then banked and turned back. Two green-uniformed shooters were at the open door, weapons at their shoulders.

Link tapped the brake hard, grasped the pack that he'd carried for the past two days, and, as the Rover slowed to a crawl, cranked the wheel toward the roadside thicket. As the vehicle entered the dense foliage he eased the driver's door open.

Plan? If you don't have one, fake it!

As the Rover came to a rest in the bushes, he propped his Stetson on the headrest.

Bap-bap-bap—brrraaaaatt—bap-bap-bap. Holes zipped through the Rover's top and stitched the seat as he slithered out. *Bap-bap-bap—brrraaaaatt.* Leaves around him jumped frantically as he crawled away, then curled behind a sturdy maple trunk and became immobile.

The firing continued as the shooters sprayed the earth below, periodically coming too close for his comfort. He remained still, and hopefully unseen.

The helicopter maneuvered, flew away down the road, and then returned.

Brrraaaaaaatt—bap-bap-bap—brrraaaaatt. There were tinny sounds of bullets penetrating metal. They were shooting up the Rover again. *Bap-bap-bap—brrraaaaatt.*

Land, he willed them. *Land the damn chopper before you accidently hit me!*

The pilot flew very slowly as they examined the ground below.

Land!

The Jet Ranger's engine surged and the rotor blades clopped noisily. He reached into the pack, found the handle of the ax, and moved his head just slightly for a look. The forest green helicopter hovered over a clearing only thirty yards from the Range Rover, which was pocked and dotted with bullet holes.

The craft slowly descended, the two men in green staring at the Rover from the chopper's opened door keeping the muzzles of their assault rifles lowered, frowning and obviously not enamored by what they'd done. They were obviously unaccustomed to such action, yet Link had no charity for the two who had nearly taken his life—and still might.

As the helicopter touched down they cautiously exited and crouched beneath the still-spinning blades. They looked back. The pilot made a curt motion, waving them toward the ruined Rover. "APPROACH THE VEHICLE," came a booming female voice.

Link started at the sound, then realized it was from the helicopter's PA system.

He eased the hand ax free from the pack and brought it up, moving slowly so he would not startle them with abrupt motion. He told himself again to take at least one of them alive.

Link gave himself an A plus in on-the-spot planning.

The men approached with hesitation and suspicion, which added to his problem.

Link hugged the earth and crawled behind a cluster of bushes that concealed him but offered no protection from bullets.

"DON'T TAKE ANY CHANCES," said the PA voice. "ANDERSON'S A PROFESSIONAL."

"He's still inside!" The first, taller one raised his assault rifle and fired a long burst into the vehicle. *Brrrraaa—aaaaatt.* The rounds shattered the remaining glass in the side window and blasted the Stetson into bits of felt.

As the sound echoed, Link decided the scarecrow ruse had worked for a second time after all. He also determined he was beyond the men, and turned to crawl directly toward them.

"LOOK IN THE VEHICLE," said the booming voice.

Things happened very swiftly then. As the lead man approached the Rover and the second stared about, Link eased to his feet and crouched, now in the open behind them both.

"WATCH . . ."

Link threw the ax at the taller man and rushed the second, heavier one.

". . . OUT!" boomed the female voice.

The second man was startled, but came around with the M16 as Link leaped.

Bap-bap . . .

Link bowled him over, grappled, and found him to be strong. It took all of his available muscle to hold the muzzle aside as the weapon was fired. *Bap!*

"WITHDRAW! WITHDRAW!"

Link held on as the stocky shooter gritted his teeth, got a new grip, and forced the rifle muzzle around. *Bap!* The round passed so close to Link's face he felt its wind.

He slammed the butt of his palm into the shooter's jaw, heard a wet gurgle as he pulled the M16 free, and turned to face the first one.

He was leaning against the side of the Rover, slack-jawed and wide-eyed, clutching the handle of the ax embedded in his bony shoulder.

Link turned his attention, as well as the M16, to the helicopter.

The engines squealed and the blades churned as the pilot prepared to take off. Link aimed the rifle at the woman's head and watched her expression turn to fear.

"Shut down!" he called out, mouthing the words distinctly since they could not be heard.

The pilot spoke into her headset mike, and stared back at Link as she listened to something being said. She made her choice. The engine surged.

Frighten her! Link shifted his aim point just slightly and fired a warning round through the Plexiglas into the bulkhead by the pilot's head.

She visibly flinched, but the metal skids continued to lift from the earth.

Link fired a second, then a third round, now trying for the transmission above and aft of the pilot to disable the craft. The helicopter continued its climb as if mocking his marksmanship—and then wobbled, and a shrill whine sounded. The chopper began to yaw wildly.

"Oh *damn*!"

Link turned and sprinted as fast as he could possibly run. He took a backward glance as the craft tilted more ominously and then flew directly into the big maple tree that loomed over the stricken Range Rover.

He dived and rolled desperately off the road.

There was no fireball, only the stripping away of rotor blades as they impacted into the tree, and crashing sounds as the fuselage fell to earth, impacting on the Range Rover.

There followed the deep silence that marks the death of an aircraft, occasionally marred by the sounds of debris falling through the trees.

Link released a pent-up breath, and his eyes came to rest on a tail rotor blade that had skewered the trunk of a small pine—no more than four feet distant.

He stood on shaky legs, stepped back onto the road, then warily trudged closer to the wreckage. A fire had ignited upon impact and spread to the heavy jet petroleum that was pooling under the fuselage.

After a brief search he decided that both M16s—including the one that he'd dropped—were lost in the burning wreckage.

The fire and smoke would draw attention. He started to return to Turf Siegel, whom he'd left two or three miles distant, when he saw the gut-wrapped handle of the hand ax protruding from the debris. It did not dislodge from the dead man's torso easily.

As he ran along the shoulder of the road, Link decided that his planning abilities were wanting. He had no helicopter, no crewman to question, and he'd lost the Range Rover—even his sleeping bag.

He reduced the grade he'd given himself to a C. Not an F because he'd eliminated a threat. Link did not dwell on the three lives that had been lost. They had declared themselves by taking Jenifer.

33

Wilderness Forest, North Side

Turf sprinted desperately through the forest, directly away from the road, moving as rapidly as he possibly could yet knowing it was not nearly fast enough to save his life.

He'd heard distant gunfire, but because of his situation he did not possess a shred of curiosity. A man facing horrible death concentrates only upon escape.

Branches whipped and bloodied his face; he ran on, unheeding, his mind filled with how he was about to perish in a cold, lonely, and inhospitable place. It no longer held beauty for him, only the dark heart of the giant back there.

Would anyone care when he died? Who would even know? He was hopelessly lost, but what did it matter if one was lost when he was run down and slain. And who cared that it had been his own stupidity that led to it?

Turf had not hidden as Link had told him. Instead he'd dawdled at the tree line, watching the road but listening so intently to the sounds of the helicopter that he'd not noticed the Explorer that had idled along with its occupant peering intently at the sides of the road.

The Junkman had braked to a halt, staring directly at him with a look of such satisfaction that there was no slightest doubt that he'd been seen.

Turf had left his sleeping bag and pack behind and run wildly, away from the huge man, heart pounding as if it might burst in his chest.

*   *   *

Billy Junkins strode through the forest, hefting the sawed-off shotgun that he preferred, nostrils flared to savor each subtle scent of his fleeing prey. While the trail Siegel left was distinct, Billy was also relying on his sense of smell. He discerned the man's fear, caught it in the stirring of wind, and wondered whether to kill Turf Siegel outright. He decided it was better to cripple and leave him tethered, investigate the gunfire, and then return. Paquette still wanted him to search for the gym bag.

He broke into a trot, feeling the anticipation of the end of the hunt, and . . . he slowed and frowned, for the tracks of the fleeing man dwindled and disappeared.

Billy stopped after a few more steps, wondering how it could be. Siegel was not woods wise. If he were pursuing Lincoln Anderson he would expect difficulty, but this one had been leaving more sign than a mob of clumsy clowns.

He backtracked for a dozen feet, staring at the earth and puzzling for a long moment. Then he looked to one side and saw where the tracks resumed in a new direction, and smiled. His prey had taken evasive action, however small, by walking back in his own tracks. Not a bad job of it, but he had not gone back far enough.

Billy would pursue a little slower and more warily.

A hundred yards farther and the trail diminished once more and again stopped.

That time it took several long minutes before he located the spoor, and he went slower yet, becoming irritated as he wondered how the man who had stumbled through the forest could so abruptly become so clever. Also, Billy no longer smelled the fear, just . . .

Acrid odors wafted in the cold breeze. Billy Junkins lifted his head, frowned, and gave an abrupt, harsh shake of his massive head.

He recognized kerosene smoke, and the sweet stench of burning flesh.

A few moments later the human tracks ended, and that time they did not continue.

*   *   *

Link Anderson trotted down a narrow game trail that would take him to where he'd left Turf. He tallied up the score. One Range Rover and comfortable hat in exchange for a helicopter and crew. The thought offered little comfort for he was no closer to finding Jenifer.

He stopped to listen, heard a whisper of sound, and saw a momentary flash of buckskin. By the time he was sure of the sighting, it had disappeared.

Link waited patiently, and a moment later heard someone laboring on the trail ahead. A long minute passed before Turf Siegel came into view, gasping breaths and stumbling. He stopped and uttered a small shriek. His face altered as he recognized Link.

"He's . . . back . . . there," he gasped.

"Who?" Link asked, looking past him.

"Junk . . . man."

"Where?"

"Real . . . close."

Behind Turf, Nek-kah partially emerged. He silently motioned northward, then glowered in imitation of the Junkman.

Link tuned his senses and heard a vague and distant sound. When he looked back, the old hermit had vanished into the forest.

Turf was desperately trying to regain his wind. "Junkman," he repeated.

"He's nowhere close," Link said, and led him along the game trail.

"You think I outran him?" Turf said in disbelief.

"I think the hermit outfoxed him. You owe him."

"Who?" A few feet farther they found Turf's day pack and sleeping bag.

"I'll be damned." Turf winced and touched one of the bloody scratches on his face. "Jesus, these *hurt,*" he said, as if noticing for the first time.

They walked for a while before he spoke up again. "Where's the Rover?"

"Gone." After a moment he added, "My hat too," and told him about the helicopter. "I wanted her to land."

Turf took the news stoically. "You're hard on their choppers. Where we going now?"

"Looking for more answers," said Link.

"I'm hungry," said Turf.

Rock Lake

Sly Paquette got the radio call telling him more about the helicopter crash.

"Just the three dead," said Rose. "No sign of Anderson or Siegel."

"Damn!" When he'd heard that the chopper had landed atop the vehicle, Sly had dared to hope it had killed Lincoln Anderson and removed the thorn.

He pressed a button connecting him with the Warehouse. A *hard line,* Howarski called it, which could not be monitored.

When Sly had first told him about the helicopter, the terrorist genius had already known. He'd been in radio contact with the pilot when a man stood before the helicopter aiming a rifle. Tall, wide of shoulder but gaunt, with intense eyes and military bearing. All of which described A. L. Anderson. Howarski had ordered the pilot to take off—telling her Anderson would not dare shoot. He'd told Paquette it was either that or let Anderson have the helicopter.

Now Paquette said, "We'll need the other helicopter."

"The Black Hawk has problems, and I won't get a replacement for the Jet Ranger until Sydney can talk one out of Tonio Gracchi."

Good luck, thought Sly Paquette. To meet Carmine Gracchi's deadline they were scrambling to amass every dollar they could get their hands on—casino earnings, income from dope manufacturing and Tonio's guests, even money strong-armed from Spirit Lake merchants— taking every penny to the casino counting room. Tonio Gracchi felt that even if they didn't yet have the gym bag, his uncle might settle if they had his cash.

"Anderson can't get into the ecol-rec zone and screw with things, can he?"

Howarski chuckled. "Not unless he can become an invisible cold-blooded creature."

Sly Paquette hung up feeling tired. It had been a long day. He decided to lean back in his most luxurious chair and catch up on his reading. There were reports from the casino: income and expense sheets from the various gaming divisions, and observations of suspicious activities by Spirit Lake citizens.

Paquette wearily picked up the top such report, this one from a bartender at the Hatchet Club, and noted the name: JASON TOUSSAINT.

Garden Entrance, Weyland Building, Manhattan

The Garden Entrance was the most obscure of the huge building's portals. For security's sake Erin arrived only two minutes early. When she saw Gordon Tower's Suburban, she hurried out and climbed in.

"You're working too hard," he said. "It's Saturday."

"Johnny's got a basketball game at seven thirty. Could you drop me off at his school?"

"No problem." They had forty-five minutes. He pulled into traffic. "You sent a diskette to my office for a comparison analysis."

"A digital recording of Gloria Vasson's voice."

"Who at last report was visiting the Manido reservation, where you were told to stay away from."

"Scout's promise. I haven't left New York."

"The second voice on the tape is Link's."

"Doesn't it seem odd that everyone's being told to keep away from the place?"

"For the past few years we've been ordered to avoid a lot of people and places."

Did she note bitterness in his voice? They drove in silence for a moment.

"The lady was not Gloria Vasson."

She was surprised. "Did you get a match on the voice?"

"Maybe. How about I tell you a story."

"Damn it, who was she?"

"Erin, I intend to tell you my story, let you off at Johnny's school, and go back to following orders and not see you again. If you'd rather not listen, that's your choice."

She felt duly chastised. "Sorry."

"Are you carrying any recording devices?"

"No."

"Good." He pulled in a breath. "Once upon a time there were these clandestine and undercover agencies. Let's give them names like CIA, DEA, FBI, ATF, and sundry military organizations. One need their agents have in common is to be able to disappear in plain view, so to make that happen, an office at Langley is set up to train and assist them. The people assigned to that office don't advertise. They're deep cover themselves and have a tradition of being extremely good at what they do, which is deception, disguises, makeup, wigs, latex facial structuring, acting lessons, and any other things that help turn people into people they're not."

Erin judiciously held her tongue. The Weyland Foundation had its own such group, called the Special Activities office.

"On the surface they're bureaucrats. They get a check from the uncle just like I do and have titles like chief of this department and that branch, but to insiders since the days of the old OSS, their division chief has traditionally been called the Master of Disguise. While that may not sound agency-like, it's a great honor within their little circle.

"A couple of years ago, the Senate Intelligence Committee learned of irregularities with their funding, and ordered a very secret investigation."

Gordon paused. "Think about it. Any ideas where I'm going?"

"None." Then it came to her. "Senator Adcock was involved?"

"He was one of three senators who had access to all of the files. They zeroed in on the Master of Disguise and his assistant, a woman slated to replace him. She was said to be the very best, better even than her mentor, and her life was wrapped up in taking over the post. But Senator Adcock discovered that seven million dollars of discretionary funds had been diverted, and there was likely more. A *big* problem was that real, no-kidding national security issues were involved. These people knew most of our deep-cover agents—domestic and international—by first name, and everything about the investigation had to be done behind closed doors."

"The woman . . . the assistant?" Erin asked. "Was she the one . . ."

"Let me finish. The director at the CIA was finally briefed by the subcommittee, and a trap was set. What the senators didn't know was the fool was sending classified E-mail files home over insecure phone lines. Remember the scandal? What the press didn't learn was that the assistant was intercepting the director's mail. She warned her boss about the trap, and disappeared. The Master of Disguise wasn't as well prepared and was caught transferring money to his offshore account. He's become a prison mushroom but the assistant's still out there. She's a fugitive, but that's almost a joke, because there are so many high-ranking people helping her. She has more power than ever because of the information she carries. She has dirt on everyone from politicians to big-time mobsters, and she uses it as a weapon."

"Her name?"

"Irene Bumgartner. Age thirty-four, five six, ash-blond, and nondescript. Now forget all that because she exchanges faces, body shapes, postures, and identities like pairs of shoes."

"And it was her voice on the tape?"

"Eighty percent probability that it's not Gloria Vasson, sixty percent that it's the assistant. There are things she can't hide, like tonal inflections on certain words. I got lucky."

"Yeah, right. Out of a few million voices on file, you just happened to get a match?"

He thought that one over before answering. "I was the senior agent assigned to the Senate investigative committee. That's why I was so interested in Senator Adcock's death, and this woman. By the way, she prefers gender-neutral names, like Gale or Francis."

"Is there a chance you can help us?"

"If I did I'd be fired and prosecuted. I was officially

advised that other federal agencies are involved, that if I interfere it'll blow a DEA or ATF operation and endanger lives. Breaking that kind of order is considered a criminal act."

"There's mob involvement at Spirit Lake. They've taken over the tribal patrol and casino, and the Indians are at their mercy. What's the answer for the Manido tribe, Gordon?"

"Wait until a new administration's sworn in on January twentieth, and hope someone new at Interior will listen."

They arrived at Johnny's school. Gordon Tower double-parked.

Erin had an idea. "You said two other senators were involved in the investigation?"

"I can't give their names; it's still that secret. Since Senator Eddie's death, they've lost interest. There's a lot of fear going around. The former Assistant Master of Disguise has dirt on half the people in Washington."

It was time for Johnny's basketball game.

"I've got to go in," said Erin. "Can we stay in touch?"

"I don't think so. I've already told you too much."

"Link may be in trouble," said Erin. "He's your friend."

"There's nothing I can do to help. Spirit Lake is a bad place to be right now." He paused. "It might be nice if someone with clout could get the word out."

34

There were sixteen laborers in the sleeping quarters. Most were Manido, cranked on their nightly ration of meth. A man was wound up in his speeded-up brain, talking incessantly to no one. A small number of them tried to sleep, knowing tomorrow's labor would be brutal if they got no rest. Others were giving dissertations and answering their own questions.

Gloria purposefully rested near the new man, Ron Doughty, still deciding whether to share her information. She could not escape alone.

From his breathing she knew he was awake, and wondered if she could take the chance.

Before she could make up her mind the door to the quarters banged open. The couple barged inside, flashing lights about, walking among the restless workers, who except for the blinding light hardly noticed their presence.

The woman paused at Doughty, illuminating his ruined face for a long moment as she decided. Finally she went on, nudging Gloria out of her path with a swift kick, and then stopping when she came to two men. Both were rail-thin, skinnier even than Gloria, and they sprawled on the filthy bedding as if oblivious to the world.

"Those," she said, stabbing the light at first one, then the other.

One at a time the man grasped their legs and dragged them out.

The woman slammed the door, and the muttering and illogical conversations resumed.

"That's the last we'll see of them," Gloria told Ron Doughty, thinking none of the others were coherent enough to remember and report her words.

"Where are they taking them?"

"A place half a mile from here called No Bottom Marsh, where they and their biker gang buddies throw the laborers when they're too weak to work."

"My God!"

"Not so loud." She pulled him nearer the door, farther from the others.

"What's the biker gang about?"

"They're from a California chapter that specializes in knowing a dozen ways to cook methamphetamine hydrochloride in huge quantities."

"Aren't you afraid they'll bug this room?" he whispered.

"And listen to a bunch of doped-up Indians? The engineers wouldn't waste their time."

"You're not Native American."

"I'm the toilet-cleaning woman. I'm also hideous and not worth a second look."

"Aw, Mrs. V. I saw you in the light at the door today, and . . ."

"Please don't. My appearance is what I make it. Twice now I've found that my nose was healing, and rebroke it. That's why I can walk around in their midst and they look through me and don't care what they say. I'm not a *real* human to them."

"You're amazing, Mrs. V."

"I prefer determined." Gloria liked Doughty, but she had not been sufficiently trusting to give him more than the initial of her last name. It was not easy after holding everything in for so long, but she'd made up her mind. "I need your help, Mr. D."

"Shoot," he said. "I owe you."

"I'm going to escape. Want to come along?"

He paused, as if getting used to the idea. "Didn't you say it was impossible?"

"Nope. They think that, not me."

"What are you DOING?" The male chatterbox was stumbling through the darkness toward them.

When Mr. D started to draw away, Gloria clutched his arm. "Stay put."

"What are you DOING?" the man cried again, and went by them in the darkness. He stopped several feet distant and began to cry.

"Jesus!" Doughty muttered.

"Too much lumpy meth and too much grief made him crazy," she said. "They keep a lab and four kitchens going, making meth. His job at the lab was to mix phosphorus and acid, and his wife's was to cook sludge at kitchen three. He was hauling a cart loaded with lumpy meth here to Building Three, when she let the sludge get a few degrees too high."

"What does that mean?"

"It blows like dynamite. That's common enough that the supervisors take a hundred-yard hike whenever sludge is heated."

"The explosion interrupted production?"

"Three hours and a new shack was thrown up, and they had a third kitchen back to cooking sludge. It is a very large operation."

"What are you DOING?" the man cried.

"I'm with you on the escape business. When do we get out?" Doughty asked.

"If I can get to their console, sometime tomorrow. When they come for the laborers in the morning, act like you're in great pain so they won't put you to work at the meth lab."

"That one's easy. I *am* in great pain."

"Attaboy, Mr. D. Good acting."

He started to chuckle, then groaned. "Laughing hurts like hell. My body's more or less intact, but my face isn't good. If I work at it, I can get one eye open a quarter of the way."

"The good news is you're thinking clearly."

"As clearly as before, which was never much to write home about. My wife said I was the only man alive who could lose socks between the bedroom and the hamper."

"You're married, Mr. D?"

"Widowed. Five years and six months now."

"My husband passed away two months ago."

"My condolences." He sounded sincere.

"Thank you," Gloria said. "Now let me try to explain their security system, which was brought on line today. What do you know about artificial intelligence?"

"Absolutely nothing."

"Computers?"

"I was just beginning to understand how to set up margins when typewriters went away. My computer expertise includes the ability to peck out letters to clients by using two fingers, and ordering cigars on the Internet."

"There are a bunch of geeks here who can do anything with software. I'm no genius like them, Mr. D, but I watch and listen closely when I scrub their floors."

"You're amazing, Mrs. V. Just go slow and repeat everything, and I'll work at understanding. I'm motivated."

"Let's start with the letters *M-B-I*. Those stand for motion, body heat, and . . ."

Sydney left Building One in the hooded coat, hefting her wooden artist's case in one hand and the blue briefcase that had once belonged to Gloria Vasson in the other. She felt buoyed of spirit despite the early morning hour and the fact that Lincoln Anderson had succeeded in destroying her mode of transportation to the casino-hotel. Still, she did not despise him as did Howarski. Anderson was a worthy opponent, and aside from Senator Eddie Adcock, since her days in the Agency there'd been few of those.

As she passed by the laborers' quarters, a dismal hut across the covered roadway from Building One, she heard one of the crazies crying, "What are you DOING?"

The laborers were so heavily drugged that they needed no guarding. That had been Tonio Gracchi's idea, and Sydney admitted that it worked. The only downside was the blatancy, and the fact that sooner or later someone from the outside would surely catch on that the people were disappearing. It did not really matter. By then she would be long, long gone. Passing on to a new adventure in yet other personas.

Sydney entered the security control center, keeping the hood up to shield her face.

"So who shall we be today," the Master of Disguise had said as she'd come to work. He had grown too old and too slow of thought. She had *told* him they were investigating, looking at the operational funds they had moved about in secret accounts, but he'd had blind faith that he could never, ever be found out. Not the Master of Disguise.

"Have someone take me to town," she told the female engineer who was on duty.

Despite the fact that the system operated without human inputs, Howarski had begrudgingly taken her advice to keep someone in the security control center night and day.

"You're not spending the rest of the night?" the female engineer asked, sticky sweet nice.

She was too weary for this. "I was working. Now I'm finished and need a ride to town."

"I can put you up in an empty guest quarters. They're quite nice."

Sydney turned on her. "Did you hear what I said, or are you a *complete* fool?"

The woman gawked at Sydney's face. "You've—changed."

Sydney was pleased, but she kept her cold facade. "Get a driver and the van, now!"

She could hardly wait to get back to Spirit Lake and try out her new identity. *So who shall we be today?*

3:00 A.M.—*Moose Lake*

Link had led the way northwest, the direction Jenifer had thought she had heard a helicopter taking off on the night of his reconnoiter. When it had become too dark to go on without Turf Siegel stumbling about like an aimless child, they'd stopped and slept on the floor of an abandoned cabin, under furs from one of Nek-kah's caches.

Although concerns for Jenifer had tortured his mind, Link had forced himself to sleep, just as he had done when he'd flown combat missions during Desert Storm.

A vital tactic to use against any enemy, they'd taught him at the realistic air combat exercises at Nellis AFB, Nevada, was to be more rested. He had learned to descend into slumber easily, and to awake at a predetermined hour. Thus he came alert at two minutes until three.

At the stroke of the hour he was outside with the sat phone to his ear, listening to Helga's R-O transmission: *"Still nothing from nephew. Break. The voice of Gloria Vasson was not genuine. The person is a chameleon at disguise, a fugitive charged by Senator Adcock in secret proceedings. She is influential, dangerous, and uses either-gender aliases. She is . . ." BLEEP! . . .*

Link glanced at the readout. The screen was blank. There could be no more R-O sessions. The flip-top sat phone was as useful as a stone.

The revelation about Gloria Vasson being replaced by Sydney came as no surprise, for he had reached the same conclusion. Gloria had likely been killed so Sydney could take her place. Now she had Jenifer!

Tomorrow he would enter the ecol-rec zone, drawn like a magnet in the hope that he was not too late.

6:15 A.M.—Rock Lake

Sly Paquette had fallen asleep in his easy chair while reading the reports. The phone rang beside him and he looked about with a groggy panic before picking up.

"Yeah?"

He had not anticipated the gruff voice on the other end that captured his full attention. "You find the gym bag?" growled Tonio Gracchi.

It took a moment for Sly to collect his wits. "We're lookin' hard."

"Know why I'm phonin' this time of morning, before
the fuckin' robins take a piss and go lookin' for fuckin'
worms? I got a call from my uncle Carmine, who can't
sleep because he keeps havin' this nightmare about waking up and seein' all that stuff from Senator Eddie's gym
bag on the front page of the *Trib,* and he asks, 'Nephew,
why don't we have the fuckin' bag?' and I tell him you
have that big shot expert back to hunting for it, but
Anderson's givin' your people fits, shooting helicopters
and burning cars. He says one thing then, 'Kill the fucker
and find the bag.' "

Sly rubbed at his aching empty socket, wondering how
worried he should be. He thought of the casino reports.
"We're going to have his interest money by his
birthday."

"Of course you will, but he wants the gym bag too,
and now this Anderson has him so he can't sleep. That
upsets me, Paquette. You know what that means, or you
been back on your reservation with all them Geronimos
too long?"

Sly Paquette understood precisely what that meant.
When Tonio Gracchi was upset, people died. "We'll find
him," he said, trying to keep the fear from his voice.

"Here's some valuable advice. Don't fuck around
much longer, 'cause right now I'm thinkin' who I might
send up there who can get things done better'n you're
doin'."

The line went as dead as Paquette knew he might
soon be. He looked out the window, feeling the chill of
the words, wondering who Tonio Gracchi was considering as his replacement. Would he have Billy Junkins
make the hit?

Abraham Lincoln Anderson was the most troublesome element in the affair. Before Paquette had sent
Doughty to the Warehouse, the private investigator had
revealed that Anderson had him looking into the death
of Senator Eddie. Why hadn't Rose and his men, and
even the Junkman with all of his muscle and woods
skills, been able to find Anderson?

Paquette remembered a newly discovered connection

with Anderson, reached over and snatched up a report
from the Hatchet Club bar, and mouthed the words as
he read.

A punk named Jason Toussaint was looking for a
marsh where people were disappearing. He'd also mentioned a pilot friend, and the bartender had overheard
the name Anderson. There was the mention of Senator
Eddie. There was muddled talk about the Bear Society,
and Indian words had been spoken that the bartender
had not understood.

The punk's aunt, Jenny Toussaint, had fallen into Sydney's trap, but Sydney didn't share information. Now
he'd have his own source.

Jason might even know where Anderson was hiding!
Sly decided to bring him in and discuss the matter over
a length of steel pipe.

35

Frank Dubois, chairman of the Weyland Foundation, had postponed a conference with the secretary of the Interior in response to Erin's request for a meeting.

Link Anderson was much more than just one of his executives. He was his closest friend, and from all indications, he was also in trouble.

As Erin told him the latest, obtained from ADIC Gordon Tower the previous evening, Frank doodled key words on a scratch pad: "Irene Bumgartner"—"Asst Master of Disguise"—"Sen. Adcock"—"Ecol-Rec, Ltd."

"Did Gordon make any suggestions?"

"Not directly. As he left he said Spirit Lake's a bad place to be right now, and it would be nice if someone with clout could get the word out."

"Get the word out about Spirit Lake? About the fugitive assistant?"

"All I know is what I just said. I wanted to call him, but he asked me not to."

"Get it out to whom? The press?"

Erin shrugged. "I don't even know if Gordon was sure himself."

Finally, in hesitant voice, Erin suggested a route of action.

"I'd sound like a raving idiot." Frank Dubois pondered for a moment, then shrugged. "What the hell."

He switched on the speakerphone and pressed the memory button that dialed the private line for POTUS, government idiot jargon for the president of the United States, who was preparing for yet another overseas tour, this one to Japan, China, and Vietnam.

Surprisingly, the president was available. "I was just talkin' about you, Frank. As you know, a few friends are raisin' money for the library being erected in my honor, and I told them you might want to help."

"That's certainly something to consider. In fact I'm calling about a matter concerning blackmail."

The answer was abrupt. "Frank, I'm gonna have to hand you off. Remember that lib'ary." Bye."

While anyone without the vast resources of the foundation at his disposal would have been ignored, Frank was transferred to the president's chief of staff.

"What can I do for you, Mr. Dubois?"

When Frank was finished there was a pause. "Mr. Dubois, while I'm sure you have a basis for these—accusations—they seem extreme. Umm—do you mind sharing your source?"

"A woman named Irene Bumgartner who once worked for the CIA. She blackmails people now, possibly a few in your office."

"Oh I doubt that. Umm—you said CIA? And you mentioned the Mafia?"

"As a matter of fact I understand the mob has taken over the Spirit Lake Indian Reservation and the FBI was told to look the other way."

"I'll have someone get back to you," the chief of staff said, and did not openly imply that Frank sounded as nutty as an upside-down fruitcake.

Frank disconnected, and looked at Erin. "Did I mention all the buzzwords?"

"Yes, sir."

"In a few minutes I'll get a call that no one in the White House knows anything about anything, but they'll look into the matter."

"Yes, sir. Probably from the White House legal staff."

Frank made his next telephone call to the attorney general. One by one he would send his message to all of the cabinet officers. Because of the Weyland Foundation's influence, the recipients would not dismiss his calls out of hand. Confidential queries would be made throughout the various departments, but with less than three months remaining in office, the most scandal-ridden administration in memory would want to just ride it out.

No one would open the can of worms at the Manido reservation or look hard for the onetime Assistant Master of Disguise who had taken so many of their files with her, but it was doubtful that either the Chicago mob or the assistant would receive continued support.

7:00 A.M.—Turtle Lake

Sergeant George Rose had dispatched three patrolmen to help Joseph Richards with the increasingly frantic search for Senator Eddie's gym bag. While the expedition leader was frightened of them and working feverishly, Rose knew they weren't going to find the bag.

Sly Paquette radioed, sounding more nervous than Rose had ever heard him.

"You got Richards out lookin' for the gym bag?"

"Yes, sir, I do, and three men with him."

"We've gotta find that fuckin' bag, Rose."

"We will." *Like hell,* he thought. He tried something. "I thought we might send 'em over near the ecol-rec zone."

Rose was wondering if he'd gone too far when Paquette answered, "Forget that place. They use space-age shit to detect people, then blow their balls off."

What did he mean by space-age shit?

"While we're talking, what do you know about Jenny Toussaint's kid nephew?"

Rose's heart skipped a beat. "Except for the fact that he drinks too much and sometimes I have to pull his car keys, he's okay."

"Bullshit! He ain't okay. A bartender at the club heard him talkin' about checkin' out marshes for bodies and cars. Also about bein' buddies with Lincoln Anderson, who he said was from some big organization in New York, which is what Sydney says too."

There. He'd mentioned Sydney again. For Rose she was a loose end he'd been unable to pin down.

"The background check we ran on Anderson didn't mention that." That part was true.

"Then your background check wasn't worth diddly." Paquette was quiet for a couple of seconds, as if reading from a note. "Know anything about a Bear Society?"

"No," Rose lied.

"We've had eagles and loons and all the old societies trying to get started, but I thought I put an end to all that crap. Jason Toussaint's part of this one."

"Might be some kid thing." Rose rubbed his forehead. Although he had anticipated it, things were coming to a head, and *fast*.

"Lemme talk with Billy Junkins. I'm gonna pull him back into town."

Meaning that Sly Paquette wanted help beating information out of Jason.

"He's still out looking for Anderson and Siegel," Rose told him truthfully.

"I'm surprised he hasn't found them." Paquette hesitated. "If he ain't there, put Willie on."

A moment later Willie was grinning like he'd won a lottery as he spoke to Paquette on Rose's radio. "Yes sir, we'd be real pleased to come and give you a hand."

Willie and his scarecrow partner hastily loaded a black and white with plastic bags containing their loot from the expedition camp. As they departed without a backward look, Rose decided he was pleased. They would not be in his hair during the next few critical hours.

Rose would warn Young Storyteller, and that would set many things into motion.

Game Trail, North Side

Since his arrival on the north side the Junkman had been puzzled at every turn. He would think he was closing in on Anderson and Siegel, only to find he'd been misled by distracting sounds and odors, and bogus trails leading in wrong directions. Footprints sometimes led into a circle or abruptly stopped—and when he'd return to a previous path, sometimes it too was altered.

He'd felt as if his senses were betraying him, but now, just as he'd begun to doubt everything about his abilities, he was finally closing in. There were fresh imprints on the forest floor, obviously made by humans. Two sets of them, he decided. Then the prints were obscured, likely by Anderson as he erased their sign. He'd done a good job, and Billy found it difficult tracking. He sniffed the air to try to identify their odors but he was too near the helicopter crash—his prey had doubled back twice during the morning—and the residual acrid smells obscured that sense. But Billy's hearing and eyesight were intact, and—*there!*—he heard a whisper, an answering vague grunt, and allowed a rare smile of triumph to capture his lips.

There were rustling noises of movement, and he imagined his quarry stealing through the forest—not realizing he was near. Should he simply charge ahead and kill them? He considered a second option, to encircle and take them from the side.

Billy carried the twelve gauge. A single blast should gain their attention. Kill Anderson, and take Siegel back so Rose could put him to work as Sly Paquette wanted.

He quietly slipped off the trail into the forest, took in a breath—then charged wildly ahead, enduring branches that lashed him, undergrowth that tried to cause him to stumble, making more noise than he wanted but feeling that with his great momentum of speed they'd still be confused when he arrived.

After just fifteen yards, when he was sure he must be abeam them, he turned sharply inward—and using the shotgun to plow aside branches, burst onto the trail.

A pair of six-month-old wolf pups yipped and scampered down the path as a massive dark-colored bitch whirled about, baring her teeth in a fierce snarl. Two other adults turned to join her. There was motion from both sides as other eyes peered out, and the bitch advanced on stiff legs to protect her young.

Junkins considered shooting her, but the others were crowding forward and growling ominously. Too many!

His mind whirled with confusion; he wanted to run but was reluctant to turn his back on them.

The bitch sprang! Billy swung the shotgun to fend her off, missed by a foot, and she bit into his leg with slashing teeth. He shoved at her as he danced back, then turned and fled down the trail. Another adult howled as the pack gave chase, and cold chills shuddered up Billy's spine as he lifted his knees chest-high and ran, praying he'd not stumble. He had never run harder or faster, crashing through the brush, branches whipping and bloodying his face—feeling malevolent yellow eyes on his back.

He slowed finally, listened intently until he was sure nothing was back there, and stopped to fearfully look back. When convinced there was no pursuit, Billy leaned against a tree and huffed breaths, heart pounding from the exertion and adrenaline rush. As his breath slowly returned his anger stirred, and he realized he had once again been taken for a fool.

The hermit had not been close enough to see the Junkman's confrontation with the ill-natured alpha bitch, but he'd known of her cantankerousness from personal experience and had heard enough to feel satisfaction. He smiled as he toyed with the shiny tape strung about his neck as ornament and considered the mother wolf's outrage.

Again he had confounded the giant. Was the huge man beginning to realize that Lin-kya was not the only one he dealt with?

Nek-kah idly twisted the strands of videotape. It was nice, but not as handsome as the shiny wristwatch he kept in the sturdy canvas bag that had been left by his friend Ed-yah.

He set out at his loping, distance-consuming gait, for a meeting he must not miss.

Wilderness Road, North Side

Sergeant Rose drove past the helicopter wreckage, looking out at the gangsters who went through the motions of acting like policemen. He nodded brusquely to one of them, wondering how long he could have gone on without being discovered. Sending the Junkman out to be fooled by the hermit. Dispatching the patrols in odd directions. Keeping the policemen's focus on the north side while Young Storyteller prepared the Bear Society in town. The taking of Jenifer Toussaint had been a mistake beyond his help.

He would continue fooling them for just a little longer.

Rose switched to base frequency on his radio and raised the station dispatcher.

"Yeah?" She was sullen, like many of the criminals Sly Paquette had foisted onto the tribal patrol, had punker-style spiked hair, and refused to conform to uniform regulations.

"Connect me to an outside line, please."

"Got a number?" she asked in her uncaring tone, as if she had better things to do.

He gave her his home phone and waited. Knowing the dispatcher would listen in, as Paquette had them do. Feeling melancholy about what he was setting into motion.

His wife answered hesitantly. "Is everything all right, George?"

"It's time for your visit," he told her softly.

She was quiet.

"Did you hear?"

"Yes."

"Before you leave, would you put the aluminum case on the porch. Someone will be by for it."

"I'm worried for you, George."

"I love you." Rose hung up, feeling the lump in his throat, wanting to tell her so much more. She would do her part, place the rifle case on the porch, take the kids out of school, and drive them, along with the family collie, to her brother's home in Lac du Flambeau. He prayed he would see them again.

He raised the bored dispatcher and asked for a second phone number.

"Hello?" came Jason Toussaint's youthful voice.

"This is Storyteller," he said clearly. "It is time to announce the rattlesnake."

"We're not ready!" Jason blurted.

Sergeant Rose's voice became as cold as ice. "A *naud-o-way* named Willie left here at seven o'clock, and is coming for you. You must either go forward as we said, or tell the *Muk-wah* to hide and wait for other times and braver Storytellers. It is up to you."

Jason hesitated.

"You betrayed them just as I said. Now it is time for you to lead. No one else can do it."

The young man sighed. "I won't let you down. You can listen for our call."

"I will. Now there are other tasks for us. We'll meet you where the Dakota and Manido made their peace." He had related that story to Jason the week before. "Come quickly, and bring the case on my porch. One last thing. Do not trust Eddie's widow. She's not who she seems to be. She is a *naud-o-way*."

Rose started to tell Jason about the kidnapping of his aunt, and decided against it. Young Storyteller had enough on his mind, and there was nothing they could do about it until later.

He broke the connection. As he was replacing the radio in its bracket, it buzzed in his hand. This time the dispatcher sounded interested. "What was *that* conversation about?"

"Just Indian talk," Rose said.

"Yeah?" She sounded wary, as if he was pulling something over on her.

He drove toward the distant rendezvous with Nek-kah the hermit, thinking about his next radio call, upon which so much would depend.

Rock Lake

Sly was nervous, pacing the floor and running a hand through his hair, considering the threat by Tonio Gracchi. The phone rang; the police dispatcher told him that Sergeant Rose had been on outside phone lines, speaking strange words.

"Strange like what?"

" 'Indian talk' was what he said . . . I don't remember exactly."

"You heard Indian words? Last I heard this was a fuckin' Indian reservation." Paquette slammed down the receiver thinking she was an idiot.

Since Tonio's call, he'd found it difficult to think clearly. He'd had dangerous ideas he would never even have considered before, like pulling everything out of the bank and running. Or, since it was expensive to run, dropping by the casino and taking the nineteen million they were gathering for Uncle Carmine.

Dumb idea. The managers at the casino would call Tonio. *Calm down,* he tried to tell himself, but it was not an easy thing to do.

When the police radio buzzed, he considered throwing it against the wall so he would not hear more bad news.

"Yeah?"

"This is Rose." The sergeant spoke in a near whisper.

"Did you find Anderson?" He tried to keep the pleading sound from his voice.

"Yes."

Sly Paquette was at first stunned—then he felt such relief that he felt like dancing, which he had never done, and shaking Rose's hand.

"I'd talk louder but I'm so close I'm worried they might hear. Anderson's with Siegel, and they have the gym bag."

Wonderful! Then Paquette remembered Anderson's resourcefulness. It was not a done deal until he had the bag in his hands. "Make sure they don't get away."

"They're camped on the back side of the old cranberry marsh. I suggest we surround them and move in slow and easy so there's no chance they'll get away with the bag."

"Sounds good." *Anything sounded good as long as Sly ended up with the fucking gym bag.* "Do it."

"My problem is, even if I use everyone out here, I don't have enough people."

The horrible picture of having to tell Tonio Gracchi

that they'd *almost* had them ran through Paquette's normally unimaginative mind. "So get more people, for crap's sake!"

"I'd like to bring out every patrolman we've got on the force and have half deploy around one side of the marsh and half around the other. Circle them, you know, then coordinate it so they all move in at once."

"You wanta get all the cops out there?" Paquette asked dubiously.

Rose sounded apologetic. "If there's a problem I'll use the people I have. I just thought you wanted to make sure they don't get away with the bag."

Paquette changed his tone. "You bet I do. Take as many as you need."

"Good. I don't want Anderson slipping through after we have them surrounded."

"Think Anderson might move while you're getting all those people out there?"

"I doubt they'll move at all. The Junkman had them on the run all night."

"Yeah?" Paquette was grinning like a kid with a new toy, which was okay because no one could see. "Call the station and tell them you want everyone. They give you static, have 'em call me."

Rose paused. "It might be better coming from you."

He did not hesitate. "Yeah, I'll make the call. You stay put and don't let 'em get away. This works, I'll have you promoted to captain, Rose." He grabbed for a pencil and pad. "What you want me to tell the cops?"

Rose kept his voice low. "Soon as they arrive at the old cranberry bog, have them split up. Tell them to use four-wheel and . . ."

Sergeant George Rose provided specific instructions on how to get the reservation patrol vehicles mired in the viscous mud surrounding the deserted cranberry bog, while Sly Paquette took notes and kept gushing how great it would be to get the gym bag.

36

Jason received the call from Storyteller at 8:20. Since they were alerted and standing by, it took only fifteen minutes to spread the word to the Bear Society.

A life-threatening state of emergency had been declared by council, according to their 1854 Manido-Chippewa Articles of Treaty Rights and Tribal Law. Each *Muk-wah* had been individually deputized in writing, the order signed by the chief and several members of the Manido Council and by George A. Rose, sergeant of police and leader of the Bear Society, commanding them to uphold all rules of treaty and council, and applicable laws of the United States of America, until the current state of emergency was terminated. Now they dug out the treasured silver badges of office that had been taken from the museum, the star shapes worn by tribal lawmen of past generations, bearing the inscriptions PEACE OFFICER, MANIDO-CHIPPEWA.

The Manido had never trusted snakes, and in early times had called their enemies *naud-o-way,* meaning "snake people." The code for the present call to action was *"Che-she ningo donik,"* which implied that rattlesnake was moving.

The battle between rattlesnake and bear was imminent. The *Muk-wah* assembled at the gathering places, homes of selected individuals, and awaited the word to attack.

Jason and Lonnie arrived at the Wigwam Smoke Shop

in their separate vehicles at eight forty-five and observed the busy police station across the street. The recalled patrolmen were pouring in and few looked happy. Seven black-and-white Explorers were being loaded with supplies.

Carole Yellowbird, the Smoke Shop clerk who had once been the night police dispatcher, examined across the street with a cold eye. "Including the ones deployed, that's all their vehicles. Some hardly start up. They're scraping the bottom of the barrel."

"Is that all of their people?" Jason asked.

"Most of them, anyway. I'll try to keep track of numbers as the scumballs leave."

Carole was a *Muk-wah* leader, third in line behind Sergeant Rose and Jason, and some felt she should have been named Young Storyteller. She was in charge of communications. While she called them all scumballs, she and another woman of the Bear Society were especially bitter toward a particular thug named Willie. She'd learned that he'd killed her brother. The other clerk's daughter had been repeatedly raped by Willie and his scarecrow-thin partner.

"It's going to be a walk-through," Lonnie blustered, observing the vehicles.

"I don't think so," said Carole. "The scumballs are armed for people-hunting, and we have deer rifles and duck guns. They'll shoot us for fun, and our people will hesitate."

Jason had a short speech. "I'd like to avoid deadly force until we're sure it's necessary. That leaves them no choice but to . . ."

Carole spun and glared. "You want us to back off? Bullshit! Like Storyteller taught us, the only way we'll succeed is to hit the scumballs so hard they want to run. They understand violence so we'll give it to them. Frighten them with their own blood, like the old Ojibwe warriors did. Chop a guy's head off and show it to his buddy, and there's a chance his buddy's going to lose interest. If you're going to try to change the attack this late, forget it, Jason."

"That's not exactly what I meant," he tried to argue.

Lonnie stopped him. "I agree with Carole. All the *Muk-wah* are risking our asses, not just you. If you hadn't blabbed at the bar, we might have more time to think about it, but it happened. Now you want to make changes? Too late, Jason. That could get us killed."

Jason was dismayed by their reactions.

Carole glared angrily. "Jason, follow the plan. Either lead, or get the hell out of the way."

"Storyteller put me in charge during his absence." As the words came out he realized they sounded as if he was pouting, or even pleading.

"Let me tell you something," Carole snapped. "If you keep going this way, start looking for someone to lead. I'm not joking, Jason, either follow the plan, or I'm out."

The problem was escalating out of control. "We'll go with the plan."

"Good."

Carole Yellowbird was no wimp. She was equally accurate with throwing knives and small-bore pistol, and had been especially resolute since her brother's death. While Jason did not like the idea of her rebellion, he also knew she was key to the taking of the police station.

She turned to Lonnie, as if it had been a minor interruption. "Like I was saying, the scumballs're better equipped than we are. They have radios and can talk with one another. We better buy Zippos, because all we have right now are smoke signals."

"Can't we get the radios from the patrol station after they leave?"

"They just loaded their spares in a black and white. Don't worry about them using them because I'll turn off their switch, but it would be nice to have some of our own."

"We'll have them soon enough," said Jason, trying to get back into the conversation.

"You're talking out of school," she snapped. "Lonnie isn't supposed to know about that yet." Her tongue remained razor sharp, and again Jason felt chastised. *Some leader,* he thought.

As the Explorers began to depart, one halted in front of the Smoke Shop. Jason and Lonnie interested themselves in the stock of cigars while three thugs sauntered in to purchase cigarettes, complaining about going to the boondocks.

"Getting cold out there. Hope you got on your fuzzy undies," Carole bantered cheerfully as she took one's money.

He reached across the counter, grasped a fleshy breast, and squeezed.

"Jesus!" Carole cried as she tried to twist free. Finally she set her mouth and endured as he grinned and felt her.

"Why don't you come along and keep us warm, Pocahontas?"

"Yeah." Another grinned. "He'll hold you down while I poke your hontas. Get it?"

"Yes," said Carole, gritting her teeth and still wincing.

"You got a problem with something?" asked the third patrolman, observing Jason and Lonnie, who were solemnly examining cigars.

"No," they mumbled dutifully.

The patrolmen played grab-ass until they went out to find their Explorer had stalled. When the engine refused to turn over, they waved down another vehicle. They used jumper cables, connected them in reverse polarity, and one screamed as if he'd been electrocuted.

"Fucking scumball," Carole groused, rubbing her breast. "Did either of you see how many were in the second three vehicles?"

"Three in the fourth and four in the sixth," said Lonnie. "I didn't get the fifth one."

"I was the one getting felt up. You guys should have watched. Jason?"

"No." He felt sheepish. *Again!*

Carole added up numbers on her pad. "If everyone showed up for the recall, there are from two to four of 'em still in the cop shop," she said.

They waited impatiently. A long moment passed before the stalled Explorer in front of the Smoke Shop was driven away. It was the last police vehicle. The time was 9:22.

Each driver had been instructed to stop by the Amoco

station to top off, and pick up two five-gallon jerry cans filled with gasoline.

At 9:50 the Amoco attendant called the Smoke Shop. "They're gone." He was *Muk-wah,* and had added water, used oil, and half a cup of sugar to each jerry can. When added to the tanks, the engines would continue running for a while, belching, smoking, and ingesting the sugar solution so it gummed carburetors so badly that they'd have to be dismantled and the injectors cleaned—if the thugs figured the problem out.

A driver stopped by the Subway, where fifty foot-long hero sandwiches had been prepared. The makers had been told to be imaginative by their manager, a *Muk-wah*. The Quik Mart had had a run on Ex-Lax.

At 9:53 the Subway manager called the Smoke Shop. "They just left."

At 9:57 a *Muk-wah* housewife called from her home on Spirit Lake Road. "Six Explorers passed on the road, headed for the north side."

"There should be one more," said Carole Yellowbird. "They left the Subway."

She waited. "Yeah. It just went by."

Carole put down the phone. "The scumballs are all out of town. We can begin timing."

The three *Muk-wah* waited to see if any of the patrol vehicles might return. They did not discuss the ill words that had passed between them, or Carole's treatment by the thugs. Twelve minutes, the time Storyteller had allotted in the plan, passed very slowly as Jason watched the sweep second hand taking its laps.

"Go ahead," he said to Lonnie.

One by one Lonnie made five prearranged telephone calls. "*Che-she* has departed," he told each person who answered, and went to the next. He completed the fifth one at 10:12.

Again they waited for what seemed hours—until a decrepit sedan carrying four males and a female parked on the street fifty feet from the police station entrance.

Carole handed her day pack to Lonnie. "Carry that. I need my hands free." She positioned a throwing-knife up her sleeve so the blade nestled between jacket and sweater, the handle in her hand. She was very accurate with that particular knife, a gift from her brother, Marvin.

A Suburban filled to bursting with *Muk-wah* pulled in behind the sedan.

"Let's go," Jason said, heart pounding so violently he felt giddy.

He'd started out the door when Carole said sharply, "Car!"

Jason hastily drew back inside just as a dust-laden Explorer skidded into the police lot and slid to a halt. There were two patrolmen inside.

Willie climbed out, looked sullenly about, and said something to his skinny partner. He started inside, then stopped and acted as if he could not make up his mind.

"I'd love to go over and say 'hi' to the murdering bastard," said Carole, handling the knife. She picked up the ringing phone, spoke a couple of words, and hung up.

She said the *Muk-wah* housewife had seen Willie's black and white coming into town at high speed. She'd been trying to warn them, but the phone was busy.

Jason stared across the street, sheepish again. Storyteller had warned him that Willie was on his way, yet he had not remembered to tell the others. For a fleeting moment he wondered if he shouldn't turn command over to Carole.

Across the street Willie turned, staggered, and climbed back into the driver's seat of his black and white without going into the station. Thus far he had not noticed the two vehicles filled with *Muk-wah,* all trying to duck out of sight.

"He's stoned," Carole said with disgust. "I could've taken him easy as pie."

Willie and his partner pulled out and turned east on the highway, toward Rock Lake.

"Now where the hell are they going?"

"Sly Paquette's, betcha," said Lonnie.

Carole grumbled, "I wish we knew how many scumballs are left in the station."

"You said two to four, so prepare for four. Let's go," said Jason, making his voice firm.

As they crossed the street, *Muk-wah* emerged from the two vehicles. The majority carried hunting rifles and looked warily about as they walked around to the back of the station. Two went to the front door, where one stood on either side. Each held a Ruger semiauto twenty-two rifle. Compared with the 9 mm and .45 autos carried by the patrolmen, they looked like toys.

Carole Yellowbird was first through the station's double doors. By the time Jason and Lonnie entered the lobby behind her she'd gone around the end of the counter, a maneuver that took her to the rear of the bulletproof cage containing the communications console.

They were alone in the room except for the dispatcher, a punker who wore her uniform shirt half open, showing off apple breasts. She was colorful, with blue and orange hair and bright blue lipstick. Silver rings pierced every imaginable bodily protrusion. She looked up from her magazine to observe Jason, then twisted to glare at Carole.

"The sign says stay in front. That means get your red ass outa here."

Carole motioned vaguely. "I thought I'd empty Marvin's locker."

"It's already cleaned out. Go away, bitch."

Carole nudged the cage door open. "Who got his things?"

"You don't hear good?" She thrust her hand out of sight—toward a pistol Carole had briefed them was kept in a holster mounted under the desk.

Carole pulled the door fully open.

"Carl!" the dispatcher squealed to someone. She drew out a 9mm Browning auto and simultaneously snatched up the radio headset.

Lonnie banged on the front of the Plexiglas cage to distract her.

"Problem at the station!" she yelled into the headset, and brought up the Browning.

Carole's knife was a blur in the poorly lit room. The dispatcher dropped both headset and pistol, and clawed at the handle protruding from her throat. Carole grasped a handful of bright hair with one hand, a skinny arm with the other, and dragged her out of the cage so violently she smacked hard into the metal doorframe on her way by. Carole jerked the haft of the knife free, spun her about, and propelled her at a run down the length of the counter away from the communications console.

The two men from outside hurried through and into the back, looking for "Carl" or anyone else left behind.

In the rear area was a locker room, as well as a cell-block area that after Sly Paquette's arrival had been vastly expanded to hold wayward Manido residents.

"Somebody got a problem at the station?" came a lazy call over the radio.

Carole Yellowbird picked up the headset and mimicked the dispatcher's voice. "Would you believe I broke a friggin' fingernail?"

The caller gave a suggestive response.

A wide-eyed patrolman emerged from the back, followed by *Muk-wah* riflemen. "He was on the pot," one announced. "Said he's got diarrhea so he couldn't go with the others."

"You're Carl?" asked Carole, but the patrolman's eyes were transfixed on the punker who stumbled about, clawing at her brightly painted neck.

In the cage Carole prepared to take her seat. "One of you shove her into the closet."

A fresh jet of blood spurted with each heartbeat.

"Damn it, *do* it! You guys'll leave and I'll have to work in this mess."

"She's still alive," argued a hesitant rifleman.

"Aw, for God's sake." Carole stalked around the desk, guided the flailing dispatcher into the closet, and slammed the door. "Need somethin' done, send a woman."

She looked about as if expecting no argument, ignoring the dispatcher who thrashed and gurgled in the closet. Satisfied, she took the helm of her old post and waited for Jason.

"Muk-wah deebuh eegan," he said. Meaning, in old Ojibwe, that it was time to proceed.

Five men and a woman hefted their hunting rifles, and cried, "Ha-ee! Ha-ee!"

The old war cry meant nothing, but Storyteller had encouraged it all the same. U.S. Marines cried "Semper Fi." Ojibwe yelled "Ha-ee."

Other marksmen had deployed to other key locations, but these departed for the roadblocks just abandoned by the patrolmen. They were good hunters and superb marksmen, and could keep anything short of an army from returning to town.

Carole dialed a number and handed the phone into the pass-through to Jason.

"This is Young Storyteller." He repeated the phrase, *"Muk-wah deebuh eegan."*

Concrete barriers would be set up at both roads leading into town. Outsiders would be told of a dangerous pipeline leak and reminded of a gas explosion in Duluth the previous year. They were considering evacuation, and until further notice no one was to enter the town.

In other words, turn around for your own safety. Bona fide Manido-Ojibwe residents would be allowed to enter. "Go home and stay there, and you will be notified."

Outbound traffic could leave unhindered.

Carole punched in another number, and Jason spoke the same words to the *Muk-wah* who supervised the telephone office two blocks distant. She would disable all but a few of the electronic switches providing outgoing phone service. She and others in her office would screen for emergencies and forward critical calls to the fire hall, EMS, or Carole at the station.

Spirit Lake was fast being isolated from the outside world. A team was going from door to door, telling the Manido-Ojibwe to load their rifles and shotguns. Any businesses that were open—it was Sunday and those were few—were to close their doors. Alcohol and unauthorized drugs were verboten on the reservation for the duration of the emergency.

Jason tried to clearly think of everything that was ongoing, and to ignore the blood that puddled under the closet door and the fact that there were no more thrashing noises from within.

"Did we remember everything?" he wondered aloud.

"Yes," Carole said evenly, waiting.

Jason went through it all one more time. It was not an easy thing, sending lifelong friends into danger. "Now the radio call," he finally told Carole.

One by one she depressed all eight transmit buttons on the radio system—each tuned to a primary or backup frequency—and handed him the microphone.

Jason spoke slowly and clearly. *"Muk-wah ningo donik!"* In old Ojibwe the words meant "The bear has taken a first step." Storyteller had just been advised that the police station was neutralized and the plan initiated. No response was anticipated until later.

A patrolman's voice came over the radio, asking what was meant by the oddball call. Others were conducting conversations over the network, chatting, joking, cursing, and complaining, all in flagrant violation of police radio discipline.

"Pull their plug," Jason told Carole.

The aging radio relay system was equipped with a nonvoice mode of operation, now obsolete, that used a circuit called a beat frequency oscillator. Dispatchers were instructed to keep the BFO switch turned off, for it generated a squeal that blocked all conversation.

"Everyone continue to your destination. We have radio problems," Carole transmitted to the chattering thugs, and flipped up the BFO toggle.

An obnoxious, piercing noise sounded.

She turned the audio control to minimum so they heard only a hum, and sat back. The police relay radios had been rendered useless, as she'd promised. The patrolmen had no backup or alternative systems and were without communications. That state would continue until she momentarily switched the oscillator off so Storyteller could tell them all was well.

"The time is eleven ten," Carole said aloud, and noted it on a fresh log page.

Jason continued to focus on the activities taking place across the reservation.

Storyteller had predicted his weakness, and he'd borne him out when he had talked too much at the casino bar. Now it was too late to dwell on any of that, and he had to make the best possible decisions for the *Muk-wah*.

Jason's reluctance to accept the original plan—suggesting that they use more finesse—had been proven wrong. They controlled the place, didn't they?

Rock Lake

Paquette hardly listened to the mindless chatter on the radio. Twice he had tried to raise Sergeant Rose, wondering if there was anything more he could do to help, but there'd been no response.

While he liked to keep Rose off-balance, the sergeant was in no danger of losing his job. Sly needed a real cop running the force. It was hard to imagine one of the gangster punks in charge—even Willie, whom he liked—and getting anything done.

He had called the dispatcher and told her to recall all the patrolmen who were well enough to walk, even those who had worked the previous night. "Have 'em meet Rose at the old cranberry bog," he'd told her. The idea made sense. Encircle Anderson and move in slow and easy so he couldn't get out.

He heard a nonsensical broadcast over the police radio. *"Muk-wah ningo donik!"* Some kind of old Ojibwe gibberish, like he hadn't heard since he'd been a kid on the north side. He was reaching for the radio to ask the dispatcher, "What the fuck's that about?" when he heard her say, "Everyone continue to your destination. We have radio problems," followed by a squeal so irritating he shut the thing off.

He walked to the window. A vehicle was pulling into his yard. Willie, driving one of the marked Explorers, along with his skinny partner.

Oh yeah! Sly remembered. He walked onto the porch and watched them get out.

"You wanted me?" Willie's eyes were wild from smoking too much pot.

Paquette pondered about sending them to help the others with Anderson. He decided to use them for an errand first. "Go find this Jason Toussaint punk and bring him here."

"Mind if I hurt him some?" Willie was grinning in his spaced-out way.

Sly liked his attitude. "Not so bad he can't talk."

Willie laughed and crawled back into the Explorer, smacked into a tree as he turned around, and drove slowly out of the yard.

Sly watched him leave, looking forward to beating on Jason Toussaint. Anderson too, if Rose took him alive. First burn his fuckin' eyes out since he'd been such a problem.

Pow! came the echoing report of a gunshot. *Pow!*

Willie's Explorer careened toward the house in reverse, slid off the road into the ditch, and almost rolled. He and his partner scrambled out and gawked toward the highway.

"Some asshole's out there with a rifle."

Paquette hurried in and tried the telephone. It was dead, like someone had shut off his service or cut the line. He tried his cell phone and got a NO SERVICE message. *Shit!*

Wilderness Road, North Side

"Muk-wah ningo donik!" Rose heard over the radio, and relief flooded through him. His Bear Society deputies had taken the police station. He felt easier, despite the fact that much more remained to be dealt with and the mob would not give up easily.

They gripped their victims' throats like rottweilers, bled them dry, and never let go.

"That was Jason," he said to Nek-kah, and the hermit looked back as if he understood.

Rose had grave concerns about leaving the *Muk-wah* in Jason's hands, yet he could have done nothing else. Despite his weakness for alcohol, which Rose knew the youth must fight forever, he had the vision.

George Rose had driven west—directly away from the old cranberry bog where he'd ordered the gangster-cops to proceed. When the others from town arrived, he pictured them changing to four-wheel drive to continue around the bog, sinking to their eyeballs as their Explorers took nosedives. Even as ignorant and overconfident—some drunk or drugged—as they were, he doubted they'd actually drive in, but it was enjoyable to think they might.

When Carole Yellowbird announced a radio problem and switched on the beat frequency oscillator to disable the net, he switched the useless thing off. In two hours she would shut off the BFO and he'd make his own call, to let them know all was well.

"It's working," he told Nek-kah. For years Sergeant Rose had tried to converse with the hermit, a task at which only the previous Storyteller, Senator Eddie, had succeeded. Still Rose had gained a degree of the old man's trust. The past few mornings he'd walked in the forest until the hermit appeared, and they'd used gestures to determine where to send the patrols and Billy Junkins. Through his signs, the hermit had confirmed that Anderson and Siegel were near Moose Lake, where two hundred years earlier the Manido-Ojibwe and Dakota-Sioux had decided that coexistence was better than pounding on one another's heads with axes. It was a good location for the meeting with the *Muk-wah,* close to the objective he had not yet told them about.

He stood at roadside with Nek-kah, looking down at the filthy canvas gym bag, the sides of which were pocked with bullet holes, the bottom stained with old blood. Rose had not looked inside, although he was interested in the contents that had caused so many deaths.

Rose motioned for Nek-kah to get into the Explorer. They'd join Anderson and Siegel at Moose Lake, and guard the gym bag until Young Storyteller and the others arrived. There was no time to waste. This part of the north side would soon be swarming with unhappy mobsters in uniform. While they didn't have a clue and posed a real threat to no one but themselves, there were other considerations. For instance, he did not know the status of the military helicopter operated by the people at the ecol-rec zone.

Nek-kah grew excited, exclaimed, "Nyah! Nyah!" and aimed the old rifle at the forest.

Sergeant Rose stared with slitted eyes. Was the old man announcing danger?

"Get in," he told Nek-kah, and reached for the gym bag.

Instead the hermit turned and fled.

Boom! The blast was tremendous in the enclosure of trees, and Nek-kah shrieked in agony.

For the split second that doomed him Rose hesitated. The sound of the rush of heavy feet was upon them when he released the bag and reached for the butt of his holstered Beretta.

The Junkman burst from the forest and halted, breathing fiercely, his feral gaze fixed upon George Rose. The shotgun was held steady, trained on his chest as Billy Junkins took in the partially drawn pistol, now frozen into place.

Rose remained still as Billy looked down at the gym bag, his expression flooding with realization. Rose was the traitor who had sent him on the fool's errands.

He tried a bluff. "Where've you been?"

The Junkman stared at the pistol that he clutched, still in its holster, and made a disdainful motion with his head. The choice was Rose's.

It was no easy thing to purposefully give up one's life, but no man could withstand the terrible torture that Sly Paquette and the Junkman would inflict to learn the secrets he carried. The location of Anderson, the plan being executed by the Bear Society.

The *Muk-wah* called Storyteller—Sergeant George Rose—made his decision.

As he pulled the Beretta free, he heard the terrible roar of the shotgun.

37

Gloria had already been out of the laborers' quarters twice, making cleaning rounds to various buildings of the Warehouse compound. She had visited the security control center for short periods both of those times, spending time on cleanser-reddened hands and calloused knees as she cleaned various portions of the tile floors, casting a vacant stare when anyone looked her way, hoping to work her way to the console unseen. Thus far that had been impossible.

Gloria made her way to Building One, where she did a quick dry-mop tour of the hallway, and stopped at the far end, at the still-locked heavy steel door of the room where she believed Jenifer Toussaint had been taken.

She rapped. If someone she did not know opened, she would give her vacant-eyed look and say she was there to clean the toilet and floor.

There was something she'd thought of the previous night, something her dead husband, Eddie Adcock, had often done. If the woman inside was Jenifer, she might remember.

Gloria tapped out the theme of the "Colonel Bogey March": *da-dum da-dum-dum-dum.*

The response was slow to come. Finally, *da-dum da-dum-dum-dum,* followed by a plaintive cry: "Let me out."

It *sounded* like Jenifer's voice. What should she say?

Gloria leaned close to the heavy door. "Do not give

up hope," she called just once, then turned and began mopping her way back to the entrance.

Although her mind was filled with questions, Gloria did not dare remain. Unlike the laborers' quarters, the Warehouse hallways and rooms were monitored by video cameras. While it was improbable the duty engineer was watching at that moment, it was possible.

Gloria went back out and pushed her gear toward the security control center. She passed Arnie, the obese guest she'd been offered to on her first night. He showed no sign of recognition.

This time she found only the on-duty engineer, seated at a console at the side of the room, studiously intent on whatever was on the screen. He glanced up, saw her but did not see her, and went back to composing computer code on his keyboard.

She started in an area beside the console, scrubbing industriously with her mop, and within a minute had worked her way around and behind.

Gloria felt little fear. She'd been this far a dozen times before. He made a grunting sound. She looked over with her vacant nonexpression, and he stared back, eyes and mind focused on something far away. A lover? Family? She thought not. The engineers seemed happiest when discussing the writing of "very smart expert system code in high order languages," as if they were a breed apart and those were life's only important accomplishments.

She wet the mop and continued swabbing, slowly and surely edging her way behind the panel marked, WEAPONS CONTROL.

Gloria got a first good look at the panel, and was dismayed. While there were a few switches, none were labeled missiles, cannons, or mines as her mind had imagined.

Forget it. It's not there.

Don't give up—think! *How would high tech nerds build a weapons panel?*

It came to her then that if everything here was computer controlled, it was likely that some menu or other would be controlled and selected by a mouse or keyboard input.

The duty officer went on with his typing and frowning, deleting and retyping, occasionally whispering aloud.

She pressed a key labeled WORK STATION PWR, and the screen blossomed to life.

PASSWORD: _____

From behind her vacant countenance, Gloria had watched the blond genius log on at another station. Would it work with this one? She kept her head down as if observing smudges on the floor, noting that the engineer remained intent, and between motions of the mop, she typed in HOWARSKI, which appeared on the screen as XXXXXXXX.

A new screen appeared, but she deflated, feeling cheated and confused. There was no menu like she knew, such as a list of words—only a vertical series of meaningless symbols.

What did they mean?

Gloria hit the down key a few times, highlighting different symbols.

The engineer muttered something, rose, and started around the computer station.

Gloria did not panic—she'd faced similar perils in the past several days—but she knew her session was over. She pressed ENTER for what it was worth and, when there was no reaction, did so again. The engineer was approaching the console.

Exasperated she depressed WORK STATION PWR, and the screen obligingly went blank.

The engineer pressed past her and muttered something akin to " 'scuse me," and took a seat at the rearmost, main console.

With him seated behind her there was no way to continue. Gloria accepted her bad luck and pushed the rolling bucket around the console, then toward the door.

Outside she gathered her equipment, rolled it all back toward the laborers' quarters, and put it away in the shed.

The brutal couple who administered the laborers approached directly toward Gloria, and for the first time that afternoon she was truly afraid.

Ron Doughty fastidiously ignored the man who had joined them in the laborers' quarters, and was practicing opening both swollen eyes and discerning shadowy objects when he heard the first terrible scream issuing from outside.

He believed it was Mrs. V, but the sounds were so agonized and loud they may have been produced by an animal in its death throes. After a full minute of it the door opened, casting light on himself and the laborer who was blinking with surprise. An angular form was harshly shoved inside—Ron was sure it was Mrs. V— and emitted another piercing scream.

As the door was still closing, he scuttled over and knelt.

"Don't touch me!" she shrieked, and crawled toward the laborer. "Oh God, it hurts! My legs, my arms! Help me, won't you?" she asked.

There was no answer.

"Please? They broke my leg, and that man is trying to force me!"

Force her? Ron wondered.

The new laborer spoke in an anxious voice. "Get away from me."

"Please?" She sidled even closer. "I need your help."

The laborer rushed to the door, opened it, and left. That time Ron heard the lock being thrown, which was not done often.

There were more groans from the terribly maimed Mrs. V. Then Ron heard an amazing sound. She was chuckling.

4:00 P.M.—West Perimeter Road, Ecol-Rec Zone

Link walked slowly, letting the bear know he was still back there by making occasional sounds, turning him back periodically and driving him toward the center of the zone. He had left Turf Siegel at Moose Lake with no instructions except not to follow him, intending to penetrate the zone and learn a secret or two. From everything that had come before he believed the ecol-rec was a key to the mob's activities at the Spirit Lake Reservation. It made sense that it would be protected.

He'd come upon the grumpy, elderly black bear methodically stripping away and eating tender shoots at a small pond, hogging it to prepare for hibernation.

"Better you than me, old bear," he'd said, and felt no small sense of guilt.

Whenever the bear tried to go in a different direction, Link feinted and huffed, and herded him ever deeper into the zone. Thus far Link had encountered no security devices, and he was beginning to wonder if there were any, if he might walk in without hindrance, when he noted slight movement in the trees fifty yards ahead.

Link stopped. *It wasn't a bird,* he decided as the bear plodded on, periodically glaring back. He was about to continue when a mechanical voice resonated: "MOTION DETECTED."

Link's eyes remained narrowed. The movement had come from a platform in a tree. He stared intently, and discerned two bug eyes and a small horn. Sensors? Below those was a directional Claymore mine like the ones he had taken, this one gimbal-mounted and moving.

The mine stopped, directed precisely toward the bear.

He remained still. The bear was uneasy at the sound of the computer-generated voice, and milled about, unable to decide on a course of action.

The monotone voice sounded again. "BODY HEAT DETECTED."

The Warehouse, Ecol-Rec Zone

The broken and terribly battered woman chuckled quietly in the laborers' quarters.

Mr. D spoke in surprise. "You're okay?"

She joined him. "Convincing, wasn't I?"

"Sure had me fooled," he acknowledged. She discerned just a trace of anger.

"The couple told me to clean the toilets in the guest quarters, and I told them no. You should have seen them, Mr. D. They turned bright red! The woman was furious. When she pushed I fell down and flopped around like a fish, and when she kicked me, I screamed and rolled around like she'd broken every rib in my chest. You heard me?"

"Yeah, very convincing. Mind telling me *why*?"

"For starters we got rid of our visitor. The more I thought about it the more I knew he was a snitch planted by the couple. He wasn't a Manido, and he wasn't hooked on meth."

"*You're* not Manido."

"My husband was Manido-Ojibwe, and they made me a member."

Ron was quiet for a short moment. "Jesus, I know who you are."

"It doesn't matter, does it. Only that we make our move before nightfall."

"Tell me again why we're not waiting for dark?"

"The laborers would be here to snitch on us. The system also uses low-light image enhancers, so they'd be able to see in the dark and we wouldn't. It makes good sense to leave sooner. They think we're hurting too badly to escape. We have two hours before they open the door for the workers, and even then I doubt they look in to see if we're here."

"They locked the door. How do we get out?"

"With this." She pulled an implement from her baggy clothing and pressed the wrapped end into his hand. "It's a blade from a meat saw. The cook put a ding in it when he hit a bone or something, and threw it out in the refuse."

Doughty gripped the handle she'd fashioned with a strip of towel, and felt the business end. "It's sharp, and heavy," he said in a happy voice.

"The other buildings are inflatable, but this one's built by stretching the same metallic material over framework. If you can cut through it we'll exit out the back, and into the forest."

"When?"

"Right now. It's going to be dark in another hour and a half, so the sooner the better."

*   *   *

They gathered every scrap of their meager clothing—
the night would be terribly cold—at the inky dark rear
of the single room. "Ready, Mrs. V?"

"I have been ready since the night I arrived, Mr. D."
She was excited, her nerves atingle.

He shoved and pressed until the point was through,
then worked the blade like an old-fashioned can opener.
"If someone's waiting, I'll skinny on out and take the
heat."

Gloria snorted, as if that were not an option. There
could be no turning back.

"Aluminized canvas," he said with a grunt, and continued to work. "The other buildings are inflated. We
should give them a little puncture before we go."

"I'd rather use our time getting away."

When the opening was large enough he pushed it outward, displaying a two-by-two-foot portal, and slithered
through.

"It's clear," he announced, but by then Gloria was
already halfway through. She laboriously gained her feet,
feeling light-headed and more giddy and weak than normal. "Close it," she said. "When the others come, it
won't be so obvious."

"Poor bastards are treated worse than slaves. I'd like
to get them all out, and have someone lay a nuke on
this damned place."

Gloria's mind was fixed on Jenifer Toussaint. There
was no way to extract her—not yet. "Remember what I
told you about the locations of the sensors?"

"Pretty much."

"We're going to thread our way through for a while."

She led the way into the thicket of maples, now barren
of leaves, that surrounded the immediate area. After a
careful pause at the road that she remembered from the
map, she took it. "We take this for three hundred meters. How are you at gauging distance, Mr. D?"

"Pretty good. A meter is a thirty-nine-inch yard. A
hundred meters is the length of a football field with one
end zone."

"Tell me when we're there."

Gloria faltered. *Not now!* she cried out to herself. *Keep going!* She stumbled again, and almost fell. There was little energy remaining, and it really did hurt where the woman had kicked her in the ribs.

"Allow me, Mrs. V." He picked her up and began to carry her.

She remembered something. "Didn't you tell me you had a bad knee."

"I was on the force in Milwaukee and took a bullet. It was a career stopper."

"It must be painful with my added weight."

"My old physical therapist would have approved. Anyway, you're light as a feather."

It was nice to be off her feet. "It's worse today," she admitted. "I feel weaker."

"It had to come, starving yourself like that. Good God! What's that smell?"

"We're passing their dope factory. A lab and four kitchens. The couple brag that they manufacture more methamphetamine than anywhere east of Nevada. From here it's two miles to the barrier."

She had explained the barrier to Mr. D. They remained quiet for a while, thinking of the danger to come.

West Perimeter, Ecol-Rec Zone

Two miles distant, Link Anderson noted wafts of the same foul odor as he listened to the mechanical voice: "BODY HEAT DETECTED."

He examined the sensors in detail. Two were bug eyes, one clear, the other dark. Electro-optical and infrared. The third was a metal cone. A high-frequency motion detector?

The mine had stopped moving, trained precisely on the bear.

"ONE NONHUMAN DETECTED—PROCEED."

The mine on the platform moved on its gimballed mount, this time all the way to the side so the bear was no longer threatened. The management at Ecol-Rec,

Limited obviously valued the lives of nonhumans over those of humans. It was something to remember.

Link began to back away, and again noted motion on the platform. The sensors moving?

He stepped behind a tree, out of the platform's field of view, then backed directly away.

Doughty looked down at Gloria and said, "We just walked two football fields."

"One more, then we turn hard left."

"East."

"Yes. I'm surprised you knew."

"I'm like that. Gotta know which way I'm going and how far. It's something built in. How are you doing, Mrs. V?"

"I'm fine. My name's Gloria."

"I know. You were Senator Eddie's wife. I saw you with him at a rally in Wausau. I thought he was a great guy and you were a lovely lady."

"Not any longer."

"It'll come back. I've never met anyone with your determination. The French call it *formidable*. The English equivalent just isn't the same."

"My father was a Frenchman from Quebec. He called me his *formidable* Gloria."

They walked in silence, and he did not seem to tire. Finally he slowed. "We turn here."

"I don't expect you to carry me through the woods, Mr. D."

"It's good for me." He picked his way through the dense foliage for two dozen yards, then found a game trail going their way. "See, we must be living right."

"Fifty meters and we turn right," Gloria told him.

"South."

"Yes." For the next half hour they continued, slowly and surely, turning back eastward, and twice crossing roads that were very close to where Gloria forecast them.

"We *must* escape, Mr. Doughty," she said once with conviction. "There are things here that need to be exposed."

"The dope factory?"

"That and much more. It's an evil place."

They came to the third road. "Stop. We're at the point of decision."

He deposited her onto her feet with all the care due fine china.

Gloria had trouble standing, and had to put extra effort into the task of putting her thoughts into proper order. "Until here the sensor platforms have been scattered, and it's been possible to work our way through. Here they're placed so the coverage overlaps."

"The barrier."

"Yes." She pointed to their forward right. "There's a platform in that direction and another straight ahead— a hundred meters apart. If we try to go between them, we'll have two sets of sensors and two focused mines to deal with. I suggest we go directly at one of them."

"Makes sense."

"If we make it past the barrier, we can get around the others."

"Gotcha. Are you ready, Mrs. V?"

They had discussed it all earlier. There were several shaped-charge mines on each platform; when one fired, the computer would arm the next. If they used separate paths, the software would pick them off one at a time.

Mr. D, who knew some about alarms, felt it was smart to stay close together, hoping the double-image presentations might baffle the computer long enough to get through. Gloria had been unable to come up with a reasonable argument.

"I'm ready," she said primly, noting that daylight was waning.

He lifted her, adjusted his grasp, and walked straight ahead. On their normal sensitivity settings, the sensors could reach out sixty meters. The lethal-blast radius of the mines was even greater.

"Can you see the platform?"

"Not yet," he said, continuing to walk. "Course I'm not seeing too good."

A dozen steps and the forest thinned dramatically.

"We're in the most lethal zone," Gloria said. "They clear the final field of fire."

"I've got it in sight. It's attached to a lone tree straight ahead."

A mechanical voice boomed: "MOTION DE-TECTED."

Despite the fact that they'd anticipated it, Mr. D started so violently she feared he might drop her. He did not pause though and continued forward.

The computerized voice sounded again: "BODY HEAT DETECTED."

They hardly breathed.

"HUMANS DETECTED. STOP FOR EXAMINA-TION."

"Oh, damn!" Gloria whispered. Their ruse had not worked. The computer program had determined they were people and not some giant, oddball mammal.

"Hold both arms up!" Mr. D began to run straight ahead as she stretched her arms high.

"NEGATIVE MATCH. STATE YOUR PASS-WORD."

She tried to remember what Sydney had used. "Revenge!" she tried.

"INVALID PASSWORD." The mechanized words hung in the air like a death sentence, and Gloria prepared to die. She wondered if they would hear the sound of the exploding mine, whether she should say a final word to Mr. D.

"Keep your arms up and try kicking your feet."

She fluttered her legs.

"It's still trained on us!" he said unnecessarily.

"MOTION DETECTED," announced the mechanical voice.

She continued to kick and wave. "The system's recycling!" she exulted.

Finally he slowed, huffing breaths. They were beyond the platform, out of range of both the sensors and the mine.

"We're past the barrier," she said. "Put me down and rest."

He did so. "We beat it," he gasped.

"Yes." She felt giddy with their grand success.

"How long before they come for us?"

"Depends on how long it takes them to study the imagery and decide we weren't a giant rabbit. We have tweaked Mr. Howarski's nose, and he won't like it. Now I suggest we find something to eat and regain some energy so we can decide on our next step."

Mr. D motioned his thumb over his shoulder. "Maybe something might try to make a meal of *us*. When we were running back there, I almost smacked into a bear."

"The bear's gone," said a calm voice. "Mind telling me where you just came from?"

38

Carole Yellowbird was exasperated at Jason's reluctance to act. For hours he had brooded and waited, periodically jotting words into a fresh notebook lifted from the administration locker, and she was convinced that while he dawdled, success was slipping through their fingers.

She'd shut off the oscillator at the stroke of every odd hour, and they'd waited vainly for Storyteller's radio call, telling them that all was prepared for their arrival on the north side.

Storyteller had impressed upon them that everything was dependent upon timing. Hit hard and fast, he had said. Isolate and destroy. Instead Jason did *nothing*.

Despite everything, Carole was hesitant to take over, for Storyteller had also told them that in the most terrible times a capable Manido leader will arise. That had been true since the first sunrise, when Crane had taken to the sky proclaiming the birth of the People. Storyteller had explained that the greatest Manido leaders had shown a failing, and then rose to the occasion.

Carole believed she was the most capable of all the *Muk-wah*. She had expected to be named as Young Storyteller and had been disheartened when Rose had picked Jason.

"He'll need your strength. Help him overcome his failings, and be his right arm."

Carole had held her tongue and agreed, but that was

before her brother had been killed, before she'd become callous of thought and hell-bent on vindication. Storyteller had made the wrong choice. They needed a warrior like herself. She would lead the *Muk-wah* to kill the bastards, then return the reins to Jason and his even weaker buddy Lonnie.

Jason Toussaint stood at the station's front window, the notebook left on a nearby desk, staring out into midnight darkness as if he heard other sounds and saw other visions.

The *Muk-wah* still manned the roadblocks barring the return of the patrolmen, and those keeping outsiders from entering the reservation. Sly Paquette and two of the worst thug cops were bottled up at his home at Rock Lake. The phones were turned off. Casino bosses had called the telephone office incessantly, trying to get lines out, and Carole was amazed they weren't suspicious that something more than "temporary technical problems" was going on.

"Jason," she called in her reasoning tone, "we should be deploying on the north side so we can ambush the scumballs at first light."

"We'll need radios and better weapons. They've got those at the casino."

She could not argue. Their communications consisted of sending *Muk-wah* in vehicles to check on everyone. "Then let's take the casino."

Lead us, for God's sake! she thought.

"Soon," he said quietly.

Carole had pleaded with him a dozen times, always away from the ears of others. Now she decided it was time to do more. She would take over before everything was lost. She had decided to appoint a replacement at the dispatch console. Then she'd take her pistol and knives, and as many *Muk-wah* as she could muster, and lead the raid on the casino, the scumball patrolmen on the north side, whatever. *Fuck it! It's time.*

Lonnie and three other deputies strolled from the back room. "Anything happening?"

She stood. "I'm declaring an emergency," she began,

and then paused, for Jason had turned to face the room. Tears glistened, wet on his cheeks.

"Storyteller is dead," he announced in a sad voice.

Lonnie called for the others in the back. Two women and another man emerged.

"You can't know that," Carole said.

"He suffered for hours, since just after I made the radio call."

"Damn it, you can't *know* that."

"Listen to him," Lonnie said.

"You were on my side," Carole snapped at Lonnie. "Now you're on his?"

"Storyteller told me to back Jason up. He said he would betray us, and then he'd have a vision. He said to tell the *Muk-wah* to listen and believe in him."

Lonnie looked at her squarely. "Storyteller said he'd asked you to help him too."

Jason acted as if he hadn't heard any of it. He regarded Carole somberly. "Bring in the volunteer firefighters—all of them—and the janitor and clerk from the casino."

"Firefighters?" she asked, frowning.

"I need to learn from them, and tell them what I want done at the casino."

"But—firefighters? Are you trying to change the plan *again*?"

"Don't argue, Carole," said Lonnie.

One of the women *Muk-wah* teared up. "Oh, God. Storyteller's really dead."

They *believed* him. Carole Yellowbird set her mouth angrily, but she called the telephone office and asked them to call out the firemen and tell them to gather at the police station.

Jason had decided they must take the casino first, and that the attack plan needed revision. While it had sounded okay as an abstract notion, the old plan was sorely lacking.

He'd wondered if he was being overly cautious—as he'd been earlier. Then he realized it did not matter. If he saw an accident about to happen, shouldn't he try to stop it? If the lives of others depended on him, shouldn't he point out flaws? Yes, and yes. The plan must be changed.

Storyteller had stated their goal in the simplest terms: Get rid of the mob and their influence, forever. The north side is our heritage—the soul, the past and future of the Manido.

They would end it there, but Jason had decided to take the casino first.

Storyteller's focus had been on the north side—always the north side. His scenario bypassed the casino until later in the game. During the last conversation Storyteller had said to "come quickly." Yet Jason had decided the *Muk-wah* first needed the radios and firearms stored in the casino vault.

They'd also take the cash. It belonged to the People, not the mob. If they eliminated the casino's profit, the mob would have no reason to stay in Spirit Lake. It made sense to go there first, and he could think of no argument against it.

Storyteller had not dwelled on the casino, as if it was of secondary importance. If they *had* to take it, his sketchy plan was pure confrontation. Enter the casino with weapons, herd everyone out, and if necessary use the six sticks of dynamite they'd got from a local farmer on the armored vault door. There was too little subtlety in the old plan, and too much danger.

By one o'clock in the morning, twenty-nine firemen and eleven of the available *Muk-wah* had assembled in the warmth of the station. They drank coffee from the big urn Lonnie had prepared, and were intent and quiet as Jason outlined what had happened so far.

"You're doing all of that and no one's wise?" a fireman asked incredulously.

"You saw the roadblocks. What did you think?"

"There's a natural gas leak in the pipeline. I saw all the trucks from Northwoods Gas. We got a notice up at the fire hall saying it's temporary."

A *Muk-wah* took his feet. "That's all part of the plan.

I work for 'em and moved their trucks from the parking
lot to the pipeline."

"We'll take the Hatchet Club next," Jason said. He
outlined the old plan, then told them of his doubts.

"If you didn't like it, why didn't you change it before?" asked a *Muk-wah*.

"I thought Storyteller—for you firemen, that's what
we call our leader—would be here to lead us. Now that
I'm in charge, I want something I can agree with."

Jason outlined his ideas, and they listened. Then he
asked questions and he listened, and they shared
thoughts of how the takeover could be done.

There was a degree of friction between *Muk-wah* and
the firefighters. The Bear Society members did not know
how many of the VFD they could trust as implicitly as
they did one another. When a fireman argued about Jason's leadership, Lonnie told what Storyteller had said.

"He has the gift. If you don't agree with him, go on
home, but don't stand in his way."

At two thirty, Jason mentioned a final factor. "Our
duty is also to protect civilians. Not just the Manido-
Ojibwe, but also the tourists, no matter what you think
of them."

A *Muk-wah* woman spoke. "You mentioned Gloria
Vasson."

"Watch out for her. Storyteller said she's not who she
seems to be. She's *naud-o-way,* an enemy. If you find
her at the hotel, take her to the station so Carole can
ask a few questions."

Everyone knew their parts. A final question was
asked. "When?"

"Three o'clock," said Jason. "Half an hour from now."

He told the janitor to return to the casino right away
to prepare the way.

3:00 A.M.—*the Hatchet Club Casino, Spirit Lake*

Jason and fifteen other *Muk-wah* pulled up at the
kitchen entrance and parked their several vehicles
helter-skelter in the darkness.

There was no more time to talk; they either understood their roles or did not. Not only did they face the nine casino bosses—all but two asleep in their hotel rooms—but there were fourteen armed casino guards and seventy-two other employees. Fortunately only a fraction of those were on duty, and half were Manido Indians who he prayed could be relied upon to help.

Most of the *Muk-wah* who poured out of the vehicles hurried around the building to take positions at various entrances. Others gathered behind Jason at the side entrance. Some carried firearms. Two were Volunteer Fire Department members, already clad in full response regalia: helmets, masks, boots, and heavy fire-retardant coats, trousers, and gloves. Two other firemen were crawling up the side ladder to the roof, and the remainder awaited the alarm at the fire department, just two blocks distant.

Jason rapped three times, then twice, then three again. There was an expected delay before the door was cracked open, and the janitor who was *Muk-wah* peered out. He showed the aerosol can of black paint he'd just used on the video camera lenses. "They're blind."

Four *Muk-wah* bearing hunting rifles dashed inside, their task to gather the skeleton crew of kitchen employees and usher them outside.

The firemen wrestled in a pair of industrial box fans, used by the fire department to eliminate smoke while fighting conflagrations. A set of double doors led into each of the restaurants serviced by the kitchen. Those were propped open. A fan was deposited before each.

The industrial fans were switched on, blowing in rather than out.

An employee, this one a Manido, hurried in to investigate the stiff breeze. A *Muk-wah* escorted him out to Young Storyteller.

Jason knew him and used his first name. "We're taking the reservation back for the People. Will you help?" He had to repeat his words to the confused man, who looked dubious.

"Cuff him," said Jason, and they marched the man

away to join the others they would have to watch over as the operation continued.

Smoke flares were ignited and placed in front of the fans. The initial issue was sparse, but it soon billowed, and dark, dense smoke was swept through the doors by the fierce draft.

Other flares were being set off on the roof by the firemen there, placed so the smoke was drawn into the intakes of the two huge heating units.

They waited for another full minute while the smoke accumulated.

"Fire!" a *Muk-wah* woman shrieked from the kitchen, so her voice would carry into the casino, where only a handful of dealers and die-hard gamblers manned tables. The cry was picked up by several panicked customers as the smoke continued to pour in.

An alarm began to jangle; then others chimed in until the accumulation of noise became deafening. The off-duty bosses would awaken, dress hastily, and hurry to the cash room. The *Muk-wah* clerk said it was a matter of mob greed. Save the money!

In the dining room and coffee shop, both of them dimly lit and closed, the smoke was already so thick it was impossible to see more than a foot or two.

The firefighters had brought Scott air packs, which they, as well as Jason and the janitor, strapped onto their backs. They all positioned the clear masks to cover nose and mouth, turned on the air, readjusted their straps, and practiced breathing as they waited. The janitor carried a heavy pry bar, and Jason had a leather tool kit on his belt.

"Ten minutes from . . . *now*," announced the fire lieutenant, in charge of timing since he was the only one with a speaker mounted in his helmet.

For that period of time the smoke and alarms would encourage the building's inhabitants—staff, mobsters, and hoodlum gamblers—to evacuate before the actual fire was set. On that the *Muk-wah* were agreed. The casino represented the evil that beset their people, and must be destroyed. Burning it to the ground was some-

thing that would have been approved by both Senator
Eddie and Storyteller.

The four entered the wall of smoke, Jason and the
firemen following the janitor, since he knew every turn,
nook, and cranny. The janitor was their guide, the lieutenant provided expertise in emergency fire actions, but
all knew that Young Storyteller led the operation.

Jason felt claustrophobic. *Breathe evenly and don't get
excited,* they'd told him, *or you'll consume the air in your
pack too quickly.* He fought to calm himself.

They walked cautiously through the smoke-obscured
dining room, then down a wide hall toward the stairs,
passing a number of panicky gamblers hurrying for the
front doors, encouraged by alarms that rang so vocifer-
ously they pained human ears.

Video cameras were set up throughout the casino, and
if they'd been unobscured, the mob bosses might have
been alerted to the scam. Fortunately the cameras in the
kitchen could not view through the black spray paint,
and the ones on the floor could not penetrate the smoke.

The sprinkler system would not activate until 148 degrees of heat was detected. That condition must be rem-
edied since Jason believed the bosses would not vacate
and jeopardize the cash in the vault unless they were
sure a fire existed. This early in the game the trick was
to create heat, and not a fire.

The vague figure of the janitor stopped and pointed.
The lieutenant firefighter popped a thermal flare that
spewed hot flame, and raised it toward a sensor in the
ceiling. The retardant material became warped and dis-
colored. "No fire," Jason whispered hopefully, "just set
off the spray," but with a flash and *whoof* the tiles began
to blaze.

Jason's heart began to pound, and his breathing became loud in his own ears. The fire was started four
minutes ahead of schedule.

Breathe evenly! he chided himself.

Several more seconds passed before water began
spewing from ceiling nozzles.

The smoke immediately abated, as they'd been told

would happen due to the damping effect. Still they remained unseen, now obscured by the spray.

They climbed in single file to the second floor, increasingly drenched by the downpour of water that was pumped directly from the ice-cold lake, and stopped at a steel door above which a camera was mounted.

The lieutenant fireman stepped before the camera and waved his arms to alert whoever might be observing from inside. "Get out!" he called ominously on his helmet speaker.

A fire siren wailed outside, signaling them that the casino had been evacuated. Other firefighters were entering the hotel side to ensure an orderly departure from there as well.

There was still no reaction from the vault room. *Are the bosses really inside?*

Another long minute passed, and Jason was considering alternatives when the door opened and a cash cart was pushed through, handled by a uniformed casino guard. Another cart was wheeled out, and then two others, which was two more than they'd anticipated. Were they all filled with cash? A train of four men trailed behind the guarded carts, coughing into handkerchiefs held to their mouths: the top-level casino bosses. Some were yelling for naught into handheld radios, not knowing that the *Muk-wah* had relieved employees of their radios as they'd exited the building.

The lieutenant appeared before them, speaking into his helmet microphone. "You can't go that way," he announced. "Follow me." He then led the bosses, guards, and carts down the hall, the second fireman following to make sure there were no stragglers. When they emerged they'd be met by armed *Muk-wah* and taken to the police station and the overnight lockup.

There were also five midlevel casino bosses, hopefully already rounded up.

The janitor caught the vault door before it closed, and he and Jason were quickly inside. That room was filled with smoke as well, still being pumped in through heat vents.

Jason quickly took stock, then began pulling new two-way UHF radios and batteries from wall-mounted charger units, placing them into the opened bin of an empty cash cart. When he had them all, he pulled a Phillips-head screwdriver from the tool holster and began to disassemble the charger itself. He moved awkwardly and seemed to have to work twice as hard as anticipated at the simple task.

The unit wouldn't come free! *Oh shit, oh shit!* With effort Jason forced himself to calm down, then to feel along the side until he located the screw he had missed.

As he began to remove it, there was a resounding bang as the janitor jimmied the door of a locker with the pry bar. Inside was a collection of shotguns, machine pistols, and ammunition, which he methodically added to the bin. He folded down the panels of the cart, and Jason hefted the wall charger into place on top.

The janitor added more weapons, until the cart was piled high.

Hurry! Jason's thoughts screamed as the janitor released the wheel locks.

They'd pushed the cart into the hall and the spraying water, the janitor leading the way, when Jason heard the first gunshot from outside, then after a moment, another. His heart pumped wildly as they maneuvered down the ramp for the disabled.

The water stopped spraying, and he felt the heat intensify. "Hurry," he shouted, although his words were muffled by the mask, and fought an impulse to desert the cart and run for an exit. They turned right, went a dozen feet, and waited as the janitor felt around blindly for a door he had said was there. They dared not delay, for the heat worsened by the second. A new whooshing sound came from behind them, and the heat became even more intense.

The first door was opened now and they were quickly through, hurrying straight ahead, blinded by the roiling smoke, the heat unbearable.

The janitor stopped, and the cart banged against a solid wall.

Where's the damned exit!

Jason's air supply dwindled, as they'd warned might happen. He reached out and began to claw the wall, searching for the exit door—thinking he would surely suffocate!

The janitor found the panic bar and dragged the cart through the door. Jason followed, was caught in a new blast of heat that blew like a gale from inside, and gave the cart a mighty shove as he went through the portal into the glare of lights.

He was choking in earnest, for the air had utterly run out. Jason gave the cart a final hard push and, after stumbling along for a few more feet, pulled the mask up and off. He breathed desperately. It was still hot, this close to the inferno, but even roiling superheated air was better than none.

Jason could see very little, for the fire department had switched on generator-powered lights that bathed the casino in illumination. Hands grasped him and drew him farther from the building. Finally he stopped, put his hands on his knees, and drew in delicious cool air.

Everyone was busy, so Jason took reports as he could get them. The attack on the casino had gone as well as anyone could expect. The ones outside had worried when they'd spent too long getting out and the fire had spread faster than anticipated.

"You okay?" he was asked by a concerned female EMT medic.

"Yeah," he said, and after breathing more fresh air he did feel better, although the skin at his exposed neck, face, and hands was feverish hot.

Jason stayed close to the cart, which bristled with gun barrels like a metal porcupine. It was guarded by a *Mukwah* who wore his deputy's badge openly and stared about with hard looks as he listened to the janitor tell their hairy tale. Another sixty seconds and it would have been over. The janitor said Young Storyteller had not wavered.

Lonnie drove up in his pickup, talking excitedly. Jason ignored his questions and asked his own. "How are things on the hotel side?"

"All the guests made it out. They were half asleep and too scared to argue."

"I heard shots."

"One of the guards pulled a pistol so Rosalie shot him with her four-ten. Just bird shot, but he's blubbering like a baby. A couple of floor bosses may have made it out without being caught, but we got all the big fish."

"And Gloria Vasson?"

"We checked every female who came out. She wasn't inside." Lonnie started toward the cart. "Maybe we should hand out the radios."

"No," said Jason. He turned to the *Muk-wah* guarding the cart. "Take it all to the station. Carole's in charge of communications, and Richard's the armorer."

Richard had spent an enlistment in the U.S. Army as a small-arms instructor.

The EMT medic finished looking over the janitor and came over to Jason. "You both have second-degree burns. I'd like to get you to the clinic and treat them before they blister."

"Later," said Jason, helping to load the contents of the cart into Lonnie's pickup.

"Then hold still," the medic groused as she smeared white unguent on his face.

During the next hour the casino parking lot was steadily emptied of vehicles as hotel residents and guests were told by the *Muk-wah* deputies to go home to Chicago or Milwaukee—or wherever. Do not return. The casino will not reopen.

Those who argued that valuables had been left behind were told to send their claims to the secretary of the Interior because the tribal fund was empty. When some complained that they'd left their keys, a *Muk-wah* who knew about such things hot-wired their vehicles.

Now please go.

Only Manido-Ojibwe residents were allowed to observe the spectacle of the flames that leaped skyward as the fire engulfed the building. The firefighters let it burn, dousing nearby buildings to keep them from catching.

As the excitement waned, several *Muk-wah* stopped by to speak with Jason, proud to have done their parts.

"It's not over," he told them. "There are still a lot of patrolmen up on the north side."

At five o'clock, when everything appeared to be under control and there was only smoking rubble remaining of the casino, Jason drove his Firebird to the station.

Carole Yellowbird was still in the dispatcher's cage, taking call after call to assuage citizens' fears about the fire and the gas pipeline leak.

A deputy told Jason about the seven pudgy casino bosses in the lockup in back. "They were demanding to see lawyers when one of our guys pulls out his pocket-knife and gives out a real loud whoop-whoop, like an old-style war cry in the movies. When they shut up, he says he hates bald guys because they have lousy scalps."

Jason was too weary to find humor. "Tell our people to stop. It's no game."

"What do you want done with the prisoners?"

"Storyteller said the jail should be neither cruel nor comfortable. Give them water and offer them bread and cold vegetables if there's no talking. If they cooperate they'll be released when council declares the emergency over."

Carole read from the log to fill him in on events. Limited telephone service was being restored. She'd distributed half a dozen of the UHF radios to critical positions, such as the *Muk-wah* manning the roadblocks and guarding Sly Paquette's house. Richard had passed out machine pistols and given crash courses on their operation. Traffic was moving, mostly out of town. The three cash carts were under guard at the council building.

The council members hadn't yet counted it, but the total amounts of U.S. and Canadian currency appeared enormous. Maybe millions.

Carole said, "Storyteller never checked in. Do you still want to make the radio announcement?" When he nodded, she switched off the squeal, turned up the volume, and handed him the microphone.

He spoke clearly. *"Muk-wah nizho' nik."*

The bear had taken a second step.

Carole Yellowbird switched on the yowling oscillator and returned the volume to the minimum setting. "Some feel we should call you Storyteller."

"Let's keep things the way they are."

She handed him one of the UHFs and an extra battery. "The manufacturer's booklet says the radios can reach out to thirty miles or more, according to the terrain. We're using channel eight for general conversations. If you want to talk privately, I'll be monitoring channel nine."

It all sounded appropriate.

"I have you listed as *Muk-wah* One."

"Change it to *Muk-wah* Two. You weren't wrong, Carole. I'm not sure about Storyteller's death. He told me to always try to interpret the dream-times, and that was what I did. I hope he's up there waiting for us.

"You'll be in charge while I'm gone," he told her, and gave her the list of fourteen Muk-wah he'd picked to accompany him to the north side.

Carole scanned it. "Good people."

They talked over what was to happen. As soon as he caught his wind, he would pick up Storyteller's aluminum case, then lead the *Muk-wah* warriors up the west side of the reservation to Moose Lake, the site of the peacemaking where Storyteller had said to meet.

If Storyteller wasn't there, they'd proceed east to the old cranberry marsh and take on the patrolmen.

Carole noted that Jason's reddened eyes were drawn to an entry on the police log.

"Your aunt Jenifer was seen leaving the reservation at four this morning."

Relief flooded through him. "I thought she was still on the north side."

"Well, she's obviously back. They said she looked fine."

He was pleased at the thought. "Did she say where she was going?"

"She didn't stop. Just waved and drove past the roadblock."

39

5:15 A.M.—Moose Lake

Link had found enough animal skins in the hermit's closest cache to keep everyone reasonably warm in the abandoned cabin where they'd spent the night. He was most concerned about Gloria, who was skeletal and much weaker than the rest.

They'd eaten well enough. Link had taken sun-dried venison jerky, potatoes, and carrots from another of Nek-kah's caches, gathered a small pile of crayfish from the lakeshore, and pulled a walleyed pike and a couple of crappies from fish traps that he'd constructed of woven branches the previous day. Although saliva had glistened at the corners of her mouth as the food cooked, Gloria had consumed her share slowly and in small amounts, exercising more restraint than Link believed possible. At survival schools he'd attended, those who had gone a week without food wolfed it down voraciously. She had gone even longer, yet had eaten sparingly.

Ron Doughty's face was so badly beaten that he was hardly recognizable, yet he regarded Gloria, whom he called Mrs. V, with awe, and catered to her whims. When he imagined that she needed anything within his capability, it was done.

She'd talked and rested, then talked more, and Link had listened diligently.

The Warehouse would soon be a Mafia diamond mine. Gloria had explained a huge methamphetamine factory,

where outlaw biker club supervisors used Manido-
Ojibwe addicts as slaves to do the heavy lifting and dangerous work. She'd told about Warehouse Building
Three, where they stored the stuff on heavy palettes,
separated into kilo bags of crystal meth, lumpy meth,
powder, and pills.

"Two tons of it will be dumped on the market in Chicago suburbs, given out like free candy at street corners
and school yards, like they did in Spirit Lake. They'll
hook new users and run other suppliers out of business.

"They use the same building to store hijacked ship-
ments. Their Mafia boss in Chicago likes high tech, so
computers and electronic gear are stacked to the ceiling.

"The next one, Building Two, is called the Resort,
and the people there are their 'guests.' If you've listened
to the news, you know that a lot of rich criminals have
been disappearing along with all their money."

Link had thought of Erin's interest in the mystery of
the disappearing crooks.

"Dishonest CEOs, judges, murderers and thieves from
wealthy families, narcotics kings, all dropping out without a trace. The mob puts them up at the Warehouse,
and helicopters a plastic surgeon in from Saint Paul.
After they've healed they place them in a new life and
a new home. It's like a witness relocation program for
criminals. A guest complained that it had cost him five
million just to get in." She'd told how the Mafia sucked
their cash, pimping women slaves, taking them on outings to the Hatchet Club to gamble in a private room.

Link had recalled the green Ecol-Rec, Limited van,
with Howarski and his engineers, and also the two men
with bandaged faces—fresh from the plastic surgeon.

"How many guests?"

"Eleven, presently. Two disappeared. The rumor was
they were liposuctioned to death."

"What's in Building One?" he'd asked.

"The engineers—they've dropped from sixteen to
twelve in the last few days—live in the front. There's an
open area, a few two-man rooms, and what Howarski
calls his monk's cell. Then, in the end room . . ." She'd
paused. "Remember Jenifer Toussaint?"

The mention of her name had hit Link like a hammer blow. Jenifer's condition was unknown. Gloria had described her location and said they kept the heat off. "She must be very cold."

"I'll be going for her," he'd said grimly.

Gloria had rested for a short while, then come awake and detailed all she knew about the security control center.

Gloria had even tried to recite the locations of the platforms, but they were numerous and she said it had been easier when she was there. She had explained sensors and explosives, and how they were controlled by software encoded into a heavy-duty server computer.

Link had decided to leave in morning darkness, to approach the barrier of platforms at the nether hour when shadowy grays prevail, and IR and low-light detectors work marginally.

Link was awakened by a distant clamor, and slipped out of the still-dark cabin to investigate. The temperature had plunged, and the restlessness of the wind in the treetops promised snow.

When he walked to lakeside he found Gloria staring across in the direction of the ecol-rec zone, listening to the faint *wee-eeep, wee-eeep* cries of a siren.

"I've only heard the Code Red once, during a test," said Gloria. "They're threatened."

"Because of your escape?"

"No. Howarski would never believe lesser mortals like us could make it out."

He waited for her to continue.

"Code Red is a multi-tier warning, with three levels of alarm."

There followed an *oo-gah,* which was repeated after a half-minute interval.

"They've just declared Level One. The sensors are reset to maximum sensitivity, and the discrimination codes are bypassed. If the system sees anything warm bodied and larger than a rabbit, a mine will detonate."

She regarded him solemnly. "It's just become impossible to get into the zone."

There was a not-so-distant *Crack!* of a detonating mine.

"They have a large stockpile of explosives, and they're deadly serious, Mr. Anderson. Howarski values the lives of animals much more than those of humans."

"There *must* be a way in," Link said.

"Perhaps, but I can't think of one. Just thank God they've only declared Level One alarm. It could be much worse."

5:50 A.M.—*Wilderness Road, North Side*

It remained murky dark, with no hint of the impending dawn. Jason was in the passenger's seat of Lonnie's pickup, his friend at the wheel. Behind them trailed other four-by-fours. The *Muk-wah* were armed with weapons of silence—axes, knives, and compound bows—as well as rifles, and the police shotguns and machine pistols removed from the casino vault.

When the odometer showed they'd come twenty miles, Jason gave a position report. "*Muk-wah* Two checking in. We're passing east of Frenchman's Lake."

"Any sign of the scumballs?" Carole Yellowbird asked.

"None yet." He'd started to terminate when Lonnie braked hard to avoid a horde of large, strutting and pecking black birds in the headlights.

"Aw shit," Jason muttered into the radio.

Carole asked if anything was wrong.

"Stand by."

The ravens, the efficient cleaning crews of the North, screamed raucous complaints as Jason dismounted. He walked closer, lunged, and waved his arms. The birds scattered amid squawks and a rush of wings, abandoning their meal, a human curled into a fetal ball.

As the others approached, Carole queried again. "What's happening, *Muk-wah* Two?"

Jason took a moment before responding. He raised the radio and spoke in a halting voice as he read the obvious sign, sharing the scene with all who listened.

A shotgun blast had torn a grapefruit-sized hole through Storyteller's abdomen. The ravens had eaten

most of his face and . . . intestines . . . he looked away
from the awful scene revealed in the headlights, clenched
his eyes for a moment, then narrated more. Storyteller
had moved about for a long while, undoubtedly in excruciating pain, leaving aimless trails of blood.

Footprints were everywhere around the body; he
guessed size sixteen or larger.

The Junkman had left him to suffer.

"That's all. We've got to take care of the body."

During the following hush over the radio net, they
wrapped Storyteller in a tarp and placed him in the bed
of Lonnie's pickup, beside the metal rifle case he had
asked for.

As they prepared to mount up, a *Muk-wah* nosing
round with a flashlight found a gout of blood in the
nearby brush. After a search they found no body.

As they prepared to leave, Jason radioed, "Someone
else was wounded as well. The Junkman's out there.
Let's keep our eyes open."

"Where to now?" Lonnie asked.

"Moose Lake, like Storyteller wanted. Then we'll go
after the patrolmen."

6:27 A.M.—Moose Lake

Link continued to listen to Gloria, gaining information, trying to come up with a way to penetrate the ecol-
rec zone.

The distant *Oo-gah!* was repeated every half minute.

Gloria was first to notice the sounds of vehicle engines, drawing ever closer.

"We'd better get out of here," Turf said.

"Maybe not." Link judged that the engine sounds
weren't those of Explorers, such as the patrolmen drove,
or Humvees like the ones Gloria had seen at the ecol-
rec zone.

By the time the first vehicle turned off to Moose Lake,
Link had sent the others down the lakeshore and remained behind to observe.

The lead pickup that halted at the end of the narrow lane was familiar. Jason Toussaint climbed out, face and neck lobster red and marred by blisters. He was joined by others, all grim of countenance and carrying an assortment of firearms.

Link called out in a low voice, identifying himself.

Jason responded warily, "Link?"

"Here." He stepped into the open, and became the aim point of a dozen weapons.

40

Yesterday had had its high points, like getting the gym bag, but Billy Junkins had been through a bad night.

After spending a few satisfied minutes watching Rose, half alive and flopping around like a headless chicken, Billy had loaded the bag into the sergeant's Explorer because it was in better condition than the one he'd parked a mile away. He'd tried to call Sly to tell him about Rose and the present he was bringing but heard only a squeal.

Since it was a long way to town, he'd gone to find the dumb-ass cops to make the call.

He'd found them at the abandoned cranberry marsh, half of them stuck in mire they should have avoided, all waiting for someone to tell them what to do. Cops everywhere, stumbling over one another, asking which was the north side of the marsh and which was the south because they'd been told to go one way or the other.

When he borrowed a radio to call Paquette, all he'd got was static, same as Rose's.

"Where's the fuckin' sarge?" a couple of them had asked.

"He ain't coming back from where I sent him," he'd told them, then decided to shut up about it because Sly might want to break the news some other way.

After topping off his tank from a couple of jerry cans

in back of a vehicle that wasn't going anywhere until
they brought in a bulldozer, he'd set out toward town.
One mile and the Explorer was hiccuping, two and it
was lurching and jumping. Three and the engine stalled,
and he'd cranked on the starter until the battery went
dead.

Still twenty miles from town, he'd taken the gym bag
and walked back to the marsh and the useless cops. By
then the sun was down. He had taken another Explorer,
evicted the three punks inside, and glugged in a few
gallons from another jerry can.

As he was fueling, they'd made a big deal about the
gym bag he was carrying.

"Does that mean we can go back?"

How the fuck would I know? he'd almost said, then
thought about it and decided Paquette must have had a
reason for sending them. "Better if you stay here."

He'd spent an uncomfortable night in the Explorer,
wishing it was bigger and not letting the three guys back
inside to get warm. When they'd kept him awake with
their complaining, he'd climbed out, caught two, and
thumped them together. They'd squealed about broken
noses and teeth until he'd run them off, got back in, and
finally slept. He'd awakened early.

This morning the Explorer had made it a single mile
before giving up. By then he'd been tired of the drill.
The one he was in now—taken from two guys who had
been asleep inside—was a bucket of crap, but it had not
broken down. He would have filled it with gasoline, but
he'd felt there was enough to get him to town, and by
then he'd pissed off so many of the cops he felt they
might try to shoot him. He had driven for two hours.
Now, as he finally approached the roadblock, he had a
feeling about things not being right, so he parked and
decided to take a look.

Billy slipped into the forest and went quietly. It had
taken half an hour before he came onto the three at
the roadblock.

He spotted a woman and two men, all Indians armed
with rifles. He thought about it all for a while, wondering
what was going on. It was too hard, trying to figure it

out. *Better to be safe than sorry,* his mother had always said. *Take the cripples first,* his uncles had told him.

Billy crept closer, not liking the way they were parked away from the thicket, too far for a good kill. He lined up on the nearest one, too long a shot for the sawed-off but close enough to slow the man down some while Billy moved around and tried to pick off the others.

7:00 A.M.—*Moose Lake*

The two groups, the *Muk-wah* and the four survivors, soaked up information from one another like thirsty sponges. Jason was outraged to learn of the murders in the forest, while Link was pleased to hear of the Manido-Ojibwe's thus far successful rebellion.

Link remained anxious about Jenifer. "How do you plan to get to the Warehouse?"

Jason blinked, puzzled. "What do you mean?"

"The ecol-rec zone."

"First we have to deal with the patrolmen before they can get back to Spirit Lake."

Gloria's gaze remained fixed across the lake. During the cold night the broad-leaved trees had shed their final foliage, making the yellow-hued ecol-rec zone appear even more stark and foreboding. Despite her awful condition, Jason had regarded her with disdain.

"Mr. Toussaint," she said in her cultured voice. "Five miles from where we sit are a group of desperate people. They're holding your aunt and your people as captives and . . ."

"My aunt was seen in Spirit Lake before we left this morning," he said coolly.

"It couldn't have been Jenifer."

"The ones who saw her have known her all her life."

"It's not her." Gloria regarded him. "Let me explain what happened to me."

Jason's look was unyielding. "Storyteller said not to trust you. I'm not interested in . . ."

"Listen to her," said Link.

"Go ahead," Jason finally told her.

"It began in my suite at the hotel," said Gloria. As she explained how Willie and the scarecrow had cropped her hair, and what they'd done thereafter, Jason appeared uneasy. She told about the dying woman in the marsh, and of being sold to the fat man. She explained how she had survived. Her story was terrible, so damning of the woman called Sydney that Link's face turned to stone, and a *Muk-wah* wondered aloud if she had human blood in her veins.

Gloria regarded Jason Toussaint solemnly as she pulled away the towel, exposing her scarred head with its scant tufts of hair, now turned to white. "The Jenifer your people saw was Sydney. Your aunt's at the Warehouse, her hair cropped like mine so Sydney could make a wig."

Jason stared in speechless horror.

"Your people saw Sydney on her way to the Warehouse to warn them."

Jason's voice was a croak. "What are they protecting?"

"Mafia businesses." Gloria began with the meth factory, speaking slowly, concisely.

"You've seen these—slaves?"

"I lived with them," she said. "The couple keeps them drunk on speed and disposes of their bodies when they burn out. They're treated worse than animals."

"So that's where our people are taken," said Lonnie.

Gloria explained the other businesses at the Warehouse.

Jason shook his head dolefully.

Crack! Another mine went off in the ecol-rec zone.

"What's the best way to get in?"

"They've made it impossible." She explained the three tiers of Code Red.

Level One: Tighten defenses, and load the drugs and hijacked goods.

"Load them into what?" Lonnie asked.

"They have trucks and trailers."

Level Two: Eliminate evidence.

"The guests and the engineers board the final trailer,

and everything's trucked out. The mob owns temporary warehouses somewhere, Milwaukee, I think.

"The meth factory supervisors will have the laborers dismantle the lab and kitchens, and dump the chemicals and sludge into the marsh. Then they'll dispose of the laborers."

No one asked what she meant by dispose. They knew.

"The biker supervisors will leave on their motorcycles, and Howarski in his helicopter."

"We've got to stop them before they reach Level Two," said Jason.

"That's what Mr. Anderson and I were discussing when you arrived. Unfortunately, they've made it practically impossible. Now there's another problem to deal with. Yesterday they received replacement parts for the military helicopter."

"An MH-60," Link explained to Jason. "Sensors, mini-Gatling guns, rockets. I damaged it once by tricking the pilot into landing, but they wouldn't fall for it again."

"They're scrambling to repair it," said Gloria. "And now that Sydney's told them about this group . . ."

"The *Muk-wah,*" one said proudly.

Gloria finished, ". . . they'll use it to destroy you."

Link mused. "First they have to make it fly. They're engineers, not mechanics. Repairing a complex aircraft isn't like writing computer software."

"They did seem to be having trouble," she said, "but they'll eventually succeed."

Everyone grew quiet, ill at ease with their thoughts.

Jason asked, "Do you know where their roads merge onto the highway?"

"Very precisely. Their telephone lines too. I memorized their maps," she said.

Jason keyed the radio, identified himself as *Muk-wah* Two, and asked someone named Carole to prepare to send people to block intersections and cut a phone line.

Carole said no problem; more volunteers were reporting to the station every hour.

Jason handed his radio to Gloria, to provide directions. As she gave detailed instructions, Jason walked to

Lonnie's pickup to observe the canvas-wrapped body there.

Link joined him.

"Storyteller didn't call us here to attack the lousy patrolmen. It was the Warehouse. Then I let them know we were coming by burning down the Hatchet Club."

"Don't be hard on yourself. You have a group who'll follow you to hell, and you don't have to watch your back for mobsters from the casino." He regarded Sergeant Rose's body. "Do you think he knew a way into the ecol-rec?"

"It's likely," said Jason. "Storyteller was meeting with the hermit. Both he and Senator Eddie trusted Nek-kah with important things, some of them Storyteller didn't tell me about."

Link lifted an oblong aluminum case, bearing a ZEIGEL logo. It was heavy.

"Storyteller's rifle," said Jason. "He was into target shooting and asked me to bring it."

Link tried a latch. "Do you have the key?"

"No."

Gloria came to return Jason's radio.

"I apologize for doubting you, Mrs. Vasson."

"My husband spoke well of you, Jason. When this is over, we must talk." She touched the wooden flute that extended from his jacket pocket. "Eddie had one like it."

"He gave me this one and taught me to play. It's called a *bibig-wun*. We use it for signaling, like the Manido in the old days."

Crack! sounded a mine explosion from the ecol-rec zone.

Oo-gah!

Link regarded Gloria. "We've got to get into the Warehouse. Can you think of anything that might possibly help?"

"Nothing. I didn't mention Level Three. If they're about to be compromised, Howarski will blow the place up to destroy any loose ends."

Turf Siegel had joined them, and now paled. "Jesus, it just came to me. Howarski's the guy who blew up the

WTO meeting in San Francisco? According to the *Times* he's smarter than the Unabomber or even Charles Sloan. We're up against *him*?"

Link ignored him. "Are the explosives already in place?"

"I'm sure," said Gloria, "and Howarski would set it off with a smile."

"But would he endanger himself?"

She humphed. "He'd offer anyone else, but *never* himself. Howarski is heroic only in his own mind."

Link wondered if they could confine Howarski in the Warehouse while they removed Jenifer and the laborers. The problem was as before, they had to find a way in.

"I been thinking," said Turf. "One of the sensors is a video camera, right?"

"Electro-optic tracker," Gloria said. "Like a black-and-white TV with bad contrast."

"Sure. They use vidicon tubes. I have a couple flash units in my pack. *Flash, flash, flash,* and they'd be blinded. What do you think?"

"Here's what else they said. The sensors work in redundancy. They also use thermal imaging and RF motion detectors. There, you now have the extent of my knowledge."

Link was listening. *Think!* Link told himself. *How do I beat him?* His mind moved in circles. Getting past the platforms meant outwitting the sensors—controlled and interpreted by an artificial intelligence program—and if he foiled one, another would take over.

I have an engineering degree. I can walk the walk. What's the answer?

The others argued about defeating this sensor or that one.

How did I defeat Howarski the last time? I got in his head and beat him at his game.

As the fuzzy edges of an idea began to emerge, he spoke to Jason. "Can you transport the others back to town?"

Crack! Another report from the ecol-rec zone.

Gloria wagged her head in the negative. "Not me. I'd prefer to return to the Warehouse. I know it better than anyone, and I don't like leaving all of those poor people behind."

"If *you're* going back, Mrs. V . . ." Doughty began.

After only short hesitation, Link agreed. Their knowledge would be invaluable.

Link asked for an introduction to Carole. Jason provided it, then handed over his UHF.

"Can you connect me with a long-distance phone line?" he asked.

"Our rules are to involve no outsiders."

Link stared hard at Jason. After a moment the younger man took the radio. "This is *Muk-wah* Two. Do what he asks," he told Carole.

When Link took the radio back and repeated his request, Carole hesitated. Finally she said, "I'll have to relay for you. Do you have the number?"

"It's in New York." He dictated a message. She took down his words and read them back.

"Wait two hours before you place the call," he told her. Telephone conversations were too easily monitored, and he could not take the chance that Howarski might tap in.

He returned Jason's radio. "I'd like to examine Sergeant Rose's body."

Before Jason had time to answer, Carole's voice interrupted over the UHF. "*Muk-wah* Two, we have trouble at the Lake Portage roadblock. The Junkman just shot and wounded Brian Small Turtle. He has a bag with him he isn't letting out of his sight."

Jason responded without hesitation. "Have our people pull back and let him through."

41

When he was certain that the three who had manned the roadblock were gone, Billy Junkins returned to his vehicle, thinking how easy it had been. Just when he'd thought they were preparing to put up a fight, they'd fled like frightened antelope.

He went by the place where they'd been parked and wondered who they'd been, and if he shouldn't have tried talking his way past. He decided he had done the right thing. Too many people wanted the gym bag in the seat at his side.

As he drove on, Billy wondered what Paquette would say when he walked in and casually dropped the bag in front of him. "Easy as pie," he'd tell him, and hope he wouldn't be too upset about him killing Rose.

He passed the first homes in Spirit Lake, and a minute or so later approached an intersection. A pickup was parked sideways in the road at both left and right. Quiet-looking, expressionless men and women stood outside, carrying rifles but not threatening. Billy had no idea why they were there, but since they did not block the way to Rock Lake, where Paquette lived, he kept going, wondering what it was about.

With the dumb-ass cops all up at the marsh playing submarine with their vehicles, it looked like something he'd have to handle for Sly after he handed over the gym bag.

He turned left at the main intersection, accelerated on

the highway, and noticed more pickups and a Suburban blocking other intersections. Still they did not interfere or try to slow him down, and he continued on without restriction. By the time he made the turnoff to Paquette's house, he had to admit that he was becoming nervous.

He drove slowly down the long driveway and after a hundred yards eased off the gas to a crawl. An Explorer was off in the ditch. *What the hell?*

Billy took the gym bag, got out, and looked around. The house was dark, which seemed odd because there were lights that Sly left on day and night. No big deal, he decided. Paquette was obviously in since his Lexus was parked in its usual place.

He went up the stairs to the door, almost went on in, then thought about it and knocked.

Bam! A fist-sized opening exploded through the massive oak door. Junkins jumped aside, swearing and yelling, "Hey, it's me!"

After a moment, during which he heard someone ratchet in a fresh shotgun shell, Sly Paquette's voice floated out. "Billy?"

"Yeah, man. What the fuck? You almost shot me."

"You carrying?"

"A sawed-off, in the car." After a moment's silence Billy added, "I got the gym bag."

"Bring it in." Sly was not nearly as exuberant as he'd thought he would be.

Billy opened the door warily and went inside.

Sly was crouched by his stuffed easy chair, blankets clutched about himself, looking out through a single bloodred eye and holding a shotgun.

Billy deposited the bag. "Easy as . . . what the fuck happened to your eye?"

"Splinters. I tried to look out the back door and they shot the doorframe. We're trapped."

"Aww," Billy said. He went back to the door he'd just entered, opened it, and peered out. "I didn't see . . ."

Pop!

"Shit!" Billy yelled, as a fire bee sliced into his biceps.

Pop! Another bee stung his thigh, a graze but it hurt worse than the pierced arm.

He danced back into the room. "What the hell's going on?"

"Women," said Paquette, from under the blankets.

"No good *bitches*!" The cop named Willie rose into sight from where he'd been hiding at the end of the couch. He too had blankets wrapped around himself. There were small dark splotches where blood drained from shoulder wounds, and more on his trouser leg.

His scarecrow partner crept in from the other room, eyes wide and frightened. He limped, and both hands were wrapped in gauze. "I saw the one who shot you."

Billy touched the bloody hole in his biceps and winced. It had been something small, like a twenty-two. "It's cold," he observed, realizing that was the reason for their blankets.

"They turned the power off at noon yesterday. I tried to go out and get wood, and they sh-shoot me," said the fearful scarecrow. "We burned a couple of kitchen chairs."

"This is bullshit," said Billy Junkins. He walked to the window, pulled the curtain back, and cautiously looked through, trying to spot one of them. No way he was going to sit in here and let a bunch of women . . .

Pop! He bellowed and grabbed his ear. The bullet had shorn off half of the lobe as cleanly as if it had been severed by a sharp knife. *Pop! Pop!* His cheek stung! Billy scrambled away from the window, spitting blood and pieces of teeth, and releasing involuntary whimpers.

8:00 A.M.—*the Warehouse*

Sydney, who knew she looked more like Jenifer Toussaint than the injured and battered woman in the room next door, had talked to Tonio Gracchi twice since she'd fled the hotel fire.

She'd been unable to contact anyone before leaving Spirit Lake. Neither the phone at the hotel lobby nor the pay phone at the Quik Mart had worked, so she'd driven all the way around the reservation at ninety miles per hour—damned lucky she didn't hit a deer or bear—to the Warehouse to warn Howarski and call Tonio Gracchi on the dedicated hard line.

Sydney had awakened Tonio before five o'clock to tell him his casino had been burned to the ground by a bunch of Stone Age mentality Indians who had also, by the way, taken over the town. No, she had not seen any of Sly Paquette's hoodlum cops. He had screamed at the possibility of losing the money and said he'd send a couple carloads of badasses to get it back.

"The sooner the better," she had told him.

After an hour Tonio had phoned back, still unable to raise anyone in Spirit Lake. There were only busy signals and a voice saying the phone line was temporarily out of commission.

"How are things goin' there at the warehouse?" he'd asked.

Sydney had told him about ordering the Code Red, despite the fact that Howarski was upset. "We're destroying innocent animals!" "Fuck the animals," she'd said.

She'd ordered the big-rig trailers to be loaded with dope and stolen computers.

"Good. Don't take no chances with losin' that shit."

"I don't intend to." She'd hung up.

Crack! Another mine had exploded, wiping out another Bambi or whoever.

She'd gone two doors down to the Resort to reassure the concerned *guests* that everything was fine, explaining the explosions as a phenomenon of freezing trees, which some of the fools actually believed. But of course, she was good at that sort of thing.

In the event she'd need a safe haven, she'd telephoned the Washington numbers of some of her most reliable contacts. Only one call had been completed. An undersecretary of Labor said to call back in the distant future. Her name was being mentioned, and he couldn't be involved.

An assistant deputy attorney general had hung up on her. The others were unavailable.

Sydney seethed, and vowed that they would be very, very sorry.

The trailers were now loaded with meth and contraband, and Howarski was out at the Black Hawk, supervising final repairs.

Sydney called Tonio, informed him of the progress, and asked about his badasses.

"I had 'em flown up to Wausau. Couple of carloads. They won't stop kicking butt until I tell 'em, and I don't plan on tellin' 'em soon." He paused. "Is Anderson behind this crap?"

"I doubt it."

"His girlfriend still alive?"

"I think so." Sydney had not checked.

"I don't like what the asshole's done. Like my uncle Carmine says, getting even is better'n getting laid. Take the bitch out and shoot her."

"With pleasure," Sydney responded. It was best if there weren't two Jenifers around.

The line suddenly went dead.

"The damned telephone quit," she complained to the on-duty engineer.

Howarski entered the room, observing her with his intense eyes. "I like your new face, and the hair's great, but aren't your tits smaller?"

"You're an idiot," she said amiably. His presence was reassuring despite his whining about killing raccoons and such.

The on-duty engineer spoke from the communications panel. "The phone line's broken at the west highway intersection."

"Could someone have cut it?" she asked.

Howarski scoffed. "Breaks occur all the time. We're surrounded by forest. Trees fall, and we send a crew to repair the line."

Crack! The sound of another exploding mine made Sydney feel better.

Howarski was confident. "It would take an Abrams tank to get in. When the Black Hawk's repaired we can handle those too. Now if you don't mind, let's stop killing animals."

"I do mind. Are Mom and Pop around?"

The biker couple took care of small work, such as dealing with Jenifer Toussaint.

"The aborigines finished loading the trailers. They're taking them to the factory."

"Tell them to see me when they return. I've got something for them to do."

8:30 A.M.—*Spirit Lake Township*

The large, dark vehicles crossed the reservation line at seventy-eight miles per hour, not slowing when they passed the first homes.

A *Muk-wah* observer transmitted, "Two of them, a blue Town Car and a black Suburban. Looks like many *naud-o-way*."

Two miles farther the vehicles were forced to slow down for a concrete highway barrier blocking the road. The driver of the Town Car cursed as he braked. When he had negotiated the circumvention he cursed again, for other concrete barriers obstructed the left lane. A Caterpillar D-9 bulldozer was directly ahead, other heavy highway construction equipment gathered on the sides of the road, and a fireplug-shaped Indian flagman wielded a handheld stop sign.

"You'll have to turn back, sir. We have a possible gas line emergency."

The driver pulled a .45 ACP auto. "Get the fuckin' dozer out of our way."

"Sure." The flagman backed off. "They're *naud-o-way,*" he confirmed into his radio.

"Dumb shit," said the driver to his four companions. They checked their weapons over, ready to kick ass as soon as they got to the town, which was only a single block distant.

As the dozer in front of them revved its diesel engine,

there came other heavy-engine sounds, from behind and both sides.

The driver craned his neck. "What the fuck?"

A second bulldozer crunched into the back of the Suburban, shoving it ahead as the one in the front smashed into the engine compartment of the Town Car. The inhabitants were first surprised and then terrified as the vehicles were compressed. Roofs buckled. Windows popped from their frames.

Out of their sight the flagman waved his sign.

The bulldozers stopped, and a pair of massive backhoes lowered their heavy buckets and rumbled forth until they were pressed firmly against the doors, cutting off all means of escape.

The flagman observed their handiwork, careful to remain out of the line of fire. He motioned that everything was proper, and the operators set their brakes and shut off their engines.

The gunmen, trapped in their metal cocoon, screamed about injured arms and legs.

The flagman called for quiet, identified himself as a peace officer, and cited the tribal laws as his authority. They were under arrest for failing to comply with his orders.

He would allow them to talk it over for an hour. Then, when he was convinced they'd thrown out all of their weapons, they'd be extracted and hauled off to jail.

Some cursed and called futilely on mobile phones. Within ten minutes there were teeth-chattering complaints that they were cold. At fifteen minutes firearms started dropping out of various broken windows. At thirty minutes they mournfully pleaded to be hauled to a warm jail.

The flagman said the deal was for a full hour and advised them to share body warmth.

Tonio Gracchi's "badasses" were subdued without incident.

8:45 A.M.—*Ecol-Rec Zone, Perimeter Road*

Link's luck held. He'd found the key to the aluminum gun case in Sergeant Rose's trouser pocket. Inside was a Winchester model 70 bolt action in .25-06 caliber, with a Redfield 4X-12X scope and a one-inch-diameter bull barrel. While too heavy for hunting, the rifle was perfect for its intended purpose—target shooting. Now he held the case upright as the four-by-four pickup wallowed through the ditch and onto the perimeter road.

After a mile they halted, climbed out, and prepared for the trek. Everyone except Turf Siegel and one of the *Muk-wah* would proceed.

Crack! The explosion was louder, closer.

Also in the rifle case were a collimator, a bipod, and eighty rounds of hand-loaded ammunition in plastic Speer containers.

Link slipped the collimator's rod into the barrel and peered through the scope. It was still true, boresighted for two hundred yards. The .25-06 caliber was an excellent choice; the bullet would not rise or fall appreciably out to twice that distance.

Oo-gah! The Code Red alarm sounded every half minute.

He packed ammunition into his jacket pockets and handed two boxes to one of the *Muk-wah* to carry. Finally he loaded the magazine with three rounds and ran the bolt forward to chamber a fourth. The action worked smoothly, the weapon obviously well tended.

The *Muk-wah* were gathered on the perimeter road, speaking in low tones.

Link looked squarely at Jason. "Killing is not always an easy thing to do."

"They've made our people suffer. We won't hesitate." Jason looked very sure.

Link nodded to Gloria Vasson and Ron Doughty. "It's time."

She made a shooing motion at Link. "I'll only need Mr. D."

Link joined the others, leaving the two alone.

As they peered intently at the forest, Gloria and the detective talked over their strategy, like longtime partners discussing a hand of bridge.

"The sensors are all reset to maximum sensitivity, about a hundred meters."

"One football field plus an end zone."

Crack! A mine exploded ahead and to their right.

"We mustn't get that close."

"What's the lethal range again?"

"About the same, a hundred meters."

"That makes it easier. At my age I need simplicity, Mrs. V. So when we get to the barrier, we may be in range of two platforms?"

"Yes." She pointed. "Tell me when we've walked two hundred meters, please."

"I'll carry you."

"Not until I weaken." She looked resolute. "Shall we begin?"

Weyland Building, Manhattan, New York

Erin stared at her screen as she answered the phone. "Twenty-seven seventy-five."

Her mental red flag was up. The readout said the call was coming from Spirit Lake, Wisconsin. Previous indications had been that all phone lines there were down.

"You're the Giants fan?" A woman's voice.

"Yes?" she said tentatively.

"I have a message from a Broncos fan."

Link was a devoted Denver fan.

"He said to tell you he's fine."

Erin felt like celebrating. If the woman spoke the truth, Link was okay!

"I'll read the rest from notes. He wants you to send the—umm—Mike Charlie Papa?"

"Why didn't the Broncos fan call?" she tried.

"He's busy. There's more. The Warehouse is located at RC one, three fifteen at eight."

Erin brought up a computer map of the reservation—easy for she had been fretting over it so often lately—and found reference coordinate one, known only to Helga and Link Anderson. She instructed the computer to plot a point 315 degrees for eight miles.

Was it truly the location of the elusive Warehouse?

"You're in contact with the Broncos fan?" she asked.

"Not at the moment. Like I said, he's busy. He said there's another Helga at the Warehouse, and . . ." The caller from Spirit Lake proceeded with the request.

"What he's asking for is unorthodox," Erin responded. "I'll need permission."

"I'll call back in ten minutes for your answer." The line went momentarily dead, then showed a busy signal. Erin punched the callback button. The busy signal returned. A moment later a digitalized voice said the number was temporarily out of service.

She buzzed Frank Dubois, to tell him Link was likely alive and pass on the request. As she waited for him to leave a meeting, she contacted John "Rabbit" Rabeni, the pilot-engineer who was babysitting the MCP airplane at the Appleton, Wisconsin, airport.

Erin had ordered them there in anticipation that Link might need support.

The MCP had begun life as a chopped-down wide-body 757 airframe. It had long legs, and was suitable for all-weather, short-airfield operations. It was rugged and adaptable to primitive field conditions, yet state-of-the-art. The MCP carried the very latest electronic warfare systems and could thwart all known air defenses. The directional brute-force jammers were so powerful that they were not to be activated within the borders of the U.S.

If tuned to the resonant frequency of the molecules of explosives or volatile gases, the substances would flash and detonate.

At precisely ten minutes, the woman called back as promised. "Giants fan?"

"Yep." Then Erin told her what they were proposing was illegal.

"Damn it, we need your help!" The voice was filled with emotion, just what Erin had been after so the V-A program could make its determination.

"We'd have to get permission from the FCC," she answered absently.

"I'll tell your *friend* what you said." Erin could tell she was about to hang up.

There! The V-A showed a ninety-two percent probability that she was truthful. The caller was legitimate.

Erin smiled. "What I want you to tell my friend is that the Mike Charlie Papa will be on station at eleven hundred hours, one hour and forty-three minutes from now. Tell him Rabbit will be driving and awaiting his signal." When there was no argument, Erin repeated the estimated time of arrival of the mobile command post.

"Thank you," said the woman from Spirit Lake, and again the connection was broken.

42

Link and the others followed in Gloria's and Ron Doughty's footsteps precisely, not wavering from the path lest they trigger the sensors mounted on one of the deadly platforms. For a while Doughty had carried the frail woman, but she was back on her feet. She stopped periodically to look carefully about, then would point in a new direction, and Doughty would resume his estimations of the distance they'd walked.

Oo-gah! croaked the alarm from the Warehouse.

Periodically they heard explosions, some distant, others closer as they approached the barrier. Once there was a tremendous report followed by sounds of shrapnel crashing through the trees. The duo before them hardly paused.

Gloria looked back at the group of followers. "We're at the barrier."

Link and Jason joined them, Link carrying the heavy-barreled rifle.

Jason's radio came alive. He had it turned down, but it still seemed loud. The vehicles guard relayed a message from Carole: "ETA is eleven hundred. Rabbit's driving."

Carole Yellowbird obviously did not believe in unnecessary chatter.

"Was that the answer you needed?" Jason asked Link.

"Yes," said Link.

"Two hundred meters," Gloria said, pointing to their forward right. "There's another to our left, but this one should be first."

"Two football fields and two end zones," muttered Ron Doughty. "Don't get too close."

Link walked cautiously. The others followed at a safe distance.

Crack! More shrapnel whistled through tree branches.

Link continued, pleased about Erin's response, but also worrying about the MCP flying in the face of missiles and the rapid-fire cannon Gloria had described.

He stared intently ahead, searching for the symmetry of a man-made platform in the trees. He shouldered the Winchester for a look. The riflescope was set to X4. More magnification and the sight picture was often unsteady. He kept his left eye squinted open to maintain his bearings.

There! The platform was not fully visible, but enough to see that a Claymore mine was moving on its gimbal mount, coming to bear!

Link dived for the protective base of an oak.

Crack! This sound was louder, and a spray of shrapnel whooshed by.

He immediately rolled over and sighted through the scope.

The platform was still; he was out of the sensors' direct line of sight. Link could see neither the bulbous shapes nor the horn antennae. He rose slowly—until they came into view.

Another mine began to move. He had been spotted, his presence provided to the computer for analysis. He squeezed the trigger gently.

Bam! The dark bulb shattered.

The mine was still moving as he shifted the aim point to the horn antenna.

Bam! The horn lurched.

He was still altering the sight picture as the mine came to rest, pointed directly at him. He dropped, and was in midair as the explosion sounded.

Crack! He felt a breeze on his scalp, and for a moment wondered if he had been hit.

"Link?" he heard Jason's concerned voice.

He rose and aimed, the sight picture steadied, and he squeezed off a round.

Bam! A miss.

The next mine began to move.

Bam! The clear bulb shattered like a clay pigeon.

He took a shallow breath, then a tentative step into the open, and watched. The remaining mines were immobile. At this platform at least, the computer was blinded.

"Link?" Jason again.

"One down," he replied.

He estimated distance and decided that he was within the hundred meters Gloria had warned about. Too close, but there had been no way to see the thing from farther out.

If the last of the leaves had not fallen the previous night, it would have been impossible.

Gloria and Doughty approached. "Where's the next one?" Link asked. The first one had taken fifteen minutes. There was no time to waste.

10:35 A.M.

Jason and his *Muk-wah* followed Gloria and Mr. D much closer now that they'd wended their way past the final platforms.

Gloria paused at an intersection of two overgrown paths, looked about to be sure of her location, and gave a nod and a finger to her lips for silence. She and Mr. D had led them safely through the maze. They were close enough to the *naud-o-way* that they might be overheard.

Oo-gah! Oo-gah! After fifteen seconds, it sounded again. *Oo-gah! Oo-gah!*

"They've gone to Level Two!" Jason whispered unnecessarily.

The signal had been given to eliminate the "evidence."

Link tapped Jason's shoulder for attention and flashed

all five fingers once, twice, and then three times. *Wait fifteen minutes before attacking.*

He watched Link move with catlike grace as he disappeared into the forest, and felt a pang that he might not see his friend alive again. Still he could think of no better candidate to go to the Warehouse and do what must be done. Jenifer could have no better champion.

The *Muk-wah* were to take the meth factory, subdue the supervisors, and round up the Manido slave laborers. They would try to accomplish that quietly, using weapons of silence.

Oo-gah! Oo-gah! brayed the alarm.

The eleven minutes that passed seemed like an eternity.

Jason lifted his flute and created the *ch-ch-ch* sounds of an angry squirrel.

The *Muk-wah* moved forward, positioning for the attack.

Gloria had described the factory so accurately that they had no trouble with the layout. As they closed in, the stench of the cooking drugs worsened, and they saw specters with darkened eyes, people they'd known all of their lives yet were hardly recognizable, moving in spasms and starts, carrying pails of chemicals from the lab to the kitchens, hauling loads from the kitchens to dump into a fetid pool of waste.

Men in studded leather jackets swaggered among them, barking orders and giving a shove here, a kick there, urging them to move faster and lining the idle ones up to one side. There'd be six of them, Gloria had said, all easily distinguishable. He spotted the brutal couple she'd told of, the woman urging the man on as he beat a laborer with a heavy belt. The woman was as she had described, all bone and gristle. The man just looked mean.

Jason crept closer, using the shadows of a great maple for cover, and looked again. He saw only two bikers, and had lost track of the couple.

"Soon as they dump the shit, get 'em over in the line," a supervisor called.

The Manido slaves would be easier to murder that way.

Oo-gah! Oo-gah! came the relentless call for death.

At fourteen minutes Jason used his flute to make final adjustments, as they'd practiced. The *Muk-wah* crept closer with their throwing-knives, slashing knives, and hand axes. Lonnie and one other carried compound bows and arrows tipped with jagged steel.

Jason played the sound of the nervous squirrel again, then of a chickadee, signaling the leftmost ones to move closer. Two *Muk-wah* were at the laboratory shack, two others moving into positions at each of the four kitchens. The remainder guarded the path to the Warehouse, cutting off that route of escape.

Jason waited. They were almost there, almost ready, and still undetected. Still only the two supervisors were in view, and for a final time he looked for the others.

A third supervisor, black bearded and wearing Lennon granny glasses, walked from the laboratory door, motioning to one of the *Muk-wah,* thinking he was a laborer.

"Get your red ass over in the line, boy."

On the flute Jason made the high trill of an attacking hawk—instructing an archer to take the new target of opportunity—and before the note faded Lonnie had released an arrow.

Thwack! The supervisor opened and closed his mouth, soundless. He wilted, the feathered shaft protruding from midchest. The *Muk-wah* the man had called to went closer, eyes focused on the door beyond the dead man, gripping a throwing ax. He cautiously went inside.

Jason made a chirping sound, then another, and a supervisor at the leftmost kitchen was taken from behind, head levered back and throat slashed in a single motion.

The arrow meant for the third visible supervisor was unaccountably delayed. He saw his companion falling to the ground, life's blood gushing in a bright red fountain, and became the first *naud-o-way* to react. He screamed a warning and was clawing to unholster his pistol when the arrow struck with such vengeance that it passed through his side.

He squealed, eyes wide, searching for a path of retreat. As he staggered back toward the meth kitchen, he fired a round at the nearest group of laborers. One of the Manido slaves fell.

Jason blew repeatedly into the flute, making raucous sounds of northern ravens, the signal for all-out attack.

The one who had been skewered remained alive for only two more steps before Lonnie impaled him with a second hunting arrow. Another *Muk-wah* snatched the pistol from the supervisor's hand, and drove an axhead into his neck.

As the raven sounds continued the *Muk-wah* found nothing to attack.

Where were the other supervisors?

The *Muk-wah* who had entered the laboratory pushed one of them, blood pulsing from an ax wound in his shoulder, outside. In no mood for niceties, they shoved him harshly to the ground and searched for weapons.

As Jason started to look away, the biker staggered to his feet and tried to flee.

Lonnie had an arrow nocked and ready. *Thwack!* The *naud-o-way* was dead before he impacted the ground. That was four. *Where was the couple?*

The Manido slaves stared about nervously, not taking sides.

"You're free," they were told. A few tried to continue working, but the *Muk-wah* stopped them, and herded them together.

"How many more of our People?" Jason asked Gloria.

"This is all of them." Gloria had observed the attack with satisfaction.

"I saw the couple earlier, but I don't know where they went."

"I do." Gloria's grim smile did not fade as she walked to an outdoor toilet.

The door that had been cracked was now pulled closed.

"Be careful," said Gloria. "They're armed and have killed a lot of our people."

Jason did not question that Gloria said "our." He nodded gravely to Lonnie, who nocked and carefully drew an arrow, aiming at the center of the flimsy building.

Thwack! The first screams issued from inside.

10:50 A.M.—the Warehouse

Fifteen minutes after leaving Jason, Link Anderson
was a mile distant, observing the buildings of the Warehouse and remembering all that Gloria had told him.

He was hidden in plain view, standing beside a collection of denuded birch trees. They'd been poisoned, like
all the flora in the ecol-rec zone, and appeared pale
and yellowish.

At the far end of the compound was the air defense
suite: the TEL, with its white-and-black Paul Revere II
missiles mounted and ready; the 27 mm cannon, particularly deadly in appearance due to the scorpion stinger
muzzle; and the eyes of the outfit, the dual-faced fixed-
array radar. The brains were the computer located inside
the command center.

Oo-gah! Oo-gah!

Three engineers who had been working on the Black
Hawk helicopter had gone into the control center. Two
others within his view carried rifles. He wondered if they
were as unfamiliar with them as the shooters on the ill-
fated Jet Ranger. Regardless, he was badly outnumbered.

Several men and a woman with bandaged faces had
emerged from the Resort, loudly asking about their
promised transportation. The so-called guests.

Two tractor-trailers were parked before Building
Three. He wondered who would drive them, and decided
on the pair of dweeb engineers standing beside one. Did
they get vicarious thrills from flying in choppers and
driving big rigs?

Crack! A report echoed from an exploding mine.

His vision moved to the security control center, Howarski's domain, then to the inflated building beside it,
where Jenifer should be in the farthest room, locked
behind a steel door.

If he miscalculated, she would die.

Bam! He heard the abrupt report of a pistol from the
foul-smelling meth factory. He waited, hoping Jason's
Muk-wah would not become involved in a noisy firefight,
and heard nothing more. No one before him was inter-

ested in the single gunshot. The guests continued calling out, wondering about transportation, using abrasive and bossy tones.

If things had gone as planned, four of the *Muk-wah* would be escorting the Manido slave laborers to the vehicles parked on the perimeter road, using paths that had been rendered safe. Jason and the remainder would await Link at the intersection of the two overgrown paths.

Oo-gah! Oo-gah!

He observed his watch. The MCP plane should be in the northern sky, turning toward the Warehouse. He moved back a step and picked up the target rifle. Except for the pushy guests demanding transportation, things about the Warehouse appeared business as usual.

During the next minute that would change.

10:55 A.M.—*Security Control Center, the Warehouse*

Sydney looked down from the rearmost console, wishing desperately that she could phone out. Things were not all bleak. By now Tonio Gracchi's "badasses" had surely arrived at Spirit Lake to put things into order. Also, Howarski had just been told the Black Hawk was ready for flight.

Three engineers were manning consoles. The one at the radar screen—operated in limited-range mode with the overhead net only partially opened—spoke in a monotonous drone.

"We have a single aircraft seventy miles north, turning toward us."

"Get rid of it!" said Howarski.

The airplane might represent a witness, and its survival was an unnecessary risk.

"Load two KW missiles!" said Howarski, no longer smiling.

"They're loaded," said the SAM specialist. His voice was unsteady. The U.S. Army Paul Revere missile system was deadly.

"Set up for communications jamming, then open the net. We'll . . ."

Bam! That one was a firearm. Someone was firing a rifle, and it was close. *Bam!* Again.

"Take a look around," Howarski ordered the on-duty engineer.

The engineer switched on video cameras that panned throughout the Warehouse area.

Sydney observed the different monitors. In one an indistinct figure stood with a raised rifle. In another the twin missiles came into view. One was spewing vapor, obviously damaged and releasing rocket fuel under pressure, and the other—

Bam!

The second missile exploded on the launch rail, spewing tentacles of fire. The concussive wave shredded the fabric of the building and inflicted sharp pain in Sydney's ears.

While the figure in the monitor had been indistinct, his identity was not in question.

As the others emerged from their shock, Sydney was already hurrying toward the door. Jenifer Toussaint was in the adjacent building. Lincoln Anderson must not be allowed to save her. When Sydney escaped there must be no telltale doubles left behind.

Howarski was slow to recover his wits, but as he did so the first things on his mind were survival—and Lincoln Anderson. He had noted the rifleman and knew it could only be Anderson.

He worked the keys at the weapons console and called for a functional check of the computer: OPERATIONAL. His fingers flew as he entered the main weapons menu, selected the scorpion symbol for the 27 mm rapid-fire cannon, then ARMED/FULL RANGE OF FIRE.

The monitor before him blinked on, showing the bore-site view of the cannon, which could be slewed up, down, and in 360 degrees with the joystick. Whatever he saw at the center of the screen could be destroyed by depressing the trigger. The stinger-tipped cannon expended a thousand rounds per minute and would destroy anything in its path.

Howarski ignored the inane questions of the engineers, who only now returned to life. As he moved the joystick the video camera showed the buildings, and Sydney scurrying next door. He considered using her for the test firing, then switched to one of Tonio's *guests,* a pudgy man who emerged from the dining hall to look frantically about.

He pressed the trigger.

BRRRRRRR.

The centroid of the video picture erupted in flying debris. When it settled he picked out a torso and a leg, all that remained visible of the guest.

He slewed the picture to locate the rifleman, but saw no sign of Anderson. No sign of—*there*! A lean figure strode down the path between buildings, past the tractor-trailers, carrying only the dreaded hand ax. Howarski could not quell an erotic shiver as he nudged the joystick to keep the centroid on target, and moved his forefinger to the trigger.

11:05 A.M.—*Twenty Thousand Feet, over Upper Michigan*

Rabbit Rabeni's eyes were glued on the flat-screen display; six hundred miles distant, Erin watched the same coordinates on the monitor in her New York office.

The mobile command post had all sensors set to maximum resolution, and he stared hard at the location on the earth that was obscured by thick clouds.

A flare flashed momentarily on the screen.

"Was that it?" Rabbit wondered aloud.

"Right place and the timing's good," said Erin.

"Want me to activate?"

"Negative, wait until I get a spectral analysis."

Long seconds passed.

"Hey, I'm seeing something new."

"Initial analysis identifies it as auto-weapons fire."

"Damn it, we can't just sit here and . . ."

Erin's tone changed. "Helga just confirmed a fuel explosion. Same spectrum as the Paul Revere II missile that Link wanted us to look for."

"Want me to switch on?"

The brute-force electronic jammer was set to blast a signal with an illegal intensity of a full megawatt of power, directly at the location that Link Anderson had passed on to Erin. The frequency would skip from 233 MHz to 266 MHz to 300 MHz, the operating-system speeds of large-scale, modern computer servers.

"Helga just did," Erin said. "Say good night to their computer."

Security Control Center, the Warehouse

As Howarski triggered the cannon the display went blank. He hastily looked about. None of the readouts or monitors were functioning.

"Computer's down!" yelled the on-duty engineer.

"That's impossible."

A malfunction light blinked on and off at the computer's power supply: SURGE! SURGE! SURGE! Smoke issued from the power supply that was built to withstand a nuclear attack.

"Fix the damned thing!"

"It's fried," said the engineer. He lost his composure and bolted for the door.

Howarski was left alone. Above him the ceiling began to sag downward, ever downward, as the blowers were unable to keep up with the deflating building.

Oo-gah! Oo-gah!

As the lights dimmed, Howarski reached across the master control panel and lifted the guard to what he believed was the SYSTEM RESET button.

Nothing.

Howarski imagined Lincoln Anderson striding purposefully toward the control center, as he had done the night he'd attacked the Black Hawk.

He jabbed the button repeatedly—and did not realize his error until a spectral voice from a loudspeaker permeated throughout the area of the Warehouse: *"Ten*

*minutes remaining. Evacuate now. Ten minutes re-
maining. Evacuate now. Ten minutes . . ."*

It came to Howarski slowly that he had activated
Level Three! As he frantically went through the procedure for deactivation, he remembered that he must first
bring up the menu.

With the computer shut down that was impossible.

In ten minutes the Warehouse would be obliterated!

43

Ecol-Rec Zone

One mile distant, at an intersection of overgrown paths, Jason and his *Muk-wah* heard the broadcast clearly: *"Ten minutes remaining. Evacuate now. Ten minutes remaining. Evacuate . . ."*

Gloria Vasson stared toward the Warehouse, her battered face turned to stone. "Howarski's activated the Level Three sequence."

"I'm going back," said Jason.

"You couldn't possibly get there in time. I suggest we move back. The meth factory will be destroyed with everything else, and we're far too close."

The Warehouse

Jenifer huddled by the door in the darkness, chilled to the bone and wondering what the announcement was about. She had been battered when the Jeep rolled, but the bruises and broken ribs were not her worst debilitation. For two days she'd been denied food or water, and she was terribly dehydrated, reduced to a single emotion: loathing for the woman who had looked like Gloria Vasson. The woman called Sydney had had her stripped, sheared her hair, taken a cast of her face, and all the while exulted at her helplessness. Jenifer had clothed herself the moment the woman left, yet she still felt violated, still naked and exposed.

They had taken her coat and cut off the heat to the room, and she was continually cold.

For the past hours there had been explosions, some loud and others distant, and she had no idea what was happening outside the pitch-black cell. She'd heard frightened people in the hall and had called out for someone to release her, but no one had responded.

She had pried a rail loose from the cot, a thirty-inch length of wood, and tried battering the door and punching at the heavy-fabric wall, but to no avail. Still she clutched it, the only semblance of a tool or weapon that she possessed.

"Nine minutes remaining. Evacuate now. Nine minutes remaining. Evacuate now. . . ."

A key moved in the lock, and she wondered if she was hallucinating. No one had visited, although she vaguely recalled a voice calling from the hall, telling her not to lose hope.

The door opened, and a woman entered. Jenifer was startled as she recognized her own features, even her hair. Sydney! The woman she despised stepped farther inside, squinting so her eyes might adjust, holding a pistol and wearing the look of one who was determined to use it.

Jenifer desperately swung the bed rail at the hand and the weapon.

Sydney squealed, more a sound of rage than pain, and the gun skittered away.

Jen fell upon her, desperately grasping and clawing. Her weakness was immediately apparent, for the woman easily shoved her hands aside, then grasped her neck and held on, throttling her, pressing her to the floor, repositioning and gaining a death's grip around Jen's throat. Squeezing, cursing her, telling her to die. "There is no reason for you to live!" she spat.

The final vestiges of Jen's energy faded. She managed a croaking noise from her parched pharynx. The utterance was repeated by the mimic who choked her.

"Eight minutes remaining. Evacuate now. Eight minutes remaining. Evacuate . . ."

Jenifer vaguely discerned a ripping sound. Sunlight was cast into the room.

She turned just enough to see a man's figure step partway through a rent in the fabric wall. The figure's hand wielded a hand ax, and the tear became larger.

Sydney raised her head, not releasing her death's hold. "Darling," she said in Jenifer's voice. "I thought you'd never get here." She mimicked Jen perfectly, despite the fact that the latex mask was so askew that she spoke through an eyehole.

Link Anderson swung the hand ax, smacking the flat side hard against Sydney's temporal bone. Then he cast her away so forcefully that she literally flew across the room.

Jenifer mouthed silent words, wanting him to kill the hated woman, but he didn't waste a second before hefting her and stepping through the rent into the light.

Bam! Her heart beat wilder. Sydney had found the dropped pistol. *Miss,* she prayed.

Bam! Link shuddered and staggered, obviously hit.

"You're hurt. Put me down," Jen croaked.

"Never." As he continued into the forest her last vision of the place was of two huge buildings that drooped dangerously as they deflated.

Jen clung on as best she could, teeth chattering. "Water," she managed.

"Soon," was all he said, as he hurried through the forest.

"Seven minutes remaining. Evacuate now. Seven minutes remaining. Evacuate . . ."

Howarski desperately tried to rein in his terror. He had mistakenly triggered the Level Three doomsday sequence. Tons of explosives would be detonated in seven minutes, and without the computer there was no way to reverse it. He'd tried resetting it, pounding relentlessly on the emergency override switch, but to no avail.

As he fled the security control center, he was not

alone. Engineers, guests, even the kitchen staff had left the buildings.

"Go into the forest," he cried to the fools, but they were too fearful of the explosions.

"The computer's down," he told the engineers. "The security system *can't* work." A few listened and tried to pass the word along. Arguments began.

Howarski had a single objective; the Black Hawk was his ticket to freedom, but he mustn't attract the mob.

The overhead net was drawn only enough to allow the radar system to operate, not nearly sufficiently to allow the Black Hawk through. His idea was to get airborne and blast his way out with the Gatling guns.

An engineer hurried by.

"Give me your weapon," Howarski snapped, reaching for the man's M16.

"Go to hell," snarled the engineer, snatching it away.

Howarski went to the MH-60's sliding door and furtively slipped inside.

"Six minutes remaining. Evacuate now. Six minutes remaining. Evacuate . . ."

He climbed into the right seat, switched on the battery, then held his breath as the gauges came to life, gyros humming as they spun up to speed.

Two engineers climbed in back, then two more. He knew that arguing would only waste time. The Black Hawk had sufficient power to take them.

"Don't let anyone else aboard," he called back as he switched on fuel and hydraulic pumps. Everything seemed to be working properly. He brought the flight instruments on line, deftly exercised the controls, depressed AUXILLIARY AIR and then both START ENGINE switches.

"Yes!" he shouted happily as the turbines began to whine.

"Five minutes remaining. Evacuate now. Five minutes remaining. Evacuate . . ."

More people climbed in back. He looked there, shouted for them to leave. They remained, and he decided there should be enough power. Get them to the highway, ditch them there, and get out of Dodge City.

As the RPM gauges rose to twenty, then thirty percent—still nowhere near the green operating zone—he
looked out, saw others running toward the craft. A cook
was at the sliding door, shoving and screaming for those
inside to make room. A female engineer squirmed her
way aboard, was cast back out, then tried again. One of
the guests, a crooked stockbroker, shoved his way forward into the copilot's seat.

"Don't touch anything," Howarski warned him as he
nudged the throttle forward.

He could wait no longer. At eighty percent he maneuvered the controls to lift the craft off the ground, felt it
sway and labor, and decided it would be difficult. Rising
slowly, hovering now at twenty feet, which was very hard
to hold, he elevated the gun sight reticle by use of the
thumbwheel on the stick.

He could not hear the announcement over the engine
noise, but estimated that they had less than four minutes.
Plenty of time if it was not squandered.

Howarski set the gun sight on a particular section of
netting and depressed the FIRE button. Nothing. He tried
again, and again there was no response.

He was close to panic when he remembered.

"Circuit breakers!" he cried. "The ones just over my
head. Push them all in!"

The stockbroker was rigid with fear. "What?"

The craft was increasingly difficult to maintain in the
wobbly hover.

An engineer reached forward, shoved in all of the circuit breakers, and yelled, "Go!"

Howarski cycled the weapons panel off and back on,
and pressed the firing button. *BRRRRR-AAATTT!* The
netting was blasted this way and that. Chunks of it
flew free.

Almost!

He held the button down again.

BRRRRR-AAATTT!

Instead of being blown clear, the entire huge net
began to pull away from the tracks, then fall directly
toward them.

The blades were immediately entangled, and the pow-

erful craft twisted violently, like a game fish caught in a
seine. The Black Hawk tilted over, over, until for an
instant it was inverted upside down—and the last utterances Howarski heard were his own screams of terror.

Ecol-Rec Zone

Link held Jenifer as tightly as he dared, running, ignoring the pain in his shoulder.

Not fast enough! Not far enough!

He heard the sounds of the helicopter taking off, a
while later the racket created by the miniguns, then a
grand *whoomp* as the chopper went down.

*"One minute remaining. Evacuate now. One minute
remaining. Evacuate . . ."*

Link ran on, using trails, ran directly toward the places
he knew platforms were mounted, since the computer
that controlled them was dead.

The first sensation of the explosion was the earth
trembling beneath his feet. He dived, trying to protect
Jenifer as best he could, when the long rumble sounded.
He covered her, anticipating the blast, then held on as
the concussive wave swept over them and on through
the forest.

Branches and trees were flung outward from the
source. A heavy limb smashed onto his injured shoulder,
and after a moment of numbness he realized he was
pinned.

Link waited for a while longer before trying to extricate them both.

Jen asked for water. "Soon," he said as before, and
managed to pull her free.

He picked her up, giddy with elation that they were
alive, ignoring the sharp pains that spiked like fire
through his shoulder and back.

"We made it," he said, walking slowly, holding on and
not about to let her go.

44

Since the afternoon following Billy Junkins's arrival, it had periodically snowed. Heavy snow with big flakes, the kind that accumulated. There were several inches of the stuff.

He had claimed his own position in Sly Paquette's house, huddling behind the dining room table he had overturned and dragged into the kitchen for protection. Paquette had wanted to hide there, but he'd shoved him out. It was only fair; Billy was larger, an easier target.

The women who shot them no longer waited for them to show themselves. Sometimes they'd come onto the porch and shoot them as they lay curled up, and while they howled and pleaded and tried to crawl away. They were no threat to the women; they'd been shot so many times in the arms, hands, and shoulders that none could handle a gun.

Despite his size, Billy was no worse off than his companions. They'd shot him thirteen times, but unlike the others he could still walk. He'd wondered if they were purposefully avoiding shooting him in the legs or feet, but could think of no reason for it. The bullet he'd taken in the mouth on the first day had made things worse, for with so many upper teeth missing, he could not have chewed if there'd been anything to devour, and the pain was intense.

Sly Paquette had only a dozen wounds, but two were

festering and beginning to smell, a nauseating odor made worse by the fact that he'd fouled his pants. The record was held by Willie, who had taken nineteen bullets. Willie's partner, Scarecrow, had somewhere between those numbers, but he no longer kept track. It might be that he was unable, since a twenty-two long rifle bullet had struck him smack in the forehead and his brain was slowly but surely leaking out. Dark, ugly, bloody matter bulged from the small hole.

Billy Junkins had known of such things with animals. He'd heard of an elk that lived for a season with half of its brain shot away. A bear had killed his mother's grandfather after its head had been half chopped away with an ax. Before, he'd guessed it was something that was possible, but now he knew, because Scarecrow was able to talk and beg like the others.

Both Willie and his partner had cried for the past two days, since Scarecrow had been shot in the pecker and Willie in the groin and butt, as if the women were concentrating their wrath on their most offensive regions.

When Scarecrow had sat up, somehow able to raise his rifle, one of the women had shot him in the forehead. Now all he did was hold his hand over the leaking hole and beg and cry and beg some more. Like Willie, promising anything if they'd just stop.

Billy heard the women coming into the living room and cringed behind the table.

Pop! Willie screamed from the living room.

Pop! Pop! Pop! He heard Sly Paquette shriek and flop around. Likely fouling his pants some more. He lived in his wastes. *Pop!* Paquette shrieked again.

Pop! "Oh God, oh God, oh God!" That from the brain-drooling Scarecrow, and Billy supposed they'd shot him in the crotch again.

Billy began to chant one of the old Aleut death songs and slowly rose to his feet. Think pleasant thoughts, the old ones had advised the dying. Think of warmth and your friends.

One of the women came to the kitchen door. *Pop!* A new bee stung his chest. He shuddered, but continued to sing as he made it to the back door, shoved it open, and continued out onto the rear deck. *Pop!* The bee stung his elbow, and he cried as shamelessly as Willie.

A woman in a parka stood a dozen feet away, her small twenty-two rifle only half raised, threatening but not interfering as he staggered to the steps.

The snow was deeper than he'd thought, a foot of it or more. He slipped on ice, lost his balance, and tumbled down the stairs.

The woman, one of the Manido-Ojibwe from the reservation, walked above him on the deck and stared down, face voided of expression. She turned then and went inside, to shoot and torment the other men.

Billy laboriously made it to his feet and slogged through the snow toward the lake, whimpering shamelessly as the various wounds came alive to tell him of their presence. He could not move the arm with the wounded elbow.

He wanted to sing more, but he had forgotten the words, and he knew there was no warmth and he had no friends to think of, so he continued on, staggering and periodically falling. He stopped then, chest heaving from effort, for Nek-kah the hermit stood in his path.

The old man wore furs, a shiny necklace about his neck, rings on his fingers, a bright silver watch on his wrist. He raised his ancient rifle. "Nyah!"

Billy remembered that he had shotgunned him and thought he had died.

"I know your secret, old man," the Junkman rumbled. The words sounded mushy and odd because of his damaged mouth.

He took another step, although the hermit stood his ground and continued to aim.

"Nyah!"

Despite his many wounds, Billy felt the meanness surge back into him. While he was deathly afraid of the women, they had not followed, and the old man before him was a lesser being and posed no threat. Someone to hurt, just as he was hurting. A last killing before he died.

The old man cried, "Ed-yah! Do-rah! Stor-ah! Nyah!"

Billy managed a sneer. "You don't have bullets.

You're too stupid to know how to load it if you had them."

The sound of the rifle's shot echoed in the forest. Billy Junkins felt as if he'd been struck by a hammer, and stared down dumbly at the crimson that blossomed on his massive chest. As he fell to his knees and started to die, the old man walked on past.

Pop! The sound of another twenty-two rifle's report inside the house, followed by a scream from Willie, were the last things the Junkman heard.

Willie held himself and screamed as the woman who had just shot his testicles lifted the muzzle of the small automatic pistol, and leaned over so he could see her clearly.

He screamed again; the pain was horrible.

"Remember me, Willie?"

She was a hag, had a broken nose in a metal splint and a white cloth turbaned about her head like some raghead swami. He'd never seen her before in his life.

"Remember telling me I should pay you after you raped me?"

He began to babble nonsense, anything so she'd believe that he'd never seen her, not in his life, and wouldn't do anything like that. "I never! I wouldn't!"

She sighed deeply, then pointed the small pistol back down at Willie's privates and formed the same pursed-lipped serious expression. "I'm going to keep doing it until you remember."

She *wanted* him to remember. "I do," he blubbered happily. "Oh shit, yeah. I remember you. Just don't shoot me anymore."

"That's good," she said. "Remember where you did it?"

He thought hard, wanting to remember. It came to him then, the turban! She didn't have any hair! He'd cut it off with his semidull knife. "The hotel. I remember. You're the rich—" He stopped himself.

"I was the rich bitch. That's me, Willie."

"Just don't shoot me anymore." He started to bawl. "Please don't."

"I wouldn't dream of it. I want you to keep on hurting and thinking about me while you bleed to death."

She stepped over to Scarecrow and smiled as she aimed. "Remember me?" she asked.

11:00 A.M.—Spirit Lake Township

The sedan rolled toward the town, going just over the speed limit. The *Muk-wah* watched it pass by and lifted her radio. "Another big car," she said. "Gray. Wisconsin plates. Could be more *naud-o-way.*"

They'd had five more carloads of hoodlums try to get onto the reservation. Tonio Gracchi's version of the cavalry. None had made it past the bulldozers. All were in jail, dining on lettuce, bread, and water, their crunched vehicles summarily deposited in Big Marsh.

The Cadillac, dark gray in color, proceeded to a concrete barrier, slowed, pulled around it carefully as the signs directed, and drove up to a flagman wielding a handheld stop sign.

Two heavy barriers blocked the left lane, and a Caterpillar D-9 bulldozer was in their path. The stocky Indian flagman wore gloves, a knit hat, and a yellow vest over a woolen coat.

The Cadillac stopped, and the driver rolled down the window.

The flagman noted that he wore a suit and tie, rarely seen in the Northwoods. The other two in the vehicle, an older man and a woman, were equally well dressed and looked not at all like the gunmen he'd encountered.

"You'll have to turn back, sir. We have a possible gas line emergency."

"We have business at your council building," the driver said. "This gentleman is chief counsel for the Weyland Foundation. We've been asked to represent the people of the reservation in some—umm—legal matters?"

The flagman was confused about the counsel-council business.

"Lawyers," the driver hinted. "On your side."

The flagman wondered why he had not said so in the

first place. He radioed for *Muk-wah* deputies to come and escort them into town.

Manido-Ojibwe Council Building, Spirit Lake Township

Link sat at the side of the room, an observer at the proceeding. It was an honor accorded to no other outsider.

The council president of the Manido band, most often referred to as their chief, sat at the head of the conference table, which was in fact four very plain and modest collapsible tables, lined up end to end. On other days the room was rearranged and used for pottery, art, and basket weaving classes.

The remainder of the council members were also seated about the table, as were Jason Toussaint and Carole Yellowbird, leaders of the Bear Society.

Waiting in the room outside were the legal team provided pro bono by the Weyland Foundation. The three lawyers, led by a former U.S. Circuit Court judge, had read through the old treaties and proclamations before departing New York. After their arrival, just an hour before, they had pored over the information contained in the gym bag that had been recovered from a location none of the Manido, not even Jenifer, would discuss.

When the chief asked Jason for a status report, the youth rose. Link noted that he was calm and sure, with little of the impetuousness observed only two weeks before.

"A lot of unwanted people are still leaving the reservation," he said. "Only Manido and bona fide residents are allowed in."

"And the patrolmen?" the chief asked.

"The last of them left two hours ago."

Link knew most of that story. The *Muk-wah* had gone to the old cranberry bog, where Storyteller had sent the hoodlum cops and found the place smelling as foul as the ecol-rec zone. The cops had suffered from diarrhea all night after the laxative poisoning, and had frozen half to death trying to free and start their stalled vehicles.

There had been no fight remaining in them when the *Muk-wah* took their weapons and encouraged them to walk, rounding up strays along the way. The trek had taken two days. When they'd arrived, footsore, exhausted, and spiritless, the chief had given them a speech about the charges they'd face if they returned, handed them the keys to a broken-down old school bus, and provided an escort to the reservation line.

Today a second bus, in the same condition, would carry away the repentant casino bosses and frostbitten gunmen sent by Tonio Gracchi.

The chief looked over at Link. "You have a question, Mr. Anderson?"

"What have you done with Councilman Paquette?" He'd been unable to get a response from Jenifer or Jason on the matter, and was again answered with silence.

Finally Jason responded. "There is an ancient Manido custom that our worst criminals be turned over to the ones they harmed the most. When someone was dishonored like that, no one spoke of them, or mentioned their name or what they'd done in life, like they'd never existed."

The chief spoke. "We're trying to do everything legally and according to treaty, but there are certain old customs to consider. Of course there's another good reason for silence. Law enforcement officers might consider us a group of backward vigilantes."

Link disagreed. "If they knew what you've endured, every agent, marshal, and state trooper I know would applaud."

"We feel it's best to keep our secrets."

"What about the lawyers outside?"

"We need their help to write an important letter." The chief nodded to Jason.

"From the beginning the *Muk-wah* have recorded everything, the extortion to get the casino and its operation, the free drugs and our people who disappeared, even videotapes of mob people visiting the casino. Sergeant Rose detailed every meeting with—the nameless one."

"What was Senator Adcock's involvement?"

"He was our leader, someone we call Storyteller. After he was shot he came looking for his Young Storyteller, Sergeant Rose, to pass on evidence about the Warehouse that he'd bought from the informants. When he was running out of time and blood, he gave it to Nek-kah to hold."

"And now you have it."

Jason nodded. "The letter will detail what happened at the casino and the Warehouse. When the time is right the chief and I will deliver it along with the tapes and depositions as proof, as Senator Eddie would have done."

To whom? Link wanted to ask, but he supposed that Jason would have told him if he'd wanted him to know.

"All we want is to be left alone, and for the old treaties to be honored. We'll use the casino money to educate and provide care for our people, and we will live on the north side as our ancestors did, not where some Washington bureaucrat wants us."

"How will you ensure they'll let you do that?" he asked.

"By offering our silence. No one will go to the media with all the tapes and depositions about the way the government turned its back."

Jason noted that Link looked troubled, and smiled wryly. "I'm a storyteller, and words mean much to us. Blackmail is not a good choice for an honorable purpose. Senator Eddie called it leverage, and said it's the language they understand best in Washington. Decency and honor mean little there, only leverage. We have that now."

45

The handful were mulling over the report Link had submitted. He had included most of it, but not all. There were secrets he would keep for the Manido. Still he'd provided a thorough outline of Eddie Adcock's heroism, and about the mob operation on the reservation.

Link was troubled by his shoulder, both from the heavy branch that had fallen on him during the explosion and the bullet that had broken his clavicle. He claimed to have a problem operating the computer—so Erin begrudgingly accepted the task.

"The Manido asked us to keep quiet about what happened. I agreed."

"What about the others? The expedition?"

"Turf Siegel's happy to just be home in the Bronx. Joseph Richards was making waves until our Habitat Earth division offered him a position on an excursion to Siberia."

"And the investigator?"

"Mr. Doughty isn't the sort to talk unnecessarily. We paid enough for his services that his daughter's expanding their alarm business, and he's more than pleased."

He didn't add that Mr. D was flying to Washington with Gloria Vasson, to help her recover the fortune that the woman called Sydney had spirited away. The Weyland Foundation's legal counsel would provide a team of attorneys to assist them.

"You did a commendable job," said Ambassador Baker. "Still someone in government's responsible for turning off the investigation of my son-in-law's death and ruining his name."

"The FBI weren't totally to blame. They were told to stay away by Senator Eddie's investigating committee while they looked into irregularities at the reservation. When Sydney began tinkering with Senator Eddie's mind, he became distrustful of the others on his committee and no longer shared his intelligence. When he died, so did the investigation."

Link continued: "The Manido will do their part. Tomorrow they'll discover that the missing treaties were misplaced and never left the museum, and acknowledge Senator Adcock as the greatest champion of their modern history. Gloria Vasson was pleased."

"I must meet her again," said the ambassador.

The octogenarian of the group raised his voice. "What about the despicable practices at the Warehouse? The losses suffered by the Indian families. Will the mob go unpunished?"

"The Manido took some skin off the Mafia and liberated a lot of cash. That's language the mob understands. Tonio Gracchi, the nephew of the Chicago mob boss who was in charge of the casino and Warehouse operations, disappeared from his home two nights ago and no one is grieving.

"For their part the Manido consider what they went through as the price of freedom. They don't want more investigations. Frankly, they don't trust much of anyone on the outside."

"That's understandable," said the octogenarian.

"So it's over," said the woman from Wyoming.

"Could we talk about that vacation?" Link asked as Frank called the meeting to a close.

Epilogue

Boudie Springs, Montana

The town was nestled at the foot of mountains so picturesque that even longtime residents drew breaths of wonder. At six thousand feet Boudie Springs was the epitome of the high country and local entrepreneurs advertised it as God's offering of respite.

The earliest settlers had been migratory peoples called Salish and Flatheads, who endured harsh winters and devastating raids by fierce Blackfeet to remain near hunting grounds with abundances of moose, elk, deer, and bighorn sheep. Then came white trappers attracted by the abundance of beaver—and later, raucous, hell-raising miners drawn by the lure of gold. The town was founded by a man named Boudie who set up a trading post beside a hot spring lying smack between the soaring Lewis and Whitefish Ranges of the Rocky Mountains.

Link told all of that to Jenifer, who fell in love with the town and the cabin at first sight. He let his ancient Dodge pickup—a slab of steel on front served as a bumper, so no one argued—idle down the fifty-foot gravel driveway as he stared at the place he called home.

"You left this for New York?" She sounded like he was crazy.

"A friend needed help."

"The one you said was chairman of the Weyland Foundation?"

"Yeah. Poor ol' filthy rich Frank. We'd made a pact to help one another."

When they went inside he found fresh wood stacked in the bin, and paper, kindling, and a log in the fireplace ready to light. An open matchbox was even set out.

"You always get this kind of treatment?"

"Only when I'm bringing a sexy woman."

As he knelt to start the fire, she bumped him with her hip. He laughed.

"Hey, buddy," she said. "That wasn't easy to do with bruises and a broken rib."

"I get special treatment from you too?"

"You bet. You want that special treatment now or later?"

"I'd better bring in our bags."

"To heck with luggage. In your gimpy condition you'd take all day."

"We can't make love. Your broken rib." Link was smiling. He already knew better.

She humphed. "Don't be silly. Just don't lie on me. That's not my favorite anyway."

"I noticed."

"You don't like women drivers?"

"I didn't say that."

"You just have trouble keeping up with me. Once I found you, I decided to not waste it." She smooched him. "Bet we can think of all kinds of solutions."

He felt good as he watched the flames already licking at the log.

Jenifer went into the bedroom and called out, "It's already made."

"My friends I told you about. Neighbors, a couple who run a bar in town, an old Blackfoot guy who looks after my mare."

"Ms. Stubborn, right?"

"Yep. You'll meet her tomorrow."

"How many women have you had in here?"

"Hundreds. It would be rude to count." He heard himself babbling on, like he could not remember doing in a long time.

"Bet you never had one ready as *this* lady." When he came to the door she was disrobing. Her voice turned husky. "Come and lie down. I want to show you something."

He did—and she showed him. When they had finished Link groaned piteously, not only from pleasure but from the pain in his back. Honestly.

Someone knocked on the door and they scrambled into their clothing. It was the neighbors, bringing over hot lunch, hauling in the luggage and welcoming Jenifer to Boudie Springs. While the couple talked, she stole a look at Link and let her happiness show. They had three weeks to get to know each other much, much better. She planned to use it wisely—if he didn't wear out.

During the night Jenifer awoke to find his side of the bed empty. She put on her robe and found him sitting in the darkness in his stuffed easy chair.

"Back bothering you?"

"Some," he said. "Mostly I find myself thinking too much."

"About the Manido slaves?"

"Sydney," he said. "I have a feeling that she's alive."

"She was very lucky if she made it out of the Warehouse."

"What I felt was sheer hatred. I'm afraid she'll harm you to get at me."

"I can't see her coming anywhere close. I know what she looks like."

"She changes."

"She can't change *that* much." She ran her hand through his hair and kissed his cheek. "Come back to bed. I have another idea about how to solve our problem."

Palma, Isle of Majorca

The clinic and spa were known across Europe as neither the swankiest nor the poorest, but among the most utilized and thus safest for the woman called Sydney.

A fleshy, orange-haired, and brightly lipsticked woman, from her accent a Londoner, walked among the Mediterranean-style buildings. Her shorts were so tight her belly swelled over the taut waistband, and a too-small push-up bra made her breasts look like a pair of pale melons bulging from a skimpy halter. A small lake of sweat puddled between.

She gave a passerby a coy smile and openly pouted that he did not notice. A woman emerging from the spa looked away, as if embarrassed to be a member of the same sex.

Palma was big in human alterations. Breasts, noses, cheeks, lips, ears, lifts, liposuctions, you name it, if you had one it could be altered. You could get a sexual transmutation in either direction. Giggling guys and macho girls fulfilling fantasy dreams. God-work.

She smiled at their stupidity, her own cleverness. True change did not involve surgery, but attitude. Three nights before she'd been a good-looking, distraught widow, let herself be seduced, and fucked a business-man's socks off. Last night she'd been an angry-eyed male at the bar who didn't take shit from anyone. Sydney liked to stay in practice.

So who shall we be today?

TOM "BEAR" WILSON was a career United States Air Force officer with three thousand hours of flying time, mostly in fighters. During his five hundred hours of combat flying he was highly decorated. Since leaving the military Mr. Wilson has worked as a private investigator, newspaper publisher, and program manager for a high-tech company in Silicon Valley. He has published eight novels and recently appeared on the History Channel's *Suicide Missions, The Wild Weasel Story*. When he is not visiting locations to obtain background material for his books, Mr. Wilson resides in the Big Thicket country of East Texas.

JAMES FRANCIS

DANGER'S HOUR

The submarine USS Tulsa is silently tracking a Russian nuclear sub when another sub collides with the Tulsa—sending her to the ocean floor. Now, Captain Geoff Richter must struggle to maintain order inside the crippled ship—as the oxygen is slowly depleted, power systems begin to fail, and time runs out.

0-451-41041-6

To order call: 1-800-788-6262